A Place of Stone

Charles McRaven

A Wings ePress, Inc.
Contemporary Fiction

Wings ePress, Inc.

Edited by: Jeanne Smith
Copy Edited by: Heather O'Connor
Executive Editor: Jeanne Smith
Cover Artist: Trisha FitzGerald-Jung
Image: Pixabay

All rights reserved

Wings ePress Books
www.wingsepress.com

Copyright © 2021 by: Charles McRaven
ISBN-13: 978-1-61309-530-0

Published In the United States Of America

Wings ePress Inc.
3000 N. Rock Road
Newton, KS 67114

Dedication

To the other Caney Creek pioneers: the Murphys, the Darbys, the John McRavens, the Lambs and my wife, Linda. We took the road less traveled.

* * *

...and like a laughing string
whereon mad fingers play
amid a place of stone...
                    —Yeats

One

The words from last night still crashed in my ears, despite the drumming of the interstate, the rushing air-shocks of the giant trucks. The new-green leaves, mists rising from deep Virginia hollows, water threading off stone ledges, all blurred in that remembered hostility. The scorn, the contempt, the anger in her voice cutting, raw like a knotted lash, across my mind. All our days together had come to this: a continuous confrontation, a shouting-down over the smallest details. My wife was a pretty woman, but our time together had become anything but pretty.

And this morning I had made a half-dozen calls, and it was over. Not with a sense of finality, the way I'd begun to envision it: the contracting business shut down cleanly, a logical break, the crew headed off into other jobs, the accounts closed. No, Bob, my foreman, would have to finish the current contracts out, letting each man go as he could, winding it down. He'd collect his bonus then, maybe in three months. Judy would close the office. And Liam McLeod Construction would cease to exist.

And Sharon could dispose of the equipment any way she liked. Auction, maybe. Or get with Bob and Judy to sell it off. I really didn't care anymore. Sharon would scream, rant, rage and cry: I didn't *care*.

I was seventy years old, and I was tired. Deadly tired.

The little Ford Ranger was old too, eighteen years old, but when she had it, Judy had spent money on it every time it'd sneezed. The 200-plus thousand miles on it didn't mean much, with new paint, engine, transmission, bearings, just about everything that rolled inside it. The camper cap was high-dollar: I could sleep in it. So I'd bought it from her. Hadn't been sure why, then: I'd had a company pickup to drive.

This morning I'd thrown basic tools in, sort of at the last minute. I hadn't planned on doing it like this, even if the idea had run across my mind a lot in recent months. Fleeting, like racing feet across a wooden bridge. Not neat, thought-out, sequential ideas, but a jumble of half-formed flashes that all added up to one thing:

Walk away.

The coffee mug had sat against the joint the table leaf made. The clean curve of the cup base came exactly to the straight line. But not over it. If I let my eyes follow the curve, I didn't fall away; I clung to the sweep of that arc. Safe from spinning off into the crack in the wood, the tangent, where the table chestnut joined but didn't match the leaf.

I remembered finding the table in an off-the-road antiques shop with Sharon. It was labeled "oak table" because few people know the difference. The man who'd fitted the replacement oak leaf hadn't had just the right router bit to match, either. And I'd never gotten around to gluing up a pair of the rare chestnut boards in the shop for a new leaf. One of those things I was going to get to when I retired.

Retired, yeah. I hadn't even remembered to register for Social Security till almost a year after I'd turned 65. Too busy. My trade wasn't building subdivision houses, or anything I could turn over to a crew. We did specialty restorations, everything from plantation houses to covered bridges to log cabins, and I could never be far from the hands-on work. But I loved it—the history, the feel and smell and rich sight of the ancient wood, the old, painstaking craftsmanship.

But that junction of the cup curve with the crack... was I clinging to the arc, afraid to let go? What would happen if I spun off into that straight-line trajectory? Off the course I'd been on for way over thirty years? Off to where?

It was before seven in the morning, and Sharon would sleep another hour, at least. I'd be gone anyway, to one of the three jobs we had going. And the shouting wouldn't start, then, till maybe eight or so tonight. And it'd be over something stupid. Like that infuriating computer I had so much trouble with. Nothing evoked Sharon's contempt like my not getting some simple step in the e-mail, or the word processor. I stayed distant from anything advanced, like spreadsheets. That's why we had Judy in the office. And of course, the kids had grown up with computers. Had laptops now, at who-knew-how-much a pop. Or those damn iPhones, that did everything but make coffee.

The corkboard above the phone table was filled with pinned pictures of the children. From way back till recent shots, from L.A. and Denver and Chicago. We'd had our family late, but now they were grown and scattered. June was trying to make it in theater combined with graduate school, Melissa was—had been—a geologist, now a housewife, and Kyle an engineer. Good kids. I guess that was mostly Sharon: she still tried to do everything for them. Lately, I seemed to be the only object of her wrath.

Well. Nobody ever said this life would be easy. I'd drained the cup, then noticed my latest Social Security check pinned up with the photographs. Judy must've done that; Sharon had always put them in some account as soon as they'd arrived. I didn't even know how much each monthly check was.

I stood, feeling the floor through the worn, familiar contours of my work boots as my weight settled into them. I was tired from yesterday, up and down those ladders. I reached for the brown window envelope, the pin dropping somewhere into the Rolodex below. I tore it open. $1430. What a joke. Was that what a man was supposed to live on? If we didn't take in fifteen, twenty grand a week, the business, the lifestyles, the livelihoods of a dozen people were blown away.

$1430. I guessed a man *could* manage on that, if his place were paid for, he didn't have a car or a lot of payments. I didn't want to think how many payments we made. Judy gave me stacks of checks to sign every time I stuck my head into the office.

Might be nice to keep this check a while, pretend it's real money for a change. I put it in my pocket.

Then, and I'd never know the details of just what my reasoning process was, I went quietly up to the attic, the open finished part Kyle had always slept in, next to June's room. In the cabinets under the sloping roof I'd built twenty years before, were sleeping bags, rolled-up mats, air pillows. My flyrod case and vest.

I carried these down to the truck, then went back up to our bedroom. Sharon was totally out, having been up till two, after our last row, after she'd awakened me coming in, as usual. I quietly filled a small bag with clothes and a pair of old sneakers. On the way out, I looked at my wife (a last time?), but she was turned to the wall, a blanket over most of her head. Peruvian weaving we'd brought back, actually. She always slept cold.

For the briefest moment, I remembered the feel of that soft body responding to my touch, that smooth skin, the early years of our marriage, the way we'd been with each other...young, in love...

I stepped out, pulled the door gently shut. My eyes took in the rabbeted-in stiles of the door, its recycled heartpine grain, the wear pattern around the hand-forged latch. My hands remembered building that door, forging that latch. *Long since.*

There'd been the Coleman stove in the shop, a medium-size ice chest and some basic camping cookware. I took an ax, chainsaw, foot adze, handsaw, and some other non-power tools. I had no clear plan at all, but I was loading up the kind of stuff I'd need on a really remote construction job.

There were racks of other tools: power nailers, shop tools, planer, saws, shaper—on and on. I wondered how much money they represented. Probably a good twenty grand. *Well.* Maybe I'd be back in a day or so. Pick up right here, again. But I really knew that the look, the feel, the smells of the place...the paint and the oil and the wood shavings, would stay with me only in memory.

~ * ~

June had dreamed of her room in Virginia again: the attic end of the house that looked out a dormer window and one at the gable end onto deep woods. There was no plot to the barely-remembered images, just the collection of stuffed panda bears and the pinned pictures of the grinning casts of the plays she'd been in growing up. And that big warm smiling sun her best friend had painted on the sloping ceiling.

As the middle child, she'd been in Melissa's shadow—Dad's girl until teenage—then Kyle had taken the older sister's place. But now out on her own in L.A. she seemed to be the one who missed home most. Melissa had her own family, and Kyle hadn't gotten past the fascination with his engineering career enough to make much time to go visit the parents.

But she hadn't just imagined it: her increasing closeness with her father now that she was so far away. Their times together since her move might be few, but they were treasured. She'd made time to go fishing with him since Kyle had left, a little to his surprise. And she liked just being with him on the projects he always seemed to have going around home. Like that pond and waterfall they always found time to add to with more stonework, or the quiet hikes back toward the mountains through the deep forest. He was a busy man, but shelved a lot of that for her.

Home. Yeah, didn't matter how frantic things got here, with importuning undergrads, deadlines, the pace of her life, she could always get recharged with a few days there. How long that'd last, with Dad now seventy, she didn't know, but she'd hoard those times as long as she could.

It was unsettling, the bickering that seemed to surface between him and Mom, and she tried to ignore that, afraid to acknowledge that it was probably worse when she wasn't there. She wouldn't take sides, just savor what she could of the haven of home. Of course,

Mom still treated her as if she were six, lecturing her on everything from dating to diets, while hinting not too subtly about wanting more grandchildren. But she knew by then that just came with the territory of mother/daughter sparring. She could let it slide off.

April. Be more or less free in a few weeks, and maybe the fish would be biting when she raced home.

~ * ~

The land in Missouri was only eleven acres, a remnant of forty that'd been our share of a divided 200-acre tract at the edge of national forest. Thirty-odd years before, five couples of us had bought it and divided it, all surprisingly drawn to different pieces, different sections of Caney Creek, the crystal-clear stream that wound through it.

When the Mallorys had wanted more creek frontage after we'd moved to Virginia, Sharon and I had sold them all but the remote eleven acres. I remembered the taxes on that were less than fifty cents a year per acre. Rough land, with scant topsoil, twisted trees, not much good for farming.

Just wildly beautiful.

And now I was headed there. It'd been six years since I'd seen my brother, Jim. He and Kelly had the section nearest the highway, the only one that had electricity and a well. The well was beside the ledgerock road down to the creek, with a freeze-proof faucet so the others of us could get drinking water on our ways to our parts on weekends.

Caney Creek was probably as clean as any waterway, with mostly national forest land upstream. In the limerock country, the soil is thin and runoff is swift. As far as I knew, our bit of land had no spring. I remembered being so impressed that the Virginia hills ran so much water. Southwest Missouri would dry up before June was out.

Our creek ran, though, and less than a half-mile below, it joined Beaver Creek, a sizeable stream. In all but the driest time, the little side stream on our part, with the three waterfalls, was musical and enchanting in falling water, dripping fern falls and eroded limestone eddies. I remembered it as hidden, deep in a cleft, hard to get to.

Magical.

The drawback to this corner of ground was just this inaccessibility. It was beyond steep. Some of it was hand-hold steep. I thought I remembered semi-levels on the Mallorys' part, ledges that ran to the west boundary and came near level with my little stream there. Maybe I could work my way down close to a cabin site.

Because that's what had been in my mind when I kept the land. A tiny shelter, for a week or two of fishing, or just to get away to, whenever. Or maybe one of the kids would want it someday.

"No way in hell will you get me back there," Sharon had vowed, when I'd insisted on keeping this boxed-in leftover. "You wanta be a hermit, *you* go live there. Do some reverse-evolution or whatever. Not me."

Sharon. What changed a dynamic, sophisticated, creative girl into a desperately social-climbing shopping spree like that? Empty nest, I guess. Shock of middle age. Menopause, maybe. But spending money had become a disease. With both our jobs, we'd taken in over a hundred-fifty grand last year, every last cent spent. And on what?

Well, there was the fifty-plus Gs on her new Yukon. And the kitchen remodel. And well, I hadn't bought clothes for myself in the 33 years we'd been married. Loved to shop, that woman did. There were shirts in my closet still unwrapped, at least five years old. And her shoes: couldn't count 'em. And bags of giveaways every spring, a lot of 'em new. And always her trips to town, with one or two meals somewhere, with whatever club or committee or girlfriend.

It had all depended on an increased inflow of cash. No matter how well the business did, it was never enough. A weekend in D.C. or with her cousins in New York could blow a thousand bucks easy. Yeah, and the times she and one of the kids had done Italy, or England, or Japan, even. But yeah, I guess the kids'd needed that culture, widened horizons.

The Peru trip was the only major thing we'd splurged on together. I'd always wanted to go there, so we finally managed it. Cost me a big job, too, when the crew screwed it up beyond saving while I was gone. Well. Water over the dam. You rolled with things like that.

And Peru—stonework that'd made me salivate, jungle, and almost-vertical peaks with temples clinging to their sides. Crafts, silver, art for sale way above the tinsel stuff I was used to seeing. Ancient pre-Inca fortresses, and the later Spanish missions. It'd been a once-in-a-lifetime experience to treasure in memory.

Even if it hadn't brought Sharon and me closer together.

The screaming, the ranting. Why did every little exchange turn into a fight? Well, I knew part of the reason was that I'd never just rolled over that way. I couldn't just let things wash over me. I had a cousin who'd married a guy she could run like a toy train. How that poor wimp survived, I'll never know. She was unbelievably lucky to find him; a real man would've taken her head off the first week. But, different strokes...Bottom line was, Sharon and I both just knew how to push each other's buttons, I guess.

I'd called Jim, said I was getting away for a while. Maybe it *was* just for a while...

No, it wasn't. Whether I stayed on the creek or not, I was out of Virginia. I guess...well, yeah, I guess I was retired, really. What else would you call it, when a seventy-year-old dropped out? Good a label as any, I guess. Never planned to retire. Liked working. Liked being good at what I did...

Interstates. All alike: gray, even in April, before the leaves were well out. Featureless, turning the hills, even the mountains, into unreal stage backdrops. You had to take an exit, get off onto a narrow road for them to become real. To get close to them, stop and get out and climb them among slender trees budding, dig your fingers into them, make them actual by the actuality of you. Interstates always made the Appalachians seem as inaccessible as the Rockies...idealized mountains, not for human consumption, view only.

A thousand miles to Caney Creek. Always two days, except those early trips when we both drove, or later when the kids could take shifts. To Nashville first, or to Louisville, and a sterile motel. The thrumming of the trucks barely muffled, and short, no-rest sleep troubled by highway food and the vibrations of the road.

Then more highway, more noise and lurching and mind-numbing travel. Finally, the turnoff from twisting U.S. Highway 160 in Missouri, the ledgerock road through the scrub cedar, welcomes of sister or brother or friends, and the other crammed visits, overdue and never what you expected, and everything changed.

Always so changed.

Those years ago, we'd all been broke, back-to-the-earth people. Trying to make livings throwing ceramic pots or doing leatherwork or painting canvases of the grudging hills. I'd been the blacksmith before getting into construction, slamming hot iron, never making any money at it. But we'd been together in our poverty, building friendships closer than any we'd had in affluent Virginia. Then, two by two, all but Jim and Kelly had gone back to whatever jobs we could find, where there were schools and telephones and running water and ice cubes.

I tried to think of the old days, the good times, the sharing, the staying over at one cabin or another, kids everywhere, mountain music, laughter. But it resolved into the here, the now, the fights, the deadly frustration.

The shouting.

Maybe the final break had something to do with my old dog's dying, too. Sharon'd kept pushing me to have him put down, and maybe I should have. But that old boy had gone to every construction job with me for fourteen years, and I just hadn't been ready to admit all that was past. His eyes had followed me each morning lately, but he just lay there. So, two weeks ago, he just didn't wake up, there on his pad in the utility room.

I'd buried him in the woods out back by myself; Sharon'd been at work. It was the middle of March, and buds were swelling, about to burst forth with new life. The turned earth smelled like life, the stirring, almost-warm breeze brought the promise of life. But now his life was over. I guessed it was a good time to die, really...spring.

Sharon had never mentioned him afterwards.

You can't go home again. But sometimes you have to try. Sometimes it's just time to go. No plan, but the vague trust that what's supposed to happen will happen. Even at seventy. Who in his right *mind* goes out into the woods at *seventy?* Crazy people. Like the homeless who flock to the streets of D.C. and Baltimore and New York, to drop out and cop out and dodge life and cling to life and then die.

Maybe that's what I was doing, on an interstate heading back a generation to something I thought I'd overlooked. A part of me lost in the avalanche of years. Lost down a lost creek of hardscrabble life that took all your waking hours to survive.

How could I possibly live? Okay, I could build some sort of cabin for a few hundred dollars. Not like I didn't know how. I could hew beams and logs and lay stone, long as they weren't too big. I could build windows and doors and a roof. Yeah, and hey, no expensive plumbing or electrical stuff. No heating system. Cook on wood.

Maybe so.

Could I even get that road close to a cabin site there? Find out. Find out just what was actually on my land. I remembered a fun weekend early on. We'd rented a surveyor's transit and found the perimeter property lines. Jim knew some surveying from college. We'd camped on the creek and got snowed on, a wet, late March snow. One girl, somebody's friend but odd-man-out, got so wet sleeping out, we took her into our tiny tent. Sharon got in the middle, so both the girl and I got soaked against the wet rip-stop nylon of the tent, Sharon staying dry and warm.

Okay, call this trip a feasibility study, then. If it wouldn't work, do something else. *But what? What can I do on $1400 a month? Make it work.*

Guess I can climb in and out of there if I have to. For how long, though? Five years? I wouldn't even be able to get another truck when this one wore out. But did I really need a truck? Old people got rides, walked everywhere. Jim was 65: old, too. But he'd be going in and out, and he was less than a quarter-mile up the hill.

~ * ~

I supposed Sharon and I could have gotten a divorce, and I'd have ended up with half of everything. After the fight, after a lot of lawyers' fees and a lot of time, and a continued battle. And of course, the kids would've been in on it, and Melissa's husband, Grady. No. *If she wants to divorce me for abandonment or whatever, she can have everything.*

She could have everything anyway. All I wanted were this scrap of land and my Social Security checks.

And some peace. Seems like a man should be able to have some peace after seventy years of hassle.

And well, maybe Sharon could have some, too.

I had a couple hundred dollars in my wallet. Barring a breakdown, I shouldn't have to use a credit card. I wanted to cut those up into little pieces, but not yet, I guessed. Maybe this wouldn't work. And just what was 'this'? Well, it wasn't just a trip, with the instructions I'd given to Bob Neal.

Bob was that rare construction type who could see a job from the management viewpoint. He knew there was no magic money tree to keep the operation afloat when things got slow. I'd known he'd wanted to go on his own soon anyway, so this wasn't pulling the rug from under him. Maybe it was for Sharon...*No, forget that.* Anyway, Bob had bought some equipment, I knew: backhoe, portable sawmill, shop tools. Sharon would surely let him buy whatever else he wanted from our business...

I'd send her a note in a few days, soon's I saw what I was up against. But yeah, call today and leave a message. Owed her that, I guessed. Come home and find me gone...no telling what she'd do. Well, then she'd know where I was. Probably burn up the phone to Jim's place, fill Kelly's ears with outrage.

Maybe I wouldn't tell her where I was. Just say I'd gone fishing for a few days, not sure where.

Yeah, that.

So okay, I stopped at a little gas/grocery off a highway exit, left a message on her cell phone, since she hadn't picked up. I don't have one of those—too complicated now—and a lot of places I'd worked didn't get reception anyway.

Southwest Virginia is big hills—old mountains, actually—once you get past the towns. I-64 roller-coasts into West Virginia through empty, high-humped, rounded rises, with traces of old logging roads.

The poplars were just now coming into new leaf, but you could see between the trees. Redbud and serviceberry, and on the south slopes, some early dogwood was thinking about getting ready to flower.

The streams were full of runoff, with those stone ledges spilling veils of water that wafted in the breeze. A shower had left pockets of mist rising from the hidden hollows up the slopes. I was beginning to notice them now, beginning to be aware of what was around me, not just inside.

Beginning to feel free, I guess.

I remembered again how I'd welcomed so much the water here, after the dry Ozarks summers. But the cold here, not as intense as the other, seeped into you worse, with the dampness. And yes, while the summers weren't that hot, the humidity soaked you.

~ * ~

Now just what the hell has that old goat done? No note, no explanation, just this short message on the phone: gone for a few days. He's never done anything like this: married to his work; lives for it. Sure hasn't paid any attention to me for years.

How many times have I had to fight the temptation just to walk out of here, see if he even notices I'm gone? We used to have a marriage—yeah, used to. So what do I do now? No way to reach him, and if I did, what could I say? Guess he's finally cracked, gone over the edge. Lives in his own little world anyway, where nobody's ever been able to get inside. So he's indulging himself in something, I guess.

Well, just leave it alone a couple days. He'll come dragging back in here when he wakes up. Unless he's really lost it. Damn, he's seventy: got no business going off like this without...

No, this can't be a spur-of-the-minute thing. Probably planned it all out, has to prove something to himself. Or to me, maybe? No idea.

Couldn't have gone to one of the kids: too far, in that old truck. They have been all that's kept him human, these last years, and now all gone. What, empty nester? That's a joke: I'm the one misses them. Girls out of patience with me, Kyle, my baby, off in his own place, job, life. Lucky to see any of them once a year.

And now my old man's what, left me? Nah, he couldn't survive without me. But I won't try to find him, beg him to come back. Give it time; it'll work itself out.

And I've got to get to work...almost late, with this thrashing around. Then there's that SPCA thing...

~ * ~

I'd make Louisville by night, I figured. And if I was starting to live frugally, I should sleep in the truck. There'd be campgrounds. I used to grab a couple hours' sleep at a rest stop and drive through, but that was then. No, a shower, the pad in the back of the truck... it'd be okay. Get an early start, and I'd be on the creek tomorrow well before night.

The settlers used to travel west early in the year, I'd read, to get to new ground in time to clear small cornfields, get seeds in the ground between the stumps. Then, with rail fences up and maybe a dog to keep out the varmints, they could turn their hands to building shelter, but not before.

I couldn't hope to plant anything on my near-vertical land. And I was also the only one of my family generation who wasn't a gardener. Jim could grow anything, the compost king. And our sister Nan had a green thumb, always sending Sharon stuff for me to plant, then watch die. Our parents had both possessed some magical green touch with plants too, none of which I'd inherited.

So, would I have to live out of cans? Not very appetizing. But without refrigeration, what could I keep, long-term? Potatoes, rice, oatmeal, flour. Surely carrots, onions, some kinds of squash. Have to eat any meat soon, or eggs.

How'd I bake anything? Oh, I could probably find an old Dutch oven somewhere. I used to have black cast-iron skillets, pots, all that stuff, back when I lived by myself not far from those same hills. Sharon didn't like cast-iron; she had enough designer cookware to fill three kitchens. Most of it never got used, even though she'd been a good cook, back when.

One thing I'd have to insist on...I wasn't going to sponge off my brother and his wife. They were well-settled in their ways, with their two children gone, what, twenty years? About that long. Grade school grandchildren. I hadn't seen those nieces and nephews forever.

Sharon and I'd married late, and ours were a half-generation or more younger. Two grandkids now: Melissa's. Kyle would probably play the old bachelor a few more years like I had. Didn't know what June had going. Well, awkward enough if I did stay dropped-out, with those three wondering whether to come see me, or avoid the crazy old man.

Funny how so many details pop up, once you've set a course. Things—too many, I was sure—I hadn't considered, would take on importance, now they were gone.

For some reason, I thought of Sharon's hands, rubbing my back, easing the aches. Boy, how long ago had *that* been? Now we only slept in the same bed out of habit. The rare intimacies always seemed to get turned off. I was always asleep when she came to bed, and always gone when she awakened.

She'd grab coffee and race off to her job by nine, and was never through before maybe eight at night, and usually later. There were meetings and late work and whatever else she did all week, and I'd find something to eat and maybe read and get drowsy.

I never watched television, so I wouldn't miss that. I'd catch the news and weather on my truck radio, then turn it off. She had to have noise all the time. Two minutes in the bathroom, and she'd have her radio on. And the television on while she did paperwork. All those things we didn't have in common had made me wonder just what we *did* have.

Not much, apparently.

Eastern Kentucky had always seemed to go on and on. After Huntington, and the river bridge, there seemed to be a lot of nothing until Lexington.

I'd gotten a sandwich in Charleston. Now I idly multiplied its exorbitant cost by a month of days. Couldn't afford that, for sure. Well, junk food was out, anyway. I'd had to learn basic cooking in the old days, and again, since the kids left. I could manage.

But just what exactly was I going to *do* with myself, down in that lost hollow? Once I'd gotten shelter built, settled, found a routine? Well, all that'd take a big chunk of time, so I guessed not to worry about that far in the future. I could surely find something to do to fill my days. Go back to the crafts thing, the blacksmithing, maybe some woodwork.

Have all the time I needed: discretionary time, always a nonexistent luxury before, with all the demands of family and business. So yeah, it'd work itself out, for better or worse.

And I guessed I really didn't care all that much.

Two

Well, six years *will* change people. Kelly's hair was white, she wore granny glasses, and she didn't zip around as fast as I'd remembered. Jim had lost his hair early, so that hadn't changed. But the wrinkles were deep, and I had to remind myself that this was my little brother. My son Kyle looked like me, but had some of Jim's characteristics. Both had studied engineering, both were quick-witted. Both loved a good joke.

I had forgotten that my brother had discovered religion late in life. Sort of a surprise, since he'd taken the whole '60s rebellion thing more seriously than most of us. They'd raised their boy and girl in these woods, and both of them had run, not walked, off to St. Louis and Dallas as fast as they could. So I'd thought of Jim and Kelly as aging hippies, till the religion bit. But they were both bright and inquisitive, and I supposed the intrigue and the no-pat-answers of it all challenged them.

There were books on their shelves with titles like *21st Century Christianity*, and *A Guide to Judaism,* and a matched, slender, red-bound set of the New Testament books. Yes, and our mother's old inherited family Bible, which must've been more than a hundred years old. I'd thought our older sister Nan had that.

"So, what're your plans?" Kelly asked me, after they'd fed me stew and homemade dark wheat bread. "Fishing trip?" Her eyes had always held a twinkle. She was one of those people who're very much at ease with who they are, and I doubt if she ever had an enemy. Well, Jim was mostly that way, too. A great pair; I'd really missed them.

"Some, I guess. Like I told you on the phone, I need to get away. How long, I don't know. I may be retiring, but that's kind of a foreign concept for me. Been wanting to walk that piece of land down on the creek again; see what's there."

"You talked about a cabin there years ago," Jim remembered.

"Did. Never got it out of my mind, really. I don't remember what kind of timber's on it, or what the building stone's like. Do remember it's steep."

"Yeah, you'll more like climb it than walk it." Kelly laughed. "I don't think we've been on it since we surveyed it that time."

"Spread out flat, you'd have twice as much." Jim grinned. "You planning to build that cabin?"

"Maybe. Don't really know what I want. Just no more of the back-East carousel, for sure."

"What about your building business? Everybody thinks of you as the rich relative."

"Hah! Lots in, lots out. I always said if I could get back up to broke, I'd quit the trade. More we made, the quicker it got spent. But house is paid for, Sharon's got a job she likes. Seemed like a good time to walk away."

"From...everything?" Kelly asked.

"The business, for sure. Virginia, for now. Sharon? I really do not know about that. But I'd say yeah, looks that way."

"Not really? What happened, shoot-out?"

"Oh, no. More of a wear-out. Less and less there. She loves the social thing. On committees, in groups, going all the time. Classic empty-nester, I guess. You know she's fourteen years younger than me. Got too much energy."

"I remember her mostly as always wanting to do things right," Kelly mused. "No matter how small an event, it had to be just so."

"Yeah, with a price tag, too. And whatever else it may be, upscale Virginia's not cheap."

"So...no real plans then, bro? Just hang out for a while?"

"If it doesn't rain tomorrow, I wanta see if I can get a sort of road down from above Mallorys' cabin. I seem to remember a ledge running west to the property line, and a way down maybe to somewhere above my side branch..."

"Rocky and steep. You got four-wheel drive?"

"Yeah. Figure if I can get close, just to park the rig. It's little, but I can camp in it. Lot depends on what I see. It's maybe ten years since Kyle and I camped there? Nine, anyway. I gotta see what's possible. Right now holing up sounds good. Maybe it won't, after tomorrow."

That night, asleep in the loft of their tiny house, where Sharon and the kids and I had stayed often 25 years ago, I had a dream. One of those vivid, gripping, sweat-drenching dreams that blasts you upright, gulping for air.

Sharon and I were in her Yukon, careening down the steep Caney Creek road. She was flooring it, swerving on the gravel, laughing hysterically. I wanted to jump, but knew I'd die if I did. Surely she'd slow down, stop. There was a hairpin turn ahead, high on the bluff above the creek. We'd never make it. I tried to yell, reach the brake, anything.

"Coward!" she screamed at me. "Wimp!" And she whipped the wheel. The long slide started. She didn't even try to control it. We left the road, crashed through scrub cedars into space. It was ninety feet to the rocks below, nine stories. The heavy nose of the SUV dropped. I was weightless, falling, falling...

~ * ~

I guess I was really a mountain man, come down to it. I'd lived alone in a little cabin over a creek that ran into the Buffalo River in the Ozarks for several years, driving out to do whatever work I could find when I needed a few bucks. Helped neighbors butcher hogs, plant corn, cut firewood, and they helped me. Maybe I was just marking time, sort of waiting for whatever was to come next.

And finally, she did. Sharon's parents bought a farm some miles upstate, not so backwoodsy, closer to a town. I ran into her one day at, of all things, a laundromat in Harrison, Arkansas.

"Hello, you live around here?" About the oldest non-pickup line in existence, but hey, mountain men ain't cool.

"Not really. Just visiting my folks, and their washing machine quit. Doing the daughter thing, helping out. How about you?" Not really interested; just making conversation while the machines did their act. But whatthehell, I hadn't seen a grown woman with all her teeth in years.

"Back down in a dark holler with the bobcats and coyotes, just come out when I can't stand my own company any more: forced civilization. So, your parents move here from some real place?"

"Yeah, New England, parts of which are a lot like here, only colder. We're from Vermont. Dad was an Army officer."

Now, I knew absolutely nothing about Vermont, other than I'd heard that people moved a lot faster there: had to, with just a couple months of summer and a whole lotta snow buildup. So, nothing at all to talk about with this pretty girl, who I guessed wasn't that long out of college. Well, I'd had some college too, didn't quite rank myself with the average redneck. And whatthehell again, I might just as well give it a shot.

"Where'd you go to school?"

"Couple of places. Started at Boston U., then finished at George Washington in D.C. You?" Playing the game.

"Few courses at the U. of Arkansas, then got tired of the games students play. I was older, out of the Marines. Shoulda stayed to finish, I guess, but I'm an outdoors type, so setting myself up for some office cell didn't appeal too much." *Yeah, that about sums it up.*

"So you hibernate where? Your 'holler'?"

"Down off the Buffalo River, place my older brother and I bought to hide in, on back. I kinda look after his place, since he's never left his bean-counting job. Fish a lot, blend in with the other wildlife."

"That river was supposed to be dammed. I heard some locals got together, worked with the Sierra Club and some other conservation groups to get it made into the national park." Eyes asking if I'd been in on that.

"Yeah, a bunch of us locals stood up to the powers that be. Took years. I'm far enough away I won't hafta move out, and the park service gave folks lifetime tenure there anyway. But I may actually try civilization someday again."

"What do you do for a job down there? I mean, the Davy Crockett thing's long gone."

"Well, the story is we hillbillies steal from each other, but I do some blacksmithing, crafts fairs, leave my work on consignment in shops around. I don't need much."

"That's...that's so, well...unexpected these days. But you can't make a living at that. Can you?"

"Not really. I build cabins for folks retiring from the grind, do carpentry, stonework. Built my own place, back before I really learned how."

And against all odds, we found ourselves having lunch at a place some friends of mine had opened on the town's one main drag. And talking. A lot of talking. What this service brat saw in me I never knew, unless it was just the change from what she was used to.

She had to go back to her publications job in D.C., which was more than a thousand miles away, but we managed to keep in touch. I made excuses to travel up there, and of course she came to see her folks more often than expected, and yeah, me. We spent a lot of time on the phone when I could find one, wrote letters, with things in them we probably wouldn't have said face-to-face.

I was pretty sure she was comparing me to those upwardly mobile lawyer types in that town, just like I was with her and the rare women I'd see. Apparently with positive results, both of us.

That went on for a year, until I got up my nerve and asked her to marry me. Still a little surprised she did that, but she made the move, first to the little cabin, then to a place near Harrison where she got a job and we had plumbing. I got serious about building stuff, and pretty soon developed a sort of following, even if it didn't pay much.

So much so that a writer for *The Kansas City Star* labeled me the "log cabin guru of the Ozarks" in a write-up. That brought in a little business, and not just in the boonies. I had to hire help, and became what I'd sworn not to be...a manager, although I still hit the hands-on stuff every day. Had to, to set the pace, since guys on a job like to talk, waste time, goof off if you let them.

~ * ~

It was a Thursday, just into April. Clouds scattered before a puffy breeze, and green things pushed up and leaf buds unfurled. Jim had some county extension thing to go to, and Kelly was doing something at their church. I was glad for the solitude.

The road was better than I'd remembered it, with brown creek gravel and even some culverts. We used to bottom-out on it in the old Volvo wagon, where the runoff had cut across and left one deep rut and the other high. But the couple across the creek then, and the Mallorys and Jim had pooled their time and somebody's tractor and truck to engineer and re-route the road. I'd have to do my maintenance part, too.

Just above Mallorys' cabin was the ledge I'd remembered. They'd jackhammered the stone down to create a driveway that cut back below to their log cabin. We'd found that house in Arkansas thirty-odd years before and moved it. The cabin-raising took successive weekends and I remembered the Mallory son, then just two. He was a lawyer in Kansas City now.

I took my axe, a compass, a peep-sight level and hundred-foot tape measure. If I could locate the property corners with Mallory land, I could run the lines myself. First thing, though, was access. We all had an agreement to go through each other's land if necessary, so I could just about pick any route I could handle.

Even if I could strike the stream at the west fence, though, there were the steep drops at the waterfalls. No, have to get down through the ledges somehow, to just above the juncture of the streams. Seems there had been a possibility, but it was steep. Today I'd see just how steep.

The west fence was mostly gone, but visible. Grids of rusted web-wire caught leaves and brush, and rotted posts with lichens lay under leaves. Some wire had grown into trees and still stood for a few feet at a stretch. *Let's see, Jim said my southwest corner was right in the streambed*; I hadn't remembered that. Should be an iron bar somewhere. Car axle? Rebar? Something that'd last, be visible.

It was there, driven into a crack in the limestone. My corner. So, 660 horizontal feet north over the hollow to a pile of stones high on the point between this side stream and Caney Creek. There'd never been a fence up that almost-bluff face. *Okay, double back down this bare rock, along the stream, till it drops too much.* Which it did, just fifty feet along, angling north from my line to the east. But I was one ledge lower, here: follow this.

Could shift some soil here, few big stones to hold it above the stream. Bad stretch, though. Couldn't picture Sharon ever trying to drive down here, dream or no dream. *Better on past here, now. Not too tippy. But now the stream's way down there. Gotta get lower.* Ah, break between big stones. If I could get the truck through and down here...

Finally, I reached the diagonal slope I remembered from below. Okay, a week's handwork, I might get to here, but the mouth of the stream was still fifteen, twenty feet down. Find a more-or-less level place to park, then. Never turn around here, though. Okay, go onto Mallorys' again, where I'd sold them my part to the east. There was a wide-spaced grove of oak trees there, and the land wasn't as steep.

I didn't like it much. I worked my way down the slope and shot the grade with the level. It *was* steep. But if I could back down this, the grade lessened a little right over the main streambed. With some big stones as a retaining wall, I could just level enough slope to perch the truck. Then it'd be eight feet down to the side stream, another four or so to Caney Creek. I could do that first part with stone steps, get down into the little streambed.

Maybe. So now, where to put a cabin? I'd liked a wide place up the side branch, where a bench of higher ground hugged the much steeper north slope. Out of the weather there, and hidden from old fields across Caney Creek. Hunters came there often, and I didn't want curious visitors.

The side stream was running about an inch of water here, over solid stone two feet wide. It'd dry up completely in summer, but what would a flash flood do? The thin soil of the cedar glades above couldn't absorb much water; it'd all come rushing down this narrow chute.

The bench hadn't washed away, though. It was five feet above the water now, and at that height, the stream would have forty feet of width in flood. The bench was about fifty feet long and maybe twelve deep. I'd have to dig back into the hill to fit even a small cabin in.

I'd thought about logs, since I knew them best, but I hadn't seen that many straight trees I wanted to cut, let alone manhandle into place. Some thickly growing cedars above that had reached tall for light, but they weren't big. And I'd have to wait while the wood seasoned, shrank, and the set-up cabin settled before I could finish it. No.

I turned back downstream. The little branch widened from a low fall onto a solid stone basin the four feet above Caney Creek, at an outside curve in the bigger stream. Floods there could spread out a couple hundred feet beyond before water at this bank rose above gravel bars and willows. But Jim had said it did get up into this branch a little in flood couple times a year.

Stones were everywhere. Big ones and little ones, squarish limestone, edges rounded by the creek. Make one solid cabin. And there was a sandbar upstream along the main creek, where an overflow channel deposited it with every flood. All I'd need would be cement then, and a lot of time. Well, I had the time.

Nothing much but time.

Prepainted metal roof, stone, the place wouldn't burn in a forest fire or rust. And backed up into the dug-out hill, it'd be warm in winter, cool in summer. Seal that wall against moisture, then backfill like all the basements my crew and I'd built. Sure.

I hefted an eighteen-inch rock, a six-inch-thick rectangle. Heavy. Have to get these one at a time from across Caney Creek. Set them on the ledge at the side stream's mouth, then climb up, carry them on up. Be slow work. Might bring a few down in the truck after I had a road from up the hill, tumble them down. Then maybe wheelbarrow them the 200 feet up the little branch to the site. Could be done, but it wouldn't be fast.

But then—sure—there were all those rocks up the side stream, too...tumble them down. Easier: gravity. Should've thought of that sooner. Cabin-in-the-making: just some assembly required.

~ * ~

Childbirth classes were about as far from the life I'd led as being on Mars, but I wasn't gonna let this woman of mine go through this alone. I did okay until they showed a film of a Caesarean section, with the scalpel and the spurting blood. Then this tough old boy about passed out, and the women conducting the classes giggled at me. No, they howled.

"I need you here," Sharon had told me, and I was okay with that. Scrubbed, gowned, masked, I held both her hands during the contractions, sponged her forehead with a cool, wet cloth, counted the durations. For hours. And realized why it's called labor.

The shift changed at the hospital, and a bunch of tough old girls came in, replacing the solicitous young things who'd been so concerned. The late shift mostly sat, stoic in their resignation, talking about their truck-driving husbands, grandkids who never called. Now and then, one would check Sharon, then noncommittally sit again. I got to hear a lot of troubles that weren't ours. Guess we were lucky to be simply on the verge of parenthood.

Then a doctor appeared, not the one we'd been seeing. Coulda been the janitor, for all we knew. He examined, nodded, walked out. One of the nurses exhorted Sharon to push, and she did. Repeatedly.

Doc came back, stayed three contractions, and caught this bluish shape in his rubber-gloved hands. It caught its breath and rent the air with a primeval howl that brought grins to every face but mine. It, a girl, was then placed on Sharon's stomach, where it registered her heartbeat and voice, and grew quiet for a bit: *Mom*. And she began to get some color.

That was Melissa, our firstborn, who turned out to be my best buddy, up to teenage. Then of course she began to treat me as a barely necessary embarrassment (Oh, *Dad!*), the father a girl had to put up with till she could escape to a real life. Sharon handled both girls well, I had to admit, looking back on it all now, but of course Melissa fled early to Grady, a promising young man with his head on computers.

~ * ~

There was a climbing path up the point of land north and west of the creek junction. Once, I'd thought of that access, but it was a good 250 feet up, then steep still to the county road, through a quarter-mile of national forest further west. Coronary hill. But some of that up there was mine, and faced south. I thought of the dizzying drops in Peru, terraced in stone walls for crops. What soil there was here was black and rich, if it could be held in place. And watered.

I climbed up. The path was worn in old use. Maybe a game trail, or a log-skidding path down from above. Steep for that, though. Looking back down, I could make out the clean, circular curve of Caney Creek, and the straight line of the side branch coming into it. Another tangent off the contained, predictable curve.

Was this a sign? My cabin site up the spun-off line from the sweeping creek? Coincidence, maybe.

Maybe not.

This hanging, south-facing slope would get a lot of sun I'd never see down below. I dug my hands into the black dirt. Pile this up and you could grow stuff in it, for sure...

Later, if at all. Growing things had to be last on my list. I had till fall to build the house, if I really wanted to do it. And yeah, I could do it, if I didn't break an arm or leg or something else vital. But okay, did I actually want to? What were the options, really? I started to figure, picking my way back down.

The land was almost impossible, but it was paid for. And under five dollars a year in taxes. Water would be a problem, but I could get a purifying filter for the stream. Boil it. Bring some from Jim's. There *could* be a spring maybe, up the branch. Never climbed all the way up. Rough getting around the falls, I remembered. One eight feet high, another maybe ten, the last about six, and all boxed in tight. I hiked up. Nice flow now, thin sheets of water over the fall. Probably hear this first one from the cabin when the water was up. Could hear the four-foot one drop into Caney Creek from there today. There were dripping ledges, with moss and new ferns unfurling, but nothing promising real water that I could see. I'd come down from above, then later look for a spring. Didn't like the idea of climbing past the falls, slipping on wet rock and falling, here by myself.

That had been a new and unwelcome realization just in the past few months. I'd really never thought much about stumbling, falling, hurting myself badly. I'd always been sure-footed, and the fact that I was seventy and should watch it hadn't really soaked in. I'd never fallen off a roof in a lifetime of building. Only broken minor bones in construction's freak accidents. Once, I'd broken two fingers and didn't know it for a month, until a doctor friend noticed. Healed crooked, and I couldn't close my hand all the way for a while, but that hadn't lasted.

I guessed this wasn't such a hot idea, really: old man planning to put himself out of touch, in harm's way, where nobody'd miss him for a week if something did happen. But what was the alternative? Go back to Virginia and the shouting matches? Fight for half the property there to be sold and the money split? Rent a room somewhere and wait to die?

No. Whatever it'd take to make this place work, I'd be free here. For how long, I didn't know. And no, that really didn't matter much.

I climbed the eight feet to the proposed parking spot and took some more levels. If I could angle the road, I could get some of the steepness out of it. Have to build that retaining wall below, but even a foot of soil high, and dig another foot down on the uphill side for it would do it. Assuming there was a foot of soil there, over the solid rock.

Some big stones up there I could pry down with my long digging bar. Set them solidly, move the dirt, and get some gravel on it. Take time, but then I'd be right here with the Ranger.

Rocks are heavy. Cement sacks—a cubic foot each—are 94 pounds. Up till a couple of years ago, I could handle them okay. Here I could fill a spackle bucket at the truck, carry it down steps for my mortar.

Okay. I could do the stone cabin—hut—whatever. Better than logs, which would have all those drawbacks. Stone cabin. Take longer, but I'd learned that in stonework, you had to look back at what you'd accomplished instead of ahead to what still intimidated you.

There were some fairly flat rocks in the creek that'd make a floor. Keep my eye out for more. Jim probably knew sources, too. I could haul from anywhere, as long as I didn't haul much. The Ranger had a bedliner, and stones would be easy to slide into and out of it. Haul the gravel for the road too, a little at a time.

I cut a few sprouts to outline the road. With care, I could tee up into the lowest ledge I'd follow, and use that as the turnaround. Couldn't do it in snow or ice probably, but I'd just have to live with that.

Going back out seemed shorter, and I made mental notes on the places that'd need work. Well, all of them, some worse than others. But I could drive over dirt till the fall rains, and surely by then I could gravel the worst places.

So that was first, then. Grub out the road, such as it'd be, then start the cabin. By winter I should be in, then let it snow all it wanted to. I should be able to do it a lot sooner, but I'd learned to multiply the time you estimate for a project by three to be realistic. And then the cost: add twenty percent for the things you hadn't counted on. Judy and I'd called that additional twenty the JFTHOI charge (just for the hell of it).

Have to cut firewood, but there was a lot of dead stuff all along here. Scrub oak trees overgrew the shallow soil and died. Only the cedars seemed able to find cracks in the rock, down to dirt and moisture somewhere.

Going back to the Ranger, I hacked a few more small sprouts out of the way, pried a few rocks. Once there, I cranked up and eased along the ledge most of the way to the back fence. Clearing that switchback would take some work, but it was on bare rock: solid. One 18-inch stone, almost a cube, was in the way.

Make a good cornerstone, if I could get it into the truck.

The stream was a lot smaller here, so it must have a spring down there somewhere. I sat on the tailgate and ate a sandwich Kelly'd insisted I take, along with water and some ice in the chest. Didn't really need that, but yeah, with the sun out, the cold water was good.

Water. Humankind's history was written in it, really. The uninhabited places of the world were that way because there was no water there. The wells in the desert were deep and rare. Like springs here, really. I knew this side stream began on an old farm high above, and that cattle were there. Bad water.

Just now there'd be seeps and wet ledges that'd be bone dry later. Well, the couple across the creek had always brought water from Jim's well. They'd sold their place to...Eric Something, a single carpenter who traveled a lot. He'd never had a well drilled—no drill rig could get across the creek ford.

I eyed the sun, then remembered to check my watch (I still had a watch). Two. Time enough to explore some more: I needed to find out all I could if I really planned to do this crazy thing.

Yeah, crazy. That's exactly what Sharon would say, soon's she heard. Kids too, probably. Well, maybe not Kyle. He rock-climbed, mountain-biked, camped and backpacked a lot. The girls had been outdoorsy too, till they'd discovered boys.

When they were small, I remembered they'd listen wide-eyed to the stories I'd tell of growing up not far from this country. Pretty ordinary really, but it'd been far away and strange to them then. Like my father's stories of Depression times in the mountains of California, where they'd gone looking for work. That time had left such a mark on my parents, they'd pushed all four of us to find security, get away from hardscrabble. Get educated, move up.

Yeah, up...to subdivisions, killer jobs, heart attacks. Our oldest brother Sam, the accountant, hadn't made it to retirement.

What chill there'd been earlier was gone now, even in the shade. But not a lot of sun made it into this streambed, and there would be less in winter. That'd be something to think about, all right. This north-facing slope road would probably keep the first snow till spring. Well, I'd never scoped out the hill on the other side; maybe I could get close that way.

No, I'd never pass the falls.

But it was time to look, anyway. So I picked my way among bushes growing from cracks in the rock, across the streambed. There were ledges here, too, but the slope was much, much steeper. Like Peru. The only way I could ever get a road here would be to blast it out. I couldn't climb most of it without handholds. I gave up.

I worked my way down the streambed on that side, though, looking for a spring, since there was little I'd be able to do with the slope. Oh, maybe plant something on a terrace or two up higher, where there'd be sunlight and it wasn't as steep, but the effort would be monstrous. And I'd have to pump Caney Creek water hundreds of feet up there with a gasoline-driven pump when this branch went dry. I remembered the stone water channels in Peru, each piece fitted without mortar so tightly there were no leaks. But they had springs uphill. So far, I hadn't found a drip here. In wet April...

It was a little grotto, hidden in dense briars and bushes, and it was hard to get to. I heard the water falling before I saw it, the hidden source of almost half the flow of the stream. It came out of that high northwest hill nobody'd ever lived near. A little limerock cave, actually, one of many channels eroded by leaf acid over millions of years. Maybe a bigger cave back in there, but when I worked my way back to it, there was only a narrow crack with water coming out.

Who'd ever seen this? So close to Caney Creek, nobody'd needed the water. And did it run all year? Probably not, or if it did, the water sank into cracks somewhere. Then I saw a rusty piece of pipe jammed back into the crack. Now, what in the world was that? Then I remembered.

The rumor was that a long-dead former owner of this land had been a moonshiner. And you needed cold spring water to condense the whiskey after you'd boiled off the fermented mash. So he'd set up down below somewhere, and piped the spring water down. Well. I sure wasn't the first one here, then. Maybe a hundred years or so too late. Did Jim know about this spring? Probably did. He'd hunted here for thirty years.

~ * ~

Sharon opened the door, fully expecting to see Liam slumped in his easy chair, asleep over a book with pages rumpled under his restless hands. It was—gosh—ten o'clock, and had he forgotten to eat anything? *Be just like him.* There was that stuff in the fridge...

No, he's not here. And sure, she hadn't seen his truck outside, but maybe that was because she really hadn't noticed. She glanced out a window: dark. Yeah, she'd had to stumble in. He'd always left the light on for her. *Hmm, took that for granted, I guess.*

She flipped on the porch light, to see the empty space where he always parked his truck. So no, he wasn't upstairs asleep, either. Early riser, he shut off his mind around nine anyway. Never ready to go out, do anything fun. Like his social life was over. Only people he talked to anymore were Bob and the other construction guys on the job.

So okay, hasn't raced back then. And it's only been a day, anyway...what'd I expect? He'll show up. I guess he will. Of course he will. Hell, he lives here. If he hasn't forgotten the way home. Wonder if he's just losing his memory? Nah, that doesn't happen all at once.

And dammit, maybe I'm better off without him...try for a real life...

~ * ~

"Got a surprise," Kelly told me when I checked in near dark. "Trish Mallory called, said they're coming down tomorrow night. Be here around six for the weekend."

"Okay! I was thinking I might drive up to see them. Save me the trip. I see they've been working on their cabin."

"Yeah," from Jim. "They've never finished it, in what, thirty years?"

"About that long. They went North somewhere every summer. Michigan, I think. Well, that's good. I got this possible way into my place, if I can fudge onto their land a little."

"Oh, they'd be okay about that. I don't think they even know where the lines are. You find your corners?"

"Did. Real climb up to the back one, but the others are easy. They tell me one thing: I've got the roughest piece of ground this side of Peru."

"Well, you're not gonna be a farmer, anyway." Jim always had that fabulous garden.

"No. Like to be able to grow a few things, but that dark hollow's no place for it. Oh, did you know about the little spring on the north slope, Jim?"

"I saw it once, years ago. Hard to get to. But the old moonshiner sure found it. I've often wondered how he got his barrels of mash down there."

"No road, that's for sure. Must've got in further down, and used a long pipe. I'll look closer. If he got in, I should be able to. You know if it runs in summer?"

"Don't know. Maybe a trickle. Probably a cave outlet. Passageways run for miles in that limestone."

"Okay. Well, I'm leaning toward putting up a stone cabin on that bench above high water, a couple hundred feet or so up the little stream. Don't know now how much I'll use it, but one of my kids might, later on."

"You're really thinking of staying, aren't you, Liam?" Kelly asked. "Are things that bad at home?" There was worry in her brown eyes. Kelly was always helping people pick up the pieces of their lives. I guessed that was what had helped bring them into the church.

"I actually don't know the answer to that. I know I had to come check it out, maybe cross it off the options. But even rough as it is, I like it. Always did."

"No way to get electricity down there, but you knew that. And water. Course you got the creek, and you'll get drinking water here, no problem."

"Thanks. I'm actually sort of looking at getting toward making it on my own. Well, at least living off my Social Security. Kerosene lamp, wash clothes in creek water, composting toilet, you know..."

"Young man's idea. But you could do it. Now Kelly's gonna ask you the inevitable question..."

"Yeah. What do you do when you break a hip, or get real sick down there? You won't even be able to let us know."

"Oh, I don't plan to be a total hermit. Except maybe in the worst weather. And I suppose I could rig a CB radio off a battery. Charge it when I drive the truck. Trade it off with the truck battery..."

"That could work," Jim conceded. "Cell phones don't out here. And I get down, check on the horses every few days. Look in on you."

"Now that's just what I don't want. You two needn't make a job out of watching out for me. The worst thing I expect is to get cabin fever. I'll read a lot in winter, do woodcarving, blacksmithing or something. Something cheap."

"Hey, yeah: you can always go back to blacksmithing. Keep you off the streets." Jim, with that grin.

"Maybe. Need a roof for that, is all. Never too cold to pound hot iron. But I don't want to get into a production thing again. Do it for fun."

"So you are planning to winter over." A statement from Kelly.

"Yeah, I guess so. If I get the cabin built, if I don't break something vital first. If a bunch of other stuff."

"Well," she said, "I'll get this in early, then. Why don't you come with us to church Sunday? That'll give you a break, keep you from going crazy later on."

"Well, you know I was never much on religion..."

"We weren't, either. Come for the fellowship, then. We have potluck suppers, gospel sings, community stuff."

"I might." I put her off. Meeting a bunch of Bible Belt local folks didn't appeal to me right then. Probably try to get me down to the mourners' bench first thing. I got a picture of that in my mind, and no, I wouldn't fit in that scene any way I could imagine it.

"Just be warned, we'll keep inviting you."

"Thanks. And you're probably right; I'll get tired of just my own company after a while." *No, I'm gonna enjoy the silence, being by myself, doing what I wanta do, when I want to and for how long.*

For a change.

Three

Tom and Trish Mallory lived in Springfield, where he did commercial art and she taught school. We'd been close, up until we moved away to greener grass. There was no way Sharon would have raised our kids here in the boondocks, and I'd refused to live in town. So, we left the region entirely. Good for the kids, and I guess for Sharon. I'd suffocated for that whole generation.

It was good to see them again. Tom was thin and fidgety, with hair gone gray, and that pair of penetrating blue eyes their son Jack had inherited. Trish had granny glasses like Kelly's and the severe teacher-look that dissolved into laugh wrinkles.

"You e-mailed us about Jack and the new granddaughter. How's Sue?" I hadn't seen their daughter since early teenage.

"In grad school...archaeology. Going out to Colorado this summer for fieldwork," Trish told me, with a combination of pride and a roll of her eyes. "Got tired of the highway department job, all the bureaucracy. Wants to teach."

"So, you here to fish?" Tom was an avid dry-fly man.

"That, too. I've always wanted to put up a cabin down on what's left of my part. Scoping it out. Mostly some way to get down to it."

"Oh. Well, we used to park in the woods down below there where the sandbar is and climb up, you know, to see the waterfalls. No problem going across our part."

"Jim tells me that gets flooded when the creek's up. I want a way to get closer, build along my branch, up below the falls."

"What're you planning, Liam?" Trish skewered me with her eyes. "Surely Sharon's not coming back to live here?"

"No, that's for sure. Well, the trout fishing's a joke in Virginia now. They stock the streams, and hordes of guys follow the trucks, hooking pen-raised midgets too dumb to live. I'd just as soon catch a smallmouth any day, and I caught more here than anywhere."

"Some big ones up in that deep hole on Jim's part. I've caught some nice ones on a barbless hook. Catch-and-release."

I thought about that...any fish I caught, I'd eat. And with what I was planning, I probably wouldn't have a lot of time to fish, anyway. Road, cabin, find out if I could really do this...

They okayed my road plan. I visited with them a while longer Friday night, then drove down to the ford to camp, where we'd all had picnics years before. A few yards downstream was a nice deep place where the creek swirled among huge boulders. Sharon and I had owned this part originally.

We'd brought Melissa and June here on hot days when they were little. There were pictures all over the house back in Virginia of those times. I suddenly wished I'd brought a few with me.

Lying on the mat in my truck, I was lulled by that moving water. The stars burned above the bluff face across the creek. There was peace here. Maybe it would last.

Maybe I could make it last.

~ * ~

As I faced the daunting project I'd begun, I realized I'd have a long, drawn-out task, and one that would give me a lot of time to think. Yeah, to think about what I'd done, and maybe to regret it. I knew the endless details of planning, building, pushing myself, would be laced with introspection, self-recrimination.

So I braced myself for that, knowing I'd never be able to keep so busy, get so lost in detailed work, to obliterate this mental/emotional journey I was on. Not that I wouldn't try; I would. *I'm gonna drown myself in building to the point where I can deny what'll eat at me every day. I'll give it all I've got to keep that door shut, locked away. But despite all the repetitive tasks, the— even boring?—details, I know I'll have to face it all eventually: leaving Sharon. Look myself in the eye and see if I can justify that. But I'll keep heaping it on, postponing, losing myself in tedium as long as I can.*

~ * ~

I got back to work on the retaining wall I'd begun the day before, where I'd eventually park the truck. I'd work a big stone down with the digging bar from a ledge above, where it'd cracked off long before, prying a few inches at a time. I'd set about ten feet of wall Friday, just one stone high, for about a foot of height. Now I could set one heavy corner in that wall to contain the fill. The other side would be my steps down. Do that next, up from the bare stone of my little streambed.

I stopped to rest often, even though I enjoyed this boulder-moving. No sense getting myself hurt down here. Plenty time to do it carefully. And I could already look back at what I'd accomplished, and feel a bit of pride in it.

As I worked, I reflected that anything high water could reach would get moved, even swept away. Stepping stones across the little branch for sure, and the first steps up. I resolved to anchor those stones with steel pins driven into drilled holes in the solid rock below. Have to get a star drill and some reinforcing rod for that.

I started a list. I could get through the weekend with the few groceries I'd bought on the trip. Shop Monday at Forsyth, the county seat, then. Wheelbarrow, cable hoist to pull those big stones with, long-term food. Cash my Social Security check...have to go by whatever federal office was there to get them to mail those here from now on. Get a post office box too, but nearer, at the road junction nearby the non-village, Kissee Mills.

I was reminded of a story one of the couples had found about our original settler near here. Sylvanus Kissee had come west alone, ahead of his family to settle in the early 1800s. He left an account of spending his few dollars on supplies, and on paper and stamps to write home. He was later to build and operate the gristmill on Beaver Creek, near where it emptied into White River, now Bull Shoals Lake. I remember he was quite pleased that he could pay for his land filing fee and the bare necessities and get established in the new land for so little.

Yeah, I'd have to do that, too. But I didn't have rich creek bottomland, or stands of virgin timber to work with. But no matter...I wasn't establishing a village.

What *was* I doing? Building a hovel to die in? Maybe. And was that so bad, really? Would it be better to die in a hospital in my late, high-overhead town in Virginia? I was compost either way.

But I wasn't ready for that yet. Maybe I wanted to prove I could still carve a home out of the woods by myself. Accomplish it. Did that mean I had an ego problem? Maybe. And didn't everyone? But most guys didn't wait this long. But really, a lot of the actuality of old age was letting yourself get into that frame of mind. I'd known plenty people still cracking at eighty, and some older.

So. The cornerstone for the wall was set deep, leaning into where I'd pile fill dirt and stones against it. Freezing and thawing ought to do no more than let it go back into place. *Hmm.* Gravel fill would be better, let the rain percolate on down to below frostline. Tons of gravel in Caney Creek, easy to get to. Yeah. Start with chunk rock, then coarse gravel, then finer on top. That's how we'd always built the driveways and roads we'd done...do it here. Be slow, but just a bucket of gravel or two a day would add up, and not kill me.

I'd learned that a big part of efficiency in construction is not wasting effort. When you walk to get something, take a thing you'll need there with you. If you don't need that thing over there, wait to go till you do. So, when I was ready, I could slide a flat step rock down when I found some, set it, and bring back a bucketful of gravel. Okay, half a bucket. Same way with tools: when you reached to set one down, bring the next one back in your hand.

I'd watched the father of a guy named Bert I'd grown up with in Arkansas work that way. He'd never hurried, but he got a lot of work done by the end of the day.

I paced myself. Dig out a pocket for a stone after I'd located it, measured it, and started it down. Like the big stones in Peru...always downhill. Then a few feet more with the stone, then rest a bit. No rush. Then go down and level the base for a stone step. Then maybe pry a slab for the step from the layered ledge above, if I could find one, where the sedimentary limestone had cracked.

I'd driven the Ranger downcreek from the ford, to as close as I could get to my place. Then carried the tools up, tossing them from ledge to ledge and climbing. I didn't want to start clearing sprouts from the roadway above while the Mallorys were there, but I couldn't say why. They'd insisted they didn't need help with their cabin, so I didn't want them thinking they had to help me with the road. Right now, I was treasuring my privacy. They probably were theirs, too. Give each other space...

For all those years, whoever owned the land further down would stop for drinking water at Jim's well, look in on them for a few minutes, then spend the day or weekend enjoying the creek by themselves. The place across the creek had been sold by the original couple, but Eric the carpenter was a likable guy, and everyone still got along. Probably remarkable, that compatibility. Our kids would probably sell out to who-knew-who after we died.

No matter, that.

By noon I'd done another six feet of side wall, on the downhill slope of the diagonal driveway/parking spot. And tossed in a lot of odd chunks of stone from above. I climbed down the drop where my steps would be, walked to the ledge over Caney Creek, let myself down, then rock-hopped up to the truck. I took two buckets I'd borrowed from Jim to bring creek-stones back in for fill.

Lunch left me drowsy, with sun trying to get through ragged clouds. Redbuds were in bloom, and some bees had decided it really was spring, so they were out. Maybe I'd build a few hives, do honey. Some people were naturals around bees. I had no idea whether I'd be or not. My grandfather kept bees, and never got stung. But Dad had tried it back after WW2, with really bad luck. Tried raising chickens, too. Ditto.

My first building job with my older brother Sam, when I was ten, was building a big chicken house of recycled barn lumber. And rusty, straightened-out nails. Guess that maybe plotted the course my life was eventually to take, all the years later.

I must've dozed off in the truck bed, because it was an hour later somehow. I stretched, feeling a little soreness. *Go slow the rest of the day.* I half-filled each bucket with six–inch creek stones and carried them across to my stream mouth. Set them on the ledge, climbed up. When I got them up to the retaining wall by hauling and dragging them up with a rope, they made a pitiful addition to the fill.

"Well," I said aloud, "Rome wasn't built in a day."

"That's because *we* weren't on that job." My brother's voice finished the old joke between us. He'd materialized from the ledge route I'd laid out.

"Hey, guy. I'm wondering if I'm having fun, yet." Wiping sweat.

"Made some progress, I see. We got back from town, so thought I'd see if you'd maimed yourself yet. Wow, some of these are big."

"Yeah. I always told my men big rocks don't take much more time to set than the right little ones, and you get a lot more done."

"These took a while." He was eyeing the paths they'd come down.

"Some. I've learned to move big stuff the easy way, though. Big prybar, lotsa time, downhill."

"Gonna put steps on down? Of course you will. Lower ones might wash away, though." I told him my plan for pinning the stones into bedrock.

"Didn't they build a mill dam like that over south of Branson that way? In the old days?" I asked him.

"Something like that. Pinned logs to the rock, then built a wooden dam out of boards against them. Can't imagine it lasted. Here, let's get that big square one up by the ledge."

"Now, don't feel like you have to help, here..."

"I don't. But you helped us build our house."

"About a hundred years ago. And you helped me with my wiring and plumbing at the Branson place."

"So, you can help me do something. Got another bar?"

"Long crowbar. Rock's mostly square, so it shouldn't roll and get away from us."

We worked the thing down. It had to weigh 800 pounds or more. Maybe a thousand. We got it set, and that section of wall was almost done. Jim's always been stronger than me, though a couple inches shorter. And he wanted to set some more rocks. So we did. The sun was hidden behind clouds, but it was about down when we finished that wall. Filled in, it'd do.

"Hey, thanks, man. But I know you got cows to milk. Better get on back."

"No, we got rid of the cows. Just the two horses now. Anyway, we got a good start here. And Eric's got a tractor with a bucket on it. He scoops up gravel above the creek ford for the road. I can borrow it any time. We trade out a lot."

"Well, maybe so, if I can do something for him. I'll do a lot of leveling where it needs it, then start with gravel. Couple more weeks, it'll be dry weather till September, anyway, before I'll need it much."

"I was thinking of this fill."

"Oh, that. Couldn't get a tractor down here yet, though. Too sidling...turn it over. I'll get the worst places, then we'll see."

"Just don't try to be too independent down here. Now, you all set for food? Kelly wants to feed you."

"Tell her thanks, but I've got it okay. Gotta eat up some stuff before it goes bad. I'm going shopping Monday too, get stocked up."

"And you know she wants you to come to church with us."

"Yeah, that. Maybe too sore to move. And I got no decent clothes..."

"Come in jeans...some folks do."

"Well, I don't have one shirt that's not a work shirt. Tell her for me I'll go next week, after I get a few clothes." I was aware I'd just been outmaneuvered, but well, how could I say no to those two? Give it a try, anyway; see what it was all about.

I was sore the next day, but not that bad. I hadn't exactly been goofing off in my construction work back in Virginia lately, although I had been leaving a lot of the heavy stuff to the young guys.

I decided to go fishing. Why not? Protein. Maybe I'd do some work later. I'd slept in, so it was maybe too late in the day, but I went, anyway. The sky was heavy with clouds, but it didn't smell like rain. Downstream were some fairly deep holes in Caney Creek, but Beaver, on down, was better. I got my vest and rod, and set out, enjoying the sights, the sounds, the scents. I'd grown used to the creek smell by now, that mix of drying mud and sycamore trees and wet moss. Here I'd have that all year.

I had to cross the creek because the bluff on my side was too close. The man who'd owned this over here on the other side had died. I hoped his heirs wouldn't do anything foolish with it. The national forest practically surrounded it, but that didn't mean it was safe from some development or other. I hadn't remembered to ask Jim for any details. Anyway, it was a long way to electricity (at least for now), and just an 80-acre pocket in the forest. Shouldn't get any building-up in my lifetime.

He had fenced it. I remembered how his cows had run all over our fields for years. There used to be these Forest Service-planted open acres for deer and game the locals volunteered to help with. Then, of course, they'd let their cattle get out and graze that rich grass. The Ozarks good old boy is shrewd, if he survives.

I remembered a tourist asking a local near here how "these poor, ignorant hillbillies ever made a living in this Godforsaken country." The answer was, "Just you move in here with a lot of money and plans to set yourself up with a country estate, and these poor, ignorant hillbillies will *show* you how they make a living." And it kept happening: some city-weary outsider would imagine he could buy this cheap land, clear the rocks, plant grass, build an expensive house, using, of course, the low-cost local labor, and live like a king. A lot of them left broke and disillusioned.

The first creek hole was under a big sycamore, its roots providing hiding places for tons of fish. I slipped past it, strung up, tied on a stonefly. I hadn't brought my waders from Virginia, but was able to get far enough out on a gravel bar for a cast upstream close to the tree.

I took a few shadow casts to get some line out, then dropped the fly, just past the deepest water. The surface was glass-like, and the faint circles moved out as I twitched the fly. Nothing. I walked in a few inches of line and twitched it some more. Anticipation high. A lot of fishing seems to be willing a fish to strike.

Wasn't working. I walked the fly past the deep place, trying to make it look like it was alive. Nope, it was dead, all right. I started a back cast, but as the slack came out of the line, something hit the fly. Something big. Of course, I jerked it right out of its mouth. Tried to drop it right back there, and got close. A bass will get mad sometimes, and hit anything that's trying to get away. It struck again, but I didn't get the hook set. *Oh boy. By now, the fish probably knows the fly's not real.*

And sure enough, nothing would coax it from those root-caves again. I went through six flies: no luck. *Okay, another day, guy. I know where you live now.*

I fished a few more holes, but gravel had washed in from erosion. The fields were undercut, and there weren't as many deep places as I remembered. I caught one fourteen-inch smallmouth, and just kept it from a maze of hollows under big rocks. Two sun perch, which I released. Get enough of those, with hushpuppies, you've got a feast. One more sizeable fish would do me, though.

On down nearly half a mile, Long Creek came in to Beaver from the right, just past the mouth of Caney. I'd never explored that stream, so hiked up it a distance. Again, the holes were deep in gravel, but there were some spots tight against some low, mossy limestone bluffs that were deep and fast from the recent April rains.

I cast up to the swirl of backwash just below such a run, and watched the fly spin in the current. Probably looked like a twig to the fish, if anything. This was in shadow, so I hoped it wasn't too late in the morning.

It was.

Then I spotted a half-submerged boulder, with some depth to the water alongside. I stripped out line, and cast long, actually bouncing the fly off the rock into the water. I had on a Coachman this time, just because it was the last thing I'd tried before. Must've looked good, because a goggle-eye hit it, hard, the way they do at first. Unlike a smallmouth, they give up soon, and I walked it home. Big enough to eat.

Then I worked my way upstream around big scattered rocks. I cast short back downstream, then let out line, to tumble the fly down the riffle. If something was waiting alongside the fast water, conserving its energy, it might just grab my offering. It didn't. But I eventually caught two more, one a sixteen-inch smallmouth that really put up a fight. I decided this was dinner, and I'd take the others to Jim and Kelly. Nothing else was interested on Long Creek, so I trudged back down.

At Beaver Creek there was a lot of water, and I hooked another fair-sized goggle-eye. The sun was far up by now, and I decided to head back. I'd taken my watch off two days before, and hadn't put it back on. No need, really. I wasn't planning to be a slave to the clock here.

A breeze had kicked up, and now it did smell like rain. I hiked on up, past where the gravel road came down to the forest trails, across Caney Creek. Two carloads of teenagers were there, drinking beer and cranking their boomboxes up. I nodded and gave a short wave as I passed. They ignored me, which was the best thing I could have wanted. Half a mile home, and I'd probably still hear them.

I cleaned the fish at the truck, burying the scales and guts, then washed them and slipped them into Ziploc bags. Folks should be home from church by now. I cranked up, eased between trees to the creek field, then on up alongside the ford and the road out. The soreness was gone, and I reflected that this had been the first fishing I'd done this year.

No excuse for that.

The Mallorys were packing when I passed their drive. I waved. Good. I'd head down my roadway then, hacking small stuff as I went.

Get in three or four hours, leave the truck as close as I could get. I'd put the tools in last night, expecting rain. It looked like it now, but it hadn't materialized. Probably wait till I had the truck in a slick place, then dump on me.

My people weren't home. I left the fish in the fridge with a note: "The heathen offers atonement." As I was leaving, Tom and Trish drove by, and on cue, it began to rain. *Okay, no work for you, old man.* I'd just park and listen to the rain on the roof.

I drove back to the ford gravel bar and shut down. *Well. Time to write Sharon, anyway.* Guessed she deserved to know where things stood. I got out a notebook and just let it pour out: "*Sharon, I'm not coming back. Bob Neal has his instructions re the company. If you should decide to keep it going, talk to him. It's yours. So's all the equipment, the house...*"

I ended the six pages by telling her I wouldn't contest a divorce, and I'd sign any papers she sent me, as long as I could keep this place. I'd have the post office box before I sent the letter, so she'd know where I was. I'd asked her not to hassle Jim and Kelly; she could write me if necessary.

And I wished her well.

That was it. I'd closed a big chapter in my life. Maybe it was a mistake. Probably was. But the fresh smell of the April rain, the sound of the creek, the utter absence of anyone anywhere near, belied that. Right then, what I'd done felt a lot more like freedom. And the bass, filleted and fried in cornmeal on the Coleman stove, made it feel even more so.

~ * ~

June punched off from the call from her mother, wondering just how much of what she'd told her was the truth. Surely Dad hadn't just walked out, no explanation, no reason. *No, there was a reason: they've been sniping at each other for years. Hard to get excited about a visit home with that going on.*

But just to leave like that? That's not Dad. Okay, so he's gone to Caney Creek to hole up for a while. Nothing wrong with taking a break from the rat race...but Mom says he's told her to shut down the business, that he's not coming back. Has he gone crazy? No way. Mom's a pain, and don't I know it. He's maybe just had it, at least for a while. Gotta get some space, like all of us do.

So okay, give it a few days, see what happens. Gotta write him, though, find out what's really going on.

She looked at the stack of undergrads' play outlines piled on her desk. They'd take half the night to read, evaluate, grade. And most of them would be bad, but you didn't stifle creativity in this business. So suck it up, nudge these kids a little, try to find a spark there, somewhere.

It all made her tired. And now this about Dad...

Four

It was after noon on Monday before I'd finished my shopping. I looked at the total I'd scrawled, and felt momentary panic. At this rate, I'd run out of money about halfway to my next Social Security check. But some of this was one-time purchase, like the wheelbarrow, the cable come-along. I'd be okay, until I needed windows and roofing for my house. And a stove. That'd cost me.

No, I could weld up something out of scrap metal. I'd done that once, a long time ago, and it'd been okay. Jim had an electric welder... Sure be handy to get a forge set up: door hinges, good hunting knife, spikes, kitchen stuff...

I'd sent the letter, with my new Kissee Mills post office box. I'd notified the Social Security people. I'd bought a pair of khakis, two shirts, and some dark socks and shoes. That'd have to do for church. I wasn't at all sure I'd be going much, but Kelly was right...it might save me from cabin fever later on. Might do something for my soul, too, but I doubted it. God and I hadn't bothered each other up till now, and I was okay with that.

I hoped He was.

The trip to Forsyth had worn me out worse than working. It had showered again in the morning, and now everything was steamy, green. You could almost see the leaves opening, the grass pushing up higher, the buds unfurling. The smell of the damp soil was so rich it made me want to dig my hands into it, sift it between my fingers, savor it.

It was a fertile Creation-time, and I felt a rising anticipation inside. Everything seemed possible just now. My hands knew the tools, my eye saw what I wanted to accomplish. I'd done enough building that there shouldn't be any surprises.

Except maybe the limits of my strength. But no, I'd done some of the heaviest work already, with no ill effects. I could handle it. *Take it slow, and above all, don't get hurt.* And I needed to look ahead more. I had to cut wood for house rafters and let it season a little, at least. Plan to take in an auction or farm sale where I might pick up a blacksmith's anvil and a forge, or at least a forge blower. I could weld together a forge. Maybe I could get some second-hand lumber somewhere, too.

Then I got an idea: maybe I'd build the shelter for the forge first, get my stove put together, keep stuff dry under there while I built the house. Live in it for a while. Sleep in the truck, probably; I didn't want snakes crawling over me. Or skunks nudging my sleeping bag, with me in it.

But yes, four posts and a roof. Shouldn't be ugly, though. The blacksmith shop should complement the house. So maybe I'd fill in between some of the posts with stone later, when I found which way the wind would blow the smoke away down my deep hollow in winter.

So much to do. Be a long time before I got bored. I ran the curves of Highway 160 with my mind already back on the creek. The anticipation was, strangely enough, a little like forty years or more ago, when I'd met a new girl and a new adventure with her was beginning. I remembered one I'd almost married, a transplant from North Carolina, whose family were living far back in the hills, like Sharon's later. It'd been a long drive to see her, and I'd caught myself driving faster the closer I got. I checked the Ranger's speed: too fast for this road.

At Jim's, I stopped in to ask a favor, and return his buckets, since I now had new ones. They were busy in the garden, the wet, black soil almost steaming.

"Could I get you to freeze this full of water for me?" I took a plastic gallon water jug out of the truck. "Then I can just put it in the ice chest to keep stuff cool."

"That's okay," Kelly replied, "I've already frozen you a plastic milk jug full. Use that one for drinking water."

"Oh, wow. Thanks. How was the fish?"

"Great. You should've stayed."

"Well, I kept the biggest one. Had to get a lot of stuff down on paper for Sharon, anyway. I told her not to bother you all with phone calls, and I hope she won't."

"That won't bother us," Jim put in. "She was never pushy." His dark eyes were on me, and I could tell he didn't entirely approve of my leaving my wife. *Not pushy, huh?* Well, I was the one who'd had to live with that...

"Oh, I got myself some half-decent clothes, Kelly, so I will go to church with you next Sunday. Where do you go?"

"Little non-denominational place off the highway at Kissee Mills. Not formal at all. Real people. Now, you need anything else? Insect repellent? These gnats are bad, after rain."

"No, I got some. I'm really okay. Thanks for the ice. I may dig me a root cellar later, to keep things cool. Ice is a temporary luxury."

"No problem. The second freezer's mostly for venison, anyway."

"You hunt a lot, then, Jim?"

"Some. Mostly just keep the deer out of the garden, and the dog does that." I remembered venison steaks here.

Down the hill, I started in on the saplings in the rest of the roadway. No breeze on this north-facing slope, and I was soon sweating. I filled a shallow gulley with rocks, then drove all the way to the back fenceline. There I took the digging bar to the big stones in the way of my switchback. If I swung wide across the stream and back, I got one ledge further down, right into the next stretch of soon-to-be road.

An hour later, I drove the Ranger nearly a hundred feet along this section without much side tipping. Then I went to work on the first bad place, laying just one height of about eight-inch stones to hold the fill. I grubbed the upper side, chopping roots as I pried them up with the mattock. I'd need fifty feet here, and was determined to get maybe half of it today. The soil was loose enough, but every inch had tree roots laced through it. Some I could cut through with the shovel, but some needed the mattock. Or the ax, even. Have to sharpen it often, with all this grit.

The sun was beginning to drop into the trees when I drove carefully in low range four-wheel drive across my dirt-and-rock-chunk fill. It packed some, but was surprisingly near-level. I got near the gateway formed by two big boulders, and shut the truck down. I'd just managed to come about 300 feet from the switchback, which meant I had 400 to go, give or take, going onto Mallory land and back.

This turn and drop ahead wouldn't be bad in dry weather. On snow and ice, it'd be a killer. The ground dropped three feet in about fifteen. I got out the peepsight level and tape measure. It was four feet in twenty. Yeah, that. I'd need to build up the outside curve below to keep from going off down the drop-off of the next ledge. Need big rocks there, for sure. But I could maybe grub some dirt here now and get closer.

No, no time for that today. And I'd still be pretty far from the site, and on a slope I didn't want to sleep on. I backed the truck all the way to the switchback, and headed out to the gravel road and the ford again. Time enough tomorrow, and yeah, I was tired. And hungry. It occurred to me that I hadn't eaten since morning.

"Must be love," I mumbled, and that struck me as funny. It *was* something like that. This whole crazy adventure...playing mountain man. Like love. Yeah. Full of uncertainties, maybe heartaches, delicious prospects, anticipation, gambles.

Okay, I'd take that, sure...love.

~ * ~

Kyle got essentially the same message from his mother: "Liam's run off to Caney Creek, trying to prove something to himself. Left everything, surely gone crazy. No discussion, no explanation, just gone in that old truck of his, out to the end of nowhere. At least Jim and Kelly can maybe keep him from killing himself."

And yes, just left her, like they'd never had anything good between them, never spent all those years sharing, building the business, raising the kids, caring for each other. So now just what was she supposed to do about it?

Well, can't help you with that one, Mom. Seems like you two could've worked it out, talked, gone for counseling maybe? You're making Dad out to be the monster here, and I know I'm just getting maybe less than half the reality, from your point of view.

Hey, we all love you, but I can imagine Dad just got some sort of overload, y'know? Anyway, I'm not passing judgment before I find out more. You want allies here, so maybe the girls will rally around you: I've gotta think this through some.

Wonder what Sarah will have to say about this. She's got that Christian slant on the world, and it seems to work for her. So what does a believer do with this: guy's dad dumping his wife and dropping off the grid. No, not dumping her so much, maybe just dumping the whole grind. Like "Stop the world..."

~ * ~

The next day I scouted out some slender cedars for cabin rafters and smithy roof poles and posts. The smithy's the shop, not the guy, though the term is confusing as it is to most folks. I remembered being called that over and over back when I was doing the craft fair circuit, starving with the other craftspeople and artists. One lady'd informed me she was a Ph.D. in English, and she *knew* I was a smithy, even if I didn't have a now-extinct chestnut tree to stand under.

"Go read the next line of Longfellow's poem, ma'am," I'd advised. "You'll find the *smith* there, 'a mighty man is he'..." She'd stalked off, nose up, highly affronted.

I cut what I needed for rafters, and some straight, smaller saplings I could slat the shop roof with. Back in Virginia I'd have poplar, straight as a gun barrel. Here there wasn't even pine, and few cedars that hadn't gone all to limbs. In the deep woods they'd shot up to compete for light though, so were usable. The sap was up, so I stripped the bark off the poles, which would turn a honey color. The axe and my hands were sticky and black with resin and dirt, but it came off with hand cleaner.

This time I remembered to eat lunch, because I'd burned up a lot of calories. Afterwards, I studied the gap again, and hit on another idea. There were big stones all along the ledges, some broken off and tumbled that I'd had to go around. I chained one about two by two feet and hooked it to the truck's bumper hitch. As I inched forward in my lowest 4wd gear, the stone moved, but at an angle downhill. It followed me, but off about four feet below. I drove past the gateway, stopped and unhooked. It was twenty feet uphill from where I needed it. Thirty minutes with the long digging bar had it in place. And had me in a sweat. Rest time.

A rock that big would hold some fill, and stop me if I slid out going up or coming down that zigzag drop. Three more would do it.

"Go, horse," I patted the truck's nose, then went for the next stone. Two hours later, the wall was in place. And I was bushed. But I threw a partial layer of six-inch reject rocks against the retaining wall to start the fill, anyway.

Then I eased the Ranger down through the gap and turned for home. Only one more sidling place, and it not too bad. I drove to it, about halfway, and stopped to rest. I hiked on, and down to the creek on my planned roadway. I took my shirt off, splashed creek water all over my upper body, then washed the sweat out of the shirt. I thought about putting it back on, but it was icy to the touch. I hung it on a branch, then climbed back up and out to the truck. Now I had to get to somewhere I could turn around, because I couldn't back through the gap on that unfinished slope.

Or, hey, just drive up onto flat stones on the downhill side for a near-level to spend the night. Did that. No creek sounds here, but early insects and rustlings in the woods and a deep sense of being really lost down there.

I slept deep, long, the weariness numbing my limbs.

Good.

~ * ~

I was doing this work sort of on autopilot, my mind more and more on the past, the way I'd heard old people do. June's first steps replayed in my mind as I stalked another stone to stabilize my road. She'd done this high-stepping walk more awkwardly than the others, and it was hilarious. Sharon had caught it on video, and of course it embarrassed the girl no end every time Mom replayed it.

Cute.

And from the beginning, Kyle was the girls' plaything. They dragged him around like a rag doll, spoiled him, hoarded him. Until of course he committed the unpardonable sin of growing beyond toddler. Then he was a pest, they complained, and why couldn't he leave them alone?

Kids. A pain and a joy, and Sharon and I ate it up. Most of the time, anyway. And when Kyle started following me around instead of clinging to her skirts, she began to resent that. Well hell, he was a little man, not a sissy. He was always fascinated by my making things, working on things. No wonder he became an engineer. I was just glad he hadn't turned out to be a hairdresser or a ballet dancer, though to be fair, I guess that'd been okay, too.

Not.

"Dad, I wanta use the table saw. Got this project for school."

"Not yet. I don't wanta see you cut your fingers off. I'll do the cutting, and you can put it together. Deal? By the way, what is it?"

"Oh, I guess so. It's a boat. We're studying ships, boats, in school, and we hafta make a model, get it approved, then make the real thing. Anything that floats, the teacher said, but I want one that's a sure-enough fishing boat. Do we have wide boards?"

"Sure, but let's build the model first. Whattya want it to look like?"

So he sketched it out: a flat-bottom, pointed-nose actual boat. I cut some very thin wood, which we bent around crosspiece miniature seats, glued to a stem piece and the transom, then we glued on bottom boards, and yeah, my nine-year-old (mostly) had his model.

The teacher approved, but was doubtful this kid could do this. I explained to him that I was only going to cut and plane boards, and he'd do the rest. Even offered to take pictures of him at work to prove he'd done it.

"Yes, better do that. The other kids are planning things like Styrofoam, and plywood with plastic jugs to get it to float. You see, the finished project has to float, and the kid must paddle it at least a few feet."

No sweat: Kyle McLeod could build this. His projects always were complicated, and his attitude was: *Hey, I can do this as well as anybody else, just get outta my way.*

Now where'd he get that?

The local TV station covered the actual lakeside gathering of the various concepts of floating stuff. I'd hauled Kyle's boat, we unloaded it, and he proceeded to install the seats, remove the temporary crosspieces, so everybody could see he was doing it himself, not me. The other kids admired his accomplishment, but the TV folks focused on the outlandish contraptions the others had put together. Most of which came apart, overturned, dumped their creators for a splashing good time.

And on the evening news that day, there was no shot of Kyle's masterpiece.

Life lesson.

~ * ~

Another day then, for road-building. This time, with less slope I opted for just the rock fill with no retaining wall. The stones would fill with soil washed down from the high side in time, and I'd just drive over them meantime. Which I did, two hours later.

Now it was the home stretch. Sliding in spots and a little scary, but with some well-placed stones, I was able to get the rest of the way onto Mallory land. Then I did a repeat of the stone-leveling act downhill, onto some fill stones to get the truck almost level again. It was nearly dark by then, but I felt as if I'd moved mountains today.

Well, parts of mountains.

That night I dreamed of Sharon again. This time she was watching me work on my wilderness roadway, taunting me with insults, rolling her eyes the way she often did. Somehow, I knew it was a dream, and she wasn't real. I was able to work away, ignoring her completely. Next time I looked up to where she'd been leaning against a tree, she was gone. Didn't come back.

Thursday dawned clear again. I turned the truck radio on for a weather forecast, and was able to get three stations. The NPR from the college at Point Lookout came in best, but I had to listen to twenty minutes of classical music first. And the student announcer kept mispronouncing the composers' names, punctuating my breakfast of corn cakes and bacon. I couldn't interpret his Artero Tooskinny for a while. Okay, weather clear till the weekend. Good. I cut the switch and got to work.

I was getting used to the soreness in the mornings, which was usually gone in half an hour. I hadn't strained anything yet, and didn't want to. You don't have to if you don't get in a hurry, and hurry isn't an old man's game.

~ * ~

Melissa had been up to her eyes in alligators when her mother had called, all frantic about Dad's leaving. She'd listened, between bouts of yelling at the kids, ages three and five, who were at the moment wrecking the house.

Then it soaked in: her father had just walked out on her mother after what, 30-something years of marriage? *What a jerk!* A momentary panic ran through her: *What if Grady got an idea like that?* But no, her husband was a rock, thank God.

"Wait, Mom. Back up a little. You're sure he's really *gone?* I mean, maybe he's just taken some time off to go fishing. You know how much he bitches and moans he's never got time for that."

"Thought so, yeah. Left a message on the phone. But then I get this long, rambling letter from Caney Creek telling me he's through. With the business, with Virginia, with *me,* for Godsake. He's gone around the bend, Mellie, and I don't know what I'm supposed to do about it." She could see her mother's angry tears.

"Oh, gosh, neither do I. *Kenny, stop that!* Listen, I've gotta get outta here, go to a parents' thing. Talk to you later, Mom. Let me think about this some. But yeah, that was a cheap-ass thing to do to you, after all..."

"He's a selfish old fool, Mellie, and I'm thinking to hell with him!"

"Okay, okay. I'll get back to you. And yeah, I'll write him, give him hell." She punched off, grabbed three-year-old Lisa just before she could pull the cookie jar off the counter on herself.

This's crazy. He's crazy. Okay, we all get stressed, but to take it out on Mom? What's happened to the old devil? He and I were so close back when I was little, the oldest, the one he spent most time with. But yeah, those memories seem a little sick, just now.

Talk this over with Grady when we can grab a breath. But I'm sure gonna run Dad over the coals soon's I can write him. What a crappy way to treat the woman who's put up with him all these years. Give him hell...

~ * ~

The snake was the color of October leaves. It was coiled just where I was about to step, and somehow I managed a sort of float over it and landed beyond. I quickstepped further, then turned to look at it. It hadn't moved out of my way because it knew it didn't have to. The head was the color of aging copper, with an almost translucence, and the pattern on the body would disappear in those fallen leaves come warm days in autumn. Now the perfect shape stood out, but I hadn't seen it till I'd almost stepped on it. The tongue was flicking out, the head moving back and forth, probably looking for a way to go.

I knew wild things didn't interact much, and that when another species paid attention, the object of that attention assumed it was about to be eaten. Eat, sleep, procreate: all of life, for them. So I was a direct threat...

Well, did I leave this denizen, who'd been here long before me, let it go its way, coexist as best I could with it? Or was I apt to find it under the next rock I picked up, or coiled next to a tool I was reaching for? Or maybe I'd step on it in the dark. I'd known a couple of guys who'd been bitten by copperheads, and the infection was bad. One, the doc wouldn't give antivenin to without seeing the actual snake that'd bitten the man. His whole leg turned black, and it was a long time before he got over it.

How much did I want to control this environment I'd come to, here? I'd already built a road of sorts, intruded with my truck, planned a house. Would I smash every snake I saw, just to be sure one wouldn't crawl into my sleeping bag? Couldn't ever be sure, I guessed. But, having to be constantly on guard, always apprehensive, knowing this guy and others were at home here...didn't like that much. And snakes liked spaces between rocks, and I was heavy into rocks...

I sat and watched this actually beautiful animal as it slowly straightened out, then began an unhurried slither up the bare limestone alongside the little stream. Minding its own business. If it just didn't have that sharp end...

I eventually got a heavy contractor's plastic trash bag from the truck, and managed to direct the snake into it with a long stick, partly flipping it inside. Then I closed the bag, carried it across Caney and downcreek all the way past Beaver, where I shook it out onto new territory. Maybe it wouldn't find its way back. Maybe it would.

I concentrated on tossing and rolling fill stones down from the woods above onto my parking area, keeping my eye out for other visitors. This went a lot faster than carrying them up from the creek, but it was still slow. I took a lot of breaks, and quit when an ache started in one hip. The truck was okay right where it was. I wouldn't be able to get it out till I'd filled this and graded the switchback up, but I had till the weekend. Or later. I could hike up to Jim's anytime, leave the Ranger here.

Sure. I didn't need wheels to be mobile.

I went in search of step stones. I wanted them three feet long by sixteen inches or so wide. Thickness didn't matter; I could bury deeper or build up under each tread. What I needed was a big, serrated boulder I could split, or better, one that'd already split into layers.

Jim had found sandstone higher up, a freak layer he'd used to floor his utility shed. But that had been far back in the woods. He and his son Mike had carried them out years before, and said they'd gotten them all. But there had to be good limestone. And there was.

The three-inch-thick top of an exposed ledge was deeply cracked from its bed below.

I checked around to make sure I was snake-free, then slipped the crowbar in and lifted. The sound was a crunch, and up it came: four feet long and wide. A lacework of roots patterned the surface underneath. Flat roots that had slipped into the barest spaces, then swelled with growth until the stone separated.

One. I needed twelve; there had to be more. Three inches down was the beginning of another fissure, but I'd need my stone chisel to wedge it open. Below that the ledge face was smooth.

In an hour I'd located five stones total, but only three were loose. And I'd have to work them to within reach of the truck. *No, wait.* This was where I could use Eric's tractor bucket later. Get two or three in and walk them down my new road when I needed them. I got the feeling Sharon was still watching, rolling her eyes at my not seeing that solution right away.

Go away, Sharon.

I scouted up the far shore of Caney Creek looking for likely boulders I might split. This time I had a stone chisel and my three-pound striking hammer. Under the high bluff there should be layered stones, fallen from the jutting face above.

What I found made me laugh out loud. There were more slabs of stone here than I could count, scattered among scrub willow on the talus slope against the bluff. I had everything I'd need, already to size. And so many flagstones for the house floor, I could do it all with just what I could see now.

I'd never come here all those years ago. The smooth gravel bars on the south creekside had always been our picnic places. Now, bees buzzed among some flowering bushes and what looked like early weeds. The sun bore in on the bluff, reflecting heat onto this jumble of fallen rock, plants, moss, and unfurling ferns. The smell was of bursting growth, like a greenhouse.

Birds were nesting in the taller saplings, and on ledges in the cliff. I saw a chipmunk racing across the flat face of a tilted boulder toward some destination, wary of predators. Water dripped from somewhere above, and I could see a fernfall greening up from a ledge that spilled large, round water drops.

These stones would require pulling across the deep water of the creek. I had two chains that should reach, if I backed the Ranger to the opposite shore. Or, if we got that tractor...Or, in dry weather, we might be able to drive up the creek bed.

Hey, I'd get these rocks.

Okay. I climbed and hiked back downstream, and hopped my way across to my branch. I took a bucket of fill stones with me, hauled them up, and added their paltry mass to the parking area, avoiding thinking about how much I still had to go. And I realized I was hungry.

The ice in the chest provided me with a cold drink and a thick ham sandwich. Have to watch out and balance what I was eating. Remember vegetables, fruit, whatever. Never been much of a nutritionist, but I'd survived. I thought again how much the family had enjoyed Sharon's cooking, back when she did cook.

~ * ~

"What's this, Mom? Pie?" Melissa was straining to see over the counter top.

"It's called quiche, honey, and it is a little like pie. But it's got eggs and vegetables and meat in it. You'll like it." Our firstborn was doubtful.

Now whatthehell's this woman put together here? Quiche? I'm supposed to eat sissy quiche? Never in my life had I tasted this dish, and only vaguely remembered something about Quiche Lorraine, or thought I did. But okay, I'd eat whatever she put in front of me, I guessed. I worked hard, had an appetite, and her cooking back then was something I never complained about.

But *quiche?*

Sharon liked for me to take her out to eat, like all women, and I could stand it every now and then. The kids were too often a pain in restaurants, though, and I'd had to whisk the worst offender out the door and wait in the car for our often-cold dinner to arrive more times than I can remember. That usually quieted the others, and my bride could at least have her out-of-the-kitchen experience without us.

So I'd gotten used to her hands-on-hips announcements as I came in the door after a grueling day's work, that I was taking her out to dinner, and we had a babysitter, so get dressed, old man. So much for hearth and home. I knew a truck driver who'd managed to survive highway food all week, to come home to find he and wife were eating out. They actually split up over that.

~ * ~

I watched an early butterfly check out my wall. Heard bees again every time I stopped chewing. Thought about all that fill I'd need for my parking place. Didn't want to figure the cubic yardage; that'd discourage me for sure. And yeah, I'd need these calories...

Now why hadn't I thought of using the truck before, I wondered. *Okay*, Sharon.

I backed it on the straight stretch very carefully, started filling it with small stones. Had a good load in less than an hour. Hadn't seen any more copperheads. Maybe the noise and activity would convince them this wasn't a good place to be.

Drove back to above my fill area, then tossed rocks. Sure beat all that climbing I'd done earlier, for increasingly distant fill stones. Two more loads and I was getting the fill area close to the near-level that was my goal. The tight turn back onto the roadway above would be hard, in snow or ice, but I could make it now, I was sure. Add to it later.

I backed the Ranger down. I was looking at treetops out the windshield, it seemed. Steeper than I'd thought. Maybe I'd be marooned here, have to rig some sort of winch to get the truck out. But give it a try, anyway.

Okay, now, up and out, maybe. I made sure the rig was in four-wheel drive, low range, and eased it forward. A few rocks rolled from under my wheels and we lurched a little, but we made it. I knew I could navigate the stone gateway, distant and way up. And all the other tight squeezes, the *maybe* places that constituted my almost-road. And out into the world.

Somehow, that realization wasn't as uplifting as it maybe should have been.

Five

It was a late summer day, and Melissa and I'd been out to a construction job since noon, when I'd picked her up at Sharon's office. She'd played with her toys in her playpen in my old Land Rover for a couple hours, which maybe was a record. Then of course she'd cried, I'd changed her, given her a bottle.

She was just into walking, in that tentative, comic getting-to-know-the-ground-under-her-feet unsure way so many toddlers her age have. So I took her out, let her discover grass and acorns and twigs around that jobsite, keeping a close eye on her.

It worked for another hour, amazingly. She never napped when she was supposed to, or maybe just when the experts said she should, so she needed entertaining. Later, on the way home we stopped so she could pick yellow Black-eyed Susans in an old field. She pulled their heads off, of course, and I helped her get the stem. There's nothing prettier than a baby girl picking flowers, and my heart was swelling against my ribs.

The Rover's rocking on our dirt road put her to sleep, something almost impossible at home until she was good and ready. I put her over my shoulder as I drove, and she never stirred. Now, I'd learned that the instant I shut off the engine, she'd bolt awake, and it'd be midnight when she finally gave up.

I eased the rig to a standstill above the little cabin, set the brake and left the throbbing power plant going. She didn't stir. I slipped out, then into the house, let her gently down on her bed and sneaked out to shut it off. Then back inside, I just stood there and watched her sleep, easily the most beautiful little girl in the world.

~ * ~

By the end of Saturday, I'd filled the low spots all along my road with stones, and had set some of the steps in place. Jim had come down Friday and helped me get step stones into the truck. Seems Eric's tractor was ailing, so we pulled them across the creek with the end-to-end chains, then worked them up into the truck on two skids of the peeled cedar rafter poles I'd cut.

Working with him, I remembered when we'd lived only twenty miles apart, and helped each other a lot. Seemed neither of us got much done alone, with all the demands of family and trying to make a living. But when either he or I came to help, the other dropped everything else and we made great progress.

"Okay, now what can I do at your place?"

"Come for church, then eat dinner with us later."

"I mean work. That's R and R."

"Maybe not," he laughed.

~ * ~

So now it was Sunday morning. I was shaven, clean after a creek-water bath, and in my new outfit, which smelled like Wal-Mart. We went in Kelly's Cherokee up the bare ledgerock road out through the other national forest section to the highway. Down to our left, the deep Caney Creek valley lay, mist rising from a shower in the night. Redbud trees clung to what thin soil there was on the limestone, fiercely blooming before the drier time to come.

"The lizards still live by the gate," Jim told me. When we'd first looked at the land those years ago, we'd seen two giant lizards near the barbed-wire gap that closed the road then. They were eighteen inches long, blue and green. "Mountain Boomers," the neighbors called them. We slowed, but none showed itself this time.

The church could have been anywhere in the world...one of thousands. Cars and pickup trucks were nosed to the cedars at the gravel parking lot's edge. Most were old like my Ranger; a few were late models. Most of these people would work in Branson at the motels or music attractions there. Or maybe in Forsyth, the nearly industry-less county seat. There'd also be the farmers, who now all ran cattle, the bulldozer operators, timber-cutters, mechanics.

The women wore dresses from homemade to fancy. The men, already red-faced from the sun, were in khakis like me, or slacks and sport jackets. Nobody wore a suit. I got introduced to almost everybody, and couldn't remember a single name.

"Oh, here's our minister." Kelly led me to a lean, weathered man of about sixty alighting from a battered Chevrolet pickup. "Bill, this is Jim's brother, Liam. Bill Zachman." The hand was harder than mine, dry and firm.

"Liam. Good to meet you. Jim's told me you ran off to Virginia on back. You here long?"

"Maybe so. Depends on a few things. I'm building a little fishing cabin I've wanted for a long time."

"Good. Lake's full of bass. We'll hafta go, sometime." He patted the hand he held, then released it, turned, took a large Bible from his truck seat, hailed newcomers.

"What else does he do for a living?" I asked.

"Farmer. Lives down on Cedar Creek," Jim told me. "Wife died maybe five years back. He's taken religion courses at the college at Point Lookout, but never went to seminary. Plain dirt preacher." I wasn't sure whether that meant he was a shouting exhorter or an earnest but unlettered storyteller. Maybe I should expect both.

We filed in. Fans were going, stirring the air that was still cool, but would heat with the bodies. About forty people found seats on the pine pews, and seven, including Jim, moved into the choir loft. It was a raised platform to the left of the pulpit, which was off-center and angled toward us. Kelly and I sat two rows back, and she introduced me to two latecoming couples.

I hadn't been to a country church since childhood, but the memories came flooding back: the thundered sermons, the enthusiastic hymn-singing, the shy children. Then there'd been the fellowship suppers, the Bible study nights, the Wednesdays when the women had hung their quilting frames from the ceiling, the pews moved aside. We kids would play tag under the quilt, running around the mothers' long-skirted legs. I got a clear picture of the rough farm shoes those women wore: scuffed, cracked, postwar country two-dollar shoes. Sixty-five years ago.

A prim-looking woman sat at the upright piano, watching the choir, of which Jim was one of only two men. Then she looked toward the minister, who'd moved behind the pulpit and was shuffling papers. He nodded, and she began a lilting, very modern tune that reminded me of the counter-culture music of the back-to-the-earth seventies and eighties. More late arrivals slipped in as the Reverend Zachman marked places in his Bible.

I knew I was going to be singled out and introduced to the congregation, and was glad I didn't have on a tie to further constrict my already sweaty neck. But Zachman only blanket-welcomed whoever might be visitors among us, and made a few announcements. Others stood and told of upcoming happenings, among them a barbecue, work on a Habitat for Humanity house project, church rummage sale. Then the pianist struck up another modern tune.

The choir members rose, and their harmony was smoothly perfect. Jim had a good bass, and the other guy, a giant in a tight shirt, had a clear tenor. The women were good. One white-haired soprano's voice soared, without a crack in it. The altos were dead-on, too. I was pleasantly surprised; we never had this back in our part of rural Arkansas.

Some of the older hymns were only barely familiar, but after one verse, I could sort of sing along. Kelly was no singer either, but we got carried along by the crowd, with the choir keeping everyone on track. They mixed oldies with that new stuff, and it was okay.

The minister read a Scripture passage about the Good Shepherd, then he called the children down front, where the eight of them sat on the floor in a semicircle around him. They ranged from five-year-olds to about twelve, scrubbed, grinning, glad to be there. The reverend greeted them, then asked if they knew what a shepherd was. Two hands went up excitedly. The older children smiled, letting the little ones answer.

"It's a dog!" one boy of six announced.

"It could be, but let's say it's a person. What does a shepherd *person* do? Audrey?"

"He lives with the sheep," the little girl said shyly, twisting her hands into the hem of her dress. She had dark hair and eyes, and would grow to be a beauty.

"Okay. But he's really there to *take care* of the sheep..."

It was cute. And Grandpa Bill was as gentle with his young charges as any shepherd. He made a simple analogy with Jesus that the younger ones might or might not have understood, said a prayer, and thanked them. They clambered through a door to the rear ahead of an older woman, and the minister stepped behind the plain board pulpit.

There was more Scripture, prayers, and a surprisingly short sermon. About how dumb sheep were, and how utterly dependent on the shepherd. His delivery was totally without artifice, as sincere as one farmer talking with another. You got the clear feeling this man was so secure in his faith he couldn't imagine anyone else not getting his message. Then there was more music. A plate was passed for offerings.

Afterwards, Zachman shook every hand, called every name, including mine.

"You come on back now, Liam," he invited. "And I meant it 'bout fishin'. I know you're buildin', but y'gotta take some time off." I mumbled something in reply. Lake fishing wasn't my thing.

"Well?" Kelly asked, as we eased out onto the country road that led the short distance back to U.S. 160.

"Fine," I admitted. "Nothing high and mighty about old Bill. And Jim, you folks are *good*."

"It's fun, really. And music is ministry, too. You do what you have a gift for." Jim had always been the musical one in the family.

"I gotta ask: do Mary and Mike go to church?"

"Well, we tried, but they were on the way out when we began to realize we can't do this life alone. We hope they'll see that, too."

Can't do it alone. Well, maybe not. But I was sure headed that way. But y'know, all those earnest folks were okay. More like the old days really, than even the back-country Virginians I'd known, once you got away from the towns. I'd often reflected on how much closer people seemed away from cities, probably from the hardscrabble lives they shared.

Kelly had roasted duck, and we feasted. Real switch from my thrown-together stew and pancakes. Needed to get myself some sort of oven. Maybe that Dutch oven...As if on cue, this fine woman brought out a peach cobbler to die for. I ate so much I couldn't waddle.

The only thing missing was the fresh milk, cream and butter they'd always had. Our kids had chattered about that long after visits, and used to want me to get a cow, too. I remembered milking cows with my older brother, Sam, often by lantern light long ago, the moths fluttering, the warm feel of the cow's side against my forehead. Melissa, our firstborn, loved all animals, and would have made a pet out of a cow. But I knew how much time had to go into caring for livestock, and I hadn't been about to go that way again.

And Sharon would have died on the spot if I'd brought home a heifer. Probably gone out the door as soon as I'd unloaded it.

We sat outside on the porch and talked about good times, and I felt some more of the old warmth coming back. Then Jim got out his guitar while Kelly sewed on something. He knew hundreds of old folk songs, and some lively bluegrass and gospel. Kelly and I joined in some, but mostly we just listened. I found myself remembering Jim's first learning the guitar, an eighteen-dollar second-hand Kay he'd saved money for. We'd suffered through "Wildwood Flower" for months. I flashed on his freckled face, concentrating, biting his lower lip.

Neat kid, always was.

"Take some of this with you," Kelly insisted, pressing a big Ziploc bag on me as I left. I couldn't protest. "And don't forget your ice."

I had the feeling it wasn't going to get any better than this.

~ * ~

My brother Jim hadn't always been this laid back and content. And I guessed you could still get a rise out of him if you managed to push the right button. I remembered the time, early on here on the creek, when he and a friend who had a heart condition were coming back from somewhere down the ledgerock almost-road from the highway. They saw smoke among the cedars and sedge grass ahead and climbing up the slope from up the creek valley. Sure enough, a forest fire was racing toward the track, and there was nothing to stop it from spreading on down to Jim's house.

He and the friend stomped the fire, beat it out with burlap sacks and the one long-handled shovel that happened to be in the pickup. As soon as they'd get a section stopped, two more would flank them. It was hot, dry, the perfect windy day for a devastating fire.

They raced to each tongue of the advancing fire, finally getting ahead of it, following it to where bare ledgerock had hemmed it in further down. Just as they were staggering back to the truck, soaked in sweat, thirsty, sooty, a ragged car skidded to a stop up the road. A teenage boy in torn tee shirt and dirty jeans jumped out, confronted them.

"Whatthehell you doin', here?" he demanded, a scowl on his face.

"Puttin' this fire out before it gets to my house," Jim told him, leaning wearily on his shovel. "Who're you?"

"I'm Raz Roberts, that's who. An' I set this here far, burn off our place, kill th' ticks an' snakes. Y'got no bizness puttin' it out."

Jim looked at his friend, who had miraculously not collapsed with a heart attack. Then he took long steps up to the kid, and placed the end of the long shovel handle against his solar plexus. Then he took another step, hard-eyed, grim, and he spoke in a deadly, calm voice.

"Now you listen, Roberts. I don't care what you do on your place—or your *daddy's* place. But this fire was about to take this whole hillside, and my house with it. Now, if you *ever* let another fire get away, or if I even hear of you setting one, about twenty of us going to come over to the Roberts place with a hanging rope, you hear me?"

"Aw, this ain't nuthin' but ole forest land, no 'count fer nuthin'." His eyes had gotten bigger, shifting, and when Jim took another step, forcing him back, they got even bigger.

"*You hear me, boy?*" He continued to push the stumbling redneck backwards. "A *hangin' rope!*"

Raz Roberts turned and ran to his car, spun the wheels getting out of there.

"Weren't you scared he had a gun or somethin'?" the friend asked.

"Wasn't, no. But now I am. Let's get on home."

~ * ~

By the third week, Sharon had called and cried on Kelly's shoulder twice, alternately insisting I was insane, and that she was worried about me. Okay, about what I'd expected. Deal with that, and so would she.

And I had the smithy up on its cedar legs and covered with galvanized metal. And some creek gravel on the worst places in the road.

Progress.

I'd found a few recycled boards at a farm sale, had decked the roof of the shop with them, and built work benches. Now I could get everything out of the Ranger and use it more like a truck—a small truck. Every chance I got, I shoveled in a load of gravel and spread it. Slow. I could have used twenty big truckloads, but every bit was helping.

Of course, this scattering would get squashed down into the dirt and I'd have to add more. And more. But hey, you gotta start somewhere, and I think I've already mentioned that all I had was time.

The house-building began with a minor ceremony. I'd worked that nice cube of stone at the switchback up a heavy plank into the truck with the come-along and brought it home. Then I tumbled it downslope and pulled it up the side branch, a little at a time to the site. It was my cornerstone, to be set on the wet concrete footing I'd been a whole day mixing in the wheelbarrow and pouring. I chiseled my initials and the date on the front face of the stone, then swung it from a tripod of poles to set it in place.

Then I went fishing again. Wasn't going to let this building binge steal all my time. Didn't catch anything but small perch, and decided to let them stay and grow a while longer. And hey, isn't most of fishing anticipation, enjoying the outdoors, getting away from it all?

I remembered taking the girls fishing before Kyle was old enough. They'd get excited when a fish hit a dry fly, and I'd set the hook and let one of them reel it in, coaching her on keeping the slack out of the line. Big fish, I'd keep the rod, walking it in, because we ate them later. But both girls enjoyed our outings, each clamoring for her turn with the next fish.

But as they grew into teenage, my daughters didn't want to spend their free time on a stream where they usually didn't catch anything. Melissa and some other girls went to a lake with another family who had a motorboat, and she'd been hooked on racing around on water instead of fishing it ever since. June just grew out of it, with all the other things she was into.

Later, of course, Kyle and I went as often as I could get away. I'd bought him a then-already-rare split bamboo rod, with my favorite action, and he still treasured it, several replacement tips later. Memories of father and son trying to outdo each other, going through all the flies in our vests, laughing, sharing.

Damn, I missed that boy.

Later that day, we had a downpour for two days that raised Caney Creek up over the four-foot side branch drop and the slope below, that was usually dry at the normal level. The roar permeated everything. Small uprooted trees thundered past, and flotsam churned the muddy water. That would've come from a dirt road crossing miles upstream. The little branch came up eight inches, and the waterfalls were spectacular. My newly-placed stepping stones were under four inches of water, but stayed pinned in place.

After the rain stopped, I found five places my road had washed, so repaired them with stones. I shaped dips for the water to cross, and lined them with flat rocks. We'd see how well that worked, next rain.

I scouted good building stone and brought some of it home in the Ranger, some down the little stream, and built a house. Well, small house. Hut.

Whatever.

The May days were long, and not too hot, and I got totally immersed in the project. It would take all summer, I figured, but I had a good start, and wanted to keep at it. I might not have the money for the roof yet, but I wanted to be ready for it when I could get it.

I was reminded of my first jobs, over 50 years before, when I had to budget the forty bucks a week I made (before taxes) to get from one payday to the next. This fixed-income business was definitely going to keep me strapped, but it should be easing after the house was finished. If by some miracle my truck didn't break down, and I could avoid banging myself up, I'd make it.

~ * ~

I didn't hear them come up the branch; they were just suddenly there. A man and three women, rounding the curve, stopping when they saw me. They were carrying cameras, tripods, reflectors. The women, two young, one not so young, were in shorts and tank tops. The guy was maybe forty, sneakers, no socks, tee shirt and shorts. They'd waded Caney Creek.

"Hey," he called. "Whatcha doin' in here?" the voice had just a little challenge in it.

I straightened from cutting a block of stone. They surely must've heard my hammering.

"Buildin' myself a cabin. How 'bout you all?" The older woman had a leathery face, hard. The girls too, had some miles on them. The man was skinny, long nose, eyes that sort of bulged.

"Didn't know anybody ever came here. That your truck up there?"

"Is. Put in a road. You come up from Beaver?"

"Yeah. Wanted to do some photography here by the falls." He looked past me up the little creek.

"Falls about dried up."

"Oh. Well, you're buildin' right in one of our favorite settings. Thought this was national forest."

"No. I've had it something over thirty years. Forest's on up a ways." The girls didn't look like models, if that was what these people were going to get pictures of. Maybe they had some kind of product back at their rig they'd planned to promote. "I'll be livin' here, soon's I get the roof on." The guy looked at the older woman, who shrugged.

"Well, I guess we'll just have to...hunt up another place, then. Hoped the falls'd be going."

"Dries up early. Always has. You folks have a nice day." I picked up my hammer.

"Yeah, well...okay." He turned, adjusting a shoulder strap. "See you." And they straggled back down the branch.

Now, what in hell was *that* all about? Sure not a family outing. Porn stuff? Who knew. Probably found this hollow, sure nobody'd ever been here. Well. I slipped down after them, hearing them now, talking among themselves. They didn't bother my truck, just climbed down off the ledge and waded Caney again. I could see an orange SUV at the edge of the gravel bar. They reached it, loaded their camera gear, started up and left.

Weird. Well, leave a spot alone, folks'd find it. Just glad nobody'd squatted on it all these years. Nah, too rough for anybody but a real hardcase. Even the core outdoorsmen I knew wanted some sort of road, or at least a trail to a place...

Okay, so yeah, I did have a road now.

In between building, I helped Jim repair fence, haul manure, replace some barn siding. And he spent entirely too much time helping me. We both would get a bang out of finding some big, long rock or other and engineering it up into my house wall. I was building these a foot thick, and there's no such thing as a lightweight stone that wide. I needed his help.

And I found myself actually looking forward to the church thing with them. Those folks were just so...unaffected, I guess you'd say,

I liked being with them. And some of what the Reverend Bill had to say started to make sense, which it really never had before.

For instance, I'd always had trouble with the concept of a God who let the kind of rotten things the world was full of, happen to people. Like wars and poverty and terrorism and disease. Old Bill explained that we had freedom of choice in this world—had to have, or we'd just be robots—and that we were bound to step in front of trucks or on land mines sometimes.

Maybe. But all our ills weren't our fault, I pointed out to him. We were standing by his pickup in Forsyth one Saturday. He'd started this, and I'd figured to get an answer or two, if I could.

"No, but try to picture this life with nuthin' ever goin' wrong," he put it to me. "Everything always just *perfect*. No surprises, nuthin' to mark our lives. We wouldn't be people anymore. We'd be just blobs— wouldn't need God. Wouldn't be *anything*, really."

I couldn't imagine that. We get used to being thinking, reasoning beings. But yeah, if nothing ever went wrong, no challenges, what'd be the point in existence, even?

I didn't have an answer to that one, but I thought it over, letting my eyes roam over the steep hills that dropped down to Lake Taneycomo below the town. Bill was loading rolls of web-wire fencing into his truck, and I helped him while my mind turned over what he'd been telling me.

"So, the old saying about the bitter makes the sweet more so, that's maybe real?"

"Seems to be. And best we know, this life's a test, see, a temporary existence lastin' just a few years, an' if we pass it, we go on to th' real thing. And what kinda test would it be if ever'thing went just right? If we didn't hit some rough spots, this test would be like havin' th' answer sheet, wouldn't it? Hey, I don't claim to have those answers, Liam. I'm just searchin' like th' rest of us. On my faith journey, too."

Okay. Test, huh? This a temporary existence? Maybe. I'd have to admit, this life had gone by fast. Too fast, looking back. And here I was, in the end game. Maybe that next life folks talked about would give us a chance to get more done. Or maybe get it right.

Or not.

Jim and I'd talk about religion, too. Between us these days, it wasn't a subject to be avoided, because I wasn't strong anti, or had a lot of iron-bound ideas. We were chopping weeds out of his rows of corn one sweltering day when he let me in on part of his conversion.

"I was having a rough time, bro. You know, getting hit with middle age, seeing greener grass everywhere else. Even thinking I'd outgrown Kelly—that's how crazy it was. I'd see another woman maybe, and wonder what I was missing. And always being broke. Not happy with having tossed the engineering, way back then.

"And I was pretty sour on a God who couldn't, or wouldn't, take better care of one of His supposed children. Anyway, I let some of that out to Kelly one time. Not the other women part, but just sort of unloaded, you know.

"She thought about that for a while, then she put her finger right on it. Said to me, "You sound like you think you're the center of the universe." Then she just got in her car and went to town to leave me time to work on that. Bottom line was, I realized I had to start thinking about doing for people other than yours truly.

"Right afterwards, I met Bill Zachman, and we spent some time hashing over stuff. Bill will always stop whatever he's doing—and he does a lot, that rocky place of his—to spend time with any of us. At the time, his wife had cancer, bad. And I could see he was hurting a helluva lot moren' me. If anybody had a right to toss the benign God concept, he was standin' right in front of me. But *he* wasn't whining. Got to me."

Long speech, for my brother. But I'd been in a hole a little like that. Not long ago, either. Hadn't reacted that way, though. Have to think about my running out, maybe in another light. Truth was, though, I didn't know yet what all the twists and turns behind my actions were. Maybe never would. Somebody famous once said self-analysis is never accurate.

I remembered something from Yeats, my favorite poet when I took time to read:

I went out to the hazel wood
Because a fire was in my head...

Six

I knew it'd happen. Matter of time. I just didn't know which one of them would be the first. I'd gotten letters from all three kids, and real long ones from Sharon. Kyle was the most likely to make the trip, but Melissa or June would probably be more outraged, and apt to come eventually, to try to talk sense into me. Or maybe not; write me off. And Melissa's letters were downright mean, I thought, solidly on Sharon's side. Okay, so much for her having been the closest to me, way on back when she was truly the firstborn.

It was Kyle, on a Saturday morning. He'd driven to Springfield the night before, stayed in a motel. Stopped in at Jim's to try to find out what to expect, I guess. Then on down to the ford in his 4wd Audi, and hiked down to the site.

"Hey, Dad." I heard him before I saw him, bent over my stonework. Long time since I'd heard that voice.

"Kyle. Good to see you, guy. Come to see if I was still alive?"

"Sort of. Wow, you've done a lot here." Eyes taking in the Ranger perched back down the branch up above, the steps, smithy, the house walls.

"Keeping busy. You know I always wanted to do this."

"Yeah. Sort of figured you'd given up on it, though. We kicked around the plan of building it before I was grown, but never found the time."

"Lotta years got away, all right. Figured I'd get it done while I still could. You got time off?"

"Not really. Just the weekend. Mom's been burning up the phone since you left, to all of us. I wanted to come see you..."

"And hear my side of it?"

"Well, yeah, I guess so. Nobody ever expected you just to...pick up and go like this." Kyle was embarrassed. I guess I didn't strike him right then as the heartless monster or raving maniac Sharon had probably pictured me to them. (Sorry to disappoint.)

Or maybe I did.

"Well, there's no 'my side' of it. Just nothing there for your mom and me anymore. Nothing but fighting."

"She's really sorry you left, Dad."

"Maybe, but I doubt that. I never saw her anymore, Kyle. Anyway, I've crossed a line, I guess." I looked him in the eye, and saw a lot of myself. "And at the risk of alienating all of you, I really don't think I have to justify this to anybody."

"But you...didn't discuss it. Didn't..." He spread his hands.

"Guilty. Tired of the yelling. Continual yelling. You could say something snapped, I guess. It just got to be time to go." It was my turn to spread my hands. That was all I had to say. So the silence just hung there, Kyle with his hands now jammed into his pockets, looking at everything but me.

I sort of waited for whatever was next.

"Well," he said after a space, "why don't I lay a few rocks with you, then maybe we can go fishing?" He was grinning.

"Sounds good to me." *Okay, this will be all right.* "Your Uncle Jim was going to help me set this window lintel stone, but you and I can handle it. Might have to set a tripod, use the come-along."

He hefted one end of the four-foot stone I'd brought from upcreek a few days earlier, loaded in Eric's tractor bucket.

"Looks like a tripod job, Dad. We could maybe get it up by hand, but it'd be easy to lose it, leaning in to try to set it."

"I was coming around to that approach, all right. So far I haven't broken any bones here, and I'd like to keep it that way."

We set one leg of the tripod I'd put together of peeled cedar poles inside the wall and the other two out, then chained the stone. The come-along works with a ratchet-handle turning the cable drum, and each click is upward progress. Like a lot of my mechanically-generated stuff here (chainsaw, truck), this one sounded out of place, a machine temporarily lost from its normally clanking environs. The stone inched up.

Once set, this lintel made my one-windowed wall look like part of a house at last. Not just a wall anymore, that could be to enclose pigs or retain soil or direct water...a house wall. And this tiny window would let in the morning sun, as soon as it cleared the shaggy cedar hill across Caney Creek.

~ * ~

Kyle has his flyrod, and we head down the creek, trying the few deep holes as we go. All those years we went fishing, and now he is better than I at flicking the deceptive flies under hanging branches, twitching their immobility into convincing struggles to stay afloat. He works the upstream end of the pools, I the downstream, despite the fact that the fish are looking right at me in the swirling current. Hey, fish can see all around, anyway. Then we switch. Even with the midday heat, we catch small bass, perch, enough for supper. I will make hush puppies.

We talk as we hike the long field toward Beaver Creek. Of his work, life in the city (I predict he won't stay there), his plans. He is enjoying his bachelor years as I did, not realizing yet that he is in fact waiting. For a hand to close over his, a voice yet only imagined, eyes for him only. So much of him is me, forty-five years younger.

It is mid-afternoon, but the light is already deepening in still-fresh leaves. We head back to the site, re-living visits here while he was growing up. One time we came in August, and the tiny, biting seed ticks swarmed over us. I'll have to remember to put out some more bug-killer, then. The grown and half-grown ones are already materializing everywhere, borne on the deer and livestock, squirrels, rabbits.

He recalls the time we all came from Virginia when he was small, to camp and swim and hike. Sharon had lost her wedding ring somewhere, near dark. Probably hauling a wet child out of the water. We'd tried to remember all the places we'd been, planning to re-visit each in the morning. It'd been low water, and we'd scouted out all the deep places to swim. Sharon and the girls were convinced we'd never find the ring, but Kyle just *knew* we would.

But next day we'd scoured all the holes we'd been in, with no results. This was gravel-bottom, and just one turned stone could hide the ring. We'd worked our way down from the ford, past the big boulders in the stream, below the hanging bluff, across a shallow stretch toward this side stream at the curve. Not much deep water here, then. But there'd been this one big tree the creek had swirled around, washing out a small, deep pocket. Kyle headed for it, optimistic. None of us had remembered being there.

And the gold band was standing on edge in three feet of the crystal water, catching the morning sun like a beacon. Why a fish hadn't taken it, I'll never know. Kyle gave a shout of delight, and dived down for it, his spindly legs thrashing. He came up with it, a grin on as wide as Missouri.

We can just see the tree now, upstream on the other side. Gravel has washed into the hole and the current has eroded more soil from around the roots. The tree is dying. A few more seasons, and it'll topple, then the slope will wash more, in the ongoing sculpturing of the stream banks.

We grill the fish, and deep-fry the oniony, cornmeal hushpuppies in a cast-iron kettle I'd found at a flea market. I don't use the Coleman stove, but a wood fire of dry sticks and creek driftwood on some sand on the ledge above Caney, a blaze that snaps in the slanting light, sending sparks. I will keep this fire going till well into dark, and we'll talk. Kyle will stay with Jim and Kelly tonight, but I've grown to belong here.

The woodsmoke curls upward in the new dark. Fireflies wink, and the creek murmurs past. Our faces are etched in the fire's glow, and the world is only this lost circle of light, flickering, shadows dancing. My son and I are sand-grains of life in a universe of stars and soft darkness. I am afraid to speak, to shatter this fragile beauty.

Finally, Kyle rises, puts bleached, bare limbs on the ebbing fire. I stir, stand.

"Have Uncle Jim and Aunt Kelly got you going to church yet, Dad?" It's asked with a little embarrassment, and I wonder why.

No, I know why.

"Well, yes, actually. And I find I miss it when I don't go. Good, uncomplicated people—well, nobody's uncomplicated—down-home preacher, good music. It's my weekly proof that I'm still human, I guess. Some weeks I don't even go out to a store."

"I've been thinking about them a lot. There's this girl I've been seeing who's a Christian. She isn't out to save my soul or anything, but the subject seems to come up a lot. I've begun to read the Bible..." He let it trail off. *Okay, new subject, all right.*

"Can't be all bad. I've given some thought to getting one myself. It's certainly had an impact on the world for the last few thousand years."

"Seems funny now," he mused. "We didn't do church, or even make time for any sort of religion. But lots of people are that way, seems like." He was sort of talking in circles: unfamiliar ground.

"We all get caught up in what's happening around us, what we're doing, planning, our own little worlds. Religion seems to be a whole other picture. Bigger one."

"Yeah. Well, I'd like to go with you all tomorrow. I know Uncle Jim and Aunt Kelly'd like that. And hey, it can't hurt." That grin.

"Well, fine. Be like family. Maybe that's something your mom and I should have done, church and all. Might have turned out a lot different. What's your girl's name?"

"Sarah Cooper. From Michigan. Came to work for our company last year, recruited from Michigan State. Sort of out of place among the more…what's the word I want…uninhibited singles in town. Told me she's the only Christian in her twenty-five-member office."

"Yeah, I read somewhere only one in three people in the country is a church member. Used to be almost a hundred percent, back before World War Two."

"I heard that. Anyway, she's got me thinking about a lot more than just work and play and all. Sharp girl."

"Sounds like it. Like the outdoors?"

"Kind of odd, that. Raised in the country till they moved to a town, so she wanted the big city. Now misses the country again. Yeah, we go backpacking, canoeing. Haven't taken her fishing. You canoe Beaver Creek yet?"

"No. Didn't bring the canoe. Jim's got his, and we may go soon. He's not much on fishing, though. Yeah, we'll probably go when there's enough water. I've been focusing on this cabin. Looks now like I should be inside it in a month or so, ahead of schedule. Then maybe later we'll get some rain, water up. I almost forgot how dry it gets here."

"You're not gonna try to get electricity, then? Or water?"

"No. Too far, and they'd be just another two expenses. Jim and I talked about a CB radio I can run off a battery. Simple lights, too. When I get settled in, I'll want to have something to work on here. Read, have projects when I'm snowed in."

"Be hard to get out, snow time. North-facing road won't thaw." He was eyeing the steep track I'd created.

"Don't plan to, much. I can hike up to Jim's in any weather, though. Won't be stranded."

"Mom's worried you'll get hurt down here where nobody'll know."

"Could happen, but hasn't so far. I'm careful, but I know things will come up. A lot like crossing a street in town, though…you can get hit."

"I guess. Well, I'll go on up the hill. See you in the morning."

"Sure. Need a flashlight? You're clear up at the ford."

"No, moon's out. I like the way you made your road. Never thought anybody'd be able to drive down here."

"Took a little redneck engineering, all right. Yeah, be up there in the morning. Keep your eyes open for snakes. And thanks for coming, Kyle. I can't say for sure how this all will turn out. Depends a lot on what your mom does. And I guess, on how hard-headed I stay."

~ * ~

Kyle seemed to enjoy his visit. He was almost charming with the ladies at church, and talked eye-to-eye with the men. If we'd had single girls over fifteen, they'd probably have mobbed him, but these hung back, giggling and shy. Crushes at a distance, I guessed. No telling how they'd act if he came back often. He liked Bill Zachman... the man's earnestness was infectious. And hey, his sermons were good.

Sunday dinner with my brother had become a ritual, and Kyle made it more complete. They'd always liked the boy, and with their Mike and Mary gone, they couldn't get enough of him. Made him promise to bring his Sarah down for a visit. I didn't know how serious that relationship was, but sure sounded good to me.

"Just not in tick-itchy August," I reminded him, "or you may never see her again."

"Yeah." He grinned. "I could sure scratch one relationship. Pun intended."

After Kyle had left for the long drive back to Chicago, I hung around, and we talked kids. We agreed they'd grown and gone too soon. None of us had realized that when they left for college, that was really about the last we'd see of them, except for visits they'd squeeze in. And now that I'd seen my son again, I knew I'd miss them all even more.

~ * ~

I was surprised Sharon hadn't jumped on the divorce. I was sure the anger would have driven her to that final act, but the weeks went by, her letters kept coming, impersonal now, avoiding mention of what we'd shared, what we'd lost, what the situation was. Like she was tiptoeing around stuff, maybe afraid to upset the status quo.

Nah, she'd never been tactful.

But she wasn't telling me a lot. Like, had she sold the business? Had Bob closed it down? What about Judy? I found myself wanting to know, after I'd been so set on turning my back on it all. Well, no matter. Not like I could or wanted to do anything about all that, anyway.

I kept getting notes from my daughters, too. June had gotten past the outrage, and was mostly just checking in. Melissa didn't like it one bit, though. They obviously didn't know how long this situation would last, but I sensed they were beginning to accept that it might well be permanent.

Okay, it might be. I didn't know yet myself. But I couldn't imagine going back to what I'd left.

No.

And the house took all my time. The days started with sunrise and ended at dark. I did take breaks; a man my age isn't a machine. But the place absorbed me. There are always a lot more details than you'd planned on in a structure of any kind, and I was relearning that.

But looking back on it, I realized I was also learning that this preoccupation with building, this very physical moving forward step by step. was coinciding with what had to be called my faith journey. Work on my road equaled the move to going to church. Putting up walls went along with my conversations with Bill Zachman. Maybe this doorway I was creating was symbolic of the opening of the door to the Word of God? Didn't know at the time, but later on it seemed clear. I wasn't much on spiritual symbolism, but it seemed to be knocking at my door, yeah.

I'd barely squeezed by dollar-wise that first month, with the new purchases. Now I found I still had a little left over when the June Social Security check came. *Save it. Never know when disaster might strike.* Murphy's Law could be very much in the picture.

~ * ~

The sound was as startling as a machine gun, or the revving of an un-muffled motorcycle. It hammered into my head from almost directly above, jolting me from sleep there on the clean sweep of flat limestone above the little stream's fall into Caney Creek.

It was almost a jackhammer sound, and I was back on a construction site, drilling stone or concrete, the shocks traveling up my arms. That pounding would shut out the sky, the air, the light, leaving me in a hazed-in circle of noise intense enough to carve into shapes.

It was a pileated woodpecker, high in a sycamore, its incredibly scarlet head driving its bill into the hard, dead wood of a limb. Some insect must have moved inside there, in its tight tunnel bored into the seasoned wood. Chips flew, and cascaded erratically among the broad leaves that shaded me.

I lay on the unyielding stone, grateful for its coolness, tired muscles flowing into it. The patterned leaves and sky above me had imprinted on my short sleep before the improbably big bird's assault. Now he—I supposed it was a male—became part of the scene but not of the pattern. He was not leaves or branches or sky, as I was not stone or stream or earth. He was just being what he was, an oversize woodpecker pursuing lunch.

That he could tear into that tough hardwood to find the source of what must be the smallest of sounds awed me. What a specialist! I'd read that each adult pileated required a square mile of forest to survive. So this branch of this tree was just one in hundreds of stops he'd make today. Maybe he'd get a grub or two, sustenance for that energy-burning, staccato attack.

I cannot tell how glad I was for the bird's visit. As if I were the reason for his driving bursts, his searching, flaming head cocked, hopping in defiance of gravity, to drill and chip and shred above me. In those moments he was with me, I realized how alone my work had been, how consumed and focused and obsessed each task had become.

Seen from above, from cocked eye: stooped man, placing stone on aching stone down in a lost hollow. Against the coming time, against the seasons, against the cold. *What a waste,* from the bird's point of view.

Remember the bird. Long after his spread-wing flight, in search of other dead branches, other minute, ticking sounds deep in wood.

Remember his favor given, giving, gift of scarlet and white-flashed black and piercing hunting cry.

Glad bird, come back. Often.

~ * ~

Well, Kyle's been to see his dad. Even went to church with him and the others. Whatthehell's happening here? He's turned into something weird out there. And Kyle says Liam's talking like he's going to stay there, down in that impossible hole. Says he doesn't sound crazy, but that's just being kind, I know. Gotta be crazy to pull this stunt. Well, I'll just keep humoring him, I guess, hope it'll all wear off.

Thought I'd enjoy having a life again, but it isn't working out that way. Thirty-three years of habit, allowances, twisted teamwork: hard to break. And I do worry. What if he gets hurt down there? Oh, I guess Jim checks in on him, but at his age, half a day under a fallen tree or slipping over a drop-off could kill him.

Sharon stacked the last of the checks from the construction equipment sales with the others, for deposit. Bob had wanted a few things he didn't already have, but the balance had gone via ads. She hadn't wanted an auction, with nosy people poking around. It'd taken a while, but it was all gone now. She accepted that even if Liam came back, he was too old to pick up the business again, get back into all the hassles.

So maybe I've actually done him a favor, lightening the load here. He can—could—come back to a decent retirement. If he ever gets his head straight, that is. So I guess it's just a marking time thing now, see where this leads. Although it's looking more like it's permanent.

But winter, now, that'll change his outlook, I'm sure. Freeze down there and that'll clear his mind, if anything can.

But the image of Liam slipping on ice on those steep slopes came into her mind, and she found herself worrying more. All it'd take would be one misstep, and her husband—yes, dammit, he was still that—could actually die before anybody found him. This wasn't the first time she'd imagined it, but the pictures were becoming more vivid as the weeks went by.

She simply hadn't heard from him lately, and guessed she wouldn't. Said he wouldn't contest a divorce, but hadn't initiated one, either.

So he thinks the ball is in my court, I guess...said all he's going to. Well, that's certainly an option, since he apparently doesn't plan to have a life here—or with me—again. But that's not a bridge I want to cross, or burn, just yet.

~ * ~

I took long breaks. Had to, or the daylong bending, stooping, lifting, moving things would get to me in more ways than tired muscles. I'd find myself weary from focusing so hard on a stone's fit, obsessed with getting it into the right space with just a half inch recessed joint, oblivious to everything else.

Okay, there was more to this life than chiseling stone—had to be.

So too much of that wouldn't do. One day I hiked on down to Long Creek again and up it into the Hercules Wilderness area of the national forest. There'd been some work done there by the CCC during the Depression, but now it was just that: wilderness, albeit second-growth timber, old traces of roads, deer trails.

The stream, much lower now, lessened even more as I climbed up through cedars shading mosses and ferns. The plentiful water of April wasn't there anymore, but there were seeps and little pools in the limestone pockets where birds came.

The occasional rabbit scampered away from my easy advance, my makeshift hiking stick striking softly into flintrock soil. Once a doe and fawn crashed away when I came from behind a stone outcrop in the old trail. They vanished in just a few feet.

This was great. I wouldn't meet a soul here, I was sure, even if I stayed out all day. If I kept on, I knew I'd reach the old Hercules fire tower somewhere ahead, and I could follow a dim road past it out to a highway.

Had no intention of doing that.

I'd provided myself with a water bottle and a couple of those energy bars, which were an extravagance, but handy on days like this. Back on the creek I'd either heat up a stew I'd put together the night before on the Coleman stove, or wolf down something else leftover, for lunch. Here I just sat on a smooth stone and soaked up the summer day, in no hurry for anything. Didn't have to be anywhere.

I had left Jim a note in case he ventured down to my site and saw I was gone; didn't want him worrying about me. He was a romantic enough soul to appreciate my taking off like this, and probably would have wanted to come with me. He and Kelly did ride this way sometimes, though they'd cut down on the horseback activities lately.

Getting old was, of course, inevitable, and yes, one did have to let go of a pursuit or two as time passed, but it wasn't a good idea to shut down too soon, either. I figured I was good for maybe five, even ten years here, if I watched myself. Probably go stir crazy with nothing to do though, that long. No, there was the blacksmithing I wanted to get back into when winter came, maybe some woodworking, put together some simple furniture.

And for sure read a lot. Making time to read had been hard, with a company to run, and before that the added demands of raising kids, too. I had borrowed books from the county library here, and made myself take enough breaks to browse through one every week or so.

Didn't matter much what I read. I'd discovered modern action story writers and old classics. Historical novels and, since I'd been going to church, Francis Schaeffer's *How Should We Then Live*. I wasn't very far into the religion bit, or at least not yet, but what this man had to say—he was dead, now—made a lot of sense to me.

Yeah, that's what I could do when the cold time came, escape into any of an unlimited number of fantasy worlds or thought-provoking treatises. Been a long time since I'd allowed myself time for those trips out of the mundane. Something to look forward to.

Jim had told me there were over 12,000 acres of this wilderness area, and it seemed to stretch on and on. Man could wander around in here for a long time and not see it all, I guessed. But as long as I followed the ravines and spring branches that all went downhill toward Beaver Creek, I knew I couldn't get lost, so I poked around some more.

Found what must have been an outdoor amphitheater, rows of stones set in a quadrant up a slope, with a big boulder where the speaker or whoever must've positioned himself. Guessed the rangers or CCC guys had meetings here. Or had there been cabins, small farms here before it became national forest? And had a long-erased country church maybe held outdoor services here? I could find out, I supposed, but I sort of liked just guessing about it. Part of the ongoing history of the place...touched by people, but lightly.

I hadn't brought a rifle with me from Virginia, figuring that was the last thing I'd need. I did suppose somebody's hogs might've gone wild in here, and yeah, getting chased up a tree by a feral boar wouldn't be fun, exactly. I remembered Jim's hunting with friends down in the creek bottoms in southern Arkansas back when he was single. Seems the locals would let their hogs run wild so they wouldn't have to feed them, then hunt them in the fall.

Well, Jim and his buddies would take their hunting rifles down into those sloughs and still-hunt, trying to avoid any good old boys who might claim the pork. Jim wounded one boar which came after him, curved tusks long and deadly. He lost his nerve and set a record climbing a tree. One of the others shot the boar, then they discovered a metal tag in its ear. Decided maybe that wasn't a sport to continue.

But I wasn't a hunter anymore, anyway. I could live on what I could afford and didn't need game. Let other guys go after the wild stuff. That didn't mean I'd give up my fishing, of course. And I suppose my attitude was a bit inconsistent, but hey, I didn't have to please anybody else with my half-baked philosophy.

And barring that imaginary tusker, there wasn't anything for a grown man to be afraid of in these woods. High wind might uproot a tree and drop it on me, but I'd stay home when the weather was bad. The old-timers called that phenomenon "wind-throwed."

No, about the only predators us moderns had to worry about were other people. And despite the movies and television, the average backwoodsman was a benign individual. Unless you got him drunk. Then he'd act just like the urban redneck, let out all his frustrations and imagined wrongs like a country-western song. Oh, I supposed I might meet some doped-up crazy out here, maybe lost, but the chances were pretty slim. And what percentage would there be in assaulting one broke old man?

I'm afraid I found myself anxious to get on back to my cabin-building sooner than I should have. This soaking up nature should have been something I could get used to, just enjoy the day, blank out my mind, play 'possum or 'coon or hound dog, with no worries beyond food. But I just wasn't there yet. Had to be doing something, at least till I learned more about relaxing.

So I headed back down a swale of forest grass between locust sprouts and vines, noting how much easier this downhill was. I'd sprayed myself liberally with insect repellent, and hoped that'd keep the ticks and chiggers off. I wasn't supposed to smell like lunch to them now, and I hoped they'd realize that.

When I reached Beaver Creek, there were the inevitable beer cans there. I'd thought about gathering them up, but knew the next carload of rednecks would bring more. It never seems to occur to a lot of my country compeers that it's easier to take an empty can away than to've brought it to the woods full. (Why, it ain't no good to nobody, then.) Well, leave these, and maybe it'd shame some future polluter into cleaning them up. Cop-out, I knew, but I didn't really care that much.

Back home, the sun slanted. Too late to mix mortar for stonework, so I just settled for shaping a few rocks and dry-laying them to get a head start on tomorrow's construction. You can't do that too far ahead, or the thickness of the mortar throws your carefully-fitted work off.

I suppose you could figure it all out ahead of time, but I didn't have that kind of inclination. Fact is, when you eyeballed things the way I did, they needed tweaking for the right fit, sure, but so did the precisely-measured stuff. Just maybe a little less.

I remembered master log builder Peter Gott in North Carolina, who could figure the notch depth for a complete log cabin beforehand, cut them, then put the whole thing up and it'd all fit. I'd always set a log, then work the top notch and fit the next one to that, figuring it one at a time as I went. Different strokes.

My backcountry vacation day was probably good for me, but now my head was filled again with calculations, figuring what came next, planning. Back into harness.

Hey, it's what I do.

Seven

The stone walls of my house were done, all the way up the gable ends. And back to that symbolism, did this mean I'd finally walled myself away from the world? Maybe. I guess that's sort of what I'd had in mind all along. Only now I'd come to treasure the time with Jim and Kelly, and yeah, even the folks at church. So maybe, with that door which would stay openable, there was hope for me. But enough with the speculative stuff. I needed a roof.

I set the hewn plate beams onto mortar-imbedded anchor bolts, and raised my rafters, a pair at a time, pinned together at the peak with a collar tie but no ridgepole. Could have gone up for Jim for help, of course, but this was a small job. Maybe I just wanted it all to myself, too. Hubris?

The really remote pioneer builders did it that way anyway, man by himself, unless he had a wife or half-grown kids to help. I found myself pretending this house was actually a couple hundred years old, like so many I'd worked on in Virginia. *Nah, nobody lived here then. Maybe a hunter or two, but surely not down in a cleft like this.* But I insisted on building as the earliest settlers would have. Role-playing, I guess.

I'd done roofs all my life, and this little, low one presented no challenges. But the very real prospect of slipping, falling, made me wary. Jim would feel left out, probably, or Eric would've helped when he was here; we could punch the job out in no time. But okay, there's more than a little stubborn streak in me.

Surprise.

I tied a rope to the first braced rafters I'd set, and around my waist. I'd leaned the other trusses against the wall where I could reach them and haul them up. They went into place in half a day. Then I began decking the roof with boards I'd bought at that farm sale. I kept the rope on, feeling a little foolish all the way through nailing on the five-vee barn tin and the ridge piece, which I finished the next day.

I'd insulate before winter, but for now my house was dried in. Well, almost. Needed to seal between the stone and rafters at the gable ends next. I took my time there, pushing the mortar into the spaces with a pointing tool. I'd considered doing the gables in wood, but less likely to burn in a forest fire...stone all the way.

Next, I fitted the second-hand window I'd bought and left space for, and began the door. This would also be a duplicate of the old handmade doors we'd found on the earliest and best-built cabins and farmhouses back East, before this land was even settled.

Then I fired up my forge to make myself that planned set of hinges and a latch. And a hasp I could padlock when I was away. Hot work, still summer. I remembered crafts fairs we'd been a part of thirty years before, always in the heat and sun. Finally got tired of that stuff and stopped doing it. Hadn't made much money at it, anyway. About all anybody wanted was hand-forged hunting knives, only the prospective customers didn't want to pay more than for hardware-store specials maybe made of old tin cans in Taiwan.

I've always liked blacksmithing. Learned it from an old smith from the mines in Arizona. He knew the secrets of hardening and tempering steel, and scoffed at the folklore the popular books promoted.

"Those fellers don't know th' first thing 'bout heat-treatin' steel," he'd told me, then proceeded to show me step-by-step how it was done.

"First of all, y'got to know how much carbon is in th' steel. Dunno that, no amount of quenchin', temperin', hocus-pocus'll getcha anywheres." He'd proceeded to show me how the telltale oxidation colors ran over the shined, heated steel, which tempering supposedly would tell how much of the brittleness was being drawn out. *After* the piece was heated to cherry red and quenched in water, salt water, or oil, which hardened it.

"But like I said, that don't mean a thing, unless y've got th' carbon in, have heated it t' red and quenched it. *Then* it means how hard yer finished steel will be. Too hard, it'll break; too soft, an' it'll bend an' won't hold an edge." He also showed me the very same colors on a piece of non-hardenable mild steel, which as he'd promised, had no effect on the metal.

I'd been an eager student. That was the year Melissa was born, and when Sharon was at work part time, I'd take her with me, starting at six weeks old, to the old man's smithy at a crafts center while I learned. This was between the small carpentry jobs I landed. She was a great favorite with the tourists, and always got along with everybody, those short periods I had her with me till Sharon came for her.

So yeah, I would put in some quality time that winter at the forge, at least to make Christmas presents for the family and any friends I managed to make in the meantime. Everybody needed a stove poker, pot rack, knife.

I also built a solid shutter, with hidden forged hinges over the window of the cabin, that I could lock from inside. With its stone walls, metal roof and heavy oak door, my house was about as secure as I could make it.

And it was just into late July. Not bad for something over three months of work. Three months uninterrupted by phone calls and owner conferences and architects and building inspectors. Amazing what a man can accomplish when he gets rid of all the modern stuff in his way.

~ * ~

The kids are long asleep, even Melissa, and Sharon and I are just dreaming before the fireplace as the snow falls outside. I find her hand in mine, warm, and we turn our eyes knowingly toward each other. Unhurriedly, we slip away, undress each other and get into the shower together. She scrubs my back, with extra scratches at that itchy spot she knows.

Then I turn to her, soap her breasts, feeling the erect nipples, kissing her mouth, neck. We meld into each other, whispering little words, touching lightly, exploring. This will never get old, this being one, this joy.

We dry off, turn out lights, slip into bed. Our stroking heightens the anticipation, and our breathing comes faster. She gives a sharp intake at the smooth entry as always, which never fails to excite me further. We find our rhythm, keeping our parent-ears out for the sound of little feet. All is quiet except the tumult within us.

And then it is over, but never over, and we lie side by side, her head in the hollow of my neck and shoulder, as the riot inside us fades. And finally, we sleep.

I had never imagined the level of sexual fulfillment with a woman till Sharon. She seemed to anticipate just what I needed, even before I knew it. And I tried to do the same with her. No matter the stresses of the day, our time in bed transported us to another realm, and it was pure heaven.

The glow renewed with morning, and our secret smiles continued the experience. Our hands would touch, I'd maybe push aside a stray lock of her hair, give her a kiss on the forehead. Damn, I loved that woman.

And now, a generation later, I find myself dreaming of those times, those magic early years when we were two against an intruding world. When we could and did keep those warm places in our hearts to retreat to, to hide in, together.

~ * ~

I scattered bug killer around my house and up along my road: serious tick time soon. And I moved myself into my cabin. Its flagstone floor was cool to my bare feet, if a little uneven. It was more of the split rock from under the bluff upcreek, laid random over gravel and grouted with masonry mortar. Maybe I'd get a rug by winter.

Jim and Kelly came down after church the next Sunday to see my creation. I'd insisted on splurging for carry-out barbecue, and laid out our dinner on the heavy oak plank table I'd built. The two straight-backed chairs were flea market items, along with the rocking chair I'd repaired.

"This is so neat," Kelly admired. "Just enough room. I see you've floored part of the loft."

"Just for storage. Don't want to climb up there to sleep. I'll have to stoke a stove later on, middle of the night when it's really cold."

"We used a wood cookstove, first few years," Jim remembered. "Heated the place, but it'd go out at night. Need to get yourself one that'll burn all night."

"Place is so small, anything'll heat it. I was thinking I might use your welder, cobble up something myself. Save dollars."

"Sure. But a cookstove would let you bake, you know." Kelly.

"Maybe so, if I run onto one I can afford. I've got this Dutch oven, though. That works for now."

~ * ~

There was more to do on the house, but it was little stuff: screen door, window screen, insulation, stuff like that. I could hit along on that during the months ahead, no sweat.

So I took some days off to fish, loaf, hike. Even invited Bill the preacher to go fishing with me, not in his lake boat, but up Beaver Creek, where I knew there were smallmouth bass. He used those big lures and a spinning reel, but he caught more than I did anyway. Man was a natural fisherman, and I wondered if he used some sort of Scriptural mantra to hoodoo them in.

He and I were easy with each other, and I could see the beginnings of a true friendship. Man my age makes friends for life, I guess, and as long as Bill didn't harangue me, we got along fine.

But he insisted that next time we should go in his bass boat, which I learned had been a gift from his congregation. Bill wouldn't have spent the money on that thing on his own, I knew. I also knew he'd almost lost his farm, paying for cancer treatments for his late wife. Helluva guy, this preacher. Probably doing more good for more folks than some high-powered televangelist, for sure.

I also knew that some of the single congregation women had set their sights on Bill, but he wasn't interested. Kelly'd told me he and his wife had lived the perfect love story, and I guess he wasn't about to do a secondhand version, now that he had her only in memory.

I'd noticed some of those same ladies, but neither was I in the market. First of all, I was still married, for how long I didn't know, but second, I had no time for a woman. Even if one were crazy enough to want to live down here in my hollow. And adapting to another human being of either of the two major sexes wasn't something I wanted to make room in my life for, just now. No, my hovel and my hermitage were gonna be it, for the time being.

Maybe from now on.

But once the house was about under wraps, I started looking more at the rest of my land, wondering just what I could do with it. Wood enough for projects, some of it dead, which I cut some of, some green, ditto, to let it season.

And I put my head on that south-facing slope up above my cabin, really for the first time. Could terrace that, try to grow some things next spring. Be a lotta work, but what else was I going to do with my time when I got cabin fever? Yeah, and when I couldn't escape memories of Sharon, which of course weren't all like those early ones.

So I explored several scenarios, even digging up there to see how deep the topsoil was. Wasn't deep, the layer of limestone being more or less solid, a foot down. Some places bare patches of it. Need a lotta dirt on top of that to sustain any growth at all. There was a reason there were so few even stumpy cedars up there. Well, put that aside for a while, along with all the half-baked ideas for moving soil, fencing, terracing, getting water up there.

I'd watched Caney Creek go through a dozen personalities since April. Cold and clear early on, then the floods—twice was all. Then the greening of the gravel bars in grass and weeds, and the sycamore leaf-smell and the willows. Now the water was down, a sort of amber tint to it. Deep summer of dragonflies and grasshoppers and reflected, unremitting blue of sky. Fish not biting here, but big holes on Beaver cool deep down, where Bill and I'd found some of them and had them for dinners.

Once I did join Bill in his bass boat on Bull Shoals Lake. Caught one lonely bass, and a few perch. I insisted he take the bass—his boat and all. Hot on the lake, not my kind of fishing, and this time he didn't catch a thing. Must've lost his mojo, I guessed. But Bill was good company, like I said. We talked religion, weather, building. Crops. Being a lifetime farmer, he had to and did, know how to do almost anything. My kind of guy.

I was also getting invitations to dinner from folks I'd met at the church. Went a few times, but found out pretty soon that matchmaking was indeed a part of that. Still not interested. But the time spent with those people was pleasant enough, if I dodged the widows and old aunts.

But again, I realized I mostly really just wanted to get back down to my little hollow and get things done. Hard to break a lifelong habit of working all the time.

So, aside from my weekly dose of humanity and the occasional trip to a store, Jim and Kelly were my worldly contacts, and I liked it that way.

~ * ~

My brother told me the heirs to the place across the creek, who'd ignored it since the old man had died, now planned to build a house and live there, and that news was anything but welcome. Here I'd just found and established the ideal hermit's cave, and I was about to be invaded by suburbia in the persons, I learned, of parents and teenage children.

I met them there on the creek one day when Jim brought them down to show them the exact corners of their property, which they hadn't known. Pleasant enough people: he a truck driver, she working at one of the resorts upstream from Forsyth on Lake Taneycomo in season. "Be glad to neighbor with yuh." The kids were three typical 21st century stereotypes, with cell phones that took pictures and videos, texted, and probably dispensed sugary drinks, for all I knew. They all had piercings in places I didn't want to be reminded of. About as out of place here as if on Mars.

But what could I do? I cringed to learn their plans included bulldozing the cedars off the slope downstream, a bit above the creek bottom field where old man Compton, the grandfather, had run his cows, to put one of those modular pre-fab things on. Basically a trailer without wheels. My least favorite kind of imitation house.

Bottom line was, I wasn't far enough away to be immune to their noise, be it rumbling SUVs, dirt bikes, or boom boxes. I began to see the end of my too-short retreat.

But I'd always believed that in a free country, a person who owned his land could do just about anything he wanted with it, even if he hadn't sweated blood to buy it, somebody back a few generations probably had. Certainly, I as a neighbor couldn't presume to tell these folks they couldn't trash my next-door paradise. They wouldn't understand, anyway. "Improvement."

Well, they'd have to come in by way of the Beaver Creek road on the concrete low-water bridge over Caney, then up through the national forest to their own land. Probably okay with the forest; they encouraged inholdings, I'd heard, to have people there to report forest fires, keep the roads passable.

I kept my mouth shut, determined to be as good a neighbor as possible, despite my visions of jarring plastic things shining up among any trees they might leave standing. And gatherings of adolescents, invited friends of these isolated dwarfs who'd insist on all the visitors the place could stand and more.

Was this a sign? Was this God I was just trying to get a handle on telling me this whole adventure of mine was a selfish mistake? Could be. The question was, would I listen, give it all up and go back home, or stay, try to stop my ears and ignore the whole intrusion?

Just have to wait it out, I guessed. Fortunately, I didn't have a lot of actual investment in my place, other than months of dedicated labor and my version of craftsmanship. I was proud of it, though, whether anyone else ever saw it or not, and it plainly galled me to have to share the environment with even the no doubt salt-of-the-earth parents.

And unfortunately, I probably wouldn't live long enough for these kids to grow up and disappear.

So, there was this fly in my nature-ointment, and I didn't like it. Just had to suck it up, though, I guessed. Retreat further into my shell and try to pretend those intruders just weren't there.

Then we got some news: the power company wanted a medium-size fortune to extend the electric line down those miles to the proposed house. The engineer who plotted the line showed them how many poles it'd take, and how hard it was to drill holes for them in that rock, and how much voltage drop there'd be, unless they went to this other plan, which cost more. That way would mean running the high-voltage wire in conduit underground to their transformer, a big box on the ground. Of course, if they could get several other people to build there, it'd be worth it for the company to extend the line free. Blah, blah, blah.

And I guess those younger Comptons just added the rest of it all up: the cost of a well, road, culverts, house, septic system. The fact that Caney Creek got up over the concrete bridge sometimes, which would strand them. And the distance out to the world, which I could tell the kids and the mother at least, hadn't liked from the first.

And hallelujah, they eventually abandoned the whole ill-conceived idea. Jim later told me he'd thought they might, given all the problems. Instead, they leased the land to a farmer who ran his cows on it, and I felt like I'd been delivered from the lion's den or something. Better the lowing of cattle than this week's heavy metal music. I began to wonder if God weren't playing around with me, with all this worry and fuss.

Nah, He probably had just let me stew myself into a snit over nothing. And that got me thinking: had He made this a test of my resolve, my budding faith? Or was it all random, the way I and most folks viewed the ups and downs of this life. I remembered what Bill Zachman had said about there having to be rough places in all our lives as part of the big test.

And compared to what he and others had suffered, my wasted-time worry wasn't even a molehill to those mountains of theirs.

Eight

The days had baked dry, and the little stream faded to a wetness from between layered stone. The dawns were cool, and the long late afterglows of sun, too, when a current of air slid from the shaded heights and flowed almost imperceptibly past my open door on its way downcreek.

Looking for something to do next, I started picking out a path with the mattock, and steps up the point between the streams in early light along the steep trail. Took three days. Then, leveling the dry earth for a usable side path at the top of the steepest part and later a course of terrace stones, was slow and sometimes dizzying work.

Stubborn roots took any soil and held it, feeding scrub and a little tufted grass and the twisted cedars. Once out on the slope, I worked a few stones down from above to begin my terrace, always mindful of the plunge seventy feet to my drying streambed below.

Once anchored, the stones defied the slope, a dam for soil and leaves and bits of twig and smaller chips of rock that'd wash down in rain. These would be the depth of woods dirt my terrace would hold, where the roots of my future planting would seek and find sustenance.

Just three courses would raise the barrier a couple of feet. Filled with woods dirt, it'd be a deep root-base that should let me grow at least early vegetables before the dry.

I wanted to grow things now, something I'd never been good at. Wanted to be as self-sustained as possible, of course, but also to plant, nourish, harvest. Contribute, I guess.

Or hell, maybe it was just ego.

As soon as the sun burned through the mists that hovered in my hollow and scorched this south-faced slope, I had to retreat, leaving the last-placed stone with drying sweat of my fingers darkening its surface. That first morning, the day after I'd finished cutting the steps, I laid only six feet of wall, one course high. Used to lay three times that. Six feet of grubbed roots and wedged stone and raked fill, beginning bed of soil.

Sharon would've sneered. Or at least I thought she would.

There wasn't much depth here, and I began to understand the stories of the Incas and the pre-Incas, carrying the precious dirt in baskets of some fashioning, to deepen the black soil of those interminable terraces. That'd be painfully hard here. Just this six feet of wall would need at least a dozen wheelbarrows of woods dirt. Or in half-filled five-gallon buckets, maybe fifty trips. For say, five rows of plants, six feet long. Labor-intensive carrots or potatoes or beans or squash.

I pictured lines of diminutive Peruvians bringing dirt down from high slopes scraped of precious soil, dumping, filling, spreading, while their ongoing work of wall-building terraces stretched the nearly-sheer faces of those hills. Enough people could do it all right, or shape the giant temple stones and rock them back unnumbered times for fitting, setting, tight each to its neighbor. Enough people could do almost anything when they had to.

I was one guy. One old pair of hands, shoving stones downhill a few feet at a time, a Don Quixote against this baked hill that could indeed begin to sway and tilt like a windmill in the waves of heat. I could be at this for the rest of whatever life I had left, and create only a few lines of terraced stone and hoarded soil above.

What in my twisted mind was I *thinking?*

But wait, now. *That's the 21ˢᵗ century mindset. Scrap that. Look at six feet of wall, dude, in one morning of relative cool.* Feel the tingle of tired arms and calves and the beginnings of back, stopped just short of aching. *You can do this.* Feet following a safe trail back down, water bottle thumping from my belt, the creek shining below, the faint singing of water over stone. The solid steps down, the side stream, and up to the little cabin of stone.

I did this. My veined hands, my patience, the gripped stones building old muscles, hardening into purpose. I could keep on doing it, too.

Sharon.

From the Ranger's perch, I could see my progress across and up the hill. A tiny line of set stones, a beginning. Yes! Maybe I'd go up again, late, with half a bucket of this black dirt from between the ledges on this sunless south rise. Never waste a trip. A half-bucket of soil would nourish a potato vine. A meal, or maybe a whole day's food.

Seen that way, the bulge of mountain began to lose its power to intimidate. I *could* do this. As long as I didn't fall out of my garden-to-be. And just what else was I planning to do with these days? Really. A single clump of earth would be one more than had been there before.

I dozed, washed clothes, lazed away the heat of day, moving slowly because there was no rush, no need. When the sun dipped, I cut black soil from the base of ledge rock, sifting roots, stones. Half full, the bucket was heavy, and yes, it was a long way up. So, a third full, at first. *See how this goes: three trips for two potato vines. That could work.*

By setting my load down every twenty steps, I worked my way to the steep face of the trail. *Okay now: every five steps.* When at last I poured this moist soil onto that behind my terrace wall, it made a pitiful, dark smudge on the dry gray. No matter...I had reversed a speck of the erosion that had taken the dirt from up here eons ago. I had brought it back to stay, this time, locked by my stones, set for my next-year's sowing. Good feeling.

But I could make more progress from above, I saw. Bring the dirt down from the top, maybe more at a time. Gravity...the Peruvians understood that. And I'd just momentarily forgotten it. For now, I'd lay a few more stones, extend my wall.

The air was still dry and hot, that mysterious layer of cool not yet formed. But if I worked slowly, I could stay ahead of the sweat in my eyes. *Oh, nice fit; need a long one now, over those two to bind this section. Saw one last trip up above. Get it down. Drag it, shove it, then quit for the day...*

But here came that cool. Maybe only a few degrees, but so welcome. *One more stone, then the light'll fade. Good time for a misstep, though, fall. No, leave that one. Get down; take the bucket. Two more feet of wall—enough. Ah.* Smell of drying willow leaves up from the creek bank. Sycamore smell, distant smell of Jim's horses from Mallorys' field. Cells of cool as I climb down, zones of heat lingering.

My wall is a good wall.

~ * ~

"What are you finding down there now to keep you busy?" Jim asked me as we mulched and watered his garden. I'd tried to make myself useful, fitting into their tightly-woven lives wherever I thought would help. Actually, I was learning a lot about planting, tending vegetables. Jim had always had the knack.

"Experimenting, mostly. I saw incredible terraces in Peru, where those people held almost vertical slopes, planted all kinds of stuff. I'm doing a little at a time on that south-facing hill, maybe try to plant next spring."

"Dry up, I'm afraid. This does, even flat, unless we water a lot."

"Try for early stuff, mulch deep. Maybe a waste of time." I hoped not, but here was the man who knew.

"If you could get water up there, it'd work. Slope like that, I'm afraid any moisture will work out from under you, no matter how much you mulch."

Water. Always that. And yes, the Peruvians had built irrigation channels in stone to their terraces from springs uphill. I didn't have that. I'd had the moonshiner's spring, but hadn't checked on it in weeks. So dry below, I'd figured it had given up for the summer.

Later, I climbed into that brush-choked recess, mindful of snakes, hoping for the sound and sight of water. All I found was some moss between layers of stone. The old pipes mocked me. Had to've been a winter-and-spring operation, moonshining here.

But this was above my terracing, high as that was. I could run a plastic pipe along the hill face, to gravity-feed water. Sure, those times the spring was running, when I wouldn't need water.

Where was my engineer son when I needed him? I could almost see him, head cocked sideways, surveying that impossible hill, the insane project I'd set myself. No, just have to fake it on my own, like always.

~ * ~

It was one Christmas, after Melissa and Grady had married, and the kids were home. Kyle was a junior in college at Virginia Tech. I'd decided to surprise everybody with a zipline I could rig with a long length of guy cable I'd picked up in some trade. The Virginia place had a steep dropoff down to a small stream, then up a gradual slope on the other side.

After a lot of searching, I located the site between big white oaks, a straight shot down and over the water maybe 20 feet above, then up to a big pine just past the cable's length. Stretched just tight enough, a crossbar with pulley should gather speed, drop quickly, then begin a slowing climb up, to stop near a turnbuckle I'd use to maintain tension. Piece another cable the remaining feet to the tree.

It'd snowed, and I dragged that heavy cable along like an obedient snake, to the site. Put up a ladder, lined the oak starting tree with pressure-treated boards so the steel wouldn't cut into it, double-clamped that. Then I pulled the rest of the cable down, clinging to saplings in the steep places, stretched it toward the pine. I was enjoying this, and the upcoming surprise would be a blast.

Kyle was always up for some wild project, and Grady was heavy into outdoor sports. The girls would enjoy this, too, I was sure. Maybe not Sharon, who by that time had lost a lot of her adventurousness somewhere.

I tightened the turnbuckle to raise the cable above the inevitable sag that might let feet hit the ground, and fitted the pulley, hang-bars. It was late when I finished, so I put off testing it.

And Kyle showed up from college a couple days early, after some class project finished ahead of schedule. Next morning, I decided to confide in him, just in case my contraption needed fine-tuning. Little mechanical expertise couldn't hurt.

"Wow, Dad." Viewing my work. "You figure the angle and all? Speed, slowdown distance?"

"Nah, just knew you go downhill fast, you level out, you start uphill, you eventually stop. Other end's close enough to the ground, if it's too fast, you just let go, walk. And if you stop too soon, I've got you to set a ladder to come down on." Sounded okay to me.

"Dad. Dad, this thing could kill you. Like what if it sways, and slams you into that tree halfway down? Or if you can't keep your grip? And you don't even have a brake on it." He was about to throw up his hands. *College students*. "Does Mom know you did this?" Almost an accusation.

"Your mom's been shopping her head off, gone either to her job or out with the girlfriends, whoever they are. No, I thought, in my naivete, that I'd make this my Christmas surprise. And I don't think it's any big deal...you roll along a cable, have fun."

"Okay, it's a great idea. But no way am I gonna let you get on this deathtrap till I've put a brake on it, and a seat. Then we can test it out together, okay?" He was almost pleading. And I was getting impatient with all this. Hey, I never got hurt—well, not bad—in all my construction work.

"Let's just take a run on it first, see what happens. I would've last night, but it got dark..."

He put a hand on my shoulder, and the look he gave me was well, sad. Okay, so the hotshot engineer was gonna water down my surprise. Not out of meanness I guessed...concern. But maybe a touch of condescension? Old man gone and done something dangerous, something way beyond his abilities? Getting old, bound to screw up? I bristled.

"Hey, just let it alone, then. Not a bfd, okay? Doesn't meet with your approval, we'll forget it. Not like I have to prove something, to you *or* to me." I turned, started toward the house.

"Dad, this isn't a pissing contest. I *said* I think this's a fine idea. Just let me keep us from getting mangled, okay? Hey, I didn't mean to put you down. And what's the harm in letting me take a few precautions? I wanta get in on this, too. How long's it been since we cooked up some piece of mechanical nonsense together?" Hand on my shoulder again.

Now how could I resist this kid? He hadn't gone off the deep end down there among the other wonder boy engineers, scrapped all the experiences we'd had. Yeah, from fixing old cars to building that rotating boom we'd mounted on an old truck to lift logs, beams, big stones. More than dad/son bonding, those adventures. Hell, I gave him a hug.

And in a little over half an hour, he'd contrived a brake and a suspended board to sit on. I could see, if this thing didn't slow enough, it'd be hard to get off the seat quickly before it slammed into the turnbuckle. I pointed this out.

"That's what the brake is for. Now, let me try it first, okay?" He was almost apologetic. *Oh, whythehell not. This's for them, not me.* I bowed him toward the ladder. He climbed up, stuffed the long cord we'd pull the thing back up with into his pocket, and launched, grinning.

He did almost drag the ground before the dropoff, but gained speed quickly, flashing past trees, no swerving. Over the stream, across a woods road there, toward the anchor tree.

And didn't have to use the brake at all. Stopped fifteen feet short of the turnbuckle. He slipped off the seat, flashed me the okay sign, whooped. I couldn't help my own wide grin.

"I wanta tighten the cable a little," he called up to me, "get it up higher off the ground, extend the run." I spread my hands, glad this was all the fine-tuning we needed.

He climbed back up, grabbing those saplings, the pulley trailing behind at the end of the retrieving line. Handed it to me, gave me a high five.

"Go get 'em, Dad. I must've been doing at least forty, the way those trees flashed by. Oh, I'll take that brake thing off...you were right...it slows by itself."

I climbed the ladder, turned, got my legs over the board, and shoved off. Tame at first, but wow, did it accelerate! One big tree looked like I'd hit it, but it flashed past safely. *Tight cable won't sway, this's okay.* I sailed over the little branch, slowed as the turnbuckle came up. Stopped about a foot from it. *Okay!*

Christmas morning, the girls had made a huge breakfast. (Sharon had complained about a headache, slept in.) After she'd joined us, gifts had been opened and exclaimed over, I led the group down to my Christmas present.

"Oh boy, that's so cool," Grady complimented, and was on the seat before Melissa could caution him. Sailed off with a whoop of joy, dismounted, applauded. Pulled the ride back up, clapped me on the back.

"I'm on it." June took the line from him, climbed, got set. Melissa had her hand to her mouth, not sure about this at all. Probably still had visions of her husband splatting himself against a tree. Not to worry, and her sister rode in fine style, laughing all the way.

Kyle took another turn, then me. I flew, wind whistling past my ears, glad I'd done this for them—all of us. Climbed back up, handed the line to Melissa, who'd never shied away from any adventure when she was little. She took it guardedly, encouraged by Grady, who helped her up, got her set.

"You'll love it, girl. Just enjoy," he assured her, and eventually she pushed off. Screamed, but I couldn't tell if it was fear or joy. Didn't matter, really: she was committed.

"Wow, Dad, that was a rush," she told me when she'd struggled back up the hill. "And I wasn't dissing your gift at all. It was just that... well, I was gonna wait to tell you all. I'm pregnant, and I thought..."

"Oh, hey, if I'd known..." *Whatthehell have I done?*

"Doesn't matter. Doctor said to keep up with exercises, anything I wanta do, till right at the last. And I love it!" She gave me a hug, just like old times.

They all went back down, even rode the zipline at night, with flashlights illuminating the trees, which looked scary. I passed on that, and Sharon, who'd come down to watch, wouldn't get on the thing at all. Hadn't built it for her, anyway. By then she was well along with the eye-rolling at whatever I did.

~ * ~

For irrigation water, okay, I'd need a big tank, then. Store it, use it only in the driest times, to keep things alive. Might work. Big tank... but I'd have to get it up there somehow. Could build one of concrete... No, be impossible to get sand, gravel, cement up there, unless I could hire a version of those Inca workers.

Well. There was a reason folks didn't cultivate these steep slopes. In Italy and Greece, they grew olives and other plants on terraces, stuff that didn't need so much water. Probably did in Peru, too. No, corn, big kernels I remembered, but then they had that irrigation.

Okay, here I was going to need it. Challenge. Too expensive to pump it up from the creek, the logical solution. Gasoline-driven pump'd cost a lot...expensive potatoes. And I'd still need that storage tank, probably.

So maybe a waste of time, all this terracing. It was August now, the driest time, and I'd run two terraces about fifty feet along, twelve feet between them. Not level ground behind the walls by any means, but enough to hold the soil from washing off the mountain. And I could lay another course of stone to raise each of the walls if I had to, deepen the soil behind them.

But *water*. A tank could be set into a dug-out pocket here, filled from the seasonal spring. Tank...modern technology could surely produce a water tank. Farmers had them, fiberglass or metal things holding a thousand gallons or so. Couldn't lift one that size up the slope without winch, long cable, some place above to lift from.

Above. Old principle again: bring anything heavy down from above. Maybe I *could* plot an obstacle-dodging road of sorts between trees on that national forest acreage from the county road to the top of my land. Bring in a tank, lower it to a place above the terraces...

That afternoon I drove the Ranger up and out to Highway 160 and to the Beaver Creek road. Using the topo map, I located the closest place to my land and parked the truck. Some place here I could get into the woods all right, but I'd have to wind around trees more than a quarter mile to my line, then on down to the brow of the hill. Let a round tank get away, it'd plunge over, hit bottom, maybe my cabin. Have to inch it down, hooked tight to a winch...

I didn't have money for a winch. Or a tank, for that matter. I was on the tightest of fixed incomes, and what would before have been a simple matter of charging off such an expense to construction jobs, now was simply an impossibility.

Didn't matter if I could get through here or not...*Well, let's just see, though.* "Space here, between these oaks." I was mumbling aloud, the way old men do. So what? Nobody around to hear. "Someone's cut dead firewood here. Oh yeah, you can get a permit from the forest people for that. So, on down this way, miss those boulders..."

Quiet here. Probably about the height of Jim's place, yeah. *My little haven's down there, hidden, under this big hill. Whole different feeling, being on top. This's really a plateau, they tell me, these mountains with eroded hollows. No matter...they're still steep, and gravity's what this is all about.*

I found the way, after almost two hours of false paths in the thickening air. Smelled like rain now finally, after almost everything had dried up. Jim's well had kept his garden green, but this limestone glade country was scorched. The cedars were browning, the oak and hickory an old, deep green, alien to the fresh newness of forgotten springtime.

I could get the Ranger to here. Then maybe yes, I could unload a tank, lower it from some sort of hand winch I could maybe build. But a tank I could haul in my little truck would hold only two or three hundred gallons. Maybe two waterings? Surely more. But just a drop in the hanging-garden bucket. Dampen a few roots; give the plants false hope.

Oh, okay, more than one smaller tank.

And well, I said I always liked a challenge. My house hadn't really been anything I hadn't done dozens of times before (if not mostly alone). This water thing *was* a challenge. Maybe a Don Quixote windmill? With enough money, I could buy a big tank, hire a big truck, winch, cable, get it into place.

With enough money...

~ * ~

We were camping on the land we'd bought in Virginia. It was early June, and water was everywhere. I'd found a spring on the land, some distance from the house site we'd chosen, which had supplied water for a settler's cabin off our part of the land. During those first days, I'd carry water from the spring, which Sharon insisted on boiling.

Melissa was two and a half, and she wanted to go with me everywhere. So we'd leave Mom and baby June at the tent and Rover camper, and explore our new domain. She seldom tired, and when she did, I'd hoist her up on my shoulders as we headed home.

We discovered wild strawberries ripening along the way to the spring, and she wanted them all. Unfortunately, they came with stems, and her hands would be stained red from tugging on them, and her mouth from eating them. She implored Sharon to make a pie from her collection, a tall order on a Coleman stove. But in those days, I still thought my wife was up for any adventure, and so okay, she contrived to try, anyway.

The result wasn't bad, except for those pesky stems, which she'd thought would soften with the makeshift baking. That experience must've started Sharon on the road to resenting the pioneer life, and she urged me to jump on building our house, asap.

But that memory persisted, here in this waterless place: tiny girl with blue eyes and ringlets gathering wild strawberries, sure to delight her mother. Delighted me, anyway.

~ * ~

I went junkyard hunting. I found gears and iron and lengths of cable. In two cool, rainy days and two more hot ones, I forged a hand winch, with locking ratchet and gear reduction. I could pull stones with it, bolted to the Ranger's back bumper or cable looped around a tree. Or, I could let out the cable, lowering a tank. Or a big rock, or a log, or a sled full of rocks, down a steep slope. Should have built this long before now.

Jim and I went in search of tanks. If one wouldn't do much, maybe three or four would. They'd have to be cheap, but maybe, one at a time, I could get them, and get them placed by say, next April. Maybe. No real hurry. Time would have to replace money, here. And yeah, I could paint them a camo green or gray, so they wouldn't stand out like relics from the Rust Belt. Maybe my watering scheme wouldn't have to destroy the mountain.

The first one was a 300-gallon metal cylinder someone had shot a hole in. Cost me twenty dollars, and some welding at Jim's shop. He wanted to help place it, so we drove the county road to the woodcutters' access to the forest. I'd lifted the camper cap off my truck with the come-along long before this, and the tank fit...barely.

Once threaded down through the national forest, I'd hacked some of my brush away to the extreme end of travel, above and back from where I wanted to be. I got into position, blocked the Ranger's wheels, hooked the winch cable to one of two welded-on handles at each end of the tank. We pried it off, sliding easily on the plastic pickup bedliner. It made a whump as it landed, slid, pulled the cable tight.

I put Jim on the winch, inching out cable as I pried with the six-foot digging bar. The tank would roll nicely from side to side, but needed prying from the cabled end to go down the rough slope. It took an hour to travel the 100 feet of my winch cable.

There we anchored the tank with stones, unhooked the cable, rewound it. Then we attached another hundred feet of cable to it and the winch hook, and started over. This time, on the steeper slope, it went faster. Except for a couple of relatively flat ledges down there that needed more prying. Then another stop, another shorter length, and we had the tank down to the dug-out pocket I'd prepared for it.

We set it in place, blocked it securely, gave each other high-fives. One set, however many more to go. Jim looked over my terraces, the minimal soil I'd filled behind. Looked like a lot less dirt now through his eyes than it had when I was muscling it down there. He shrugged.

"Might work. You coulda done that fast with a bulldozer, though, or even just a tractor with a bucket on it."

"Yeah, and lost it over the edge, besides denuding the slope and spending dollars I don't have. I'm in no hurry, Jim."

"Good thing, too. Oh, remind me to send some corn with you. Got more than we can give away."

Well, of course the corn gift ran into dinner at their place, which I was most grateful for. Jim and Kelly were just about my only family now, and old curmudgeon or not, family was important to me. Kelly had done something in the kitchen with pork that elevated it far above mere hog, and we feasted.

"Any word from Sharon?" my sister-in-law ventured, "or has she given up on you?"

"Maybe. I get these letters that are like from an old schoolmate, news I could do without, chitchat. I get the feeling she's just waiting for me to work things out, go home and pick up again. Hasn't sold the house. Has closed down the business, sold the major equipment. All of which is fine with me."

"Well, you've sure got settled in down there," Jim observed. "I was pretty skeptical of your getting it done so much on your own, but knew you wanted the solo thing..." His voice trailed off.

"Yeah. Guess I wanted to see if I could still do it. Found out I could, with your help, and a little of Kyle's, Eric's. Winter'll be sort of a strain, I guess, but I figure to lay in a lot of wood, and stay in, bad weather. Be okay if I don't get myself hurt, or catch some strange disease."

"Stay away from people, you won't get sick. We don't get colds much anymore, since the kids grew up. You'll do all right. Gets cool, you'll always enjoy blacksmithing again."

"There's that. Got a lot of reading I wanta do, too. I guess I can get through the winter without going crazy."

"Sure," Jim assured me. "And we'll hunt, too, if you want to. Put some venison in the freezer, cut your grocery bill."

Nine

"We need to talk," Sharon informed me. Kyle was quiet in his crib and the girls were settling down but still talking, fighting sleep the way kids will. It was a typical evening, even after the excitement of the boy's birth and his sisters' getting used to his presence.

"Okay, let's talk." I had no idea what this would be about, but had picked up on a vague discontent in my bride that hadn't been there before. So I sort of braced myself.

"Well, to get right to it, I don't want to raise the kids here." *Here* was now a little creek out of Branson, Missouri, where we'd relocated a cabin, added to it and put down roots. It was also my base for the increasing construction work.

"Schools? They seem pretty good to me." I was apparently clueless.

"Not so much that as the peer pressure. All this development, the booming entertainment thing on Highway 76. It's bringing in all kinds of people, drugs, drifters. I just don't think we should trust that we can keep ours from falling through the cracks, know what I mean? You know how teenagers just have to go with the flow."

"There's that, I guess. So what do you have in mind?" She'd obviously thought this through, knew what she wanted. I'd learned that about her.

"Somewhere with good schools, yes. But also somewhere with bright kids and some culture, influence them in the right direction."

"Okay, so again, where?"

"Well, I need your input here, of course. But I'd thought maybe up North, or back East." I thought about this: what, Milwaukee and snow? New England and more snow? At least she hadn't suggested California, which was about to slide off into the ocean and was populated with crazies, far as I was concerned.

"Virginia, maybe? There's a great university there in Charlottesville, and it's not that far to D.C. or to Richmond. Got mountains, rivers, lots going on." *Yeah, and high prices, for sure. Probably pay more for an acre of land there than we've put into this whole place. But rivers, maybe good fishing. Okay, we'll think about this.*

But I later learned Sharon had indeed chosen this very location, probably researched it, maybe had come to know somebody from there. She was that way...onto details, thorough, and okay, good at that stuff.

So, did I put up a fuss, having built my business here, to have to start over there, where competition was probably harsh? And what if I couldn't find construction work there at all? Have to charge more to pay the higher bills, have to fight stiffer building codes, gear up in general.

We started looking around. Made some trips to places that might also work, like Chapel Hill, North Carolina (maybe), Connecticut? (no), Georgia mountains (the movie *Deliverance*?). But the more we searched, the better Charlottesville and the surrounding territory looked to us. So, sell out here for whatever we could get, leave, travel, start over from scratch. I wasn't much over forty, so okay, it could work. Maybe.

But I did get to wondering just how much of this scheme was really for the kids and how much Sharon's maybe getting stir crazy. Didn't matter, I figured, but there was this little voice back in my head that said as soon as she got settled someplace else, she'd want to move onward and upward to the next thing, whatever that turned out to be.

But we started winding things up in the Ozarks and sold our cabin surprisingly soon, and of course for too little money. Well, most of our investment was my labor, so since I hadn't kept a record, I guessed it didn't matter much.

We loaded the long-wheelbase Land Rover, which I'd converted to a tiny camper with a fold-down couch bed, a counter with dry sink, propane tank, and a hammock for the kids overhead. Kyle could sleep in a little space at the rear wheel well, along with other storage. And we went in search of just the right place to emigrate to.

Across part of Arkansas, Mississippi, Alabama, Georgia, South Carolina, up through Virginia to New England. With lots of side trips, some camping, some staying in motels to clean up and do laundry. And to see a lot of country, which glowed in fall leaf color and often looked better than it was.

Bottom line: we bought the 22 acres northwest of Charlottesville we still owned, and raised our tribe there. It wasn't a bad choice, at least for the kids. I chafed at the politics, the high costs, the snobbery, and the just plain too many people. My ancestors had left this territory for more space, and here we were back in the throng.

But it'd been good, actually. Little lean the first winter, but then I fell into restoration jobs. Seems log cabin fever was high there, and every remote cabin was a target for moving onto some McMansion's back woods for a guest house, or for restoring right where it was. I even got to build a couple bridges, which were challenges. Especially one. The owner wanted to duplicate those great covered ones in Pennsylvania. One of my favorite jobs.

And we restored two gristmills, also challenges. And plantation houses. I avoided the brick ranchers that had moldering particle board and sagging foundations, those built to last a bare generation. And I found I was building a following.

~ * ~

It was suddenly October, and the amber air held turning leaves against an achingly blue sky. Nights were crisp, but the sun burned me at noon, working at the terraces above the house. Carpets of leaves crunched underfoot, and I raked them, gathered them, spread them over my planting beds with dirt over, to hold them in place. The air was winey now, made sharper by the realization that the year would soon be lost in cold rain and the coming dark months. It was a heady but tenuous time, full of languor, but also of getting-in, a scurrying punctuated by long rests in the sun.

I watched squirrels find nuts, scamper with them up trees to hollows, cache them. I could imagine the rare black bears fattening against their semi-hibernation, all the animals banking against the specter of winter.

Kyle came one Saturday with his Sarah, a slim girl with an aura of warmth about her I found irresistible. She had to see everything: the terraced slopes, the water tanks, the steps and paths. And she was entranced with my stone cabin. Seeing it through her eyes, I guess it did look a little like some fairytale troll's house. It had mellowed somehow, in just these months, with the graying of wood and the softening of the new, sharp edges. Looked as if it'd been there a lot longer than its one season.

We had lunch outside on the flat stone above Caney Creek, at a work table we moved there. Sun filtered through yellow and red leaves and warmed the little hollow in light the color of honey. Sarah had wide-set blue eyes, and hair that was either light brown or dark blonde, depending on the light.

Afterwards, we hiked down toward Beaver Creek with flyrods. October's generally dry in the Ozarks, but after a couple of stray rains, the creek was moving okay. Kyle hadn't shown Sarah how to use the rod yet, which I found odd. (Later, I learned he wanted to save that experience for me...nice.) And she insisted I teach her. That made the hermit feel good, I tell you. We found a wide gravel bar and I gave her the basics while Kyle fished on down.

She was afraid of the hook at first, until I pointed out that it was up there eight feet above her head if she handled it right.

"If you see you've let it drop, though, you duck down. People do get hooked. Start with only a little line out, and it's easier to control."

She did. Couple dozen tries, and she could sense when the line was out behind her far enough to start the forward cast.

"Some people count time," I told her, figuring, since Kyle had said she was musical, that'd work for her. But she soon had it, however she did it. "Now, strip a little more line out, and let it go into the cast. Drop it by that rock."

She did that, and a sun perch or something else small hit her fly.

"Wow! What do I do now?"

"Give it a jerk. You may or may not have a fish on."

She didn't, but the excitement of that little strike fired her up. The blue eyes danced, and she went at that water, dropping the fly every foot or so till she'd covered the pool. I'd shown her how to walk the line in her left hand, and she was getting it.

All that whipping the water, no other fish would hit, but one did. Must've waked it from under a ledge. Wasn't big, but she got excited again. I coached her in setting the hook, walking it in, holding her rod high to take any strain from a run. No danger of snapping a leader from this fish, which turned out to be a nine-inch goggle-eye. I explained that she'd have to give ground, step with a big fish so it wouldn't break her leader, but keep the pressure on.

Kyle looked up when she held it up, and he waved. We decided to let this one go, since we hadn't caught anything else, and I showed her how to take the hook out, which was only in the fish's lip. She didn't squirm. She held it under water for a few seconds, feeling it flex in her hand, then let it streak away. Smiled as wide as the Ozarks.

I looked for some of Sarah's religious...pushing, I guess you'd call it, but nothing was evident. Like Jim and Kelly, apparently she didn't make a big thing out of it with other people.

I hadn't been exactly resisting the whole church business myself, but it'd been for me mostly a nice, laid-back getting with people I'd come to like. Reverend Zachman didn't harangue—I'd have stopped going if he did—and his earnestness was genuine. *Fine. You do your thing; I'll do mine.*

And right now, mine is getting settled in, solo.

We did go with the folks Sunday, as usual. Sarah was a big hit, as I knew she would be. She didn't let you stay neutral about her; she sort of drew you in like a magnet. And you found you wanted to be around her, hear her laugh, hear her little-girl voice. Which she could use, we found out, in the hymns and the newer praise songs. She knew them all, and sang them in a clear soprano. Kyle's grin mirrored my own. I was proud of this girl my son had found, and hoped this relationship would last.

We'd had dinner with Jim and Kelly the night before, and now Kyle insisted on treating us all in Forsyth. New place, with big, old beamwork and some pretty good stonework, too. The food was great, and we overstuffed, of course. Nice change from my own cooking, again.

Sharon's name didn't come up once, and I was grateful. Seeing Kyle again triggered a lot of memories of home, which would be natural. I didn't ask if he'd taken Sarah to visit his mom, but I got the impression he would, soon. My boy wasn't going to do any better than this young lady, I was sure.

But this was the 21st century, and my opinion didn't count at all. Couples broke up, shifted, regrouped, for some strange reasons now. Maybe they always had.

I sure couldn't point any fingers.

I didn't want Sarah to leave without knowing that I approved strongly, though. Wasn't sure just how to do that, and it was time for them to go.

"You drag this boy back down to see us again, Sarah. And if he won't come, you just come without him." At that, she surprised me by giving me a real hug. Felt just like one of the daughters, back when they were growing up. Nice.

"Don't you worry," she told me, "I'll be back. I know there's a big fish with my name on it down in one of those holes." Gave me a wink.

I'd kick Kyle's butt if he let this one go.

~ * ~

The girls were still a little mad, I guessed, or maybe just confused. Melissa would scold me good in her letters. I'd written them both, after they'd sent me those accusatory first notes. *Okay, they're with Sharon on this, and maybe they're right.* My own thoughts of my wife more often slipped back into the good times: the little things we'd said to each other, little in-jokes, phrases, words of endearment, I guess.

And of course there was the intimacy we had early on. Sharon was, as I've said, a good-looking woman. And no matter how we rationalize our attractions, we'd all rather wake up in the morning with beauty next to us instead of ugly.

So yeah, I'd get to re-living some of that remembered sex between us...natural, I suppose. And hey, a guy's not dead at seventy, not necessarily a dirty old man either. Still sometimes dreamed of her touch, the smoothness of her skin on mine, the pure joy of our stroking, anticipation building, that ecstasy of our finally completely joining.

But every time I went there, or even close, those whispered words then hardened into the put-downs, the contempt, the insulted and insulting confrontations that had driven me off out of her orbit.

Off the circle of our life together, onto this tangent, this solo thing.

I didn't know what was in her head now, and guessed I never had. She continued to write, and had called to talk with Kelly a couple more times. Kelly reported that she had been concerned, but maybe still feeling betrayed. Okay, she had a right to be, I guessed. Old man *had* run off, after all. Not to another woman, at least, but run off just the same.

I'll admit my behavior wasn't exactly in keeping with a new awareness that was gradually sinking in from my exposure to religion, that of a...debt, maybe, we all have to those people around us. Little hazy, I'm afraid. And of course there was the "till death do you part" promise. Only that hadn't bothered me much, under the circumstances.

Probably should have.

~ * ~

With the cool weather, I got onto the blacksmithing. More to pass the time than any real need. I'd never had time these past years for any more than the strap hinges, latches, andirons and pot racks for the houses we'd restored. Now I looked forward to doing some advanced work, mostly for my own satisfaction. Found some good coal in

Springfield, and paid Jim back for what I'd used of his. I'd taught him basic ironwork many years ago, but about all he did was horse-shoeing. I'd never known enough about horses to try to shoe one, thereby escaping the image of "real" blacksmith most folks have.

Yeah, the movies always show a scruffy old guy holding a horse's hoof up, with a hammer in his hand, like that's all we ever do. Probably an actor, anyway, and that's as close as he ever gets to being a star. Reality is, we can make anything outta iron or steel, give us enough time and maybe some instruction. Even machine parts, when necessary; first machines, engines were forged by blacksmiths anyway. Who else?

I closed in the windy sides of the smithy with some more weathered oak barnboards I'd found, and it began to look as if it'd been there forever. Fit nicely alongside the little stone house, and I could again imagine myself a pioneer of sorts.

I made Jim a skinning knife, and Kelly a couple of kitchen knives from some medium-carbon steel rod I'd scrounged. Tempered just right, they'd hold a razor edge and still flex without breaking. I'd found a dead black cherry tree up the slope that was thoroughly seasoned, and carved the handles from that rich, red wood. It gets darker with age, and is hard enough to last forever. There was also Osage orange growing here, that varies in shades from an intense yellow down through streaked brown even to an almost mahogany color.

Then I made myself a Bowie knife of some circle-saw steel, and spent some time on the brass bolster and handle. Got a piece of heavy leather and put together a sheath. This knife was heavy enough to split kindling, but it'd do for a hunting knife, too. I got to wearing it on my belt...made me feel like a real mountain man. Surprising how many uses I found for it, too: hack brush, pry things, cut pegs, things I didn't know I needed before.

Thing about these handmade knives...if they weren't lost, they'd survive the original owners, become heirlooms for the great-grandkids. *Yeah, old great-grandpa hammered this outta scrap iron, must've been on back about the time of the dinosaurs.*

Next, I forged some wood chisels, a smaller drawknife, some other carving tools. I might enjoy some woodworking when I was snowed in, I figured. I was enjoying making the tools, for sure. The concentration on the hammering, oil-hardening, tempering, the honing, the handle-fitting made the hours slip by, and I found I often didn't want to stop for food or sleep.

I'd made tools like these before, but found when I used them on construction jobs, they seemed to disappear somehow, although nobody ever admitted to lifting them. That wouldn't happen here, unless I lost them under a pile of sawdust or wood chips.

November brought the rains, and the winds that finished stripping the trees. The moonshiner's spring was running again, I found when I climbed up there. And those magic waterfalls were threading sheets of silver upstream from my cabin. The thirsty ground drank the rain, then let it slip along the ledgerock into my stream, sheeting the limestone, slippery now.

I spent a couple of hours at a time cutting dead timber for firewood. It worked best to cut a skeleton tree upslope somewhere along my road in, then cut it to long lengths, drag it to the truck, then cut it shorter, load it, haul it home. Less trudging that way. The larger blocks I split with a maul I'd forged from a chipped, recycled sledgehammer head, and an iron wedge from a section of truck axle.

By the first powdering of snow, I had two cords of dry wood stacked next to the house, within easy reach of the door. I remembered the New England custom of joining house to woodshed to barn, to fight the snowdrifts. Didn't snow that much here. There'd be this light one or two, then maybe after Christmas before anything bad. Ice maybe, and that'd keep my truck grounded.

But I'd gotten to a place where that thought didn't worry me. I didn't have to be mobile anymore. And it wasn't so far up to Jim's, if I wanted company or needed to get a ride out. Always be able to crunch my way through dead leaves in the woods, avoid the ice on the road.

~ * ~

When things go sour, you look back later and try to figure where it all started, what maybe little thing could have been done differently, words that should have been said better. It's always an exercise in frustration, but you do it.

And it was pretty clear what had really set Sharon and me at odds. Or maybe it'd been on the way to that all along.

It all came apart for the wrong reasons. We'd had a million-dollar year for my construction company, which for just five guys was phenomenal. That didn't translate to a huge net, of course, but Sharon and I ended up with around two hundred Gs for our percentage. And we were paying our guys a couple bucks an hour more than anybody else, plus overtime and fringe benefits.

This was after years of building a following, taking crud jobs when we had nothing else, turning dilapidated historic structures into silk purses, even getting written up and on TV interviews. It was a milestone, and I was justifiably proud. Could send the younger kids to college too, no sweat.

And Sharon turns to me and lays this on me, out of the blue:

"Finally. Now Liam, don't blow this with taking any more reject jobs. We've worked hard to get here, and there's no place to go but up. You don't charge enough for your work, you're too easy-going, you let people take advantage of you. I haven't busted my butt all these years to go back to bare survival."

"Hey, I charge what's fair. I know when a customer's gonna back off from sticker shock, and I get jobs because I don't get greedy. We work fast and good and we save people money that way. That's why we've reached this milestone, and I'm not gonna blow the winning formula." Sounded right to me.

"All I'm hearing here is 'I.' Five times in that spiel. Like I don't pull *my* weight, here? Along with raising three kids? You'd still be living in a shack on peanuts, Liam McLeod, if I hadn't pulled us out of that. And I get a say in how this company's run." Hands on hips. *Shack? This's beginning to piss me off. But cool it, guy.*

"Well, sure you do. Haven't I always included you in decisions?"

"After the fight, sometimes, yes. And it's gonna change, starting today. First, we're gonna hire a bookkeeper slash secretary. And I'm going to get a real job, get out of the house and office, where I've been chained for years. And you're gonna be on the payroll, by the hour, in addition to our twenty percent profit. And we're marking everything, labor and materials, up another ten percent."

"That'll blow the business all to hell, Sharon. No way can we find work, charging all that. Get real, here!" *Yeah, this is crazy. Like I don't know how to run a construction company after all these years? Whatthehell's got into this woman?*

"You know what your problem is, Liam? You think small. You work small. Everything about you is small. Here you're on the threshold of real success, and you wanta keep on being *small!* Well, I'm through scrimping, almost starving, doing without. And another thing: I'm going out and buying myself a new car. I'm sick of your old patched-together heaps. You and Kyle can do your male bonding thing over some other junk, not my car."

"Hey, just what's got into you, woman? What's caused this explosion?"

"Got into me? You don't have a *clue*, Liam. You have no idea how I've been planning to drag you out of the woods into a real life, how I've pushed you, led you, even had to trick you into making something of yourself. All these years *I've* been the one with vision, with aspirations. You're just a pair of hands. *I* have to do the thinking around here, because you sure don't. You'd be content to live in a damn cave somewhere, deprive me and the kids of everything but hog lard and cornpone or something!" She stalked out of the office, slammed the door.

And of course the rage was building inside me. *Just a pair of hands? A damn cave? And she wants to wreck the business with all that shit about gouging the customers? Like two hundred thousand isn't enough to live on?* And her damn car wasn't but five years old. Or maybe six, I couldn't remember. Tried to keep her in something late-model to avoid breakdowns, but she clearly didn't appreciate that.

I heard her crank up and leave, and I went out to the shop and threw things for a while, letting off steam. So this was the way we were gonna live from now on? In a battleground? Well, we'd just see about that...

~ * ~

Thanksgiving came, and I half-expected Kyle and Sarah to come, but suspected they'd go to Sharon's, probably meet one of the daughters there. June had written me a nice note, full this time of worry. After seven months, she'd come to the realization that this could be permanent, and was dealing with it. Some, anyway. Melissa had Grady and her kids out in Denver, and I guessed she'd just write the old man off. Okay. I missed my girls, but they'd flown long enough ago I guessed I could handle it. Would like to see the grandkids, though. Probably no chance, now.

Burned bridges.

Jim and Kelly surprised me that day with a golden retriever pup that looked so much like my old dog it really got to me. This one didn't have AKC papers, but was supposedly purebred. He was eight weeks old, and mostly fur and awkward feet. About licked me to death in the first five minutes. Well. I stammered my thanks.

"Didn't want you to get too lonely down there," Kelly explained, eyes crinkling behind her granny glasses. Jim's grin was wide as a gate.

"What'll you name him?"

"Oh, I'll wait till he shows some quirk. You know my old dog Dodger could slip between our ankles and in or out a door like soap. This'n will earn some name."

Dinner with them was the usual feast. I never could figure how they ate so well and stayed slim. Work, I guess. They both had always buzzed around a lot, even if not so fast now. Metabolism.

Unfortunately, both their kids were spending the holiday with their in-laws. They'd be here Christmas, though, with the grandchildren. Well, maybe Kyle and Sarah'd come then, too. I didn't hope for the daughters, but June might just show. She'd visited with Sharon twice, and maybe she'd want to hear the other side...

Well, if there really *was* an other side.

The pup settled in the uncomplicated way goldens do. I let him sleep in, because a horned owl could nail him, or a fox. Even a coyote or bobcat. Let him grow some. He was all energy, of course, and into anything chewable. I put shoes and tools up out of reach. He couldn't do any damage to the flagstone floor, even with puddles. But like my old dog, he was naturally housebroken. I'm a light sleeper, and one whimper got me up to take him outside.

My principal occupation these days besides the forge work was bringing woods dirt down to my terraces. The pup thought this was a grand idea...he'd jump into dirt and leaves I'd raked up, and proceed to scatter everything. So I started him learning the word "no," with gradually improving results.

I was able to help both Jim and Eric cut firewood a couple of Saturdays. The three of us seemed to get a lot more done together than we could've on our own. Eric was a good guy, big, easy-going, skilled craftsman. We always had a lot to talk about. Had a girlfriend in Springfield he'd go see a lot, and all those long-distance carpentry jobs. Be here most of the winter, though, he told me. Good. Have some more company.

~ * ~

An idea I'd had for a sled worked pretty well. I'd bolted together a low three-by-four-foot thing with sides and iron-shod runners made from truck leaf springs. These got slick the first day of sliding it. I anchored the winch to a cedar and the cable to the sled. Then I'd shovel in a couple wheelbarrows full of good black dirt. Let off the winch lock, and I could ease the sled down, then lock it into place for unloading.

I'd had to take rocks out of its path, because I couldn't see it after it'd gone below the swell of the hill. I marked where to stop the cable, then climbed down my zigzag path. The sled would be there, tethered above my terraces. I could spread about fifteen loads behind my stone wall before I'd have to re-position the winch and clear a new sled run. The slick runners hardly disturbed the thin soil, and I'd stabilize the runs later with brush to keep that soil in place.

The pup would dash along from side to side, barking at the moving sled, convinced he was in charge of the operation. And at day's end, both he and I would be near exhaustion.

This was an activity that could wear me out if I let it. But I paced myself, filling the sled methodically, using a mattock to cut roots, sifting the black soil. Now it was damp, and not powdery as in summer. The sled-pull back up wasn't too bad, with the winch's gearing, but it took time. I was using only the one length of cable, working from lower on the hill than vehicle territory. And I was being careful to leave some of the soil by mulching it there, not denude the underlying stone.

~ * ~

I heard their engine from across Caney: sound came up my hollow better with the leaves off. I stepped out to see who was over there. Three guys in camo, with deer rifles. They'd started to wade across the creek from their extended-cab 4wd truck, despite Mallory's "No Hunting" signs every few yards. Seeing me, they reversed, came down to across from the side stream.

"How y'doin'?" one called.

"Fine. You boys goin' to hunt the forest?"

"Yeah, but there's signs up where we used to hunt."

"Not forest over there. Fellow owns it an' his neighbor's got horses, doesn't want one hit."

"Oh, we know th' diff'rence in a horse an' a deer." Grins.

"Yeah. Well, forest's all back on the side you're on. Thirteen thousand acres of wilderness area. Oughta be somethin' in there."

"Reckon so. See y'got a road down. Aimin' t'build somethin'?"

"Already done it, back there. Been plannin' it thirty years. You boys have a good day huntin'." I turned to leave, but one of the others didn't want to let it go.

"Shame, ruinin' good huntin', folks puttin' in roads, buildin' houses an' all." He spat tobacco juice. Big guy, red face, beer gut, looked maybe a brick shy of a full load. I wasn't feeling particularly charitable, I'm afraid.

"Yeah, I guess. But y'know, when they put in a road, and built your own house, back whenever that was, they probably ruined a lot of good huntin', too, when you really think about it." He looked bewildered, probably his usual expression.

"That don't make no sense. I live in town. This's woods."

"Wasn't always town, go back far enough. But that's one reason they got the national forest, to keep some good huntin' ground."

"Wal, we like t'hunt where we wanta hunt, not where some guv'ment bunch says we can." More tobacco juice.

"Come on, Curtis," the first man spoke again. "Man's got a right t'build on his own land, I reckon."

"Jis' don't seem right," grumbled Curtis, whose understanding of others' property rights probably ended at whatever he wanted to do at any given moment. Give him beer on Saturday and a big gun, he'd be happy as a hog in manure. As they left, I reflected that this man—all of them—probably voted in elections, too.

Scary thought.

I guessed I was getting grumpy, here away from people. But it's always irritated the hell out of me the way hunters, horsemen, even birdwatchers, just ignore fences, property lines. Hey, somebody had to buy that land, pay taxes on it, be responsible for it. Not like a suburbanite on a quarter of an acre had the right to consider somebody else's property public territory, there for his/her enjoyment.

I remembered vandalism, too...usual broken windows, trash dumped. A friend in Virginia had this land his dad had left him alongside a lake he'd created, way back in the woods. He'd been after me to help him build a weekend cabin there, but I'd discouraged him. Too hard to keep track of the place, between visits.

And sure enough, some kids decided it'd be fun to block up the overflow drain at the dam, which raised the lake's water level. Neither my friend nor any of the family had been to the place all winter, and when he went, he discovered the high water had killed all the trees along the shore. Hard to replace a forest.

Oh well, best not to get too riled up about a few hunters.

There were stretches of several days when I didn't do much at all. The drizzle would keep me inside, reading in the gray light. I knew I'd get soft if I didn't do some physical stuff, though. Good days I'd cut wood or move dirt. And keep an eye out for more trespassing hunters. And/or woods-loving porn film freaks.

The Mallorys came down once to see my place. Kelly'd told them what I was doing up my little hollow, and their curiosity brought them down my road. Trish thought the little house was cute, if too tiny.

"Where'll you put stuff?"

"You're looking at it all, right here. I travel light."

"And it looks like you're staying. What about Sharon?"

"Well, Sharon's got a life back in Virginia, and I guess I've got one here, at least for the time being." I hoped that settled that question.

"It's a piece of art," Tom appraised, the artist in him taking in the position of the little stone structure, snugged against the hill, the aged wood of the smithy, the winding, stone-lined path up alongside the branch to my door. "A little like a Hobbit house."

"Maybe. Just an extension of me, I guess. Didn't Thoreau say that?"

"Something like that...what we do and what we wear, the results of our labors tell what kind of people we are."

"That'd make me a sure-fire hermit."

"You said it; I didn't."

Pretty obvious the Mallorys didn't approve of my deserting my wife, either. I seemed to be a minority of one, here. I wasn't exactly sorry when they left.

I set out some dwarf fruit trees up behind the terraces, with their trunks wrapped in plastic to keep the deer and rabbits from eating the bark. Time to do some fencing maybe, although the deer would probably jump anything I could build. And how could I set posts in that thin soil? I'd seen stone piles around posts to hold them in place, but that'd be a huge chore in itself.

I priced web-wire fencing next time I was in Forsyth. Not too bad, but it would need strong anchoring. I tried Jim's hand posthole digger a few places on my hill. Well, I could get a couple of feet down, here and there. Other places the rock showed through the surface a lot like bone. Okay, set some posts then, and rockpile the others. Lots of otherwise non-usable stones around. No shortage of rocks, here. I remembered seeing a music album cover: *Stoney End,* by some group or other. Yeah.

I cut some slow-growth cedar posts that were almost all red heart, and started this job. The digger made my wrists sore...new muscles at work. But it warmed me in those chill days. I'd stretch the wire between the set posts, then staple it to those floating in between that I'd have to rock up around. I could build up stones around the bottom of the wire along with the posts that way too, keep small critters from pushing under. Horse-high, bull-strong, hog-tight was the old saying. I guessed, too, that if my vicious guard dog spent enough time up there, he'd mark enough territory the deer would maybe spook and stay away.

Try that, anyway.

Ten

Christmas sneaked up on me the way it used to when I was swamped in construction work. Sharon would have to get after me to get a tree, threatening to buy a manicured monstrosity at some exorbitant price if I didn't take the kids out to hunt one in the woods.

We'd always decorate it early, then leave it up till way past New Year's, all browning and shedding, even in a bucket of water. Christmas was always a bigger deal with her and the kids. Supposed to be that way, I guess. And hey, it hadn't been like I was too busy this time to get ready for it. I just hadn't gotten into the mindset yet, I guess.

So, even with the preparations at church, the Advent Sundays and the songs, I wasn't really ready. Did get a welcome note from June, saying she was flying in to see me. Could I meet her in Springfield? Sure could. But then she called Jim to say Kyle and Sarah would meet her, bring her down.

Well. Gonna be quite a gathering then, with Jim's Mike and Mary and those grandkids. Lotsa people. My place was so tiny, and I couldn't afford to put anybody up in a motel...Then I saw Eric on the creek, and he'd heard the news from Jim.

"I'm outta here for two weeks, Liam. See my folks in Kansas City. You put your kids in my cabin now, long as they want. An' no, I won't take no for an answer."

"Well, Eric, that's nice of you to offer. You never met my daughter June, did you?"

"No, but I know Kyle, and I met Sarah that time. They're all welcome to the place. Water storage tank's a little cranky if it gets too cold, but it won't prob'ly, Christmas. January's when I hafta keep it all from freezing." Eric had an engine-driven pump pickup pipe in the creek he used to fill an overhead tank the original builders had put in. That supplied all but the drinking and cooking water, which he got from Jim's well up the hill.

So. Eric's house was neat, for a bachelor's place. The couple who'd built it had been real back-to-the-earth people, not at all fazed by the washed-out road and the creek ford and living without electricity. That was the thing to do in the homespun era, I remembered; all of us telling each other how good it was to be outside the system, independent. Only then reality had intruded, and everyone but Jim and Kelly had gone back to civilization, the game over, to jobs and "life" again.

I guess you could call all that life.

And now here I was back on the creek, old man cut loose from that very system again. Except that system had provided me with my little Social Security check, and in a way even my old truck and my hovel.

But the kids' coming to see me, now that'd be really fine. Made me antsy, waiting, and I guess I began to realize I'd been lonely, really. All the work, the projects, the dawn-to-dark stuff of getting settled had pushed that back.

Almost.

~ * ~

Well, nobody's coming home for Christmas, apparently. Deserting me too, for that old goat. That's adding insult to injury, no matter how you look at it. So okay, June's been here twice, and

Melissa's promised, but after the first of the year. Don't know when Kyle will find time from his bachelor lifestyle to come see his mother. Boy was all mine when he was little, but Liam stole him early on.

Well, no use stewing about it. They all went out the door to college and never looked back, really. Gotta get used to it, I guess. Can't drag them home, and every other mother's told me it's just that way.

Damn that man! He's gonna stay down in that hole till he dies. Even through the winter, apparently. Well, let him. He's dumped me, so I guess I shouldn't care what happens to him.

Only I do.

~ * ~

The big day was on a Friday, and the kids were due Wednesday afternoon. Kyle and Sarah had time off, and they'd meet June's plane a little after noon. I got the house clean early, then went up the hill with the pup in the Ranger. It was overcast but not cold, and no snow was left on the ground. Jim had said he wanted to patch a place in his barn roof, so I'd help on that.

I remembered our putting up those sheets of galvanized metal that first time. He hadn't painted it, and the thin zinc had worn off, the sheet-iron rusted. A corner had blown loose and flapped, crinkling the metal into cracks.

The new metal was shiny in the bed of his pickup, jarring and bright next to the old when we got it up there. Jim said he'd let the new stuff age over winter—let the shine wear off—then paint the whole thing. Use the rust-converter stuff I'd put on old roofs that became primer. Some chemical action that stopped rust, or was supposed to.

The square cedar pole-barn posts that had been so red and sharp-cornered and aromatic thirty years before were now gray and round-edged and smooth to the touch. Cows had rubbed against the soft wood, hands had touched it, pitchforks of hay and shovels had bumped and brushed it countless times. The barn looked centuries old, and smelled like barns the world over: hay and manure and harness leather and rope and rusty iron. All the scents of farming. I breathed it in deep.

The sun broke through, and the December air warmed, so our coats came off as we worked. The wood under the metal, also cedar, was still good, so this was a quick job. Kelly checked on us a couple times: two old men on a roof didn't look too safe to her. But we moved slow and careful, stayed out of trouble. And got in a few good jokes, too. Enjoyed it.

We were driving the last of those plastic-washered nails when Kyle's Audi slipped into the yard. We actually heard the screen door slam before we saw the car. Kelly was out and had the kids hugged before I got down the ladder, Jim right behind me, grinning.

June always brought the sun with her, with her big eyes and permanent smile. She'd done theater since middle school, and filled a stage, all energy. Now she naturally moved to the center of things, brightening the place like she always did. She gave me a searching look, but was obviously glad to see me.

"How's my hermit daddy?" Big hug.

"Hidin' from the world, I guess. How's the crazy Left Coast?"

"Insane. I'm going to a few classes, but mostly I'm teaching undergrads...wide-eyed, deluded kids, most of whom will never get on a real stage. At least not for pay. But you're the one we're all worried about, you know, did a bear eat you?"

"Not yet. And now I've got this fierce guard dog, thanks to your Uncle Jim and Aunt Kelly." The pup, coming back from the woods, took that as a cue to jump up on her jeans, paws fortunately not at the moment muddy.

"Ohh, what a sweetie! Why, he's just like Dodger was. Hey, fuzzball." She picked him up and hugged him and he got her face with his lightning tongue. I used the pause to greet Kyle and Sarah, who'd been talking with Jim.

"Good to see you two again. This's gonna be a great Christmas, with all of you here. And Mike and Mary will be in, too. When, Kelly? Tonight?"

"Late, for Mary. Mike and his bunch tomorrow morning. Yeah, we'll fill up the woods all right. But come in. Had lunch?"

"We did, in Springfield," Kyle said. "Thought we'd go down to Eric's first, get our stuff in, then..."

"Then you're coming back here for dinner. I've been cooking all day. Think Kyle's car can do the ford, Jim? Or should they take my Cherokee?"

"Probably too deep, all right. Yeah, let's move stuff over to yours. Creek's up some, and the gravel's always loose."

"I wanta see Dad's house first." June linked her arm in mine. "I've seen Eric's place, back when we were little. Just dump my suitcase anywhere there, Kyle. I gotta see the old bear's den."

"Pretty primitive, I'm afraid," I told her, after we were in the Ranger and on the road down. "No plumbing, no electricity, woodstove..."

"Bath in a tin washtub, too, I'll bet."

"Yeah, well...too cold to skinny-dip in the creek, lately. But I manage. Your mother would die."

"She's so freaked. About...all this. I mean, nobody expected... She's sure you've gone crazy, you know."

"Maybe she's right. It just got to a point, like I wrote you. I'm probably all wrong in this, honey. Probably missing something obvious, looking for something that's not there. But I just had to do this." I shrugged.

"Okay. Enough soul-searching. I'm not on a witch-hunt, here. Hey, this road is okay. We used to bottom out along here."

"Eric and Jim's work, mostly. The Mallorys do some when they're here. Me too, lately. Here's where I've built my trail." We eased through the woods. I hadn't minded the rough places, but with a passenger along, was made aware you couldn't rush this cowpath. June was looking around, trying to orient herself. She'd probably never seen this part of the place.

"Up ahead's the little waterfall stream, where it comes onto our land. Drops on down, so I had to get down the ledges after this switchback. Took some redneck engineering, but I get out okay, till ice or heavy snow."

"Then what? Hibernate?"

"No, I can hike up to Jim's. Go to church with them, get to the store. I'm okay here, really."

"But don't you miss people? I mean, well, Mom? You guys had over thirty years, you know."

"Yeah, I was there for all of them, girl. Sure, I miss the good times, the memories. But last few years, seems like nothing good to miss."

"Okay. She can be a pain, don't I know it. Thinks I'm still six years old. But...well, you *know* she'll come out here, sooner or later. She won't like, just give up."

"I guess. Cross that bridge when it comes. Oh, I found an old moonshiner's spring over on the other side. Back in all that brush. We're close now."

"Really? Uncle Jim used to say he thought this place was one of those hollows you just didn't go into, in the old days. Ooh, I see your roof down there." She leaned over, one hand on the pup's head. He'd tried to climb onto her lap all the way down.

"Yeah. Road, if you can call it that, goes over a bit onto Mallorys', then I hairpin on down. You remember where the little stream joins Caney Creek?"

"Oh, yes. We hunted friendship rocks there. Grubby little kids always in the water. Couldn't believe how many stones we found with holes in them. Made miles of necklaces, remember?"

"And cried when your mom wouldn't let you take the big ones. We were still finding those rocks at the house in Virginia when I left." I backed, parked. The spot wasn't as precarious now, with the big stones hemming it in from the drop to the creek and the gravel I'd spread.

"Hey, neat steps. And stepping stones! Boy, you moved a lotta rock. I didn't miss all those holding the road up."

"More rocks than anything else, around here. Cabin's just up ahead. Remember a shelf on the right, before the first waterfall?"

"Mm. Not really. Been a long time. Oh, wow, there it is! Oh, it's like a Hansel and Gretel house!" Her hands went to her face, and her eyes widened. I tried to see it as she was, like I'd done with Sarah, but no, I'd been too close to it these months, building. June moved ahead almost in a trance, seeing the recessed window, the thread of smoke from the stovepipe, the stacked firewood, the smithy. The pup ran to the door, waited, tail doing a windmill.

"Wow, it's a real house! I mean, sure it's tiny, but I'd pictured a hovel. It's so...*neat*, Dad. I mean, I knew you wouldn't just throw something awful up, but this is so...well, *cute*."

"Just happened. No plan, really. But I do like how it fits against the hill. And now with the rains, you can hear the waterfall."

"I can. But down here, so...*away*. What if you break a bone or something, fall off somewhere? Got a cell phone?"

"No. And they don't work here, anyway. Jim's found most of a CB radio set. I can power it off a battery. But I'm really careful here. Most dangerous thing I've done is go fishing."

"I can't believe that; I saw you on that barn roof. At least this one isn't so high. But you didn't get hurt doing all this? No landslides, falls, bad cuts?"

"Nothing worse than a mashed finger or two. I took it slow, really. Absolutely nothing else to do but put it together. Took all the time it needed. Lotsa breaks to listen to the birds, smell the roses."

"Lucky you. Wow, your blacksmith's shop is so tidy! I remember Mom was always onto you about all the old iron you had stacked around the one at home."

"Can't afford much of a collection here. Forces me to be neat."

"About that. What're you living on, Dad? Mom said you left her everything: the business, all the equipment, the house..."

"Social Security is all I need. Don't have many expenses now the house is up. It was close for a while, but I'm okay now. Few groceries, dog food."

"Thoreau all over again. Okay, let's see what you've got inside."

The pup danced around a bit, then lay by the stove watching us, head on his paws. The pleasant smell of woodsmoke touched the air, along with the still-fresh aroma of cedar from the beams. June took in the oak counter, dry sink and shelves that constituted my kitchen, the water containers, the stored groceries.

"No running water, then. Got an outhouse?"

"Yeah, through the smithy. I'll put a little porch roof over my door, to connect with the shop, keep the way dry."

"It's like a fishing camp, Dad. And I guess that's really what it is, right? I mean, I know you needed to get away, like you wrote us, but you don't plan to stay here always?"

"Don't know, honey. Your mother, and maybe a truckload of psychiatrists, would probably say this is my midlife crisis, a little late. Didn't buy a red sportscar and do Botox, came here and built this instead. Maybe I'll work through it. Maybe not." I shrugged again.

"But *people*, like I said. You gotta miss them."

"Oh, I go to church almost every Sunday. Good honest folks there. Not out for anything from me, not working angles, making demands. You might wanta come with us, see what it's like?"

"Oh, I don't do the church thing. We never did, you know. I wouldn't know what to do, how to act. Sarah's got Kyle into it, I know, but...well...But you're going. That's good, I guess, people and all..." I could see this was making her nervous.

"Nobody's pushing, June. I guess that's a part of why I go. I expected to get harangued, get fingers pointed at me. Didn't happen."

"Well, I hope not. The way I see it, everybody's got skeletons in the closet...Well, I just might go, this once. Never been inside a church, except for weddings and funerals. What's the preacher like? Blow-dried hair and fiery eyes?"

"Farmer. I keep expecting him to show up in overalls. Been fishing with him. Really sincere guy, been through a lotta grief himself. Well, you think about it, then. Some folks only go Christmas and Easter, anyway."

"Yeah. Dad, part of why I came is to see what you're into here. Yeah, if church is part of that, I do wanta go."

"Date. Now, we just have time to climb up to where my garden will be, if you're up for it. We sometimes went up there for the view, if you remember."

"Seems like it. Miles and miles of miles and miles, the wilderness area, right?

"Yeah, a bunch of it. Jim and Kelly used to ride it a lot, and I've gone up there some. About as empty as any place gets, except for the odd bewildered hunter." We climbed the steep trail on the steps I'd cut, and got that view, up and beyond Caney Creek, the ridges getting bluer with distance. Up closer it was all brown now, except for the cedar groves, and the gray cloud cover seemed to close in on the mountains.

And that tangent my little branch made, off the curve of Caney. We just looked for a while, and I could almost feel June unwinding from her civilized pace. Her hand in mine reminded me so much of when she was small, that trusting hand counting on me to keep her from unseen scary things. But now I saw the light was fading a little.

"I guess we ought to head back, or Kelly'll think we fell in the creek. Wanta go to Eric's place first?"

"I guess so. I hear he's got plumbing."

"Does. That water storage tank thing the first people built. I'll check Kyle out on it." We went back down, across, climbed up to the truck. "So, what do you think of Sarah?"

"She's really okay. Kyle never dated much, even in college, and we always wondered what kind of girl he'd find. I hear he sort of made up for lost time up in Chicago, so we all wonder if she's long-term."

"Yeah, I guess that's a question. I like her a lot, but you know none of you has to run your choices by me."

"Well, some of the specimens I find lurking around in the theater you wouldn't want to meet. Always playing somebody else, and I'm sure they never figure out who they are themselves, really." She laughed. "You think Kyle might get serious about Sarah?"

"Who knows? This's a new age, and all the rules have changed. He's twenty-six now, and maybe he is ready to settle down. Everybody doesn't wait till he's old like I did."

We forded the creek and drove up the old fields, brown in last season's grass, rimmed by the ever-present cedars on the creek side, the oaks and hickories against the rise of the hill to our left. It'd always seemed a long way from the ford, among that first couple's cows, horses, to what was now Eric's house. It had weathered into the landscape after a generation, and was really an inviting place. I checked Kyle the engineer out on the pump system while the girls washed up.

It seemed so incredibly long ago, this house-raising, the hardly-remembered people who'd gathered here, playing pioneer sure, but laughing, sharing, working for and with each other. We hadn't had kids yet then, although some of the others had, in all sizes. I remembered them running, shouting, splashing in the creek while we all tried to avoid stepping on them, helping build this place. Another life, it seemed now.

Then we all headed back and up the hill, anticipating one of Kelly's great meals. Listening to the kids chatter away, I felt a new wave of affection for them. This would be a great Christmas. I appreciated them more than I had in years. And it looked like I was really out of the doghouse, with these three. Close, tight, great feeling.

A new car was parked in front of Jim's house...one of their kids had come early, I guessed. *Well, great: more the merrier.* We unloaded from Kelly's Cherokee as the front door opened.

Eleven

The woman who came out to the car gave us all a jolt: Sharon, of course, followed by Kelly, who turned her palms up in a shrug.

Well, now. No warning, no word, just here...I noted fleetingly that she actually looked great. *Shame looks aren't all.*

"Mom!" June was as surprised as I was. I glanced at Kyle, but this was new to him, too. Sarah threw me a quick glance as June gave her mother a hug. I was just sort of numb.

"Nobody was coming to my house for Christmas, so I'm here," Sharon explained, hugging Kyle, then Sarah. Then she fixed me with a look I couldn't decipher.

"Well, old man, I've come to see you, like it or not."

"Hello, Sharon," I managed. "Surprise."

"Why? You knew I'd come, soon as I realized you really weren't coming back."

"Why don't we talk about it later?" My face felt hot. Embarrassment? Anger? I didn't know. I just had the very real feeling that this great holiday had suddenly been bombed.

Kelly rescued the moment, the way I remembered she had a knack for, by taking Sharon's arm and motioning us all to the open door.

"Now, you all get yourselves in here. Food's hot and on the table. Jim, bring in some firewood, would you?"

I helped my brother with the wood, still sort of in a daze. Neither of us said anything. I knew I hadn't been set up; they were blindsided, too. We went inside, to at least two conversations going on. Everybody was over the initial shock, and it seemed I was the only one not chattering: Kyle and Jim were already discussing something, even before he'd put the armload of wood down. Engineers.

I couldn't tell you what we ate that night. All I was aware of was that everything had changed: my tidy little routine, my introverted, maybe selfish world. It was evident that my kids were very much in tune with their mother, and somehow this seemed almost a betrayal...

Now, stop this! You old fool. Just because you're sour on the world, you can't expect... Sarah was watching, little covert glances from her place next to me. Maybe she knew a little of what was going through my mind.

And suddenly, I was just tired of all this. All these people, this noise. Revulsion overcame me, and there was nothing I wanted more right then than to be out of there. Dumb, to think I could hole up here, with Jim and the family so close. Of course they'd all come, all invade me...I was about an inch from jumping up, storming out the door into the air.

Then I felt Sarah's hand in mine, and turned to look at her, the talk flowing on around us. Her eyes were wide, and the smallest tear was there. She squeezed my hand, and smiled wanly.

This girl was into my head.

Okay. Okay, then. I can do this. I could stay, play the game. Sharon was here, not the end of the world. My son had this fine young woman. June didn't think I was a monster. Jim and Kelly were rock solid. *I can get a grip here.*

Sharon was keeping the talk going, one of her gifts...no dead air with her around. She seemed to know just what to ask to get a real response: yes, Kyle's new mechanical gizmo at work he'd invented and built the prototype for was going into production. Details. Yes, June had cast her new production. A difficult, involved, contemporary piece. Personalities. Yes, Kelly's apple butter she always sent us was the best this year. Yes, Jim's little musical group he jammed with met every week and were still together. Yes.

Yes.

It got late, somehow. I'd managed to enter into the talk now and then. Sarah had told how I'd coached her in fly-fishing, bragged on my little fairy-tale house in the woods. Somehow it hadn't been all that strained, among the family this way. And while I realized I was the one who was odd man out, it'd somehow all come together.

In spite of me?

Kelly put the question of where Sharon was to stay immediately to rest.

"Our tribe won't be here till tomorrow, after all. Your room's all ready. We'll work something else out later."

"I was hoping for an invitation to my husband's house, actually." She eyed me, a challenge.

"Oh," Jim interposed quickly, "that place of his, you can't turn around in it. No room to cuss the dog without gettin' fur in your teeth. No heat, no plumbin'. Lives like a varmint."

"I want to see it. Tomorrow, then?" Eyes still on me.

"Sure." I shrugged. "But Jim's just given you its good points. More like a monk's cell."

Before the kids and I left, I managed to thank Kelly.

"Hey, no problem. I know we can squeeze her in at Eric's place, too. He's had a dozen people stay over."

My truck was at the creek ford, and I said goodnight there. Both girls hugged me, but my heart just wasn't in it. The sky had cleared, and stars burned the way they do here, big and bright in the lower humidity. After they'd crossed the creek, I stood listening to the sound of the water rippling over the gravel, louder rushing through the boulders on down. A faint, cold breeze moved the sycamore limbs, and rattled the few big leaves caught in their branches like dried memories.

Dead leaves, relics of the long spring and summer, gone like yesterdays. Hinting and reminding of old adventures, old disappointments, triumphs, old loves.

Dead.

Sharon's here. Almost nine months she'd had, to feel whatever she felt at my leaving. To be angry, insulted, disillusioned. To be able to pursue her meetings and committees and lunches and connections without having to contend with me. And now she was here.

Why?

Well, the kids said she worried about me. Hard to believe. Didn't seem to worry while I was out hittin' the construction work six days a week. Biggest worry then seemed to be going through the motions of cooking now and then, keeping the house. With a housekeeper two days a week, too.

As I stood there under those burning stars, I seriously considered just getting the essentials from my house and slipping away again. This time to some place totally hidden, with no links to anybody. Texas? Montana, maybe. Idaho. *No, not in December.* I didn't have the kind of bucks to take on that country in winter.

Eventually I had to face it. I'd just been able to survive here, with Jim's help, and a piece of land. No, at my age, there weren't any other options. Have to tough it out here. Or...

What did she *want* here, anyway? Me to go back with her to Virginia? Could she be over her resentment, want to patch it up? Didn't seem likely, knowing Sharon. No, probably just curious. About what had happened to me. See if I was really as crazy as she suspected. That, and see the kids. She'd have to approve of Sarah. Might want to know what I thought of her. No, probably didn't care.

Well.

But I couldn't sleep that night. Not surprising. I'd fill the stove, get the room too warm, kick off blankets, twist around. Thinking over stuff. Eventually drift off, then wake up cold. Finally, I went out barefoot and splashed icy water in my face, did some stretches. Got to sleep near daylight.

And it didn't seem like long before the pup woke me, barking. I stumbled up and let him out, found my clothes. Fire was down to coals. Kettle just warm. I stoked the stove, feeling the chill. Be rough in January, when it'd get really cold...

I looked out. Sky was bright already. Heard a voice and then saw Sharon, petting the dog and talking to him down at the bend of the little branch. She was in a suede coat, knit cap and boots, on one knee, baby-talking the pup, who was going crazy, licking, jumping, wiggling. No damn judge of character, for sure. *Hey, mutt, that's the enemy.*

Only she didn't act like the enemy. Confuses me when people don't fit my stereotypes of them. She saw me, stood, waved.

"Hey. Looks like I've found the hermit."

"Yeah, I guess so. Come on up. Coffee?"

"Sure. I slipped off from Jim's. They were still out from all the excitement last night." She came closer. "You don't look like you slept. In fact, you look like hell."

"Thanks. I don't remember you being up this early, ever. What time is it, anyway?"

"Nearly eight. I wanted out before their kids came." She stood back, looking over the cabin. "So this is it. You always talked about doing this someday." I couldn't tell what she thought of the place, and for some reason that seemed important just then. She walked up to the wall, touched it, ran her fingers over the stones I'd laid. Eyed the smithy, the huge stack of firewood. "Looks like you haven't done anything but work here, Liam. Like maybe daylight to dark?"

I shrugged. Yeah, I guessed so. Buried myself in it, really. And now she was here, right in the middle of my new/old life. I had no idea what I was supposed to say.

"Come inside. No sense freezing out here. Cold settles in this hollow. Nice in summer, though." The stove was crackling now, and it wouldn't take but a few minutes for the room to warm up.

Sharon took her gloves off and stood, warming her hands, taking in everything, her fingers working. The scent of her filled the little space, and I realized how long it'd been. She took off the knit cap, shook out her hair. No gray yet, I saw, or was that dye? She'd always fussed a lot with her hair, embarrassed for me to see her in rollers, back in those first years. Odd I should think of that. But she *was* a good-looking woman, and I remembered that first-impression attraction again, so long ago.

I got out the coffee, felt the kettle...getting hot. Found some pastries Kelly had sent down. Sort of bustled around, still not knowing what to say, so I didn't.

Finally, after noting every inch of the house, she surprised me.

"You do good work, old man. Always did." A smile.

"Well, it's what I do. Hard to shut down, after all these years. Probably go the rest of the way crazy if I didn't stay at it." She was being nice, then. Okay. Not sure what was behind that, but I could play too, I guessed. Then:

"I'd have helped, you know. You could have let me help." Accusing, but only mildly. Maybe this wouldn't lead to one of our fights, if we could keep the lid on. I wanted to say no way could she have helped, except to leave me the hell alone. She could help now by going home...

"I sort of had to do this by myself, I guess, Sharon. Delayed midlife crisis, probably." I turned my palms up. That wasn't an answer.

"But did you think you had to leave me totally out of it? No, I didn't mean to say that. I know you thought you did. I know things... got...bad, I guess, between us. But I never wanted that. I never wanted us to drift apart, Liam. Believe that."

"Okay, I can believe that, because I didn't want that, either. But like I wrote you, I just couldn't take another fight, another in-house war. I needed air, I guess. And I've found a life here, if *you* can believe *that*."

"What life? You're a hermit, Liam. Do you ever *go* anywhere? You couldn't, with all the work you've put into this place. You've worked yourself to death here."

"Not quite. And yeah, I go to town when I have to. Go to church with Jim and Kelly every Sunday. Never thought I'd do that now, but I look forward to it, actually."

"Oh, yes. Apparently, Kyle's Sarah has converted you, too."

That made me angry. There was absolutely nothing phony about Sarah. Didn't push, preach. Just a fine girl. And if this...

"I didn't mean that to sound bad," Sharon went on hurriedly, apparently catching my expression. "And I know Jim and Kelly had a lot to do with it, too. But what can you get out of a backwoods preacher? I mean, if you wanted religion, surely you could go somewhere like around that college, where the people are...well, educated, at least."

I swallowed, hard. Poured coffee. Kept my mouth shut. Same old one-way road ahead. Same beginnings of same fights. But this time I wouldn't do it. Would *not* do it. Big effort, but I capped it.

I thought I was capping it.

"Why not go with us, Sharon? Tomorrow. We're all going. Come along, see for yourself what it's really like. Be surprised." I watched her eyes for the disbelief I knew she'd show. I couldn't picture her in Bill Zachman's church, and there was no way she could, either. Or...

"Maybe I will. Got to be something to it, if all of you are into it." She sipped coffee, put down her cup, looked me in the eye. "Liam, I know you're trying here, with me. But I'm trying, too. Trying to understand, trying to see what this is all about. Trying not to argue. It's just so... *foreign*, somehow. Like we were two different people, instead of who we are..."

"Who are we, Sharon? Anymore. Who? Your life's been all your job and committee meetings and Chamber projects and political action stuff since even before the kids left home. What did we have together, really? I had my work, but you gotta know, it got so there wasn't any point to it, anymore. We spent so little time together we were like strangers."

"Not complete strangers, Liam. Our sex life wasn't over, I happen to know..."

"Believe me, Sharon, that was over, too. If there was one place we *were* strangers, it was in bed."

"And that was all *my* fault? How many times did you just turn away from me?"

I held up a hand. This was on a track to a collision.

"Enough about that."

"Okay. But why did I practically have to drag you away from home, to go anywhere with me? You came home from work and just died, Liam. Well, I wasn't going to die with you, just wither away..."

"So that's what I'm saying...we didn't have anything left, Sharon. Why pretend any longer? No reason. So now you've got your life, and I've got mine. You've got everything we had, and I've got all I need, here. End of story." I spread my hands. Sounded reasonable to me.

"Not quite. You've got the kids on your side in this. Melissa's the only one who thinks you're crazy, and she's getting impatient with me. June's always been your girl more than mine, and Kyle's your clone. Now his Sarah thinks you're God or something." She was pacing. "Families aren't supposed to be split up like this. I had to come clear out here to see my kids at Christmas! That's not *right*, Liam."

"Hey, I didn't make them choose sides. All I wanted—still want— is some *peace*, Sharon. I haven't heard an angry word in what, nine months? Yeah, and I *love* that."

"But you can't just bury yourself here. You had everything—had built up such a reputation, a strong business. You were on top..."

I held up a hand again. Wearily. This was an inch—no, a half-inch—away from another fight.

I made the time-out sign. This had to stop. Before it got really out of hand, which it had so many times in the past. *Just don't say anything more, you old fool.* But I couldn't let it go, just yet. Had to get in the last word, I guess, like some redneck in a cuss-fight.

"And I said, who needs it? I didn't and don't. And now I don't want or need another argument. This is *over,* Sharon. Let it be. If you want Christmas with us—me—okay. But accept it. This situation is real. You and I and what we once had between us are history. I've got no complications here, and that's what I want—need. What I left was all complications. Over with, now. No more discussion. None." I opened the stove, put wood in. Closed it. Realized my hand was shaking.

"So you're through listening?"

"I'm through listening, yes."

"Okay. No argument." Then she did what women are so good at...
she changed course. "But what if you get hurt down here? Who'd know,
till you maybe died? We all worry about you, whether you believe it or
not." Her eyes said that was true.

Okay, maybe.

"I'm careful. Have to be. And Jim's down every day or so. Got
livestock, chores. And we're working on a battery-powered radio set.
I'll be able to call him."

"But it's winter. You'll freeze down here..."

"Not freezing now. Snug place, you'll have to admit."

"So *small*. You don't have to live like this..." Sweeping the tiny
interior with her eyes, maybe at a loss for more words. Should be self-
evident, I guess, from her viewpoint.

"End of talk about me, remember? Now, do you want to go see the
kids? I'll drive you over. Creek's up at the ford."

Twelve

I'd like to be able to say some things got worked out over that Christmas weekend, but I'd be lying. No breakthroughs, no revelations, no deep soul-searchings that resulted in everything getting resolved. None of that.

There was some walking on eggs between Sharon and me, and the kids were careful to avoid anything that might spark us. An outsider would have seen just this great extended family having fun, sharing, catching up. Being a *family,* with all that involves.

And yeah, there was a lot of that, seen in perspective. But I was so wound up, so on guard, I'm afraid I didn't play my part very well. Despite the good cheer, everybody knew *I* was the one who'd put the fly in the ointment, was the source of whatever discord ran just under the surface. Come right down to it, I didn't have a real ally in the bunch, unless maybe it was Sarah, who had the advantage of perspective. Guess she didn't think I was a monster, because she hadn't known us all before...our situation.

But we got through it. Sharon behaved, and so did I. Jim's kids were okay with things; treated us like always. Everybody liked

Sarah. We all went to church Christmas morning, and the place was packed. Jim, Sarah and the rest of the choir were terrific, with tight harmonies all over the place on some pretty involved pieces. The skinny accompanist never smiled once, but got on that keyboard like a swarm of bees.

The rev's sermon was his usual earnest fare, clear but not pushy, simple but strong. I'd come to looking forward to hearing him. He seemed moved that Sharon was there. I don't know what the flock thought of our situation, didn't care. And they didn't pry, at least not while we were there. Just met her, talked with her, and she did her thing to keep the situation from getting awkward. That *was* a gift, really.

Back home, we pigged on every kind of food. The grandkids broke new toys, got underfoot. Like old times. Kelly refereed it all. We guys got out to split firewood as a break from the noise. Caught up on stuff, guy talk about trucks and fishing and politics. I got to hear more than I wanted to about Mike's computer job (did *everybody* punch computers now?), and Mary's Don and the insurance business. Just glad he didn't try to sell me a policy. That might've pushed me over some edge.

Then it was over. Sharon left for the airport with nothing settled between us. June left with Kyle and Sarah. Jim's kids and grandkids left. The place got real quiet again, and though I missed the young people, I was kind of glad it was over. Back to some degree of normalcy, if you could call it that.

I was glad Sharon had behaved okay, getting over the worst of her anger, finally. Or maybe just holding it all in, with the kinfolks around. Being civilized. She could do that well when the occasion called for it. Well, she was gone now, and like I said, nothing changed, really.

But I'd gotten the feeling she wasn't really liking her life too much now. Even with the house, all the money, her contacts, social life. Woman had a hole in her life, and it wasn't just me. I think she still saw my leaving as more a betrayal than a real loss. She was insulted that what I'd wanted away from was actually her, mostly.

Well, we all get insulted, time to time, live long enough.

~ * ~

Okay, that's over, whatever it was. Great to see the kids, though, and yeah, Kyle's Sarah's okay, too. But that old fool won't budge, won't take a single step toward working this all out. At least we didn't fight...not quite. He'll never see things the way I— the world—see them, and this's his answer, I guess: go hide in that hole. Couldn't believe he'd actually do it: set himself up completely independent like that. Says he doesn't need anybody...read me.

But he has Jim and Kelly, at least. And that bunch at church, for whatever that can do for him. At least not ranting extremists, and okay, he apparently needs them. Backwoods preacher...

But he won't even listen to reason anymore. Won't let me into his little world, not that he really ever has. Guess that's why we quarreled so much...No, dammit, woman, you gave him hell that time about the business, knew it was the wrong thing to do, and it went all downhilll from there. But I was right...

So okay, what do I do now? Go out and see if I can find another man? Dumb idea...most of 'em more messed up than Liam. Besides, I take that 'till death do us part' bit seriously. Apparently he doesn't.

Or, like I've hoped, will he work through this and get some sense? Sure didn't look like it. So how much longer do I wait? Or do I just write him off? Wish there were an answer somewhere.

Well, I've made the first move, going out there to see him. Tried to talk sense to him, failed. "Guess I'll just let this winter go by, which should push him into doing something, even if it's wrong," *to quote John Wayne. A year in the woods should be enough, man his age. I could see a young stud camping out, going back to nature, but a seventy-year-old?*

Wish I could just forget him, but I can't. Not with 33 years invested, three kids, a life. And it wasn't really such a bad life, all told. Just wish he could see that, all we had—still could have. Blind old man, trying to relive something, I guess. At least he won't run off to another woman, down there at the end of the world.

That's even laughable.

But Sharon wasn't laughing—hadn't laughed about this at all. Denial had given way to wonder, then anger, outrage that Liam had actually done this. *To her!* Okay, she wouldn't go there again: that hadn't gotten her anywhere.

And she should quit worrying, she knew. Let him do his thing as long as he could, which shouldn't be much longer. If he got hurt, he just did. Now *that'd* put things in perspective, for sure...

~ * ~

I can't say I got Sharon out of my mind after that. I hadn't been able to do that these past months either, even with all the work I'd set myself. And a non-resolution like we'd just gone through doesn't change things any. But you don't just write off over thirty years with a woman, three kids, a life...good or bad, but a life. We'd done it together, after all.

And yeah, I got to missing her now, alone in this dark hollow, without the urgency of creating shelter, getting set for the cold. I remembered the scent of her hair, shaking it out here by the stove. I remembered other things too, the good ones more...

The dog helped: warm fuzzy little thing, getting gangly now. I'd started talking to him, and we'd get out, no matter the weather, tramp around, explore.

Tumbled stones, sharp-edged from ledges upslope, or water-rounded in streamed from centuries of wear. Smooth, slippery in green from remembered rain, seeps among old ferns hanging. Obstacle boulder-hopping up twisting, stone-blocked course to the first curtain of falling water. Old ice hanging above where sun never reaches. Quiet, except for the dancing splash of water dropping into pool. Small creatures water here: darting, twitting birds, a flash of fur, a rustle in fallen leaves.

Dapple of sun now, long shafts over south wall of this boxed-in hollow, warming talus slope in thin light. I feel the fractional temperature rise from spangled stones at my feet. The wind is high in trees patterning sky, but no movement here. Here is shelter, safety, in this lost fold of the earth. I am as near swallowed by the roll of hill and cleft as if intentionally hidden. It would be so easy to overlook me here: the span of my years, the work, the dubious achievements, the laughter, tears.

How much do I matter here?

Anywhere?

I rest awhile against a boulder on a bed of crackling leaves. The sun is fractured above in tracery of limb and twig and clinging, crisp leaf. Twisted, stubborn oak sends roots into fissures in stone, prying, spreading, refusing to give up.

Am I that rock-ribbed, planted here in spite of all, unmoving, unreasoning as the oak? Sharon would say so. Or a silent, mossy stone in this streambed, anchored against seasonal torrents of water rushing down, cresting against me, pushing, straining, slipping finally around.

No, these things belong. They're a part of the hollow, this spare, choked canyon of green and gray and glistening. I'm fragile: old man with brittle bones, balanced here on sloping rock, as transient as the tiny birds, curious, seeking sustenance. The hawks and the foxes know I am here, the elusive deer and the stray rabbit and the furtive squirrel. Maybe in time the very place will grow accustomed to my presence, and I will claim my space here legitimately.

Time. How much of that do I have? And does it matter, really? A day or a year or five years or ten...a snap of celestial fingers. But I guess I do matter, to Kyle and June and the others. I guess I'm part of this universe, of some obscure value, in a scheme of things I don't understand.

Like the rock. Like the oak.

The pup has run back downstream, sure-footed now over ridged and shifting stones. He has sniffed all that is of interest in this cleft. "Let's go back now," he says, "maybe something's changed at home."

Maybe it has.

~ * ~

When there was ice, I'd stay close. I didn't fool myself that I couldn't fall, break something. Freeze quick, those bitter days, if I couldn't move.

Most people see age seventy as clear beyond their conception: anybody that old has got to be pretty frail. When you get there, there's little difference. You do discover you can't do quite as much, have to rest more. But, keep at it and you don't go downhill fast.

I kept cutting wood, beyond what I'd need. Went up and helped Jim a lot. Spreading manure, plowing organic stuff under. Helped him shoe the horses, which is something I had never done as a blacksmith. Big animals that could hurt you without even noticing.

Worked with Eric when he was home. He had a collection of old vehicles he tinkered with. Not antiques: old Jeep, pickup truck, the tractor. Enjoyed getting greasy, talking with him, starting to see a little of myself in him when I was younger. Sort of wondered if he and June might hit it off. Nah, she liked the bright lights too much. Or at least she did for now; might get old after a few more years at it. And if she did meet the right man, like most girls her plans would do a sharp turn. Nothing wrong with that.

I read a lot too, something I'd had to squeeze in between jobs all those years. Could always get into a classic I'd remember to get at the library in town, settle in with. Good book had always been a sort of escape for me. Now that let me get my head out of this walled-in hollow to any place in the world, in history, in great events.

Fortunately, my eyesight was still good with the reading glasses. I often thought how impossible it'd be if I'd lost one of the major senses, to try to do what I'd done here. Had kept all my fingers, and had broken only a few bones in the construction business. Try very hard to keep it that way, and this life could go on more or less indefinitely.

~ * ~

It started as a mildly sore throat, the way colds always did with me. I took some vitamin C to try to scare it off, but it settled in. Guess I'd picked it up at church, about the only place I went with people close. It moved through the stages: stopped-up sinuses, headache, sore everywhere. I made chicken soup, remembering the old adage: "It can't hurt."

Not being a patient man, I hated being sick. Just a waste of everything: time, energy, plans, schedules. Very much an enforced time-out that would leave me weak for too long. I'd noticed it took me longer to come back from anything wrong with the body, last few years. So, I resignedly blocked out a couple of weeks, read the books I had on hand, stayed away from Jim and Kelly, to spare them this.

It wasn't pneumonia or the flu, thank God. Just a bad cold that settled in my chest, and meant almost a month of coughing before it finally wore itself out. My routine was limited to bringing in firewood, minimal cooking, not much moving around, and grumbling at my sorry lot. Try as I did, I couldn't see the remotest positive aspect to being laid up, and yeah, I resented it. Good thing nobody was around to have to put up with me.

But it passed eventually, and I was able to move around again without soreness. The headache left me, along with the feeling of general worthlessness that'd been hung around my neck like a weight. And okay, I wasn't as weak now.

Did some simple smithing on quiet days. Good to work the hot iron on a chilling day, see it take shape under my hammer. Limited only by my imagination...I had all the time it might take to create a tool, a bit of ornamental iron. Made Kelly a boot scraper, a kitchen pot rack. Stayed reasonably busy.

Got through January okay, with a couple of surprise days late in the month that hinted at spring. The sunlight steamed clumped dead leaves windrowed against the ledgerock. The smell was like life, trapped down there, snug in the ground, ripe seeds waiting, swelling. Spring?

Lies, all lies. February was bleak, wet. Both the shortest month and the longest to get through. Any thaw was followed by a hard freeze, and the locking-down of sleeping life again.

Those long days of gray quilted clouds and water running everywhere, I got to reading the Bible I'd bought. I hadn't asked Bill Zachman where to begin, or even discussed it with Jim. I scanned the books, the Gospels, to get some feel for the sequence, but got bogged down in names and wars and pronouncements in the Old Testament. I'd heard all that was the foundation for the good stuff about Jesus, so got on with the Gospel of Matthew.

That first day, I read for ten hours, right though a big part of the night. I soaked up the New Testament, through the scary stuff in

Revelation, then started over in Genesis. I was surprised to run onto so many quotations I knew—had known—most of my life. A lot of the phrases in our language come from this book, apparently.

By Sunday, I'd read enough to recognize where some of Bill's sermon references came from. I could almost follow his searching out passages for his message. I'd been impressed by the sheer extent of his Bible knowledge. This man put together a complete presentation every week, year after year, researched it, connected its parts, made it hang together. And just for us, just for those few minutes Sunday mornings we were there. I'd wondered if he saved them, re-used them, recorded his sermons in any way.

"Nope," he'd told me. "They're for you all only. I hope I'm finding God's Word each week, and it's enough to try to get it to you folks. I can't claim His words."

Okay. Bill was no prophet, didn't have the answers, he'd said more than once. So he was a sort of guide, then. Somewhat ahead of the rest of us, on our respective travels through life (he called them faith journeys). A tour guide; I guessed maybe I needed that.

And the more I read, the more I began to realize I hadn't handled the Sharon thing very well. I'd known that all along, but had sort of let myself just spin off on that tangent like I had no control.

No, I'd *wanted* to leave. Maybe prove I didn't need her. Or all that rat race that had been our lives. And sure, prove I could still put together a place to live, even in an impossible location. At my age. Hubris, I guess. Pride, ego. Those motivations didn't look so good anymore.

But as always, when I tried to bring up the good times with Sharon again, the fights overshadowed everything else. We hadn't quite gone over that edge this time, but we'd come close. I guess the woman was trying anyway, like she said. I guess I could've been more accommodating, too. Maybe she was genuinely worried for me. Maybe most of the anger had passed. Anger was an emotion I just didn't want any more of in my life.

I went out into an overcast day, after sleeping in. Might have been a Tuesday, I didn't check. It was cold, damp, but not unbearable.

A few snowbirds, or whatever those little puffed-up gray and white things are, flitted in the bare branches. The limbs were black against the sky, almost shiny with the wet. No rain, but a fog had settled into my hollow, soaking all it touched. I shivered a little in my lined canvas coat, needing activity.

The pup ran on ahead, sniffing a thousand scents I couldn't imagine. No telling what woods creatures had passed in the night, seeing my lighted window, bent man inside reading his big book. I guessed the dog was envisioning them, furry scurriers, safe in hollow trees now, under stone ledges banked in brown leaves, up in nests of sticks and old grass and leaves in the forks of trees.

I was like that, burrowed in from the weather. Venturing out on quiet feet only as needed. Making the familiar and safe runs to Jim's, or the church, or the store at Kissee Mills. I hardly ever drove to Forsyth now; my needs were simpler, like those of the woods creatures.

The sound of moving water never left me in this season. The side branch sang in its gift of water. Caney Creek rippled and gurgled along, wearing the ledge limestone another gossamer-thin layer as the dark months slipped away. Soon now, the laden soil would release the thawing ice it had come to know, and the chill guests would slip down in intricate trickles under leaf-carpets, to merge and swell and slip over stone to seek the running stream.

Just days now, and the sleeping roots would feel outward, and down, sipping the moist earth, sending the stuff of swelling buds coursing along veined trunks and limbs and naked twigs. The vague restlessness I felt every day now was everywhere: in the stirring winds, the swelling creek, the freshening smell of soil renewing itself.

Cabin fever. I'd always gotten out to work somewhere till now, when the wearing-out days of late winter called with false promises. The crew and I had almost always scheduled inside work for winter, seldom being kept from a building project because of nasty weather. Now I was attuning my life more to that of geared-down winter creatures: rabbits, raccoons, squirrels, bears even. Let the cold times pass. I was warm. I was fed.

I was alone.

That part I didn't really like so well. Too much time to think, I guess. And when I got a couple of birthday cards from the kids, I admitted to myself how much I missed them. Seventy had been a sort of milestone for me, and that was a year ago. You know, realizing I was old, really for the first time. Long as I was going to work every day, doing the physical thing regularly, age hadn't seemed to matter much. Sixty-five had come and gone okay. And this past time here, filled with projects, work. Kept my mind off being old.

I realized how lucky I'd been down here in my hideaway. Lotsa chances to fall, break something important. But the few times I had lost my balance, I'd managed to roll, minimize the impact, just get shaken up a little. I'd really been careful with the back 'cause that can get you bad. Luck, I guess. Maybe experience, too. Maybe God was watching over me, or one of His angels.

Nah, I was too much of a grump for that.

~ * ~

The bride was beautiful. Really, and it had nothing to do with the fact that she was my firstborn child. And Grady was a handsome lad, a kid I actually liked. Oh, I'd had the usual father-negative reaction the first time she'd brought him home. I'd remembered all Melissa and I'd shared when she was small, and I guess I'd subconsciously resent any man who'd take her away.

But the past few years, she'd been almost a stranger, having submerged herself in the typical teenage almost-rebellion so common. Okay, later she did get homesick, came back whenever she could make the time, to sort of recharge her batteries, she said. And yeah, we got along. More than got along, really.

And Sharon and I knew we were lucky for our daughter to've found this athletic, kind young man. No matter he was what I'd likely call a computer nerd...everybody seemed to be one now, to some degree. New world order.

It was at home, and Sharon and June had buzzed around for weeks, cleaning, preparing, cooking, getting immersed in all the pre-nuptial stuff of a girl's wedding. Kyle and I'd been recruited for all sorts of tasks: moving our projects to the back of the property, opening up more parking space, painting, sprucing up the outside.

The reception would be at a Charlottesville venue, an art center that catered to that sort of thing. Melissa would even graciously allow me to play chauffeur and drive them there in the old Land Rover, so full of memories for her. Nice.

The preacher was a friend of somebody the bride knew, not at all fazed by this outdoor setting back in the woods. He'd encouraged the couple to write their own vows, which they did, and it was fine. *Just don't ever let the magic of this day fade, kids, the way it has for us. Work hard to keep what you've got now, and don't blow it.*

The current divorce rate scared me, and I tried hard to believe this match was indeed made in heaven, or wherever. Like all couples, they'd need all the help they could get, so much demanding their time and focus in this tech age.

Applause, congratulations. Sharon's hand was in mine, a truce for this occasion, and there was a tear in her eye. Then we loaded up, headed for town, leading the procession. The reception was a sort of blur, with only the memory of my trying to dance a few steps with the bride, and avoiding embarrassing myself further with Sharon.

Then they were off, and a chapter of our lives ended.

Or began.

~ * ~

Cabin fever has gotten to me in a big way. We'd had a late, big snowstorm after it was technically springtime. The calendar didn't faze the elements any. Not a chance I could get the Ranger up the road. The drifts were so deep I was out of breath after only a few feet of climbing Sunday, so I stayed in. Checked in with Jim on the new CB. They were staying home, too.

Reread John Casey's *Spartina* and Linda Greenlaw's *The Hungry Ocean*. Found I'd missed a lot in both books first time through. Mind must've been on something else, I guess.

Got straightened out on the Biblical prophets Elisha and Elijah, finally. And the all-time bad woman, Jezebel. Lot of blood spilled back in the Old Testament—everywhere, I guess. Too many people trying to live on too little barely-habitable land. I'd always reflected that you'd have to be pretty mean to begin with, to live in that dry, wasted country. And recent events over there hadn't improved things, either.

I'd heard that about my ancestors in Scotland, too. Seemed they'd always fought each other over something: land or insults or pride—any excuse. If there hadn't been a war to get in on, they'd start one. This rock-ribbed place of mine was probably a lot like Scotland: take a lot of it to survive on. Made me glad nobody'd really want this spot enough to fight me for it. Place probably make me meaner too, if I did stay here.

~ * ~

A sudden sound from the sycamore above me. I knew that sound. I slipped out into the snow. Through bare branches, I could see the pileated woodpecker working at a section of dead tree trunk. He wasn't alone, this time. His mate, not as flamboyantly bright crimson-headed, worked beside him, pecking out a hole, chips flying.

They would nest there then, right in my face. Didn't think they'd do that, close to people. Maybe to them I wasn't really people. I stood still, the spell lasting. They took turns, hammering the hard wood, hollowing this chosen tree in light that was gray and unreal, punctuated by their bold assault. A place for new life in this deep cleft of the world we shared, up this tangent off the curve of the creek, little universe of our own. What a glad addition they'd be.

Just days later, real spring finally came, marking close to a year on Caney Creek. I'd mudded-in green peas and other early stuff on my terraces, stooping over the hoe, feeling muscles that'd slept the winter. I'd worked-in some rotted manure and sawdust from a barn in Kissee Mills, and figured that'd be fertilizer enough.

I'd left the fence posts tall, and now strung three strands of barbed wire above the four-foot web-wire fence. Maybe keep deer out. I kept the pup with me up there, much trouble as he was to keep out of things. He was indeed into marking his territory a lot now, so the smell should keep other foragers away, too.

Jim told me he draped sweaty T-shirts on his fences, changing them every few days. Claimed it worked. Of course, he regularly shot the invading deer too, and ate them. And he was good about sharing that venison with me, which cut my grocery bill a lot.

I've always sort of wanted to be a farmer. The smell of newly turned earth is a compelling, sweet sensation full of promise that never fails to stir me. I remember that smell from very early childhood, when my father would plow the fields until after the soft spring dark fell. The jingle of harness would pass as he turned the last furrows in the faint afterglow of sun, sweat from the horses mixing with that teeming earth-smell. Too dark to see, the memory is of the smell, the sounds.

Long since. He had a knack for growing things that Jim inherited. Missed me completely. The few attempts I'd made at a garden had been follies of rank weeds, bug-eaten vines and sun-scorched, baked ground. Never took the time to do it right, I guess.

Now here I was again, against all odds on this hanging almost-cliff. The precious soil I'd scraped up was deep behind my stone terraces, but surely too thin, since the solid limerock could yield no moisture against the merciless sun. Would the few hundred gallons of water I was collecting make a difference? Maybe.

I expected to spend most of my days tending this garden, mulching, weeding, watering. Jim had his favorite organic pest-controls, and I'd borrow shamelessly. I reflected, as I did often, that having this brother and his thoughtful wife near was a godsend.

Speaking of which, I'd made the Bible-reading a regular thing these past weeks. The big picture was coming into focus for me, but it was showing me I wasn't doing my part very well. As a flawed creature God had brought into His universe, I fit well. But as far as my duty to the rest of humankind, I hadn't done much. And I didn't even want to think about abandoning my wife of a third of a century. Have to work up to handling that one.

It wasn't enough, apparently, to have provided materially for the family, helped produce three terrific kids. Even provided livelihoods for the men and a few women who'd worked for me. There seemed to be a special further purpose for my existence, some niche I was created to fill. I'd sometimes thought I was doing that, building and restoring places for folks to live. But that was past, now. I'd turned myself out to pasture, if you could call this vertical place that.

And yeah, I guess that'd been pretty selfish, really. Emotionally anyway, Sharon and the kids must still need the old man in a more stable role. Maybe that was it. I was supposed to get senile in my rocking chair back in Virginia, be there for the grandkids to climb on, laugh at, be drooled on, entertained by.

Maybe I could get defensively deaf so I couldn't hear Sharon's complaining. No, I'd go absolutely crazy, living that life. Just try to grow things here for now, I thought, pushing seeds into the moist earth. And if the return I got was only a fraction of what I'd put into the process, so what? Keep me off the streets. And keep me here trying to figure it all out.

But the nights were getting to me. I guess after all the other arguments, being alone just isn't the natural state of man.

When the sun westered over the budding trees, going down early, the long fingers of light stroked the deep cleft I lived in. I'd pick my way down the steep path from the garden, the dog crisscrossing ahead of me, behind me, sometimes blundering into me, precariously high over the creek—had to watch that one. Going home, even from this short distance above, was sweet enough, the smell of woodsmoke hanging in the softening air.

Home.

But once there, the cooking, the stretching tired muscles in my chair, listening to the crackle of the cookfire in the stove, reminded me I was alone. The tumbling stream outside my door sang a sad song now. I didn't know why. The pup, head on his paws, looked mournful. No reason for that; we had all we needed right here.

Didn't we?

~ * ~

So after Sharon's rebellion, if that's what it was that time, we didn't drift, we barreled apart. I tried a little...modified the business practices a bit toward what she'd wanted, but kept control...customers didn't hire her; they hired me. But the put-downs continued. I guess once she'd declared, she couldn't back down, try to patch things up.

She got the new car, a job, something to do with computers for a real estate company, and we hired Judy.

But if she'd expected me just to roll over, take that crap like I said earlier, she was disappointed. How could a man, not a wimp, stomach that attitude and still cozy up to that kind of cactus? Couldn't and didn't.

The girls were gone by then, and with Kyle in college, they didn't see much of our war. We both tried hard to act like human beings toward each other when they were home, which was happening less and less.

And yeah, I buried myself in work, stayed gone a lot, and let her do the same. She stopped cooking, and I had to revert to my bachelor meals—make time for that or starve. Hated eating out, all those chemicals.

Things could've gone on like that for years, but no, it got worse. She wasn't happy with this standoff, although I was sure she'd brought it on. In retrospect I guess I should've tried harder, but the few times I made a move toward reconciliation, she'd get caustic.

"I was thinking, Sharon, of making time for us to go down to Peru for a break. If you can get off work, I think I can trust Bob to hold that big Coleman job together for a week or two. Whattya say?"

"What, you wanta live out a fantasy or something? Go off to the tropics to drool over rocks? No, I've got a ton of work here that nobody else can do. And where'd you get such a notion? Thought you wanted to stay buried in work."

Okay, I tried. In my cluelessness, I thought getting away together might get rid of some pressures, give us a chance to try to relive a little of how it used to be. Not.

But I guess she tried, too. Must've thought about it some. So after a few days, she said her boss could maybe shift some of her workload to another woman, and okay, maybe we *could* squeeze a week, if I still wanted to. I'd already dismissed the idea, since that Coleman job was getting sticky and needed me there. But okay, maybe this could be the answer, or part of it.

We did it, despite the cost. And all she wanted to do was buy expensive silver jewelry and weavings and a trunkful of other souvenirs, while I wanted to glory in that incredible stonework. The only times we spent together, really, were when we'd hire a guide to go see some great temple or those magnificent terraces, with their engineered irrigation systems. Or in the separate beds at the hotel, where she insisted on having oxygen piped in to fight altitude sickness, which didn't bother me.

We hardly spoke on the plane home. And of course, the Coleman job had gone all to hell.

~ * ~

Okay, I guessed this lonely stuff meant I wasn't keeping busy enough, even now the cabin fever months were past. Work had always been the cure for almost all my ills, and it would just have to be again. Extend the terraces then, plant more. Go up and help Jim more. See what Eric had going. Maybe volunteer at church, one of those Habitat for Humanity houses they helped on, for poor folks—poorer than me.

Yeah, get busier.

So it was up next morning at daylight, the sun not yet probing the mist that settled into my hollow. Cook, eat, get up that path again. Dew caught the first red rays rimming the bluff across Caney, sparkling every color in pinpoints of light, changing as the tiny drops evaporated, as the sun rose and the angle changed. Spiders out already, their new webs holding dewdrops like jewels. I had to stop and admire them.

Since I'd already fenced in my garden, I decided not to extend the terraces beyond that labored boundary, but to build interim terraces instead. That way I could pile up the soil deeper just below each existing upper wall, where it was shallow. Hold more moisture that way, grow more. That is, if I were destined to grow anything at all...long chance, I knew.

The sled didn't work as well now, with the fence, so I stopped it short and used a pair of buckets partially filled with soil from it. Took longer, but four trips made a four-foot bed of the rich woods dirt, enough for a couple of hills of squash, a half-dozen cabbages.

Just now, with spring rains and the greening-up of creation, I couldn't conjure up the drought that would come. The soil teemed. Seeds burst from the black earth, eager, triumphant. Now if I could just keep them alive, those fragile green things, reaching roots into loam I'd dug my fingers into...

New life, maybe a portent for me. If I could keep it together, make it all round out somehow, this year could be the start of just that: a new life. And whatever role I was supposed to be filling might become evident, if I were patient, kept on doing my thing, trying to fit.

~ * ~

Sharon watched the budding of trees on the hill in Virginia, the tiny crocus springing up overnight, scattering, multiplying each year. The daffodils, serviceberry blooms, the promises of redbud. *Somehow, it's another year, already, although the months drag, without Liam. He's apparently weathered the winter, and it hasn't brought him home.*

She walked among last year's fallen leaves, noting the spikes of new grass pushing up, eager for sun. New life, a miracle really, and how many years had it been since she'd taken time to notice? Too busy, always too busy.

And now all the commitments, the demands, the deadlines that'd always been so important...what'd they amount to, in the whole scheme of things? Did she really care whether the Chamber of Commerce partnered with her company to put together that campaign to attract more industry? The one they said only she could handle? And were those interminable meetings that crowded her calendar really necessary?

They'd always seemed so, even to the point of taking priority over what needed to happen here at home. Now, in the light of this new season, and with her man gone probably forever, it all seemed trite, busy work, even maybe a waste of time.

So what *was* important? Was she just supposed to drop everything she'd built up all these years? What, run in circles trying to fill her days in this house, putter around like some old woman past any worth?

And no closer to bringing that stubborn old man home. Over the winter, she'd thrashed every idea to death, of how to reach him, and it hadn't worked. He hadn't seemed senile, but what else could you call it? She'd had such high hopes for the Christmas visit, and it'd gotten her nowhere.

Oh, I'm working myself into a dead-end of worry. Guess I'll just have to dig in again, drown out too much thinking, with work. Seems to be all I'm good for, anyway. Just doesn't seem to have much of a point anymore, now that I'm alone. But I've tried every way, failed, to reach Liam.

Or maybe there's one more way...

~ * ~

By April, frost danger was past. The winds dropped, the rains continued, but I knew it was mulch time. Water: keep it, use it. *Got to hold every drop of water, keep it right where it falls, preserve it, cherish it.* So, the two buckets now full of leaves and forest duff—bark, rotting wood—gathered a double handful at a time from the woods above, carried slowly and carefully down, around, in through my gate. Insulating layers of organic moisture-block, building up as the plants grew. Eager potatoes, rank green peas, turnips, squash, lettuce.

Now the sun beat hot on my hanging slope, pulling the green things up out of the soil, feeding them. But the sun was a robber, too. It wanted my hoarded water, wanted this plunge of earth to go back to stubborn cedar and lichen and bramble. Wanted to waste my labor here, cancel out the aching trips for soil, mulch, the bent-over seeding, nurturing, caressing each plant.

I sat up there in the early rays, feeling the heat suffuse my veins, my bones. Quickening the life inside me as it did my plants, drawing us up and out into the day. I could lie on my ground up there and feel the living earth under me, flowing into me, welding me to itself.

I would go back to earth one day. The brief life-span complete, full-circle, I would melt and flow in joyous return to this soil, this mothering earth. Soon? Late? I didn't know, didn't care. *Whenever, God. Whatever's right...*

Was I getting morbid? Didn't seem like it. Seemed more like a natural cycle of which I was nearing the end of this phase. Nothing fearful about it now. I guessed I was sort of coming closer to the place in the universe I was supposed to be.

Maybe.

And in those green days of spring, a year now into my exile, I lost most of my doubts. I could be calm, even against the demanding, weather-driven deadlines of seeds in the ground, deepening mulch, sweat-stained stones placed to hold my hill. Maybe this God I was gradually coming to accept was working something out in me. And just maybe I wasn't too stubborn, too prideful to let it happen the way it was supposed to.

And it didn't just become evident when I took time to think about it on my own. In the company of the church people on those projects, nailing, sawing, bringing somebody a house from the ground like a growing tree, I could feel I belonged. Those were great experiences: the putting-together, helping each other, joking. Yeah, fitting in. Those Saturdays sharing, leading, following, working in a weave of joy with others, peace would come stealing.

Maybe, then, this was what I was to do with the remaining time I was gifted with. Maybe this was it: God's use for me. Yes, I could do this, fit here, perhaps even come finally to belong.

Yes.

Sharon's letters had come all winter, friendly almost. She seemed to be settling in, too. Then one April note said she'd been attending a religious study group in town.

"They're real, Liam. Not what I'd always imagined churchgoers to be...you know, holier than thou, smug, prejudiced. I think I must've gotten a little past some of that at your church that time. You won't believe it, but I'm helping run the nursery here. It's fun, being around those little kids. I'm not sure I buy the whole faith package yet, though. Seems a little austere. Maybe I'm missing something. Anyway, I thought you'd like to hear what I've been doing to fill my days..."

Um. Now, is she trying to ingratiate herself with me here, or could this be real? Filling her days. Never had any trouble doing that before. I doubted if this'd last, but who knew? Nobody'd have thought *I'd* enjoy a country church...Well, just have to see how this went, long-term.

The pup wanted to dig up everything I planted, but I got his attention with a newly-leafed tree branch that made noise, if it didn't inflict pain. He did like to lie in the cool dirt, watching me with those big eyes, wondering just what craziness I was up to now. He was always ready to go exploring, and would wait for me to have to straighten up for a break, then romp over to the gate. We spent a lot of time walking the ledges above and beyond my little hanging garden. I named him Boswell, to my crochety Sam Johnson.

With the plentiful rain, my water tanks were filled and ready. I was sort of proud of that accomplishment: I called it redneck engineering. With luck and the grace of God, I might just keep stuff alive in deep summer. Early things I could, I hoped, gather before that dry time. And just maybe I could plant some fall stuff, the way Jim did every year. After the worst of the dry, if we could get some freak moisture then.

Wait and see, like with everything else.

Thirteen

It was morning, which would turn into one of those unseasonably hot April days of clear sky and little breeze, that would get downright chilly by nightfall. Jim McLeod had wanted to help Kelly plant today, but Eric was home after a long carpentry stint up near Columbia, and that fence needed fixing. The horses had gotten out twice, and his neighbor had made time to help replace some of the rotten posts that were letting the wire sag. It was something Jim just hadn't been able to squeeze in, with the rush of getting his garden in.

But ever since awakening that morning, something had nagged at him, as if he'd forgotten a thing that needed doing. He went over the list of necessary tasks that always piled up in the spring, things that just had to be done. But he and Kelly had gone over all that, and planned it out in her organized way.

No, must've just been a stray thought that'd come to mind and stuck there for a bit, then been forgotten. Things did that, he realized, more and more as he aged. Like everyone, he'd sometimes find himself purposefully going after something, then his mind would latch onto something else, and he'd find himself wondering what the original errand was.

He'd mumbled something to Kelly as he was loading posts into his truck, gathering his tools. She was headed for the garden.

"What's that?"

"Oh, nothing. Just feel like there's a gap in my head or something. It'll come to me; probably something I'll need that I've forgotten."

"We getting old?" Her silver laugh.

"Nah, not us. Prob'ly just middle age setting in."

"Not sure I know about middle age...when does it start?"

He grinned, waved goodbye, and started the truck, unable to shake the feeling. *Okay, it's not Liam: he's okay, was up yesterday. He'll be up on top mulching, but he's careful. Maybe climb up there in a few days, see how it's going. No chance for a decent garden on that slope, but he's gotta be doing something. I'd have given him a part of our field, but I know he wants to be totally independent, do it the hard way.*

My big brother. Really glad he's apparently come to the faith. Funny how God calls us at different times in our lives. Nobody's pushed him; he's turned the right way on his own. Maybe needed this past year to sort everything out. Kind of expect him to work his way back to Sharon before long, too. Kelly thinks he will, anyway.

Odd how we never suspected anything wrong between those two...always on top of things, always outgoing, both of them. Never know just what's in anybody else's head, for sure. And he remembered how his wife had helped put him back on track those years ago, when he'd lost his own way.

Don't think she ever suspected I was actually thinking of bailing out, that time. Tried to keep it all inside.

Or did she?

He forded the creek, began the drive up through the field and woods toward the upper ford to his creekbottom field. He saw Eric coming down from the knoll his house was on, ready for the day's work. *Great to have a neighbor—friend—there to help when we need it. Maybe he'll have whatever that is, tool or something, I've forgotten. No, it's not that... dunno just what it is, but it's picking at me. Well...*

~ * ~

I'd spent the morning planting more beans and squash—things I figured even a novice could grow. If I remembered correctly, that's what the natives grew before my ancestors came to this continent. Normally plant those later, I'd learned from Jim, but here, with the coming dry time...

After lunch I'd puttered around, not quite ready to start anything new. Stockpiled more mulch, reset a couple of terrace stones that'd slipped out of place...must've bumped them. Couldn't seem to get focused on anything, but the afternoon passed somehow.

Truth was, I was feeling more guilty about the whole Sharon business now, just over a year later. She could get into my head, more so since her letters had no bitterness in them now. I'd sent her a note now and then, mostly updating her on my homestead progress. Not much else to write about, really. I alternated between relishing my near-total independence, and actually missing that woman. Only difference now was, I was admitting it. I was also coming to remember the good times more with her. And yeah, that feel of her smooth skin, and the overall attractiveness that hadn't let her get old.

Anyway, Boswell the pup and I eventually abandoned the garden, climbed the rest of the trail, up the point to a wide ledge that ran back off my land well onto the national forest before it ended in a jumble of cedars and steep rubble. The other way, it looked like this had once connected to a woods road beyond my north property line.

Two old rusted car wheels lay along the ledge. I guessed them to be 1920's vintage. Maybe this was all that was left of a homemade cart, wood rotted entirely away, axle salvaged, these circles of iron slowly going back to earth, too.

I could look down into the beginnings of my canyon from up here, over the treetops that filled it. We were up maybe 200 feet, with another ledge above, then a low slope up through the forest land, at an angle to the kinked road I'd plotted through the trees and around the biggest stones to bring my water tanks and loads of manure down. The limerock was fractured into big chunks here, but made its own terraces above and below. Maybe I should have gardened up here. No, too far to climb. And no, this part wasn't mine.

Boswell started a rabbit, but fell all over himself stopping when it zipped through a space between boulders below.

"Watch it, boy. You'll fall out of this road on your head." I called him back before he could jump over the rocks after his quarry and break something. Or maybe step on a sunning snake down there.

We hiked to the end of the ledge, then climbed to the one above for the walk back. This one wasn't as level, and had patches of bare stone, with a scant covering of moss here and there where water seeped from the layers above. How this moss survived the baking days of July and August was beyond me, but it came back every year, green again, tough. Twisted cedars found cracks and thin soil, and somehow also survived. Or some of them did…dried-up snags attested to a lost fight for others. Their twisted remains were gray as driftwood, fine-grained, red when cut into, aromatic. So old they'd grown with almost no sapwood.

There was an especially good view of Caney Creek and my side branch from further down on the point in winter, that tangent I'd gone off on. From down there, your eyes could follow the bigger stream up to the bluff on Mallorys' land near the ford. Way too much foliage now, though, I was sure. *Well, go on back that way, anyway. Too late to do any fishing…call it a day.*

I remember thinking on that walk, how my life had settled into what I was sure it was supposed to be. How the bad aspects of my separation from Sharon had smoothed and achieved a status quo we both apparently could live with. How my kids loved me, despite the curmudgeon role I'd adopted. How my fitting into the church activities had filled a need, both in me and to some extent, that of the church (extra hands).

And I was winning the battle of coaxing plants out of the soil on my impossible slope. I'd engineered what appeared to be the answer, if my watering scheme could just handle the dry time. I had this sense of achievement: snug house, projects, closeness with great folks, and now starting to grow my own food.

And it could go on and on I knew, for whatever time I had left...a comfortable cycle of living, close to this earth, a part of it. Yeah, I was planted here looked like, and loving it.

"I've just about got it all," I said to the pup. He cocked an ear while examining a track of something: *the old man's talking to himself again.*

I stopped for a rest, choosing a separated section of ledge I could sit on above the way. Nice long rock, I observed, but big. No way to get this one down, even though it looked loose, already. I turned, put my hands behind me on it and boosted myself up onto it.

But my hands dropped in an unreal way, as the stone broke loose and started to roll off its perch. I had just an instant to realize what was happening, to launch myself off it, try to get clear. My right foot flashed out for a place to land, when I was suddenly slammed to the ground, my left leg pinned, smashed under that monster rock.

The pain was unbelievable. My leg was crushed below the knee— had to be broken. So quick—how could all that weight have moved so *quick?* Fleeting realization that I'd been incredibly lucky all these months—blotted out in unbearable pain. Sudden awareness that I was trapped there, a thousand pounds of stone on me.

Succession of images: seeing myself from some other perspective, pinned here where no one knew I was. Picture of the steep trail down to my house, distant, unreachable. Then of the long climb above through the forest to the road. No matter, I wasn't going either way. The CB radio useless down below...

Sound roared in my ears, and it was my own cry. The world was red, screaming pain. And panic. *I can't move even a bit from here.* Suffocating helplessness, claustrophobic immobility. I was clawing the tufts of grass under me, writhing.

Caught.

Okay, okay, now. No more panic. God, what pain! But bear it... you got no choice. What's to do here, now? No pole to pry with, not even a stick. I twisted, searched. Nothing. Stone was almost flat on the ground, my leg compressed to maybe an inch under it. No, no way to pry it.

Sudden nausea, blackness building. Tried to fight it. Couldn't. The system shuts down when the pain is beyond enduring. Numbness...

No sense of time passing, but tingling now, along with the pain. Slow light, like up from a well. Buzzing in my head, regaining consciousness. How long was I out? Not long, I guessed; sun about the same place. Unremitting pain. Brain fuzzy. Clearing now. What's to *do?* What can I...?

No, nothing I can do.

Couldn't cut the leg off. Could I? Small pocketknife. I'd pass out again, bleed to death. No. Yell, then. Long, long chance anybody'd hear me. Woods would muffle sound. Try it. Long, hoarse groan, more than a shout. Pup whined, tried to lick my face. *You're no help. Can't send you to Jim's. Can't send you anywhere.*

I'm chewing hard on a twig I've found. *Bite the bullet. Dig fingers in the ground. Twist, writhe, try to divert the pain.* It's worse when I try to pull out. And the leg won't move. I look: doesn't seem to be any blood, somehow. *Thank God for small favors.*

Thank God, huh? For *this?* For being pinned here, beyond nowhere, in pain that'd wipe out a young man? With the inevitable end just hours away?

Minutes?

No, this wasn't His doing. This was just a freak, dumb happening. A rock destined to move, after who knows how many million years, and I was in the wrong place when it did. Hey, I helped it. God didn't do this, even if I maybe deserved it.

I'm out of options, here. If I don't go into shock, I'll die of exposure tonight. No coat—didn't need it in this sunshine. Won't matter; I won't make it to dark. The organism can stand only so much. I'm seventy-one, no longer a strong man. Wouldn't matter...half-ton stone on me.

Yeah, out of options. The mind had been jumping around, trying to find something—anything I could do. *But there's nothing. Perfect shut-ended situation: old man trapped on a mountain, no one knowing where he is. I've heard so many stories. Hard to believe I'm the story, now.*

But I am.

The pebbles and tufts of grass were in sharp focus before my eyes. Twigs from the cedars. Dried oak leaves, crumbling back to earth. The soil, where I've scuffed it, sweet, moist, black. Back to earth. Yeah.

I'm coming, earth.

Well, pain or not, I oughta make time for some goodbyes, I guessed.

I'll miss you, Sharon. Never been able to get you out of my mind, hard as I've tried. And sorry, girls, to've freaked out these last months. June, you understand, I guess. And Kyle. My boy. Never condemned me at all. Kyle and Sarah: God's children. Yeah, and Jim and Kelly, too. Bill Zachman, you're doing a lotta good, out of your own pain. You'd tell me to pray, I know. Haven't gotten that far though, yet...

Yet? Hey, there's no more time. There's blinding pain that's gonna snuff me out real soon. I don't have a yet left. And I guess, if I'm gonna do this, I better do it now. Brain get fuzzy, soon. Pass out again. Better...

God, if You're up there...No, I know You're there. Always known that, I guess. Well, I'm more than on my knees, God. I'm humbled. Boy, am I humbled. God, if You hear me, I could use some help. Maybe a small miracle. No, I don't deserve one of those, but...well, Bill says none of us deserves Your help. You just give it, out of grace...

I didn't know how to pray, and the pain was tearing at me, denying me words, thoughts, even. Tried to remember prayers from church. I concentrated, sweat pouring off me, trying to open a passage to God. I knew I'd been the one who'd shut Him out, slammed a door, rejected Him. Now I wanted that door opened, more than I wanted to live, even. This close to death, this close to the end, I needed Him beyond any need I could have imagined.

Then Bill Zachman's words—Jesus' words from His prayer in the garden of Gethsemane, before His dying—came to me: *Your will, not mine, be done.*

And the pain moved to another place, another dimension, not consuming me now, not draining my strength. I didn't have any strength. The ground felt so very good: the earth again. I was letting go, easing back to that earth, not fighting any longer. And it was all right. I'd broken through to God; I knew that. And it didn't matter anymore.

Whatever is Your will...

~ * ~

There are no dreams when you're unconscious. I'd been there before this, once or twice. Coming back is hard. The system says *okay, we've had to shut down, regroup, but now we can come back, just barely. We're not out of the woods yet.*

Yeah, that *yet.*

The sound was sharp, loud, even jarring. Confusing, repeated. In the place I was, sounds weren't identifiable: nothing was, really. But this sound wanted in...

Oh, the dog. What could he know, here? *Senses something wrong, sure. Not hard to figure I guess, me nailed to the ground like this. Oh, that's the sun: not down yet. Can't have been that long. Well, here we go. Chilly now, no movement to keep warm. Pain, again. So good, when it got isolated that way. Can't have it all, though...like I thought I did just that short space ago, when I could walk, had two legs...*

Well, God, You haven't let me go, so far. And I'm not fighting it when You do. In Your hands now...Always was, really. I had a few years of thinking I was in charge. Forgive me, Father, for my pride, my ego. You've humbled me, that's the important thing, now. Dying? Not a big deal anymore. We all die. And I've had my share of years...

Dog. What was he barking at? Snake, looking for its hole under this rock? *Hey, go for it, snake. I don't care, anymore. No, nothing out there. Long shadows. Air kind of green, new leaves and all. Thick, near-twilight now, but it hasn't really been that long. Birds flitting, early insects out. Springtime...rebirth. Yeah, I'm beginning to see I can relate to that. Shed the old life, the one that's so far from perfect...*

Jesus, our sins are forgiven in You. All these months I've been hearing that, and it never penetrated. I believe, Lord: You're everything, and the only thing. Wish I'd realized it sooner; could've made my life mean something. Well. You reach us in different ways, different times...

I was warm. From inside, somehow. The glow wasn't any kind of outside thing; the temperature was steadily dropping. But this heat was driving the pain away again, too. Okay, so I'd go out not in raging pain, but easily.

Thank You, God.

Boswell had raced off after something. Whatever he'd been barking at, I guessed. Fox, maybe. Deer. Something. Skunk? That'd be funny now, if I got sprayed, here where I couldn't escape. Somehow, I could see the humor in that, even here, in this fix.

Well, stop thinking physical stuff; we're getting past that now. A sort of peace settling in. And I know now that I'm not alone in this. I know Who's with me...

A shout. *Do angels shout? No, wait...That was here, close...*

Jim? How...? Delirious, surely. Then the dog: fastest tongue in the West. Pushed him away, craned to see.

My brother, old man running along the ledge, yelling back over his shoulder to someone. Calling to me.

"Liam? What in the world *happened?* Oh, my God, I see what happened. Eric! He's here!" Hands on me, not clear, light weak with the coming sunset.

"He's hot. Fever? We gotta get this rock off him. Can you talk, Liam? We'll get you outta here."

"Hey, guys." Voice unsteady, distant, not like mine. "How in this world did you...? No, never mind; I know how. Need a little...help, here." I gestured. "Heavy rock." Silly thing to say. Ain't no light rocks.

"Okay. Can we lift it, Eric? Big."

"Let's both get on this end. Pull out if you can, Liam, when it comes up. They both grabbed hold. "One, two, *three!"*

Eric is big. Jim's strong, but Eric's big *and* strong. One end of the long rock came up, somehow. I shoved against it with my other foot, and the leg came free. Pain surged back, hard. But not much blood.

"*Ahhh! Oh!* That smarts. Whooee! Thanks, guys. Don't...suppose one of you has an aspirin on him...No? Okay then, I'll just jump off this cliff back home. *Ahhhgh!*"

"Okay, now. Eric, can we carry him up to where we can come in through the forest? Then I can run get the Cherokee, bring it around and down. Or can you carry him by yourself?"

"I got him. No moren' a sack of potatoes. You go, now."

"And you be careful, bro," I called. "Don't need...another broke leg, here." I was shaking now, not real clear on what was happening. "And hey, don't you all...let Sharon know, okay? Not yet." He said something back, moving away fast.

"Up we go now." Eric eased me over a shoulder into a fireman's carry. And started the climb up over the ledgerock and into the trees. Jim's voice, faint, calling the dog.

I could feel every step, my leg hanging. We were moving fast, too, considering. Twigs, small limbs brushed us. Still light in the sky: Eric could see the way.

"Just you stay with us, guy," he encouraged me. "Get you patched up real soon. Weird, how Jim knew you were in trouble. Knew where to come, too." He dodged a tree. "We were finishing up a stretch of fence upcreek. You know, end of his long field."

"He knew, huh?" I had my jaw clamped tight against the pain. But I knew how Jim had known.

"Yeah, some way. Had the tools in the truck, leaving, then he got this odd look, said somethin' was wrong. 'Kelly, you think?' I asked him. No, it was you, he said. Knew he had to go. So I said well, if it's bad, I better come, too.

"You weren't home, and Jim, he goes right to the trail up to your garden patch. Yells for you. That's when we heard the dog bark. Heard us yelling. You were prob'ly out cold."

"Couple of times, yeah. Couldn't figure the dog barking. Thought it was maybe a skunk." I managed a shaky laugh.

"Ow, that'd been bad. Not that gettin' your leg smashed isn't bad enough."

He kept up a chatter as we wound up through the scrub oak. Helped, trying to follow what he was saying, getting my mind around his words, just a little off the worst of the pain.

"Hey, Eric. Take a break. You gotta be...winded. Jim can't get here soon. I'll be okay on the ground. Got...sorta used to that, back there." I winced at a shift; he'd almost stumbled.

"Okay, I guess. How long were you there? You know?" He set me down gingerly.

"Seemed like a long time, but couldn't have been...don't know. Too long."

"I guess. Funny the way it hit Jim. He worries about you, by yourself like that. But you've been lucky, till now."

"Lucky now, too, Eric, if that's luck. Think about it."

"Yeah. You mightn't made it through the night."

"Wouldn't have."

~ * ~

Jim was running, almost stumbling. *No, gotta slow down... wouldn't do to have both of us mangled up. Take these steps down slow, then hit it up to the house. It'll take Eric a while to get Liam up through the forest, and I'll just have to get there quick as I can. Can't risk a heart attack either, racing uphill. Okay, take a quick stop, tie the dog here at the cabin and I'm gone.*

*Okay, so that's what that...premonition was all about. Should have gone up, checked on him...no, that'd have been before...*He was dodging through the trees, straight up to his place, grabbing small trunks, pulling himself along. Halfway there, he had to stop, catch his breath.

Ouch, coulda called Kelly on the CB, had her drive out to meet us. Too late now. Just take it slower, not knock myself out, I'll get there. Hope Liam doesn't shut down, too much pain or something. Okay, close now.

He stumbled, breathless, the last few feet to the car, yelled to his wife.

"Liam's hurt, Kelly. Gotta...meet Eric and him at the...forest road!"

"I'm coming!" The door slammed, she sprinted to the car, jumped in.

"What happened? He fall?" Jim was gunning the car up the rocky road.

"Big rock fell on him, pinned him. We got it off. He's bad… Hospital…"

Fourteen

They put me in a wheelchair at the hospital in Branson. Jim and Kelly had gotten some sort of painkiller into me, but it hadn't kicked in, and the pain had almost knocked me out more than once. Finally got a shot of something stronger from somebody there. People in white coats X-rayed the leg, buzzed around. Made me feel totally helpless, being handled, lifted, turned, fussed over. Set me to see an orthopedist next day in Springfield. The pain got a little less, eventually.

"Broken, of course?" I asked the ER doc.

"Oh, yes. Smashed up pretty much, too. Nothing we can't fix, though. Harry Myers, the specialist I'm sending you to, is as good as they come. You're lucky it's all there. Much longer with the circulation mostly cut off like that, and you'd have lost the leg. You got a guardian angel or something?" He patted my shoulder.

"Yeah, I guess you could say that."

You could definitely say that.

I don't remember much about that night, which was a blur of red pain and sleepless grogginess. They probably shot me full of so much numbness I was supposed to drift off, but I couldn't quite manage that. Seemed like about a year before that first night ended.

Next day, medics drove me to Springfield in an ambulance, Jim and Kelly following. I was still more than a little groggy when this Doc Myers checked me over. The leg was swollen, and a lot of ugly colors, yellow, blue, red. The skin hurt, the bones hurt, everything hurt. Along with the deep pain, any touch felt like fire running all over the surface of my leg. The doctor was gentle, but all business.

"Lot of tendon and nerve damage here. Some blockage, too. But the break is clean, for some reason. You're lucky really, you know? I'd have expected bone to be splintered all over the place. Must've been a depression in the ground just where your leg was. Okay, here's prescriptions for more painkiller, anti-inflammatory, anti-coagulant, and some sleeping pills. You're going to be off this thing for a while. Keep this strap-on cast on any time you're not asleep, and try not to thrash around. I'll see you again in a week. Any questions?"

"How long will something like this take to heal? Or will it heal, completely?"

"Depends. But at the outside, a year till it's really back right, and there's no reason it can't get back almost a hundred percent. We can usually start therapy in four, five months or less. Couple of months on crutches, then a cane probably, before therapy. Got to build up the muscles again. You'll lose that all over while you're immobile.

"Lot of stuff smashed up in there besides the bone, which as I said, is a simple fracture, and it'll all take time to heal. And all in all, it's a lot better than it could have been."

Okay. *Yeah, better.* But I sure wasn't gonna be climbing that trail up to the garden. Maybe I wasn't even going to be able to live by myself for a while. Bummer. Of course, my brother would and did insist I stay with them for the duration, but that'd get old for them. Me too, probably.

During the ride back to Caney Creek, my head clearing some, I mentally went over the options. To start with, my independent lifestyle, if you could call it that, was over for the time being. I could do crutches in normal places, sure, but those steps down to the creek? Well, folks did go up and down stairs on crutches. Maybe. But firewood? Yeah, the little I'd need, now it was warm. Water? Couldn't drive the Ranger up to Jim's with the mangled leg.

He could and would bring me water, come get me for church, take me to shop for groceries. But I'd be a constant drag on them, and for who knew how long? Didn't like that prospect much better than living with them.

So what'd that leave?

Okay, I knew what that'd leave. I could crawl back to Sharon, literally on my knees, and have the gall to ask her to take me back, wait on me, put up with the impatience and grouchiness I knew this thing would bring.

All right, as a new Christian, I could learn to lose the pride. Gonna have to do that, anyway. And hey, maybe that was what this was all about.

Maybe so.

But just what made me even imagine she'd do it? Swallow the whole outrage, betrayal, rejection?

No, I didn't think so.

So, say I'm pretty well incapacitated for what, maybe three months with luck, which would be pushing it. July, August. Summer about over, then. Forget the garden. The forge work too, that'd kept me sorta sane. And no, I couldn't hire anybody to stay with me, even part time. Not on Social Security. I didn't even know what sort of old age program this thing fell under. *Or will I pay all the bills? Wow. Better find that one out, and now. These pills aren't cheap, either. So even if I hole up, don't even go back to the doc, tough it out, just keeping the worst pain away will cost me big.*

Well, people with broken legs have survived since there were people. I could do it. Spend a few days with my brother, make them feel good about helping, then work back into the Lone Ranger thing.

Is that my pride, again? Hope not. If You're telling me to lose that, God, I'm getting the message, if slowly. But I don't want to dump on anyone else, either. And yes, You and I'll talk about this. A lot.

And thanks again, Big Guy, for Jim and Eric, and for hearing my prayer.

~ * ~

The crutches weren't as bad as I'd feared. The only time I'd used them before had been way back, when I'd been younger and stronger. But I could get around okay, even go up and down steps, long as I didn't let myself lose my balance and go over the long way.

That was good, and I knew I could live in my cabin again. So, after a few days with Jim and Kelly and over their objections, I got them to drop me off down at my place.

"Only thing, Liam," Kelly informed me, "I'm trading cars with you. You can drive my automatic, and I'll take your Ranger till the leg's better. Okay?"

"Hey, you don't have to..."

"I want to. That'll give you a way to get around, 'cause I know you won't want to be a bother. An imagined bother." She gave me a peck on the cheek. Good woman.

So they took the Ranger back up the hill, after watching me get down the steps. *Piece of cake. Just remember to lean back into the slope.* Avoid that long way down if I went over the other way. They'd stashed jugs of drinking water, and filled my ice chest. Left me eggs and other perishables, too.

Hey, I could make it. The radio worked all right, and I wasn't about to wander off anywhere.

This time.

I'd put off the heavy thinking while I was at Jim's, letting them spoil me just enough, and drifting off a lot...the drugged system sparing me a lot of the worst. Now the pain had subsided a little, to where I could sort of isolate it, at least part of the time, get my head working.

The plan, as I evolved it, had me recovering here, doing just what I could manage as I got mobile again. Keep quiet about the leg, even to the kids. Didn't want anybody rushing to my rescue. If one of them came, I'd be that much better by then. Cross that bridge when I came to it.

And Sharon? Well, that'd take some more figuring. But now I felt that God would lead me in the right direction on that. I honestly didn't know how I really felt about Sharon. It was as if I'd taken a year off, maybe to get some perspective, and I'd be able to sort out my feelings soon. Maybe. I also didn't know how she really felt about me anymore.

You see, even though I'd cast her as the bad guy this past year, I knew this woman wasn't really a shrew. She'd borne and raised three fine kids. She was a doting grandmother. Couldn't be all bad. And while she'd left me no choice but to believe we'd had nothing left between us, a lot of that was probably me.

Okay, it *was* me.

I re-read the Apostle Paul's take on marriage in Corinthians. Old bachelor, Paul. Women treated like cattle back then. Bill Zachman had explained to us that theologians now factored in the customs and beliefs of the times in interpreting Scripture. And back then women had no rights. None. Hard to believe women had put up with the patriarchal thing for so many centuries. So universal they didn't have any choice, I guess. Feminist movement wasn't but a generation or so old, even now...

Well. God and I'll thrash this out then, next few weeks. And when I'm not so bad a cripple, I'll take the next step.

The big one, I guessed.

I missed a couple Sundays at church, but did go back. Folks solicitous, trying to do stuff for me. Came bringing food to Jim's for me. Some good cooks in that bunch. Reverend Bill even drove his pickup down to my turnoff from the main ford road, knowing he couldn't turn around at my cabin, with the Cherokee there. Walked down, and spent a couple hours with me. We talked about whatever came to mind: crops and fishing and dogs. Before he left, he prayed with me, a simple, unself-conscious prayer. That warmed me long after he'd gone.

Good man.

Eventually I crutched my way up the path to my garden, mostly to see if I could do it. Hey, if I did fall, I could still crawl, this time.

Not bad, really. Out of breath soon, but that was natural, and I stopped to rest often. The weeds had grown, but not much yet. Only now in May, the rains were further apart, and soon the real trial would begin. Mulch had kept the moisture in and the weeds manageable so far, and my stuff was well up.

I'd expected wild things to get in and eat my veggies, but the fence was tight, and the stones I'd lined it with at the bottom had kept them from digging under; miraculously, destruction hadn't happened. And now top guard dog Boswell marked the fence liberally, daring them to intrude.

I managed to sort of balance enough, mostly sitting, to drive some stakes and tie some web-wire fence for edible green things to climb on. Mulched some more from a pile I'd dumped over the fence. I saw I could sit and pull weeds as they came, the way I remembered an old one-legged man in Virginia I knew had gardened for years.

Bottom line was, this activity really picked my spirits up. Needed that, too.

I did decide to put up a handrail along the path up the hill to grab if I started to fall. That was a project now. I crutched up my road to find saplings, then sat and cut them down with a hatchet. Peeled them with a drawknife, then dragged them by a rope around my waist down, across, and up to the path. The pup nipped at them as they slithered along, and I thought there must be some way to harness all that energy. Sled dog? Nah, not on this slope.

There were enough cedars and substantial bushes to rope the poles to, if I cut them the right lengths. I used nylon rope, figuring it'd last several years, at least. Probably as long as the poles.

That little exercise took a week, along with some minor work in the garden. I took a lot of breaks, lying back to watch the clouds. I realized how seldom I'd taken time to do this really, except for short rest breaks. Wild azaleas were blooming in the rock ledges, the scent a sweet, natural perfume; birds were nesting, busy at the job they'd done for thousands of years. The woodpecker chicks had fledged and flown. I was browning in the sun again. I could hear the creek far below, the rippling borne on the mild breeze.

The leg hurt constantly, and I didn't exactly enjoy that, but I had the pain in a place I could stand it. Right now, the world looked pretty fine to me again. I thanked God for it all a thousand times.

Fifteen

I've never been a suspicious type of guy. Never imagined there were baddies out there just waiting for me to give them the opportunity to come after me. I just don't do the professional victim thing well.

But not too long after I'd settled in again to the curtailed routine, I had a bunch of visitors.

Not the kind I welcomed.

A rusted pickup truck lurched and roared onto the gravel bar across Caney from my little stream mouth, roiling smoke as it stopped. About seven teenage boys jumped down and raced for the water, laughing, yelling, clad in cutoff jeans and tee shirts, mostly barefoot.

Okay, goin' swimmin', oldest pastime in the world, I guessed. And half the creek wasn't mine anyway, *so go for it, guys,* was my thought. I was just negotiating the last step down from my parking space when they stormed the creek, and I crutched the few feet onto the flat limestone slab to welcome them. Hey, doesn't hurt to be friendly, and it might forestall any mischief. My dog was just wagging his tail, glad for the company.

"Hey, who're you?" one of them called, having just jumped into the waist-deep water above the standing boulders in the creek bed. All of them turned to look.

"I live here, just up a ways. You men doin' all right?"

"Just swimmin', for shore. Thought this wuz th' forest land."

"No, on down, and up the slope. Family owns that, but they don't care folks swim in the creek. Neither do I."

"Don't care, huh? Well, they ain't here, so it don't matter they care er not, does it, boys?" Raucous laugh, which the others echoed. This particular lout seemed to be the leader of the bunch, the one who'd been driving.

"An' don't look like you're in enny shape t'say one way er t'other neither, are you, old man? Them crutches an' all."

"Guess not. Well, y'all enjoy the water," I said, and I turned up the side branch toward my cabin.

"Whatcha got up there, feller?" another boy asked, no doubt emboldened by the leader's brashness. "Camp? You campin' out?" He'd moved to get a view up the stream.

"Just my cabin. Been here more than a year. Be seein' you." I took a couple of swings away on the crutches. Boswell followed.

"We'd kinda like to see that cabin, wouldn't we, boys?" the leader persisted. "Don't reckon y'd mind none, would you, old man?" And he waded across to the mouth of my stream.

This could get out of hand, I knew, and I suddenly saw my situation in perspective. Rowdy boys, seven of them, and one crippled old man, off away from anybody else. They might think I had beer or money or anything else of value here, and who was to stop them from taking it? Bunch like that, they'd encourage each other, do things they'd never think of alone.

"An' how'd y'ever git that truck down here? Ain't no way t'git a road down that hill."

"I built a road. Not that hard, if a man's got time."

"He built a road!" the boy crowed to his companions. "This old man, all crippled up, done built hisself a road. Now, do enny of y'all b'lieve that? How'd you do that, old man? Don't look like no bulldozer's been here." He pronounced it "bullnozer." The rest of the group had clustered around him.

I looked this specimen up and down. Lean, stubbled face, maybe eighteen. Probably high school dropout or high school bully, or both. Had his acolytes with him, and was looking for any action that'd build him up in their eyes. The rest of them just followers, sneaked off from farm chores now that school was out, ranging from maybe fifteen to his age.

I didn't want them at my cabin. But Stubble-Face was climbing the ledge, not fifteen feet from me, and I didn't see any way to stop them from swarming me and my domain.

"Bobby, I don't thaink we'd oughta jist push onto this man's place," one of the younger boys protested weakly. "We got th' whole creek to ourselves."

"Now, ain't nobody pushin' nothin', Daughtry. We're jist invitin' ourselves t'see whut this old feller's got up here. Ain't no way he's done built hisself a cabin, all stove in like he is, ner this road, neither, so he's lyin' to us." He suddenly reached out, grabbed one of my crutches. That put me off balance, and I nearly fell. He let go with a grin that had a tooth missing. My vicious guard dog didn't do a thing to help.

What to do, here? Just stand back, if they'd even let me, while they ran all over my place like locusts? I did have a half-bottle of medicinal bourbon stashed in the cabin, and if they got hold of that...

"Hey!" I heard suddenly from up near my Ranger. "Got a problem here, Liam?"

It was Eric. Big, amiable Eric, and he had his lever-action 30/30 rifle across his shoulders, arms hooked over it. The boys saw it too, and fell back.

"Heard a lotta shoutin' down here. Looks like you got company." He slipped the rifle down, cradled it. But it just happened to be pointing in the kids' direction. "These boys behavin'?"

These boys had definitely not been behaving, and now they looked like they'd been caught with their hands in the cookie jar.

"We's jist swimmin' in th' creek," Stubble-Bobby stammered, his eyes fixed on the muzzle of Eric's rifle. I imagine that hole looked the size of a washtub to him, just then. And he appeared about half his former size.

"Creek's back behind you, I believe," Eric pointed out, with a jerk of his head. "I'd say you've already had yourselves a swim, from the looks of things. And I b'lieve I just saw you jerkin' this man's crutch, like some stupid-ass coward."

With that, he racked the lever of his rifle, chambering a round. If I'd been the culprit, I'd sure have pissed my pants already. "Now, it just might be a good idea for you all to head on back home about now, don't you think?"

"Y-yessir, we's jist on our way. Jist leavin', we wuz, wuzn't we, boys?" Stubble jumped back off the ledge, all swagger gone, followed by his stumbling, splashing, hastening entourage. They all kept wide of Eric, whose rifle just happened to follow them across Caney to their truck. In what must have been record time, they were aboard, staying low. The truck engine coughed to life in a cloud of blue smoke, and they got turned around, spinning on the gravel, and were gone.

"Well, Liam, seemed you were a bit outnumbered there. I just happened to be feeding Jim's horses while they're gone, heard their engine and the yelling down here. Head retard a real instigator. Shoulda maybe just shot him, teach the others a lesson." He climbed down, came to me. "You okay?"

"Yeah, just a little shaken. Afraid they'd keep pushing each other, showing off, you know, to some real meanness. Looks like you've come to my rescue just in time. Again. You just happened to have that rifle?"

"Always keep it in my truck, yes. And you never know what or who you'll run into, lotta noise like that. And hey, I mighta needed it for a snake or somethin'." He grinned.

"Or a bunch of snakes. Thanks, buddy. Again. Now come on up for at least a cold drink. Hot enough, I might get in the creek myself, if I could manage it." We ambled up to the cabin. He was thinking.

"You don't have a gun of any kind, do you, Liam?"

"No, didn't think I'd need one. Jim and I've gone hunting with his rifles a couple times, but I figured I'd be left alone down here. Maybe not."

"No, folks come across the bridge down at Beaver, they're gonna come on up, see what's here. You maybe oughta get yourself a little firepower, just for situations like this. If you'd had a sidearm showing, those boys wouldn't have come across the creek at all."

"You're probably right. Couple of times I've thought about it, but been lucky so far, I guess. And I'm not exactly in fighting trim right now." Rueful laugh, as we sipped ice tea in the shade.

"Well, on those crutches, a rifle would be awkward. I'd say get yourself a long-barrel pistol you can hit stuff with, not a snub-nose lady's gun. Looks meaner, too. Deterrent, you know."

I reflected on the statistics that proved crime went down where folks were allowed to carry firearms, and had to agree. One more complication to deal with, but today's little episode could have been avoided, if...

"Think I may do that, all right. Never know when it might come in handy." I was also thinking of just a few shots signaling an accident, say. Yeah, like maybe caught under that big rock. Either Eric or Jim would've heard that, even if Divine Intervention hadn't kicked in.

So I guessed I'd go shopping for a gun, which up to now hadn't been on my priority list. Not to shoot clumsy teenagers with, but yeah, to scare the hell out of them.

I had the notion, too, that this Bobby character might just plan a return trip. Plainly wouldn't like being shown up in front of his cohorts, and he might've guessed Eric just happened to be near, didn't belong there. Maybe get a few beers in him and come back. Didn't like that prospect much.

So I asked Eric and Jim where a man might pick up some heat, to use a term. Both said auctions were probably best, since the gun shops set their prices high. Seems there was always some sale going on in the region that included guns, of a deceased farmer or somebody else who'd managed to collect several.

Current favorites, both said, were the nine millimeter automatics now favored by police and the criminals on the TV shows and in movies. That'd make them high-priced.

"Should be a lotta thirty-eight revolvers around," Jim told me, "since the cops don't use them anymore. I'll keep an eye out for an auction."

That would be okay, but it might take time. And now that the idea was in my head, I was impatient. Didn't want to spend much money, but I'd managed to stash some away lately. Maybe I'd just drive up to Springfield one day soon, see what was available. Maybe some cheap replica or something that wouldn't leave me broke.

Meanwhile, I kept my eye open for more visitors, but none came. My plan had to be to call Jim on the CB if there was trouble, hoping I could catch him or Kelly inside, and that he could then race down to help. Not an ideal situation, and another imposition on them.

Jim did loan me his 30.06 rifle, which I kept inside my door. Couldn't carry it around very well on the crutches, but if I stayed close, I could get to it. Just how I'd manage to draw a quick bead and stay vertical was a problem to be dealt with when and if the need arose. Of course, I didn't plan to have to *use* it, actually. Mean-looking enough, it should be a deterrent only. And temporary, till I could get my own mini-arsenal.

So, I invited myself along the next time my brother and Kelly went to Springfield, just to check things out. They had a few errands to run and friends to visit, so said sure, that'd work.

Kelly wanted to go to a fabric store, so dropped Jim and me at a gun shop on some street in a seedy part of town, promising to be back in less than an hour. The place was full of firepower, and several customers crowded the counter. I'd never realized that so many people bought guns. Women handling little automatics, hunters sizing up rifles, racks of shotguns with the safety locks on them.

The handguns were in glass cases, and I just looked for a while. The prices started at around $400, and I was put off by that. But there were a few used pieces for less, and we finally got a clerk's attention. He wanted to push the new high-dollar guns, but did show us a couple of secondhand ones.

"Now some of these are cheap versions of the best names," he explained. "Okay if you don't want quality. No resale value, though.

Stick with S&W, Glock, Browning, you'll get a better gun, and if you sell it later, you can get your money back. Two things don't ever go down in value—antiques and guns."

Okay. But I wasn't going to part with seven hundred bucks or more for a name. Expected to bang away at a target till I got to where I could hit somewhere near the mark, then just have it handy. And the used specimens looked so beat-up I was afraid they'd be more dangerous to the shooter than the target.

I liked a replica of an 1800s Colt, and another of a Remington. Both pricey, though. Finally realized this wasn't the place to shop. So much business, so many on the payroll, I knew the store had a high overhead.

Down the block we picked up a weekly shopper at a little grocery store, that had all sorts of stuff listed for sale, including guns. Some not too expensive. We found a phone booth and called a couple of numbers, finding one older man at home. Yeah, he still had the .38 long barrel. Not much demand, he said, since most folks wanted a gun they could carry easier. Sure, we could come on out, and he gave us directions.

So when Kelly got back, amazingly close to the hour promised, we hunted up the old guy. First thing he said was he hadn't registered the pistol and hoped we wouldn't, either.

"Government'll know just who's got what, when they get set to take away what's left of our freedoms," he warned. "So anybody asks, I just claim my guns have been in the family since way before any regulation. You handle it any way you want. I'm not a dealer, don't care what you tell or who to."

He proceeded to break down the revolver, show me how much wear it had, its features. Yes, it had a swing-out cylinder for faster unloading/loading. Yes, it was double-acting, which meant it didn't have to be cocked first, then fired. No, the firing pin didn't rest on the detonator, so I could load all six cylinders. Yes, it was accurate.

"It ain't no cherry, but it'll last a long time yet. Mint condition, I could get three times the price, easy. Collectors wants 'em like new, y'know. Had a couple look at it, but pass. Y'want a gun t'use now'n then, this's it."

He needed to sell it because his old car needed a radiator. Then he showed us his other guns, a veritable arsenal of everything from assault rifles to muzzle-loaders. I got the notion he'd sell them off one at a time as his needs for other things arose. Sort of old age insurance, I guessed. Hey, whatever works, right?

He wanted $200.

I paid him.

Got two boxes of expensive cartridges back at the gun shop, and sort of got used to the feel of the weapon while riding around with Kelly and Jim as they tended to their errands. I liked the gun. Have to make some sort of holster for it...too long to stuff in a pocket. Play Western sheriff, I guessed, there on my own turf.

Afterwards, back home, Jim and I set up paper plate targets one afternoon against a dirt bank where the bluff ended. He showed me the classic military/police stance you see on TV shows, two-handed, feet apart. Both he and I hit well at 30 feet, passably at 60, and once in a while at 100. The gun didn't buck much, which surprised me, and it felt comfortable. Afterwards, I cleaned and oiled it, as directed.

So okay, I hadn't ruined my budget, and I guessed I could intimidate any crazed urbanites who tried to storm my castle. Or angry bulls, or snakes, human or otherwise, trying to bite Boswell or me. I eventually rigged a holster I could hang from my belt in back, out of the way of the crutches and most things I wanted to do. It wasn't too heavy once I got used to it.

And I felt a lot safer, even though I'd probably never need to use the thing.

Deterrent.

~ * ~

But I did actually get the chance to use my new toy sooner than I'd thought. I heard Boswell barking one morning before I'd really gotten started on my day, and crutched out to see what he'd found. Turned out to be a big copperhead coiled up against a boulder, not far from the house.

The dog would feint at the snake, then jerk back as it struck, so far apparently safe. I called him away to let it go on its way, again considering just what degree of threat to dog and man it represented.

But the snake was mad, it seemed, at that persistent dog, and instead of slithering away, it came after him. Not typical snake behavior, in my experience. But big as it was, maybe it sensed it could drive off anything around here and establish its own territory. If it hadn't already.

Okay, did I blast it to bits, try to bag it for relocation like before, or hide and watch till it left us alone? Decisions.

Just then Boswell started barking again, and I glanced down the stream. Here came another snake, almost identical. The hair on the back of my neck rose: was this an infestation? And why weren't they leaving, going into hiding? Some sort of copperhead homecoming? And was my house their destination? Be hard to dodge one now, in my condition.

That realization did it. I drew the gun, sighted on the moving body of the first snake, and almost cut it in two with the slug. Then I waited for the echoes of the shot to fade, sighted again and dispatched the second one. Both writhed around a lot, but they weren't going anywhere now.

I spent most of that day searching for others, and from then on, I never took for granted that my dog and I had this place all to ourselves. Funny how we'd gone so long without serpentine visitors, then those two. Well, mates, maybe. Past tense.

Of course, Jim just happened to come down to check on his horses after hearing the shots. I told him my snake story, and we both figured I'd just been lucky before this.

"Chances are they'd have just gone on up into the woods, but you never know. Could be a whole family of them around, and you or the dog just never stumbled on them. I don't mind snakes, generally, but do blast them when they're close to the house. Don't want them thinking my turf is theirs."

"Well, now I'm paranoid about them, but with my cannon here, I'm okay. Just can't jump out of the way anymore, with these sticks."

"How long did the doc say you'd need them?"

"Oh, he encouraged me to get rid of them as soon as I could get around okay. Don't know how soon that'll be, but every time I've tried it, I totter. Guess we all have to admit we don't bounce back as quick at our ages." I didn't want this to be true, but I was living proof, wasn't I?

"Well, when you get into therapy, they'll probably know all the muscles to build up to speed things up. Hope so, anyway."

We talked about stuff in general for a while, then he left, having satisfied himself I hadn't been in a war with the Visigoths or rural terrorists. I did notice he'd brought his own pistol with him, just to be on the safe side.

Sure.

Sixteen

Of course, Kyle came to see me one Saturday, bringing Sarah with him. I heard his call from the cabin, sitting up in the garden in the sun. Boswell barked, and tore out the gate and down the path to meet them. If there was anything missing in that dog's life, it was more people. I yelled back, but it wasn't necessary, since that yellow ball of fur had shown them where I was.

A few minutes later, the three of them appeared on the path, the dog bouncing around, licking them to death. They didn't see the crutches at first, and apparently Jim and Kelly hadn't let on. I was seated, pulling emerging weeds while they were relatively small and defenseless, but I didn't stand up.

"Hey, what's this, Dad? You okay? What'd you do to yourself?"

"Oh, little accident with the leg, few weeks back. Getting better. Hey, Sarah, how's my girl?"

"I'm fine, Mr. Mac, but you're the one I want to know about. Now, what happened? Really." She sat next to me, gave me a sideways hug.

"Okay, details: big rock rolled off a ledge when I tried to sit on it, up above. Couldn't get out from under it. Jim and Eric got it off me okay. Did some damage to the leg, here."

"Wow. Lucky they were with you...Or *were* they? You weren't alone, were you? *Oh*..." her hand went to her mouth. Eyes wide.

"Um, well yeah, I was. But not really." And I told them about my praying. Not to be rescued, but to accept God's will. "And His will was for my brother and Eric to find me in time. Go figure." I turned a palm up.

Sarah put her arms around me, again just like my daughters had so many times when they were small. Didn't say anything, but there were tears. Kyle laid a hand on my arm. Nothing about it made us self-conscious, up there in the sky, over my deep and hidden little world.

We had our own world, right there.

"It wasn't your time, Dad," Kyle concluded. "There's more for you to do here. Don't you think?"

"I do think, yes. But I'm getting past being a physical basket case before I find out just what that is. And it's not really that hard, now I've gotten used to it, the crutches and all. Hey, lotsa people on crutches. And I'm thankful mine are temporary."

They had to hear what the doc had said, what the program was, how long I'd be on the sticks. All the gory details. I told them all I knew, which wasn't much.

"You know, Dad," Kyle was a little hesitant to bring up whatever it was he wanted to bring up. "Mom would've been here, cared for you. Would've taken you back..."

"Maybe. And yeah, I was ready to eat my pride, which I have to do anyway. Not fair to her, though, descend on her, grumpy old man demanding all her attention."

"She'd have loved it. You gotta know, I'm sure part of the problem has been her not feeling needed."

"My son, the psychiatrist. But you're probably right, there. Just a little too soon, yet. Gotta work through to what's right on my own. Maybe that's ego...I hope it's not. Like to think it's sparing others, but I guess time'll tell..." I let it trail off, looking around for some way to change the subject to something more pleasant.

Then I saw it.

"Hey, what's *this?*" I'd just caught a glint of light, noticed the rock on Sarah's finger. Her grin was about an acre wide.

"Surprise. Your son gave me this. Like it?" She wiggled the finger.

"Well, that's *great* news! And you both let me ramble on here, some self-centered old man. Wow! Congratulations, both of you!" I took her hand, slapped Kyle on the back. "When?"

"No date yet," she said. "It just happened last weekend. But we wanted to come see you first, let you know." *Let me be the first to know? What a sweet kid.* And she was going to be my daughter. Wow.

"Well, now. I'm just about speechless, but this's the best news you could've brought me. Wow, this's so *great!*" Pulled them both to me, hugged them, hard. The pup licked everybody's hands.

"Okay, I've wasted the morning pretending to garden up here. Let's go down for lunch. Water's good; maybe we'll even go fishing. Oh, you tell your mom yet, Kyle?"

"Did. Said we were coming down this weekend. She sends you her love. Really."

"Okay. I'm finding that a little easier to believe lately, but we'll just have to see how that goes." *Okay, so I'm not the first to know...no big deal; still the best news I can remember.*

When I got to my feet, Kyle helping me, they saw my gun.

"Hey, what's this? Shooting snakes?"

"Matter of fact, I have been sort of invaded, and I can't get out of their way like I used to. But it's also for signaling, say if something else like that big rock happens to me. Jim and Kelly and I went to Springfield and I bought it from an old guy who needed money. Been practicing with Jim." I didn't tell them about the rogue teenagers who'd started me thinking about this. Just give them one more concern about me, that.

"Well," Kyle observed, "your dog here could get himself bitten, for sure, even if you didn't. Guess you've evened the playing field some." He seemed okay with it, and so did Sarah. They'd surely worried about me, down here alone, before this, and at least now they knew I could supposedly better take care of myself.

At the cabin, they wouldn't let me do anything, both buzzing around me, finding things, setting up, spoiling me. Gotta love that.

"I should've suspected something when I saw your Ranger at Uncle Jim's, Dad. All Aunt Kelly said was that she'd traded with you for a while. Boy, they sure can keep a secret." Grin.

"Well, I needed to find out whether I could live down here on my own before I spread the news and got everybody all concerned and worked up over me. Everything takes longer, is all. And with Kelly's automatic, I can get anywhere okay. Won't be much longer till I start therapy on the leg. They can do that in Branson."

We talked about their plans, mostly. Pretty obvious they'd each found the right soulmate, and I couldn't have been more pleased. Funny though, I found myself wanting to share this joy with Sharon.

Hmm.

We did actually get in a little fishing later, when the shadows were long through the leaves and the sun slanted. Some of the heat was gone, and the creek sang along, just full enough after the last rain to keep the fish awake.

I could stand fairly well on the strap-on cast with its boot sole. Big fish would probably pull me over, but we didn't hook any big ones. Didn't hobble down to Beaver Creek, where we'd have done better. Not on a life-or-death quest for food anyway today. Let the few go we did get; let 'em grow some more, so then they could be lunch.

Kelly had insisted we come for dinner, so we took the Cherokee up the hill. I was extra careful not to scratch it on sprouts and limbs, more than I was with the Ranger.

I noted a few places that needed gravel after recent rains. Yeah, with my slower pace, there'd be plenty for me to do here, even if I had to sit to do it, take my time. I'd seen woods places eaten up by the wilderness in just a few months of neglect. Nature is a hungry animal. But I was here, most of me; I could cope with the impending green takeover.

We had dinner, another of Kelly's great creations, then we talked, mostly about the kids and their upcoming schedule. They were thinking maybe December for the wedding. The engineering firm they both worked for wanted to promote Kyle, and send him to a branch in St. Louis. Great: that'd be closer than Chicago. To here, at least. He'd go in July.

"They got any restrictions about married couples working for the same company?" I asked.

"No, but they want us in different divisions," Sarah answered. "Or in St. Louis I can find another job, no problem."

"Well, you know the way down here," Jim invited. "We wanta see you whenever you can make it." Kelly echoed him.

The phone rang, and it was Sharon. *Sure, she knew the kids'd be here.* She talked with Kelly first, then Sarah. Apparently happy about the news when she'd heard. That made several of us.

"Yes, he's here," Sarah said into the phone, then handed it to me. *Whoops!* I wasn't ready for that. Wanted to know how I was.

"Okay, all things considered. Few aches and pains, but I'm mobile. How was your winter?"

"Not used to being alone yet, Liam. I don't suppose you've done your penance, or whatever it is, yet? You know you can come home..."

"Thanks. And well, I'm still working through stuff, like I told you Christmas. Maybe I'm trying to prove whatever it is I'm supposed to prove to myself. How about these kids, now? I think it's great."

"Sure. I like Sarah a lot. She's not...pushy about her religion and all. Sweet girl. I'd like to meet her family, wouldn't you?"

"Maybe. Hadn't gotten that far. Sure, work something out before long. Good to hear from you, girl. I know you wanta talk to your son, though. Here he is." I got off before she could get back onto me.

Kyle mostly just answered her questions, from what we could tell. Once he looked over at me.

"He's okay, Mom. Slowed down a bit, maybe, but doing okay. Into some serious gardening up on the slope above his cabin. We had to go up there and drag him down."

Afterwards, all of us talked about the faith aspect of my deliverance. It was as natural as any conversation, which surprised me a little. Most folks don't discuss religion outside church, and of course we never had, at home. Now I wished we had, for all our sakes. Kyle wasn't uncomfortable with it at all, and I silently thanked Sarah for that. Good influence, this girl.

Later I drove back down the hill, guilty about not telling Sharon about my leg, but content too, with the way things were going. Even if the kids decided to marry fairly soon, I'd be pretty much back on both feet.

And well, that might be the time for me to try to make some decisions, too. Whenever it'd be. We'd see each other then, Sharon and I, and the girls, too. Maybe time to be a family, again. Try, anyway.

Or not. I had no idea, in spite of Sharon's invitation, how that would actually play. She'd be hacked about my keeping the accident from her—or maybe I didn't have to tell her that...

Nah, somebody'd let it slip.

But I sure didn't want to go back to our being like two snakes in a standoff. Both of us would have to cut a lot of slack. Kyle'd said a lot of it was her being needed...*Yeah, that.* Well, that fit us both, really. Everybody has to feel important. And I guess I hadn't made her feel that way, last few years. I was feeling my share of guilt about all of this, more and more.

The kids told the folks at church about the engagement, and those good people hugged them silly. Reverend Bill asked a special blessing on them, and the amens were almost shouted. The adolescent girls kept sneaking peeks at this cool woman of Kyle's.

Well, she *was* cool.

Jim had gone over with Sarah the songs the choir would do, and she sang with them. Filled out the soprano section nicely. One hymn had a descant she and the white-haired lady did. Rich. A great experience, chills all down my spine.

The day passed, of course, and then they had to leave. Didn't want that, but hey, they had work, and now more of a life than either'd had before. But now I knew they'd both be back, or we'd get together wherever I was, and whatever was to come. And that thought was really fine.

~ * ~

Their visit left me warm for a long time. Here the youngest kid was taking the plunge, a new generation taking shape. Who knew when June would find herself the right guy in that theater crowd? She was taking classes toward another degree, though, and meeting people outside that tight little circle. I wasn't really worried about her...live her own life, like I had.

This second springtime I was necessarily slowed down, and took more time to let the wonder of my little world soak into me. I missed the pileated woodpeckers after they'd hatched their young, seeing them peeking out of the hollowed-out den as they grew, all fuzzy and ugly. Then they'd grown some more, gotten beautiful, and that was that. They did come back now and then, one at a time, on their incessant hunt for wood-eating insects. I liked to think, when I saw one, that it was the old bird I'd known from before, come to check on me. He'd always startle me with his machine-gun call.

I got to know some of the other birds, too, but didn't get into trying to identify them. Crows, cardinals, robins, jays I knew, and I lumped all those other little ones into one musical category. Oh, I did put out a hummingbird feeder, and soon one found it. Then another, and they'd drive each other away from that red artificial stuff inside. Probably find out it was really toxic, but didn't seem to do them any harm.

About birds, though: when we'd first gone to Virginia and found the land we built on, we heard and saw doves nesting in the cedars there. They came back year after year, right to the trees we'd left almost against the house. One pair even nested on a high window ledge. The kids would watch the female sitting on her eggs on that minimal pile of sticks and grass, and try not to scare her away. She'd cock her head at them through the glass, then ignore them. They went bananas when the little ones hatched, and monitored their growth a dozen times a day.

The sound of those doves had become a part of our lives in Virginia. You didn't notice it much most of the time. You'd see them flying, disappearing into the thick foliage of the cedars, hear their melodious call so often you took it for granted. They became part of our lives. Or maybe we'd just become part of theirs.

So this spring and summer, I was moved and delighted to hear that call again here, floating on the soft air in the trees around my cabin. I don't know if this was new territory for them, whether they'd been here the year before, or whether I just hadn't noticed them. They were welcome, but their mournful calls also triggered some homesickness in me.

I did have one noisy intrusion while on the crutches. Three carloads of people decided to have a picnic across Caney from my place, and of course they wandered all over, like folks will when they've gone out into the woods and left their brains at home.

Couple of them waded the creek, then saw my Ranger parked up in the bushes. I'd hobbled out to let them know this wasn't public land, but sure, go ahead and have fun on the other side of the creek.

Just to make a point, I'd shifted my belt holster around so it was visible, and I saw them register the gun as I swung my way toward them. Without a word, they turned, splashed back across the creek thinking maybe I was somebody out of the movie *Deliverance*, and had a quick parley with the rest of the picnickers. Pointing, nervously gathering up things.

I waved, turned, and went back up my branch. They were evidently relieved that I wasn't about to slaughter them over their sandwiches, cookies and ants, and they stayed for a while. Only I'd probably spoiled their concept of being in the uninhabited woods alone. Then they left, and quiet descended again. I sort of wondered what kind of tale they'd tell when they got back to wherever they belonged.

Didn't really care.

I saw and heard and felt a lot more this year than last, without the obsession of building and the self-imposed deadlines weighing me down. The moods of the creek changed a dozen times a day, its sound a constant, soothing melody most of the time. When it flooded, which it did only once this spring, it roared, but its angry waters didn't seem to threaten as much. I knew its limits, or imagined I did.

This season should have been one of more peace and tranquility, except for the constant pain of my leg and the real effort of getting around. I was resigned to it, and tried hard not to chafe at my limitations. I had a lot to be thankful for, I kept telling myself. And I believed that. But I also found myself with the shadow of Sharon in my thoughts, tempering the magic of each day. Not destroying it, maybe just shading it a little, the way a thin cloud sometimes does the sun.

But like I'd noticed, it did become easier and easier to remember the good days, the long-ago tenderness, the shared joys, the good and the hard times we'd weathered together. I guess everybody idealizes memories, hazed, softened by time.

Oh, the anger did manage to come through when I let it: the fights, the demands, the screaming. Now I tried to shut the door on all that—just not let it in. And finally, I was beginning to see that a lot of it had been provoked: words, retorts, getting in the last jab, escalating. Maybe just not knowing when to quit, both of us.

Seventeen

Well, things have a way of getting complicated, just when you're sorting them out. That's usually bad: get comfortable with your situation, then things change, and you're off-balance again.

But sometimes it's actually good. Something'll come along to jar you out of your rut, and then you realize you're better off. You'd been missing a lot and just didn't know it.

Limited physical therapy started late in July, after I'd been off the crutches a couple weeks. Apparently, I'd progressed further than expected. I'd whittled myself a cane from a young sprout that a vine had wrapped around as it grew, making it grow into a nice spiral. Took some of the weight off the leg with that.

My therapist was about fifty, a neat, attractive, efficient woman who didn't push me too fast. Right off, though, she told me there was absolutely no reason I couldn't get back 100%, and even build more muscle all over than before. Said it was a myth about older people being doomed to getting weaker. Didn't know whether to believe that...coulda been just her routine spiel.

"Of course, you'll have to work harder than someone younger," she told me. I said I guessed I could handle working harder.

Her name was Jocelyn Summers. Didn't talk much about herself at first, but was good at her job. Spent a lot of time massaging my foot and ankle, which she said were getting the worst of the leg injury. But she worked on a big, knotted-up place on the back of the leg, too, which still hurt a lot. Deep bone-ache, and a sharp surface pain, to name just two. Always felt better afterwards, though.

She asked me about myself, which I guess is standard bedside manner. Told her some, and she was impressed about my building the stone cabin, living close to the land. I did tell her Sharon and I were separated. She'd been divorced over twenty years, had no children.

Now, even at my age, I wasn't immune to the ministrations of a pretty woman. And that doesn't make me a dirty old man. Given the choice, we all like to be in the company of attractive people, as opposed to the other kind. Supposed to see past that, I know, but most of us don't. So yeah, I enjoyed being with her, busted leg or no leg.

I went to Branson twice a week for these sessions, and they got to be high points in my days. Been a hermit too long, I guessed. Jocelyn would give me a heated pad for a while to begin with, then do the massage stuff, and work with me on some stretches. Then she'd turn me over to one of several exercise people for all sorts of things I had to do to build up the muscles in the leg and ankle. Final treatment was ice for about 20 minutes.

Most of the staff at this facility, an adjunct to the hospital, were young, helpful girls and young men. They were all clean-cut, efficient, concerned kids who sort of made a pet out of me. All of them had a way of making me try harder for them.

Kelly had found some angle in Medicare that covered most of the cost of all this. She'd worked in this same hospital as a medical technologist till retirement, and knew the strings to pull. I was glad: I soon learned that without this specialized therapy, I'd probably never recover much.

"You have to know which muscles to work," Jocelyn told me. *Yeah, some I didn't know I had.* She and those kids found them all, along with the exact sore spots to work on. Sometimes I'd get the notion the cure was worse than the condition, the way they worked me over.

I'd emerge from the air-conditioned workout room into the blasting heat of Ozarks summer, and it'd about knock me over. Have to take a few tentative breaths around, to get acclimated. By the time I'd limped to my wheels and driven out of town, I'd managed to come to grips with the weather again. Well, sort of.

It was the dry time again, and the sun would fry you. At home, the creek was as low as I'd ever seen it, and my side stream was little more than a memory. I was just keeping some of the garden stuff alive between rains, rationing the precious water in my storage tanks.

But about that: in spite of my reduced mobility, the garden hadn't been a total failure. Oh, it'd take a lot more water to do it right, I could see, and the terraces needed more depth to the soil, but my labors apparently hadn't all been in vain.

I'd eaten peas and greens and other early veggies, grown before the soil baked dry. Now, in the waning summer, I'd dribble water from the tanks down through the heavy mulch, fighting the wilting leaves as best I could. Watered late, so the sun wouldn't draw it all up too soon. But the dry ground sapped the water I did give the plants, like sponges all around their roots.

Jim just shook his head. He had to water his garden from their deep well, and he had no hopes for my shallow, hill-hanging ground, this late. Probably right. I did give the young fruit trees more, since they'd probably make it, while the beans, squash, other late stuff might not, anyway.

Jocelyn Summers was an avid gardener, too, I learned. She was intrigued at my mountainside experiment, and wanted to see it.

Well okay, why not? I enjoyed talking to this woman, and admitted I'd been pretty well starved for conversation. She was smart, interested, and like I said, pretty, too. She was athletic, and except for some gray in the light brown of her hair, you'd never have guessed her age. Had these intelligent brown eyes. She was a serious outdoors person.

So, I picked her up one Saturday, and we drove to Caney Creek, me telling myself this wasn't a real date. Maybe to feel I wasn't being untrue to my wife, I mean. Hey, Jocelyn was my *therapist*. Jim and Kelly were in Springfield, so we only stopped to fill water jugs, then threaded the road down. By then, I was back in the Ranger, the clutching supposedly helping build up the muscles in my bum left leg.

I backed down to my parking perch, and we climbed out. The side branch was dry here, and only a trickle would come over the falls upcreek after a rain. Caney was slithering along, low but with some deep pools. The air smelled of willows and sycamore leaves, and the myriad, drowsy scents of deep summer. Cicadas droned, and the bird sounds that never left this place were background. Clouds tufted the hot sky, moving on a breeze that tugged the treetops. The light draft that moved up my side branch daytimes in summer, pulled by the rising ground, kept the heat just bearable.

Jocelyn flipped over my cabin. The year since I'd finished the outside had mellowed it into its surroundings so you'd have sworn it'd always been there. Boswell licked my visitor till I had to call him off and toss him a stick to fetch. He brought it back to her.

"Well, my faithful companion has apparently thrown me over. You a dog person?"

"Not really. He's sweet, though. So, it's just you two, in this great little place. You know of course, this is everybody's idea of paradise." She was taking in the jumbled, mossy watercourse up my stream, the sweep of bluff-face up Caney Creek opposite, the towering trees up on the south hill we'd come down.

"I like it. Wanta see inside the house? Or the garden? Such as it is."

"Both. This is so great...a troll's house. I hadn't exactly pictured you as a troll. And you're telling me you built all this by yourself?"

"Had a little help. Us trolls are a solitary lot, though. Tend to scare folks off."

"Why do I doubt that? Wow, this is tiny in here. You and Boswell about fill it up, don't you?" She was taking in the minimal necessities. Saw my revolver, but didn't comment. So maybe she wasn't that much of a tree-hugger. I realized I was building a picture of this woman in my mind.

"Always room for a visitor, if one's brave enough to come here." I got us some iced tea from the chest, and we went back out into the heat. "Garden's straight up above us."

"Up there? That's so steep, you get a workout every time you go up there, don't you?"

We went down the streambed, then climbed the trail, with my holding onto the railing to help the bad leg. She'd gotten me off the cane, pointing out that it was throwing my gait off. Weak on that side, though, and I guessed it would be for a long time. And yeah, it still hurt a lot, and that too, would only gradually diminish, I'd been told. I was holding off on the painkillers, not wanting to get too dependent on them. Stubborn, I guess.

At the side path to the garden, Jocelyn turned and took in the sweep of Caney Creek, down from the bluffs toward us and into the bend where the side branch shot off. Like that tangent that kept coming into my life. I had the brief thought that this woman might turn out to be another one of those...

"It's breathtaking. I'd have wanted the cabin up here. Or higher. What a view!"

"This is pretty exposed to the weather, though. Down below, I've got water over my falls most of the year, at my door. I like the music of that, and the sheltered feel of the hollow. This is always here for me, too, of course. I own up above a ways, too."

We inspected the plants, and I explained how I'd sledded the woods dirt down, built the stone retaining walls. She was a little in awe of it all.

"All an experiment, though. Not really enough depth to the soil, and I don't have enough water to do it right. Plan is to hold every drop that falls, every devious way I can."

"This makes me realize how spoiled I am, with my almost-level weed patch. You've had to create yours."

"Had to keep busy. If I sit around and brood, I start realizing how old I am."

"Not you." She gave me a smile. "It must've been hard, not being able to keep at it, these past months."

"Yeah. I gave the crutches a real workout. The accident really put things into perspective for me, though. I realize now this whole place is pretty precarious."

"But so *worth it*. Just this view is to die for."

"From up top you can see the folds of the hills on over toward Hercules. Don't think I'm up for the climb today. I can actually drive down through the forest onto my land up there, though."

"Oh. Could we? Maybe next time?" *Hmm. Next time.* That sounded good.

"Well...sure. And I could show you the killer rock that got me. I plan to winch that thing down and build something with it, one day."

"Not by yourself. Maybe I could come help." It was a question, really. And sure, that'd be nice. I told her so.

We climbed back down, then up past the cabin and smithy to the first fall. Just a few drips. Disappointment, but the pool below held water.

"This is one reason I built here. Any rain gets it going, and there's a wet-weather spring—old moonshiner's water supply—and a half-mile or so of runoff from Johnson Bald, the hill on up. September on, I have water here. In the spring, sometimes too much, with Caney Creek in flood."

"It's lovely. Oh, there's a pileated woodpecker!"

"They live around close. Nested up there in that tree. Old friend. Think he comes to check up on me." Boswell scared a squirrel up another tree, sniffed every tumbled rock. Then he came to Jocelyn for some loving. She didn't disappoint him.

~ * ~

Well, that visit was innocuous enough. Crippled-up seventy-one-year-old man and his therapist. But later I recalled the scent of her hair, standing behind her as she gazed up Caney Creek, the frank delight in my hideaway, the things I'd built and done here. I had flashes of fantasy about her—how she could maybe fit here. Outdoors type, after all...

Now, cut that out, you old fool! You're not out to get a new woman. You're just now getting it together, finding where your head is. Don't need this. Don't need it at all.

But hey, a man can have a friend, can't he? What does it matter, at my age, if it's a she or a he? *Bill Zachman's a friend, too.* Not the same, though, even if it maybe should be. And for sure a man never gets too old, like I'd seen, to appreciate a pretty woman. I remembered her firm, tanned legs in those L.L. Bean hiking shorts. The slim waist, the laugh-wrinkles. Sexy, yeah.

I liked the woman.

Next time, we drove in through the forest, on the track I'd plotted through the trees to dodge the big stones. From up here, you saw high above the deep cut that was Caney Creek, to the blue hills folding over each other to the east. Here, like local folks said, the mountains weren't high, but the hollows sure were deep. Yeah.

We climbed down to the ledge, me moving very carefully, and walked along it to the fallen boulder that had almost claimed me. The ground was scuffed where I'd struggled. And given up. And prayed. Jocelyn knew I'd been rescued by Jim and Eric, right there. Drama. She looked around, then back at that stone. She was clearly jolted by the size of it.

"What did you think then, with that monster on top of you? I mean, up here, alone? What went through your mind?" I could tell she was trying to see it: the enormity, the hopelessness, the brutal reality...

"Lots of stuff, but the pain shut out a lot, too. Unconscious part of the time. Absolutely nothing I could do, you see. So, finally, I... just prayed." That felt odd, my saying that to her. We'd never talked religion.

"Really? I've never been much on, you know, prayer and like that. Never knew much about all that..."

"Me either, really. But I'd been exposed to it, the past year. Brother and his wife have had me going to a little church with them. Sort of soaking in, gradually. So see, that was all that was left for me, prayer."

"Well, it seems to have worked for you. This religious one is the brother who found you?"

"Yeah. Said he suddenly knew I was in trouble. Brought the neighbor, fortunately. Big guy, and this rock needed muscle."

"It's huge. How would you ever move it anywhere?"

"Hand winch, a few feet at a time. Figure it owes me. Plan to put it somewhere I can sit on it forever, instead of it on me, and in a place where it won't move again."

This was after a hard rain, one of those late summer rarities, and the creek had come up. We climbed down for lunch, and there was a little water in my branch. Even a little more than a trickle over the first fall when we went up to see. Pleasant. We sat on the stone bench and ate the picnic she'd brought. I had ice in the chest, and some cold apple cider.

"So forgive my prying, Liam, but is this permanent, here? I mean… you said you and your wife were separated. Is this it, then?"

"To be honest, I don't know, Jocelyn. At first, I left the options open, but I was sure she'd divorce me. Hey, it got so bad I just walked out, came here from Virginia, left it all to her. But I knew soon I'd stay here, no matter what. Tired of the rat race, the fighting. She and the kids thought I was crazy, but the kids—two out of three, anyway—have come around. And Sharon seems mostly past the outrage. I never know what's in other people's heads, but I'd say it'll wear itself out, if it hasn't already.

"So, well…I'm sort of waiting to see what happens next, I guess. Get over the bad leg, get fully independent again, before I make any serious decisions. Maybe not then, either. Doesn't seem to be any reason to hurry things, jump to any conclusions. For now, though, to answer your question, yeah, this is it. Boswell and me. Hermits."

"Can't be all bad. I guess all of us have a dream of chucking it all, finding, building a place like this. Only most of us just don't have the nerve, are willing to take such a plunge. And you've *done* it. I'm envious." She actually reached, squeezed my hand.

I felt a rush of real affection for this woman, something I hadn't experienced in this way for a very long time. It was nice, but also a little embarrassing. Before I'd met Sharon, relatively late in life, I'd never been just friends with a woman. Sex had always gotten in the way of a good-buddy relationship. Those I was attracted to got complicated. Those I wasn't—well, I just wasn't. Probably pretty selfish, really.

~ * ~

I didn't mention Jocelyn to Jim or Kelly, beyond the reference to "this therapist who's working on me." They were solidly in the Sharon camp, and would probably have taken it wrong. I saw her twice a week at my therapy sessions, and we managed a sort of date every week or so. I thought she and I were okay with that.

But it seemed we weren't. Since the beginning, she'd wanted to do things for me. Bring me food, worry about me. Pretty clear she was interested in becoming more than just my therapist. Why, I didn't know. Woman like that, she needed a younger man, not a dried-up old codger. But I was missing her, too, those days we didn't see each other. Like I said, I liked her. Liked seeing her, hearing her. Yeah, and touching her, even if it was just a hand on an arm, fingers locked for a moment to steady me in a shaky place.

Probably sort of pathetic, at my age.

If we'd been younger, and able to, we'd probably have been on the phone to each other every day, wasting time. But here I was, the hermit, cut off from the world. No matter, I told myself, no need to rush things. Got nothing but time. No need to moon over each other with long phone calls, talking about absolutely nothing the way young people do.

Only problem was, I knew things didn't ever just stand still, particularly relationships. They moved forward, or they came apart. And a lotta times they seemed to do both. Where this one was headed, I couldn't know...train wreck, or something fine?

But another thing: I really wanted to share my newly-discovered faith with this woman, but that wasn't on her agenda, I found. She'd sort of tune out if I brought it up, change the subject. *Okay, dealer's choice.* Nobody forces God on you. One of Bill Zachman's favorite lines was "God leads us horses to water, but he doesn't make us drink."

So no, Jocelyn wouldn't be going to church with me. And I'd have to explain her to Jim and Kelly if she did. Be awkward, that, any way I went about it. And no, I wasn't really dodging them, but...

Well, maybe I was. With Jocelyn, I mean. So yeah, it made things a little simpler, not having those two complicating the equation. I felt a little guilty about that, though.

By the end of September, the balancing exercises and the treadmill stuff and all the rest of my treatment had helped a lot. Doc Myers in Springfield was pleased, and told me I'd be off the therapy in another month or so. Great. All the climbing up and down my hills had apparently helped, even if it'd been painful at first. Jocelyn had encouraged that, warning only against overdoing it, pushing myself back into the pain zone. The burn from exercise was okay, though, that was good.

When I didn't have anything else pressing to do, I'd go up and hook the come-along to a tree and pull that big rock a few feet. I'd trussed it with a chain so it was easy to tie to. Had to double the cable through a snatch block to get the necessary pull. though, heavy as it was. That thing was coming home with me, sooner or later. Well, closer to home. It became a symbol of my rehab, I guess.

As I got stronger, it got closer to the end of the ledge. I'd have to do some redneck engineering there, to keep it from tumbling down through my garden, and maybe smashing my house down below. Have to use one of the cables I'd used to lower the sled and water tanks with, to stabilize it when it came time to lower it to the next level. Be a bit tricky, but as long as I stayed uphill from it, it'd be okay.

I was thinking a leveled-out place for it, so I could pull it out alongside the trail, up where the view was. Set it solid, and it'd be the place to rest from the climb, see Caney Creek and the bluffs from. Sit on *it* and dare it to move again. There weren't many sturdy trees to tie to where the ledge rounded out, but with the cables I could reach something solid. Be something to occupy my mind and idle hours. Another backwoods homegrown engineering project to put my abilities to work on.

Whenever I was going to find I had idle hours, that is. Right then I'm afraid I was inventing time to go see Jocelyn every chance I got. Yeah, and enjoying it.

~ * ~

Well, girl, just what have you gotten yourself into? Friendship thing, or something more? Liam's not like any stereotypical old man...works, creates great things, got projects going. More like a guy my age. And what's age got to do with it, anyway? He keeps on, he'll be back tough and wiry as ever, down in that hollow defying the odds.

The wife's a big factor, though. Is she in, or isn't she? Surely hasn't written him off. Yet. But way over a year apart, you'd think there'd be some resolution. Not. So, where's this going?

No way would I have ever envisioned myself in a relationship with a man almost a generation older than me...or is this really a relationship? Well, it sure looks like it. And it's fun, being with him, besides watching him come back from being a cripple. No, Liam couldn't be a cripple, no matter how beat up he was. I see people who've given up, and that's not him at all.

He'll be going strong for another twenty years with that constitution. And I guess the question is, do I want to be a part of his life? Okay, I guess I am already, the way we've been what, dating? Not in the 21st century sense, but what else could you call it? I look forward to seeing him, being with him, and I can tell he does, too.

So, his plan is just to let it—us—ease along, no decisions, no commitments, no complications. See where it takes us. Can I do that? Well, why not? Not like I need some man to complete me...found that out a long time ago.

Hell, I just like the guy, and he likes me. And it'll get more serious—has to—the way relationships grow. So, we'll see what's next. Be simpler without the wife, but maybe she's really history.

Hmm.

~ * ~

Naturally, I found myself doing some serious comparing between Jocelyn and Sharon these days. They weren't that far apart in age, but the resemblance ended there. Jocelyn seemed to be one of those rare people who're completely at home in their bodies. Comfortable just being who and what they are.

Sharon had never been that way. She was always reaching for something, trying some new fad or craze, never content with herself. Not a condemnation, but that's who she was: impatient, demanding that everybody around her tune in to what she'd discovered, that week or that month or that day even, and you guys hurry up and get on board.

And yeah, as I've said repeatedly, that M.O. just got to be too much for me to handle.

Not that way with Jocelyn at all. She didn't seem to have an agenda, just did her thing helping people like me get back on their feet. Enjoyed life apparently, and that was okay. I did sort of wonder what her other relationships were like (didn't ask, of course). What her hopes were, you know, for the years to come. Just get older I guessed, with a lotta years ahead of her, mellow out more, not straight-arm the world like a lot of us seemed to. I've said she was easy to be around, easy to like.

But like I also said, the distinct feeling grew that, much as Jocelyn seemed to enjoy our easy relationship, she really wanted it go somewhere, too. Oh, we went to Springfield now and then, to some civilized event or other. And to gatherings around Branson. That town had grown beyond the awkward village I'd remembered from thirty-plus years before, trying to handle the tourists with way too little know-how. Now you could find about anything a big town offered, within reason. The little college helped too, with its input of culture. There were concerts, chamber music, and there'd be plays soon, with the new semester now under way.

But I was pretty sure it wasn't variety Jocelyn wanted. An old college roommate of mine—a ladies' man incidentally—had once observed that every woman, in his opinion, no matter her desire for independence, really just wanted to put her feet under some man's table. Sexist point of view. And I had to remember that guy had later gone through three wrecked marriages, so what'd he know?

But was *that* what Jocelyn wanted? Didn't know. Didn't ask.

I didn't have much of a table.

I couldn't imagine her living down in my hollow, even the outdoorswoman that she was. Hey, bottom line, I was really doing the hippie thing, from more than a generation ago. Get old for her in a hurry...no running water, electricity.

No, that budding fantasy wouldn't wash (pun intended).

Her place was a little cottage in cedar glade country south and east of Branson, pleasantly away from the tourists. Had the remains of her little garden, and some late flowers actually blooming. Those yellow things, coreopsis, I think. The house was neat and spotless, of course, and she'd collected lots of pottery, wood carvings, weavings, leather, other things from the local craftsmen. Comfortable place. I figured I'd hammer her out something nice to add to her collection.

That thought sort of made me wonder if each of those goodies might have been the gift of another man from her past, but hey, I wasn't going there...her business. Woman that good-looking hadn't been a recluse, I was sure.

She was a great cook, and had me over to feed me a lot, without a doubt the way to this old man's heart, under my bachelor circumstances. In a way, it seemed it just didn't get any better than this. Any way I looked at it, I could get to liking this relationship a lot, settle into it. Maybe even for the long term, if that description could fit a man in my position.

But it was also like waiting for the other shoe to drop.

Like I said, things gotta change.

Eighteen

When I let myself think about it, I recognized that Jocelyn was one of two possibilities: she could be the right woman for me, discovered this back-door way. The woman worth my coming out of my cave for, to share with, spend whatever was left of my life with. Could be. Or, she could be a (pleasant) obstacle on my road back to accepting responsibility again, doing what I'd been coming around to believing was right. Maybe what Bill Zachman had said about a test of my faith, even.

Didn't know which. I never had much insight, obviously. And I'd proved I sure was at sea when it came to figuring out women. What's the old joke? If a man thinks for one minute he understands a woman, that's about the right duration of that insight.

Or maybe I was thinking too much. That's how I finally resolved it—by not resolving it. I enjoyed being with her, and that was just gonna have to be enough for now. No precipitous action, no doing something, even if it was wrong.

Now like I mentioned, folks at the church, neighbors, had already tried to fix me up with first one lone woman, then another. Sharon's showing up Christmas sort of put a chock to that, though. Even with the curiosity and outright prying that matchmakers seem to have, the well-meaning busybodies here didn't know yet just what my real situation was. Jim and Kelly apparently hadn't enlightened anybody, either.

Fine with me.

I'd always made sure they were included when I couldn't dodge an invitation somewhere that looked like a setup. It'd worked, so far. Turn it into a group thing, and I could get lost in the shuffle, so to speak.

Anyway, here was Jocelyn, fine woman, and sooner or later something was gonna happen. So, let it. Never been very patient, but I was learning. Busted leg'll do that for you.

I remembered a woman we'd done construction work for some years back. Early fifties, couple years older'n Jocelyn. Had this guy, 67 I believe he was, steady boyfriend. About the same year spread as we are, now. Anyway, those two went places together, fed each other, put up with each other's quirks, needs. But gave each other a lotta space. And apparently that'd been workable. They had enough things in common to be comfortable around each other, but they sure had their own lives.

We could probably get that way, if I was wrong about Jocelyn's wanting more from the relationship. Maybe I was.

See about that.

But she did want to know all about Kyle and Sarah, and was excited about their plans for the upcoming wedding. And she wanted to meet June, and of course Jim and Kelly.

So, how'd I handle this? Show her off as my new woman, alienate at least half my family—the Sharon camp? Or keep slipping around like we were, or rather, like I was.

No, I guessed we'd have to come to some understanding between us. And that sounded a lot like "Am I in or out?" Or was I overreacting? Maybe so. Maybe fantasizing, too, given my age and the real picture. Whatever that was. What *was* reality, here? Sometimes I felt I was living a dreamed adventure, and that I'd wake up, and find myself back in Virginia, back on the job, back treading treacherous water.

Therapy was over now, in late October. Leg was still a little weak and ached some, but it was so much better, I could take it. I was supposed to keep up the stretches and exercises on my own, and Jocelyn would give me the third degree about that if she suspected I'd cheated.

"I want you back, tougher than you were. Your heart's good, so you could be running up that trail a half-dozen times a day." She was only half-kidding, too. But I wasn't about to try to be somebody's idea of a marathon runner. My life had me doing more than guys half my age, just routine daily chores. Forget the macho stuff.

I tried to help Jim often, and Eric, when he was home. Among us, we had more to do than we'd ever get to. And I got in on a few work days the church was into again, fixing up substandard houses, helping poor folks. Couldn't do the heavy stuff, but there was a lot a guy in my shape could handle. This work was simple, compared to the demanding restoration projects that'd been my specialty for a generation. Two-by-fours, plywood, drywall, paint—no-brainers.

My life was all right again. Really. I'd put Sharon on the back shelf of my mind, more or less successfully. Wasn't looking over my shoulder while I worked, smirking anymore. And not in any nightmares lately, either. Thankful for that, really. And I guess most of that was Jocelyn.

Well, of course it was. *Face reality, here.*

Sharon had written, urging me to go to Michigan with her to meet Sarah's people. I'd put her off with a vague reference to work I had to finish before fall. I expected her to insist, get pushy, even angry. Surprised me when she didn't. Guess she was sort of tiptoeing around any confrontation. Not like the Sharon I knew, for sure. And her being almost nice about it made me feel guilty, under the present circumstances.

But I managed to put off dealing with that, too. Really, things were in a sort of suspension during this time, with my hide-and-watch behavior. Complicated, along with my feeling needed and useful and I guess, being relatively happy with the way things were.

About happy. I'd found that when there wasn't a major hassle, that seemed to constitute happiness. And there were always the delightful little happenings, like Kyle's engagement, or the birth of a new grandchild, that made you realize this was as good as it was gonna get. In this life. Next one was a riddle, of course.

The only thing that made my relationship with Jocelyn seem... incomplete I guess, was her not sharing the faith I'd found. She just wasn't interested in hearing or talking about God, or coming to church with me. It was just a facet of things that wasn't going to be there. I thought about that a lot. And it did get to be more important. I reflected on Paul's "unequally yoked" admonition in Corinthians. But of course, we weren't yoked at all.

No, we weren't. Walk away from this—her—anytime I wanted, with nothing more than a smile.

Couldn't I?

~ * ~

But I couldn't keep Jocelyn a secret from my brother and Kelly. They saw me driving out more often, and must know I was into something, now therapy was over. Didn't pry...they weren't like that, but I did catch a raised eyebrow now and then.

And sure enough, we ran into them at lunch one day in Branson. Had to happen...just a matter of time and the inevitable odds. After all, Jim had those friends there he played music with, and they'd get together to jam odd times. And Kelly had worked at the hospital so long, she kept up with some of the folks there.

So then, we're at this favorite homestyle eatery off the main tourist drag well into fall, after the traffic slacks off, when Jim and Kelly come in. It's midweek, not my usual day to do my minimal shopping, so they're sort of surprised to see me—us.

I do the intros, hoping my guilt doesn't show too much, explaining that Jocelyn's my therapist. They know the schedule, (that's all over now) so things click, of course. I see Kelly getting the picture right off, the way women always do, though Jim may not be. But I'm cool, and so is Jocelyn. She's wanted to meet them anyway, like I said. We make room at the table, and proceed to visit like old friends. Jim's checking Jocelyn out, I see, so he's on board now with the relationship.

Only, what *is* the relationship? Guy my age, younger woman, sure. But she's no kid, either. Friends, just happen to be of the opposite sexes. Shouldn't be a big deal, and I can let it go at that. Or at least I keep telling myself I can. But I know Jim and Kelly won't. Sharon's been too big a factor for too long, and I sense repercussions on the way. Fat's in the fire now, and I'll just have to wait to see how far the splatters reach.

Jocelyn lets it out that she's been to see me, of course, and I handle that casually. Kelly's eyebrow goes up a bit, and I know she's feeling left out. Okay, not a big deal. I didn't consciously exclude them—or did I? Doesn't matter, because my sister-in-law does the gracious thing and invites Jocelyn out again. She accepts, for Saturday. They go on to girl talk, while Jim and I talk tires. I'd come in on my spare, ostensibly to replace a tire cut on a sharp ledge rock, and he knows the best dealers.

Afterwards, after Jocelyn has left to go back to work, no quick kiss, no touch at all, I get the not-unexpected eye from both of them. And hey, I guess I deserve it, right?

"Been busy, bro?" Jim puts an arm around my shoulders, grins. He's got it all worked out in his head, it seems.

"Yeah, Liam. Keeping secrets." Kelly shakes a finger at me in mock irritation. But she's grinning, too. So maybe I *haven't* shot myself down with my favorite contemporary relatives. Yet.

"Hey, I've been pushed and pulled and prodded by that woman most of the summer. Sure we're friends. She just happens to be a woman. Bill Zachman's a friend, too. He's a man." (I go back to that rationalization I've been using on myself in weak moments. Doesn't work here, either.) "Any reason for us not to be?"

"'Course not." She turns up a palm. "We're just so used to your being a hermit, down in your hole, you surprised us."

"Seems okay," Jim puts in. "Strong-looking girl." That's not what he really means obviously, being a guy, but I guess maybe he's trying to be non-judgmental.

"Cute, too." Kelly cocks an eye at me. *Yeah, cute. And of course, that's the biggie.* How shallow that is, really. If she were mud-ugly, nobody'd think a thing about it.

But she's not.

It is a sort of relief, though, to get our whatever-it-is out in the open. Question now is what about Kyle and Sarah, and June? The next shocks. I expect at least Kyle to come visit again soon. How will the kids take another woman in the picture?

Doesn't matter, I rationalize again. *I made the big break a year and a half ago. Die was cast, back then. Life just playing itself out, is all. They'll just have to accept it. No big betrayal here.*

I kept telling myself that, over and over.

But why did I feel that's just what Jocelyn was? A betrayal. Sure, I'd been on my way to maybe trying to do the right thing, see if Sharon and I could try again, get it right this time. But that was before. And so, was Jocelyn just new and different, or was she really right for me? I should know those things by now, if I ever would.

But, same old question.

Didn't know the answer. Time would tell, I guessed. Only I knew it'd just be a matter of that same time till Sharon found out—bound to happen—and then it'd get sticky. Well, just have to let that happen, then. Pick up the mangled pieces when they broke.

But there was still this guilt. I was having most of the trouble reconciling Jocelyn with my beliefs, and not just because she wasn't with me on that. Didn't know how much that'd weigh in the long run, but it was important. Couldn't serve two masters, as Jesus had said.

No, with any objectivity at all, it looked to anyone else like I'd just dumped my wife for another woman. Sure, that year and a half later, but aside from that timing, I was…well, having trouble with that, along with what everyone else would think.

As if that should matter.

And if it's giving me a hard time, I thought, *there must be something behind it. Something maybe wrong.* But I wasn't about to toss this relationship, without a clearer picture of it all.

No.

~ * ~

Fall, already. A year and a half, and still no resolution—I've said that before—for Liam and me. Is it really all over? I've denied it all along, but maybe some of that was pride. Like how dare that old man leave me after all we've shared. Can't deny it much longer, I guess.

Well, maybe it's just wearing itself out with time. I'm not angry now, at least. Disappointed yes, and a little sad about it all. But seems like it is over between us. He wouldn't go with me to meet Sarah's family, like he's written us all off. No, he'll always be close to Kyle, and he likes her. And the girls—June at least—seem to be right there in his camp.

Won't be long till the wedding, and I'm sure he'll go to that. See him again then, after a year. Probably won't change anything, though. Stubborn old fool.

Wonder what he thinks about my going to church, getting involved in that? Wasn't just something to fill my life, another set of obligations. Or was it? No, I really think I'm getting a lot out of that. Supposed to be the real thing—real life—to take the place of all the materialistic rat race.

Could this possibly be part of God's plan for me—us? Did it take this jolt to make us both see what's real? Have to think about that some, now. And if it's true, we've both done our penance... time to get back together. Can he see that? Can I, really?

Yeah, lots to think about in all this.

~ * ~

Kyle and Sarah didn't get down again that fall. Neither did June. Too busy, all of them. The season slid by, the first of November golden and dry, nippy nights reminding me of the cold to come. Late fall this year, and the days were still mostly full of sun, the last of the leaves scarlet and gold against that incredible sky, the air winey. My favorite time of year, always has been.

I cut a lot of firewood again, smelling the tangy, moist sawdust from the oak and hickory, feeling the sun on my back. Leg ached some, and a little weak, surprising me sometimes when I'd put sudden weight on it and get the feeling it'd buckle. Never actually let me down, because I was always extra careful. Always sort of looking for a place to land if it did give way, the way you will after a fall.

Jocelyn and I hiked a little despite the leg, fished, camped out. Jim and Kelly joined us now and then for a movie or dinner. We all got along well enough, although I suspected Kelly, at least, didn't entirely approve. She hadn't let on to Sharon, though, I was sure. Loyal, that woman, even in this conflicted situation.

There was this night, just Jocelyn and me, on Beaver Creek, the water slipping past quietly among the stones, low from no rain. The campfire was mostly embers, glowing our faces ruddy, an almost-chill between our shoulder blades. We'd roasted ears of corn not too far past their prime, potatoes, grilled perch we'd caught, made hush puppies.

Now stuffed, quiet, we lay back, gazed up at the universe's brightest stars, breathed the cleanest air on the planet. I found her hand in mine—not the first time—warm, sweet. After a while she turned to me.

"I love this, Liam. Do you realize there's not another soul for miles but us? It's like this, all this, is just for you and me. Nobody—nothing—else matters. You feel that?"

"How could I not? It's almost too much to take in, girl. As if we could shatter it all with just a wrong word, something that'd wake us up, jolt us back into the real world."

"Yeah. Let's don't let it." She pressed my hand to her cheek, turned those eyes on mine, the firelight flecking them. She was sure one fine-looking woman, and there was no way I wasn't going to react to her.

I kissed her then, lightly at first, then really. She responded, pulled me to her. I had just time to reflect that this was our first kiss, when she did it again. I felt a stirring I hadn't experienced in a long, long time.

After a time of very nice hugging, while the campfire died down, we stood, moved to the tent. This would be our first night together. I was nervous, and I could tell she was, too. Sort of like a couple of teenagers discovering each other, maybe a generation and a half later.

We fussed around then, with tooth-brushing, excusing ourselves to the brush, washing in the creek. Finally, we shucked boots and slid into our respective sleeping bags. By accident or design, the zippered openings faced each other.

And they weren't zipped.

"Keep me warm?" she asked, reaching across, kissing me lightly. *Oh boy, here it comes.*

"Actually, I had considered that." I moved to her.

But this wasn't right somehow, even with the kissing, and our arms around each other. Sure, we were two mature people who liked each other a lot, and here we were, alone in a setting that was nothing if not romantic. Nobody to answer to, have to justify ourselves to...

Well, almost nobody. I nestled her head against my neck and shoulder and thought about that. Only the scent of her hair kept intruding. It'd be so easy to let my hands explore, move over that firm body, grow hot with desire.

But I didn't. First of all, we weren't ready for intimacy. Or if we were, it'd change everything. I didn't think we could give ourselves lightly: I knew I couldn't. It'd mean a big commitment. And maybe that was what I was afraid of really, what I wanted to avoid.

As a younger man, I knew I'd have tossed any reservations, gone for it. Not now. I wasn't ready for everything to change. And yeah, there were these principles I'd acquired.

And The Man to answer to...

So we didn't take it any further, just relaxed together, comfortably drifting off in a secure sort of way, aware of each other's closeness, warmth, but...well, friends.

That.

~ * ~

But by late November, as the wedding got closer, I faced the obvious fact that Jocelyn would be a complication if I included her. It'd be up in Michigan, snow all over, everybody shut up indoors in each other's faces. I was pretty sure Sharon wouldn't be able to handle that well at all.

No-brainer.

"So that's the size of it," I told Jocelyn. "You've said you wanted to meet my family, but I don't think that's the time for it. Get awkward, and Kyle and Sarah don't need that, with this the big event in their lives."

"I see." She was quiet for a while, and I could sense her maybe thinking she was being shut out, like I was ashamed of her? After all, I'd avoided Jim and Kelly till it'd happened by accident. And now she'd be alone back here while I was up there with Sharon.

I didn't really know what was going through her mind, of course. I put another log in my stove, a stew on it bubbling in its pot, giving off good smells. My biscuits were baking in the Dutch oven, and the tiny room was cozy. She absently fondled Boswell's ears as the gears were turning in her head.

"Well, I certainly didn't plan to push myself onto anyone," she began. "It'll be a really great thing for your family, and no, I don't really belong, do I? I mean, not even as a friend, if it'll be... embarrassing."

I felt about an inch tall at that. What'd I gotten myself into, here? I searched for the right words, if there could be right words.

"Put it this way: *I'll* be the embarrassment there, Jocelyn. My daughter Melissa will barely tolerate me, Sarah's folks will probably see me as a sort of outcast, and I have no idea whatsoever what Sharon will say, or do. It'll be dicey as it is. The only thing that'd make it worse is if I don't go at all.

"I'd love to have you come with me. Yeah, show you off, if you can believe that. You know by now that I think a lot of you, lady. I just can't see dropping a bomb on my son's wedding...won't do that." I picked up another stick of firewood. *No, just did that...*

"It's okay, Liam. Really. I just hadn't thought it through before now. We've sort of let things go on of their own accord between us, and it's been great. It has. No room for—no need for—complications. I'm okay with that. I like being with you, you know that, too. But no, let's not do anything to muddy the water."

She stood, and for a second, I thought she was just barely keeping the lid on, that she'd storm out the door and that'd be that. Wouldn't really have surprised me. But no, she lifted the lid on the stew pot, stirred it, checked on the biscuits.

Good. She wouldn't lose it. That was really important to me, just then. I put Boswell out so he wouldn't beg with those soulful eyes. He made me feel guilty when I ate and he didn't.

We went to work on that stew. I don't have a recipe for it; it's never the same twice. And my biscuits are big and solid. Never liked light, airy biscuits. Sharon always said if we couldn't eat 'em, we could build walls with 'em. Funny though, when the kids would come home, they'd always ask me to cook stew and biscuits. Nice memory.

From that night at the creek on, I'd sensed a subtle difference in my relationship with Jocelyn. Nothing overt, just a touch of distance between us. And I guess it was mutual, a little, even if I found that hard to believe about my feelings.

And that about her not sharing my faith was really getting to me. Hey, I was sure by now that my one-on-one with God that'd come home under that rock that time was more important than any friendship. Or even my family, although I wasn't quite as sure about that. Yet. But if Jocelyn couldn't accept my God, maybe this wasn't really the right woman. Not like she was asking me to accept hers either, though. Somebody once said atheism is a god, too.

We still did stuff together, next couple weeks. Seen objectively, I guess each of us was just the best thing that'd come along, even if he/she wasn't the ideal. Funny that, my being anybody's ideal, at my age. Well, going on with seeing each other the way we were sure beat staying at home painting our aging toenails.

Or maybe I was making too big a deal about this whole thing. Maybe. My sister Nan had mentioned that I seemed to refer to my age entirely too much, build it into every equation. She was older, after all.

Jocelyn and I never crossed the line that'd been drawn that night on the creek. Never got that close again, quite. She'd probably felt rejected that time, and maybe did now, too. I hoped not. Maybe she figured I wasn't capable of sex anymore. Didn't matter, that. Not something to get into at all, with her or any other woman, except maybe Sharon, if and when our circuitous non-relationship wound up going that way.

Bottom line: I just wasn't going there.

Maybe I'd built in an escape, the way I remembered doing with girls I'd gone with before Sharon. With what seemed to be the wrong relationship developing, I'd subconsciously plant red flags—stumbling blocks really—to push us apart before things went very far down that bumpy road. Was I doing that now? Couldn't tell.

Did I mention I never had a lot of insight?

Nineteen

The wedding was going to be a logistical big deal. The sisters and Sharon were flying in from L.A. and Denver and Virginia to Lansing. Jim and Kelly were going to drive the Cherokee, so I'd ride with them. Kyle had some friends from work and from college who'd make it, and of course Sarah's kin and friends and fellow workers planned to converge in swarms.

I'd been saving up for the trip for a while, and had bought some fairly decent clothes. Jocelyn had gone with me to help pick them out, sure I'd put my foot in it if left unsupervised. Probably would have. She seemed all right with everything, so I was, too. See how it all played out afterwards.

I hadn't made up my mind whether to tell the family about her. Wouldn't till afterwards, if at all. And the accident? Okay, I could tell them about that, I guessed, now I was literally back on my feet.

So after leaving Boswell with Eric, we made the trip north, into already-winter. I'd always thought of Michigan as pretty much ice-bound, being from the mid-south. Didn't know just what to expect, but was glad I didn't live there.

That had been reinforced by the report of some folks I'd met who'd told me they'd had to ski out to their vacation cabin on the Northern Neck one Thanksgiving. Roads were all snowed under, and they'd only been able to locate their place by the chimney, the only thing showing above the drifts. Had to dig down to get in. Did not want that for myself, thanks.

Once there, Sarah's folks—the Coopers—solved the awkwardness of Sharon and me by putting her and the girls up in a guest house they had on their place. Not plush, but suitably upscale. Kyle and I got a motel room they insisted on paying for. No problem with that, in my financial state. Jim and Kelly were right next door.

My boy wasn't obviously nervous about this monumental change in his life, and neither was Sarah. They were two really self-assured people, and I was proud of them both. They were like anchors in a storm, with Lily Cooper racing around, marshaling the details of her daughter's big day and everybody talking at once. Getting in each other's way. Seth, the father, beamed a lot, slapped backs, talked too loud and too often. *Well, only daughter and all, this is their big thing.*

My daughter Melissa had come by herself, leaving her Grady with the two kids and whatever he did for a living with computers. I had a few minutes with her alone before Sharon and June showed. Hadn't seen this child in two years. Or was it three, now?

"Well, Dad, how's the hermit?" She was thirty already, and beginning to look like more than the fresh-faced schoolgirl she'd always been. She gave me a hug that was a little tentative.

"Okay, I guess. Missed you. Too much to bring the kids, I guess?"

"I could have, but I really needed to get some time for myself. I don't know where the last five years have gone."

"You look great. Grady doing all right?"

"Works all the time. I do the supermom thing, and we wave when we pass each other. But what about you? The word I get is that you stay holed up on Caney Creek and run visitors off with your shotgun." She actually grinned. *So okay, maybe this means she's getting past the pariah thing.*

"Not true: I use a revolver. No, I've just geared down, is all. I don't expect any of you to understand it. Not sure I do, myself. Just something I had to do."

"Yeah, well. Mom's getting used to the...situation, I guess, but she still doesn't like it. You were pretty rough on her."

"Seemed the best way to handle it at the time. Probably wasn't. Oh, here they come." June and Sharon hugged Lily Cooper, then spotted us. Sharon, another year older, had definite gray now. June looked the same.

"Hey, old man." My wife gave me a peck on the cheek. June hugged me, hard. "You seem to be in one piece." She was sizing me up. June turned to Melissa.

"I'm good. You look great, too." Awkward pause. "House okay?" It was all I could think of to ask.

"The house? Sure. You built it, you know. You build good."

"Well, old age gets to everything, eventually. And all that room, I figured you'd maybe sell it, get something smaller."

"No plans for that. It's there and waiting if and when *you* want it." Meaningful look.

"That's nice. Really. You're a patient woman, Sharon."

"Need that, with you around. And even when you aren't. I realize that hasn't been one of my better characteristics."

"Yeah. Well, I don't have to tell you this I know, but let's be clear on keeping our differences out of the kids' wedding, okay?"

"Hey, I'm no monster, Liam. I plan to enjoy the big event, not screw it up. You behave and I'll behave."

"Deal. Melissa looks good. All grown up."

"They all are. Oh, did June tell you she's landed a directing job in New York?"

"No! I haven't heard from her in a while." I butted into her conversation at a pause. "Hey, girl, what's this I hear about New York?"

"Oh, I was gonna write you, Dad, but thought I'd wait till we were here. Just a one-shot thing, and I'll be co-directing with this L.A. guy. His connections. Not that big a deal." Shrug.

"Sounds like a break to me. Making the switch from acting?"

"Not really. I'll take whatever comes down the pike. Beats waiting tables." No, she didn't look the same. More...seasoned, maybe. She was 28 now. Grown up, for sure.

That night was the rehearsal dinner at the Coopers' big house, and everybody scurried around, laughing, joking. Seth Cooper's big voice rose above the hubbub at almost predictable intervals. Jack, Sarah's younger brother, teased Kyle about his supposedly domineering sister.

"...Try to run you like a clock, or a toy train," he was saying. Poking fun, really. And I didn't think so; looked like a real team to me. And what's a barely-past-adolescence kid-brother know, anyway?

It would have been easy to feel like odd-man-out here, the country cousin, poor relation. I was out of my element in this place, all this snow, accents I couldn't always follow. The talk among the men kept coming back to business, like it always does when we congregate. Seth was in insurance, in my jaded opinion about the least useful occupation a man could have. I was afraid he'd try to sell me some. *But cut him some slack here, old man; these are the new in-laws.*

At dinner, Kyle's boss, a young guy with a crewcut, gave a toast to his favorite employees. Other toasts followed. Laughter, good cheer all around. Impossible not to get caught up in it. Sharon was having a great time, and our girls, too. And if I wasn't exactly the life of the party, neither was I a wet blanket. I did catch Lily Cooper eyeing me curiously at least twice, but I guessed that'd be my own reaction if our roles had been reversed.

It failed to unnerve me.

Afterwards, Jim got out his guitar, and with most of the crowd, sang every song anybody knew. He and Sarah did a couple of incredible duets, and I saw tears in both Sharon's and Lily's eyes. It struck me that mothers are pretty special people: it's tough for a father to let a kid go, but he hasn't conceived, carried, delivered, nourished the child. I guessed that, short of heaven, the mother/child relationship was as holy as it's going to get.

"Penny?" Kelly poked my arm.

"Oh, just thinking how...special you moms are. You give the kids everything for so long, then you just have to step back and let them go. Gotta be hard."

"Sometimes it's a relief. But you're right, it's pretty poignant, in the middle of all the celebration. Jim cried at both our kids' weddings. Don't tell him I told you that."

"He's always been the sensitive one in the family. But it's great to see the next generation getting their feet on the ground, striking out, taking over. Give us a rest."

"I've never seen you rest, Liam. You almost burned those crutches up. Slow down and you'd die."

"Maybe." Needed another subject here, besides the old man of the piece. "Sharon's loving this."

"She is. Your girls, too. And Kyle's managing not to be too bewildered by it all."

"It'll all hit him, after it's over. He did good."

"Did. She's good for him. Great girl." She looked at me oddly for a space, and I knew there were wheels turning in her head. I didn't know where this was going, because it hadn't started yet.

"So," she finally got to it. "You think you and Sharon might... work out something? Not that it's any of my business, but...or is there this complication now?" She was nervous, bringing Jocelyn up, but she was doing it anyway. Must've had a little to drink.

"Oh, I dunno. We've declared a truce, at least. Maybe we'll talk some. Depends. I've had a lot of time to think what's right for us. Never far from my mind, really. I was so sure she'd divorce me, clear the air that way, simplify everything."

"You should know her better than that. What, thirty-three years? Thirty-four?" *Yeah, Kelly's had something to drink, all right.*

"Got to thinking I didn't know her at all, Kelly. Just seemed like nothing left between us but friction, hassles."

"She sure thinks there is. Worries about you all the time."

"Maybe. That's why I didn't want her to know about the accident, of course. She'd have gone ballistic."

"Bet you dollars to...rocks, she would've dropped everything to race out to take care of you."

"I was afraid she'd wanta drag me back to Virginia."

"Had it occurred to you that taking care of you might be the important thing, no matter where it happened?"

She wasn't going to leave this alone. We were in a corner by ourselves, away from the crowd. I'd found an easy chair, and she was on one of those carved oak ones with a brocaded seat. She was leaning forward, and I could see the minute flaws in the carving over her shoulder, where dogwood flower petals weren't quite smooth. I thought fleetingly of the mountain ladies who made quilts, and always left an obvious flaw in each one, because only God makes things perfect.

"Look, I wasn't about to dump myself on her, after the way I'd...well, dumped her already. Couldn't have asked that of her. Or anybody."

"Sometimes it's harder to be forgiven than it is to forgive. I hear that's pride, Liam. When are you gonna *lose* that?"

Everyone applauded as another song ended, and I had to decide how much further I wanted to let this go. Problem was, it was just about impossible to take offense at Kelly, whether she'd had a drink too much or not...that kind of person.

"Guilty. But I'd decided first to get mobile again, Kelly, just so I *wouldn't* be a drag, so the playing field would be level again, then my plan was to try to make it work. Again. I had no idea how to start, or what I'd find, a year and a half later. And I still don't, so I haven't." I spread my hands.

"Only now there's this complication named Jocelyn, who in case you haven't noticed, also thinks a hell of a lot of you."

"Jocelyn's okay. Jocelyn's a friend, happens to be a woman. And she doesn't represent ongoing domestic warfare. At least not yet..."

"But she won't be happy just letting things drift along. Women don't *do* that, Liam. She'll want some sort of resolution."

"Hey, she and I're not kids here, Kelly. No hormone-driven passion out of a B-grade movie. I'm seventy-one..."

"And you don't have a *clue* what's in either of those women's heads, brother of mine. All I'm saying, in my nosy way, is that now's a good time to find out, with one of them." She raised a finger, before taking another sip from her glass. She looked severe, or tried to.

Neither of us had noticed when some of the guests pushed furniture back, opening room to dance. Someone was at the piano, and an electric bass appeared. Another guitar. A lively tune I didn't know started, and Kyle and Sarah were pushed onto the floor. Hands started clapping the time as they danced.

A great-looking pair. I thought as I had before, that this world would be in pretty good hands with young people like this in it, taking over from our worn-out generation. Great feeling.

The music ended to a thunder of applause, then started up again, slow. I saw Lily Cooper take Seth's hand and lead him out.

"Get your butt moving, Liam," Kelly hissed, nudging me. I looked across and saw Sharon watching me. Now why did I feel I'd been set up? But what the heck, we were the parents. This probably wouldn't kill me.

I stood with just a twinge in my bad leg, my eyes on my wife, and we threaded our way toward each other. I saw Melissa's hand go to her mouth, and I knew Kyle and June were grinning.

Sharon had always loved to dance, but I was never good at it. Another difference. We touched hands, though, and that seemed as natural as breathing. We moved together. Other couples joined us. Kyle and Sarah floated near, and she gave me the biggest smile in Michigan.

It was okay then, for a few minutes. No, it was better than okay. Holding my wife actually felt good, felt *right*. I was thinking this could...

I came down on the bad leg, in a sort of twist. It gave a little, and the ache I'd gotten used to became a sharp stab of pain. I stumbled, and Sharon saw my face. She grabbed for me as I went down.

"Liam, what's wrong?" as I felt Kyle's arm suddenly clamping me, too. Things weren't stable in my vision, which meant I'd fallen, at least part of the way. They got me vertical again, and I put a little weight on the leg. *Ouch.* Man, was *that* stupid! Kyle helped me to a corner couch.

"Easy, Dad. Mom, his leg's *broken!* Sit over here, Dad..."

"I'm okay. Just a little twist, wrong way." But I sat, giving a little wave to some of the others who'd seen. Sharon sat beside me. She looked scared.

"Liam, what...?"

"It's okay. I..." Confession time, I guessed. "Okay, I hurt the leg a while back. Haven't pushed it much. Not out clogging lately. I did something wrong out there, is all. Be all right." I was getting my breath back.

"You never told me about that! Kyle said it was *broken?* You *broke your leg?*" She drilled me with her eyes. "Tell me, now."

"Hey, it can wait. This is a wedding. Our *son's* wedding. My leg's history."

"Oh, and you down in that godforsaken hole by yourself!" Hand to her mouth.

"That 'hole' is my home, Sharon. I *live* there."

"Not anymore, you don't. You're coming *home* with me, Liam. If you think I'll let you stagger around on the ice this winter, you're *really* crazy."

I held up a hand, cutting off her fierce whisper. This had the potential of a train wreck, and I wasn't gonna let that happen.

"We'll talk about it later, Sharon. *Later.* Right now, I wanta enjoy this." I turned away from her, focusing on the dancers. The music was fast, again. I started clapping time, only partly to get my mind off the pain.

She gave me a long, questioning look, then shook her head, pursed her lips, and clapped, too. The pain lessened, but I needed aspirin, at least. I asked her if she could find some. She left. Kyle and Sarah came back.

"You okay, Dad? Sorry I spilled it about the leg."

"No, it's okay. I'd have told her. Thought it was better than it is. She's gone for aspirin."

"I'll show her." Sarah gave me a quick kiss, left. Kyle sat.

"How's it been, since we saw you?"

"Healed okay. Had a lotta therapy on it. Shouldn't have buckled like that. I've been hiking a little, cutting wood. Been good. Just a crazy twist, there. Hermits don't dance much." Grin.

Well, twisted grin.

"No. Hey, you gotta know how great it was, you two together out there. I thought June was gonna cry."

"Well, your mom and I are both really happy about you and Sarah, so we're together on that, at least. You did good, son." I squeezed his arm.

Sharon brought me some of those fast-acting big-dose painkillers and I slugged a couple. Then she wanted to hear all about this accident, but I put her off, promised I'd tell her later. For now, I said, let's enjoy this. I caught Jim's eye, dancing with Kelly. The music was ending. I got myself an idea, motioned them over.

"Bro, this lady isn't having any fun. Now, you two are the best dancers in the world, so please go do it. I'm sidelined."

Jim bowed, took Sharon's hand. She gave me a look, rolled her eyes a little, but rose, smiled her thanks to them both.

"Now we'll see some dancing." Kelly grinned. "Hey, I saw you stumble. How bad is it?"

"Not that bad, really. Doc said there was some sort of webbing between the bones that'd take a long time to heal. Must've twisted it or something, I guess. Hey, look at that."

Jim had whispered to the piano player and the guy who now had his guitar. They'd started a wild beat—some bluegrass thing—and my brother's feet were flying. Sharon's too, and I remembered these two at dances back when we were all living in the woods and dirt-poor. Somebody'd have us all to his cabin somewhere, eat, drink, get out the instruments and dance. Often on the bare ground around a bonfire. Seemed like in another life now, but this was taking me back.

Our daughters knew this stuff. Sarah's brother Jack asked Melissa, and I saw Kyle's crewcut boss take June's hand. *Okay, now: Appalachia and the Ozarks, folks! You'll see some heels kickin' up.*

Everybody was having a ball. The girls were showing their partners the steps, and they were getting it. Sharon and Jim were flying, punishing that floor. The rest of us were clapping time, which seemed to keep getting faster. Kelly leaned over.

"Sharon's heart okay? Dances like a kid."

"I guess so. She's never sick. And Jim, wow. Hard to believe my little brother's sixty-six."

"Won't admit it." Pause. "So how's it going with Sharon? Saw she was grilling you."

"No time to tell, yet. She wants to know all about the accident, of course. Did say she wants to take me back to Virginia, which was to be expected, I guess. We'll talk."

"Good." She squeezed my hand. "Maybe time to rethink the caveman role, Liam."

Wouldn't this good woman ever shut up about this? Like I said, I couldn't put her down...all concern for me, and yeah, for everybody she found who was hurting. But just now I felt the old out-of-control thing setting in. Like events were shaping me, instead of the other way around. Maybe it's been obvious I don't react to that well.

So, how to handle this, without going all defensive, throwing a mild temper tantrum? Well, I guessed in my new awareness of myself as *not* the center of the universe, as Jim had said, I could—should— just ease back and let this all happen the way it was supposed to. Not easy for a caveman.

"Yeah. Well, we'll see," I told her.

Maybe it would be.

~ * ~

Jocelyn couldn't get her mind on her work, there in the therapy section of the hospital. She'd made peace with being left out of Liam's family thing...wedding wasn't the place for her, the outsider in all this, after all.

But I've made him the center of my life these months past. Probably a dumb thing to do. He's not really free. And now he's up there with Sharon, in what's probably a very happy situation. Okay, I don't have a claim on him, and yeah, the whole idea's been crazy.

He's seventy-one, girl. What makes you think you could have a life with him? Maybe a few years, sure. Sharing, being there for each other. Both of us really lonely, and so it just happened...no plan. And neither of us fought it, backed off from it.

He's a man of principle, and long as he's married to her, he's not gonna violate that. Religious, too, and that seems to be a bigger thing than I thought. Never gotten in the way before.

Her hands worked the knot out of the patient's back without thought...old habit. She was outwardly cool, in control. But something Liam had said one time came back, a Bible quote: *A warring in my flesh*, was what one of those old guys had said, meaning a futility of control, she guessed. Yeah, that was her now, although Liam had meant it about himself. She'd taken it to mean his ambivalence about Sharon, but realized it could've been about her, too.

I know he likes me a lot, maybe even loves me. And I've tried to analyze my feelings, too. I've never had a relationship like this before: no sex, but not just friends, either. We agreed just to let it move along at its own pace, and it has, but to where? What do we have, really? Good times together, sure. Is that all it can be? And is that enough?

This week will tell us everything; I feel it in my bones. And I'm not sure I want to know which way it'll go just yet. On pins and needles, though. Am I in or out? Know soon enough.

She was telling the patient how to continue the treatment at home: keep up the exercises, build the right muscles, lean on the tennis ball to ease that tight pain just inside the shoulder blade. And sure, she'd see him again Tuesday. "Bye, now." The automatic smile, but with the sudden realization that she couldn't remember this man's name.

Twenty

The wedding was really fine. The minister gave a charge to the couple, in which he admonished them to touch often, even just in passing, to hold hands for the rest of their lives, and to find refuge in each other from the pressures they'd face. Nice. These kids would make it, I was sure. I sat next to Sharon, with June and Melissa, who kept grinning at us, like they were schoolgirls.

Conspirators.

The reception was fun, too, with toasts and well-wishing by the crewcut boss Ken, who was best man. June told me he was single, another engineer. Okay...she'd always checked out the boys.

There were Mexican musicians, way up here in Michigan, for some reason, but they were good. Several of Sarah's friends gave tributes, and Seth Cooper gave his daughter a heartfelt sendoff. Lily tried not to cry, didn't make it.

Then they were away to the airport, headed for Hawaii. Nice change from all this snow. Sharon's eyes were wet from Sarah's and Kyle's hugs. She squeezed my hand, used a tissue.

Packed couple of days, but now it all started being over. Melissa had to fly back to Denver to salvage her family, but June was spending Christmas with Sharon in Virginia, so they were booked on a flight there tomorrow. One of those you had to arrange months in advance to avoid bankruptcy. Jim, Kelly and I would leave in the morning for the long drive south. Maybe outta this iced-in world.

"Okay, Liam, now we talk," my wife announced after June had left with Ken and Jack and others for a party they'd drummed up. "And I canceled your room at the motel. Plenty room here." Here, was the guest house. And okay, no way to put anything off. I didn't think ahead to sleeping arrangements.

So she sat me down, up there in snowbound Michigan, and told me what amounted to her side of it all. How she'd dealt with the whole menopause thing by taking on all the civic stuff, filling her days with work and meetings and committees even before the children had left home.

"I got caught up in all that, Liam, when I should have been spending more time at home with you and the kids. I felt like I was finding a life beyond soccer practice and orthodontists' appointments and dirty dishes. You were always working, and I figured I could do that, too. And yeah, you did take them places, go to games, make time for them. But I felt like that was no more than your responsibility, share. We did that.

"And then they were gone. Out the door to college, and from then on, it was only visiting, and only when they felt like it. It's hard to realize that after you give them so much, they're just *gone*. Eighteen, and they're outta there. So, empty-nester, I piled it on. And I guess really neglected you. But I'm just now seeing that. It was okay, I told myself, because you were filling what I realize now was the same void, with more work. Taking on those distant jobs, being gone, coming home dead tired.

"I know you missed the girls, but you missed Kyle most. And he was suddenly off to college one minute and in Chicago the next, with a degree and a job. And a life.

"And even with my work, committees, business and all, I was frustrated as hell. It wasn't working, you see? The political stuff? They were just using me—all of us. Get the candidate elected, then we were history. Volunteers are great, but we get worn out, tossed aside, till we're needed again.

"I wasn't *getting* anywhere, Liam. Brick wall, with my life barely half over. Had to be more for me, somewhere. But where? I sure wasn't going to try for another man, like so many women around me, who couldn't handle the shock of growing up. For better or worse, I had my man." Here she gave me a look that dared me to think differently. But I wasn't disagreeing; I was listening, processing, just taking it all in.

"And you didn't see it. Any of it. And I wasn't about to cry on your shoulder. I'm as stubborn as you...but then you know that, don't you?" Rueful smile.

Okay, she was getting this off her chest. And it was obvious she'd done a lot of soul-searching about it. I still didn't say anything, just let it unroll. We were communicating—at least one-way.

"And I just didn't realize that every conversation we had was ending in a fight. Should have been more obvious, but you get tunnel-vision, I guess. I couldn't see the whole picture of what was happening to us: I just wanted you to see my side of whatever it was we were disagreeing on. Right then. And you never seemed to want to.

"Okay, take the computer thing: I couldn't see why you didn't get the simplest procedures. I was even sure you were deliberately refusing to understand, just to get to me. I made myself a victim, I guess. Never occurred to me that you don't see things the way I do—don't learn the same way. You always wanted to know *why* you pushed a certain button on the thing to make something else happen, and I didn't care: I just wanted to get to where that button took me.

"Anyway, after you left—and now I know you'd been building up to it a long time—I went into denial. I get this phone message out of the blue that you're on the way somewhere to clear your head, go fishing. Okay, I dealt with that. Then the letter. But by then I knew you weren't coming back. Bob told me about your instructions. And yes, I blamed you for everything. Desertion. Betrayal. Giving up a business and a reputation you—we—had built over half a lifetime, in a tough market. I figured you just had to be crazy, gone over the edge."

She stood, walked around. I knew all this wasn't easy for her, and I admired her for making herself do it—say it. I kept myself from interrupting, just listened, and focused on another of those dogwood-carved chairs with the flawed petals. Wood grain: I'd dealt with wood grain all my life. Layers of a tree built up, a lot like layers of events in our lives, adding up in the end to who we were, are. She went on after a bit.

"Then I suddenly realized you were *five years* past retirement age. Just blew on past it. Slamming away, like you *had* to. Where was the time for us? When were *we* going to have a life? Except for that week in Peru, what had *we* had? Kids and work, that's what.

"And fights.

"And I wanted—still want—that time we've earned, Liam. I want you back. Any terms. A year ago now, I went to Caney Creek determined to do, say, promise whatever it took to *get* you back. Brick wall, again. And I almost lost it, more than once. Same old track to the same old fights, no matter how I tried to go about it.

"But the bottom line was, you weren't ready, to talk or to listen. So I put a sock in it and left, and I waited. And was very much afraid—rightfully so, it turns out—that you'd get hurt, off down there in the woods. Or worse, that you'd never come out again.

"I knew you needed time. So did I, but I hadn't realized that, then. I needed to work through a lotta stuff I didn't even know I was carrying. You found some answers in the church, I know. I'm trying that, but it's not coming easily for me. Lot of interference, the pace I've been keeping: distractions, demands.

"So I'm unloading most of that now. I've cut the job to part-time. Gotten off the boards and committees. Taken a lot of time to work around the house, plant things, take a deep breath. This winter I'd planned to read a lot, weave, like I haven't in thirty years. And yes, get more involved in the church I've been going to. I wrote you I'd started going to a Bible study. Well, they invited me for the regular services, so eventually I went. Been going all fall. Now I find I miss it when I don't go."

She stopped, looked at me for a reaction. I guessed she was through, for now. *Okay, my turn, looks like.* I wanted to stand, pace, but the leg let me know that wasn't a good idea.

"Well, that's great, Sharon, about the church. Really. But you said it wasn't coming easily. You gotta know it didn't for me either, for a year or so. Not till the accident. That got my attention, big time."

"Tell me. I know it had to be bad, or somebody would have let me know." She sat again, facing me, our knees almost touching. I couldn't see the dogwood petals behind her now.

So I re-lived the whole thing again, and I didn't leave out anything. How I was certain I was dying, had said my goodbyes, then realized if I was going to pray, I had to do it while I was lucid. How Jim had somehow gotten the message, dropped everything and brought Eric.

Her hand had gone to her throat, eyes wide, when I described the big boulder, and where I was. And I realized again how hopeless that situation had to appear to anyone—had to me: totally beyond anybody's reach. I finished with the therapy, tactfully leaving out Jocelyn. Somehow, that woman wasn't even a factor, here in this place, in this situation.

Tunnel vision?

"So I wanted to get back on my feet—literally—before I told you, piled it on you. Jim wanted me up with them, but same thing as with you: I didn't wanta be that kind of dead weight. Oh, bad choice of words...Didn't know if I could manage back at my cabin at all, but then I found out I could. If I didn't overdo it, if I took it easy, if I used some judgment and no heroics."

She took her hand away, took mine, looked into my eyes.

"You know I'd have come. I'd have dropped everything, come to take care of you. 'In sickness and in health.'" She meant it.

"I was afraid so. But I'd dumped on you, and I wouldn't ask that of you...add insult to injury. I figured to be okay by now, when I knew I'd see you. And I am, really. Little weak on that leg, but that twist was freak. I've been climbing up my steps and path with no problem, cutting firewood..."

"But you could've twisted it just like that any of a thousand times, down there, alone again, doing all the things you can't help taking on, whether you need to or not."

"Yeah, I guess. Ironic I did it in a slow dance. But I've been really, really careful since the accident. Have the CB radio, too, and could crawl to it from anywhere on the place. Got handrails up, don't go places I did before. And both Jim and Eric invent reasons to come check on me, now. Almost embarrassing."

"And you wouldn't tell me." The beginnings of tears. "I almost *lost* you, Liam...Or had I, already? Wouldn't admit it." The tears were there, then. I don't think I'd ever seen her so...vulnerable, alone.

Well, what's a guy to do, situation like that? Maybe I'd acted like a stubborn, selfish old man, but I wasn't solid rock. I pulled her to me, hugged her close, held her. She cried a while, softly, and yeah, I did feel like a first-rate ogre. Nothing I'd done made any sense, just now... all wrong, all selfish. All ego.

None of it fit with who I wanted to be: somebody better. I wanted to be God's child.

And yeah, this woman's man.

Twenty-one

If there'd been any way to wrangle a flight this close to Christmas, I'd probably have been all over it, flown back to Virginia with Sharon and June. Pick up the pieces later. Lotsa loose ends to tie up on Caney Creek, though. And despite my epiphany, or rather when it began to wear off, I'm afraid I remembered too many of the old fights, the insults, and was afraid they'd start again.

Okay, I'd already planned to deal with that, after the leg got better: *just follow through, now. Get on the course and stay on it.* Which is always easier-sounding than it is in practice, I'd learned. My road should have been clear, now. Should have been like a big superhighway, in fact.

But doubt began to worm its way into the situation. Doubt. And that, I was learning, is an evil tool. Call evil the dark side of our makeup, the Darth Vader side, call it Satan—whatever. Doubt eats away at us, makes us question things we know are true, believe in. Undermines us. And funny thing, the more we try to live our faith, the more the cynicism, the questions.

Those doubts.

I'd asked Bill Zachman about that, and he'd explained it in his uncomplicated, direct way. When subtle, even appealing, Satan (he's succeeded in convincing most people he doesn't exist) sees he's losing you to God, he tries harder, slips in under the door like an oily rag and plays to your ego, pride, logic. It's not a frontal assault, more of a getting you to question, to use the intelligence you're sure you have, to get his wedge into you...those doubts, that cynicism.

Problem is, our knowledge, logic, is based on so little understanding, so relatively little real knowledge, it's misleading. Thin as the coat of paint on a globe, Bill said, or as he quoted some religious writer, trying to measure the whole universe with a yardstick. And I was surprised to learn he'd had to fight this battle just about every day, too, more so since becoming a minister.

"Seems like th' harder I try to follow the Lord, the harder it gets for me, Liam. All th' other stuff out there that looks like it'd be easier."

So now, when I was finally facing my shirked responsibilities, on the road back, here came the assault troops: insidious, weaseling, even appearing *so* logical. No horns, cloven hooves, red tights, tails. Just there, raiding my mind.

Twisting it.

The appealing part was mostly Jocelyn, whom I'd grown really fond of. Could I just dump her, run on back to Virginia with my truck and my dog, sounding like, living out, a country-western song? That'd be dumping two women in a row, I realized. Didn't like the smell of that at all.

Or did I owe our relationship, Jocelyn's and mine, the chance to be right, for both of us? Stay that course, despite the insights I'd just been granted. I hadn't made any specific promises to Sharon, and she hadn't asked. I guess she figured she was on shaky enough ground, not to push it.

I had going on two years without Sharon. And five months of that time with Jocelyn. What was right? What was the direction, the choice? Hey, a guy in my position wasn't supposed to be making choices between two women like this. That was for guys Kyle's age, with their lives ahead of them.

And with any objectivity at all, just what did either of them see in me, anyway? I wasn't anybody's idea of the dream man...

Gotta laugh at that one.

Have to let it work out, I guess...my usual non-decision. I worried over it all on the long drive down-country with my people. Didn't give them any straight answers, either. Even though Kelly had really worked on me, done her sisterly best, the way she saw it.

~ * ~

With all three of us driving in shifts down those long states, we got home soon enough, and didn't run into any really bad weather. No snow at Caney Creek, just overcast and nippy. Creek was up nicely, falls running. Boswell so glad to see me he about licked me to a shadow. Eric had looked after him and my other stuff, along with his own cold-weather concerns, and now was off to relatives' for Christmas again this year. I was reminded for the umpteenth time what a good neighbor, great guy he was.

I hadn't called Jocelyn while I was with Jim and Kelly, no point in irritating them. Jim would've understood, or I hoped he would, but not Kelly. It was Monday night, and I'd get to a neutral phone tomorrow, check in, but stay under the radar.

No, it'd have to be more than just that. I had to face the fact that it was time for finding out where we stood, really. Were we, or weren't we? Couldn't put it off any longer, much as I'd rather dodge it some more. This one wouldn't just solve itself. The status quo wouldn't cut it any longer...this relationship/situation wouldn't stand still.

So, in the cold rain of next day, otherwise an unremarkable Tuesday, I drove out to Kissee Mills, called her at work. Her voice told me she was glad to hear from me. *Well, sure.*

"Hey, you're back. How'd it go?"

"Great. Kids off to Hawaii, my girls gone back home. Lotta snow up there in Michigan. Glad to be back in God's country."

"How was Sharon?" I knew she'd get right to it.

"Okay, I guess. Mothers always misty when kids marry. But she had a good time. She and Jim are great dancers, really got on it together..."

"But how was she about you, Liam?" Wouldn't let it go. Okay, then.

"Well, Jocelyn, I guess you and I really need to talk about that. When can we get together?"

"Sounds portentous. Should I be forewarned?" She kept her voice light, but I knew she was thinking.

"Can't really say. Tonight?" Christmas was Saturday. For some reason, I wanted to know where we stood before that.

"Okay. Want to come over and get fed?"

"Sounds good. This rain's not supposed to freeze, the weather wizards say, get me stranded."

"If it does, you can stay, she invited, with absolutely no shame." She laughed, a little strained.

"Thanks. Yeah, around seven?"

So I'd thrown the fat in the fire again, after sort of deciding to let some time go by first. *No, get it over with.*

The way I saw it now, there were three options here: One, dump Jocelyn and go home to Sharon; two, leave Sharon dumped and stay with Jocelyn; three, forget them both and stay holed up by myself. That is, till I got too old to live there.

Didn't like that last one much, mostly the part about realizing I'd have to move away sooner or later, women in my life or not. But that was inevitable, even if I had kept putting the realization off.

Denial.

Now, I wasn't discounting the great time I'd just had with Sharon. Hey, I'm dense, but not *that* blind. But, away from her and the joy of the wedding and seeing my family again, things were just...say, getting into perspective again. At least I hoped they were. And yeah, there were those doubts, *the storm troops.*

I decided to pray about it, and spent most of the rest of that day doing just that. Boswell wanted me to go out in the rain and explore with him, but slippery as it was, I passed on that. I burned firewood and asked for the right way to go. I focused, concentrated the way I had up on that ledge with that killer rock on me. In minutes I was sweating.

I'd learned by then that God answers prayers in one of three ways: yes, no, or not yet. Not yet would take time, and I was antsy to take some sort of action. And I'd had the distinct feeling Jocelyn really wanted a resolution too, one way or the other. Well, I was pushing things to a head, I guessed, see what was supposed to come from that, since God wasn't giving me any sudden illuminations. He's got His own timetable; I'd learned that. So I prayed for His will to be done, about me and all of it.

As the time drew near, I became aware of minute details around me. The oak slab table with the snags in the wood where my hand plane had hit a knot. The unevenness in the stones of the walls, shadowed in the subdued light from my window. The weave of a wool blanket on the bed, the smooth iron door latch I'd hammered out those months ago. The ripples of Boswell's golden fur as he lay, head on forepaws, listening to the crackle of the stove. I shook off the feeling that I needed to imprint these things on my memory, that I was about to lose them.

Forever.

Once outside, I could hear the delicate sound of the waterfall upstream, and the heavier rush of Caney Creek among the boulders in the bend. The rain had stopped, but it made the forest give off a musty, secret smell of hidden life waiting out the cold time again. Water dripped from the ledgerock, greening the lichens, cold, wet. I really loved this place, in every one of its many moods and faces and characters.

Gone were the squirrels and rabbits, the doves and the pileated woodpeckers and all the night creatures that existed and competed and fought and found a living here. And in this suddenly comfortless, glistening world, I seemed really, almost terminally, alone. In spite of the fact that my dog was here, and just feet away was my home, my fireside, warmth glowing out my window.

Back inside, my canvas coat steamed in the wood heat, my hat dripped. I warmed my hands, noting how gnarled they'd become. Hard hands, old, but knowing shapings and turnings and settings of a lifetime. Hands that had touched every inch of this house and all that was in it, hands that seemed to move of themselves at tasks grown familiar and smoothed by endless repetition. Hands that had built so many shelters, including for me and my family, and that had kept us alive.

Easy to take hands for granted.

I left my dog in the shelter of the smithy where he had a pad to lie on, and eased the Ranger up the road for the second time that day, as the rain started again. Every aspect of all this was so familiar. Mist whitened in the headlights, tree trunks glistening and black, the dark forest a wall just beyond the lights' reach, letting my truck and me slip past.

I realized with a pang that I was really bound to miss this place, no matter which way I went: now or later. It was harsh, steep, remote, almost impossible to live in. And no, I wouldn't be able to handle it here much longer, biology being what it is. The odds against me would get longer every season, until I'd be forced to go *somewhere*.

I was reminded of the disciple Peter in the Bible, at the end of the Gospel of John. Jesus tells him, *When you were young, you girded yourself and walked wherever you would. But when you shall be old, you shall stretch forth your hands, and another shall gird you, and carry you whither you would not.*

But I belonged here, really, finally. I thought again about having become one with the wild things that made this place home: the furry creatures, the feathered ones, the cool, deep fish in the moving water. All fitting in, lost but not lost in this overlooked cleft of the world, snug, living out our roles in the master plan of it all. Eventually to die, naturally, part of it all.

Only as a human being, it was more complicated for me: there was more. I was privileged to have another life to look forward to, if I could hand myself more completely to God, hold nothing back, trust Him. Not there yet, but working toward it. That *yet* again. And yeah, I *was* created in His image...

That sounded more than a little conceited, just now.

And when you had to face the inevitable fact—couldn't keep on by yourself—you thought about old folks' homes, living with relatives, being cared for one way or another. It all added up to losing your independence, giving up control of your life. It would be bad enough in a boring brick rancher with everything on one floor, flat yard, shopping and medical care close. But here...this'd be hard even for someone young.

But I shook off that foreboding train of thought...wasn't ready for all that, just yet. Still a lot I could and wanted to do. My garden experiment hadn't been a total failure, I found myself thinking. With deeper soil and more water, it could work. I could do that with that engine-driven pump at the creek and enough black plastic pipe. Probably fifty to sixty dollars' worth of gasoline would irrigate the patch through those dry weeks. *Yeah, that could work...*

For somebody else. If—no, when—I got too old to get up that steep path, do the work when I got there.

My thoughts tumbled around like that on the wet road to Forsyth, then on toward Branson on the south blacktop. I tried to balance pros and cons of those three basic choices I had, but didn't make much sense of it. I kept getting images of the view up Caney Creek, of the waterfalls, of the warm, lighted window of my cabin through the rain. I guessed that was a big part of who I was now. A part of it, and that simplified, natural life didn't lend itself to deep speculations, decisions.

Maybe it should. Getting away from the hassles of civilization was supposed to clear the way for heavy thinking. *Guess I must've missed that, somehow.*

Twenty-two

By the time I eased the truck into Jocelyn's driveway, I hadn't had a single revelation. I was back at square one, not knowing which way to jump. Her little house shone warm at the lighted windows, too, like a promise in this night not fit to be out in. I carried a Christmas gift I'd made for her, a stylized flower forged from one piece of iron, velvety black in its beeswax finish.

"Hey, traveling man," she greeted me, wet and dripping as I was already, just from the few feet to her door. "Come in before you drown." The place smelled like bread baking, a haven of warmth and comfort. Fleeting thought of how nice it'd be to come home to. But home from where? I wasn't doing construction anymore. Wasn't traveling; wouldn't be.

But, home...

"Sloppy out." Brief hug, quick kiss. Like old married people. I gave her the flower, and her eyes widened. She ran her fingers over the forge marks, caressing. Then she gave me a real kiss, clung to me for a space.

"It's beautiful, Liam. Like a part of you." *Hmm, I guess.* "Well, now I'm gonna feed you up, fortify you against the elements. And you're going to tell me all about the wedding. And...everything else. Deal?"

"Sounds like one to me. Whatever you're cooking smells great. Might civilize me." I shucked the coat, hat, followed my nose toward the food. Warmed my hands at her woodstove.

It was better than it smelled, even. Jocelyn liked to cook, something Sharon had never enjoyed or made much time for since forever. Our girls and even Kyle had become cooks out of self-preservation. This was some kind of pork thing that was a long way from mountain hog-and-hominy. Veggies were great too, reminding me of the fresh stuff I'd had early in the summer from my rock patch. I savored every bite.

And that contributed to the lengthening time before we had to get down to reality. Didn't want that just yet, but finally here it was.

"Okay now, friend, how'd it go in Yankee land?" We'd stacked the dishwasher and were sipping herb tea, toes to the stove.

"Wedding was great. We're all glad our boy found Sarah, who's a treasure. She's got Kyle into religion, which is good. But she's no proselytizer. She and Jim sang some songs that made us all cry. Everybody danced after the rehearsal dinner. I managed to twist my leg, so everybody found out about it. The girls and Sharon gave me hell about all that."

"You seem to be getting around okay now. How bad was it?"

"Just a temporary thing. Came down on it wrong, apparently, stumbled. All better now, but I gotta watch out, I guess. Dumb thing, since I've been doing everything I need to at the place with no problem."

"Okay, then. Now tell me about Sharon." Jocelyn had her hands clasped around a knee. She didn't seem antsy or apprehensive, just interested. I didn't quite buy that, but okay, I'd tell her.

"Sharon started out insisting I go back to Virginia where I wouldn't kill myself. Told her I lived here, not there. Then she went over a lotta stuff she's begun to realize, about how we got pushed apart. Admitted to trying to find herself a life when she had one all along. I don't know how real that was. Anyway, bottom line she says she really wants me back with her." I spread my hands.

"I see. And you? How do you feel about that?" Eyes keen, now. Her cool slipping. Just how much did I really mean to this woman? Couldn't guess, but maybe I was about to find out.

"I've been trying to figure that, all the way home and since. I really missed my cabin, my place, you, just those few days. A whole lot of me wants to be there on that creek, till I get too feeble to climb out. Whenever that is."

"Then what? Assuming you do stay there?"

"Then I would have to come out, to some form of civilization, I guess. It'd mean I couldn't shift for myself anymore, so one way or another, I'd end up being a load on somebody. The idea of an old-folks' home really turns me off, even if I had the money for it." Image of those lines about the disciple Peter again: being *handled*.

"But you're a long way off from that. I see you still tough at eighty... eighty-five."

"Maybe, if I keep active. And that place'll do that for me, just getting by. But you gotta know, too, it gets lonely down in that hollow, just me and my dog. I stayed busy enough for a year and a half, and I could handle it. But, seeing the girls, Kyle, Sarah—all of them—I didn't like the idea of the hermit thing so well. And I'll have to admit it to you, it was easier to remember the good times with Sharon, the kids growing up, all the good things, there with them."

"Family's so important. I missed that part. And *I* can tell you about lonely. So are you saying you don't know what you'll do? Sounds like you have a standing invitation, back in Virginia."

"Maybe. But I don't fool myself it'd be all roses. People don't change that much, I know."

"So those are your two options?" She was fishing.

"One other, I guess." And here I put my eyes on hers, level, down-to-the-wire. "But I really don't know where we stand, you and I, Jocelyn. So maybe we need to get that out in the open first so we can deal with it." It was really a question.

And yeah, it needed an answer.

"Fair enough." She stood, back to the stove, hands behind her. "So, I'm hearing you don't know, then?"

"About the size of it, yeah. Clueless, I guess."

"And I'd have to say I don't, either. Yet." That *yet* again. "No way would I have planned to get involved with a guy your age. Not that that's been a big deal; I really think we're good for each other. But how that'd play long-term, I can't say. People in love will do whatever the situation requires. I'm not saying I'd look forward to pushing your wheelchair, but if we're the right two people, I'd sure do it, and gladly. And like I said, we'd have some good years before that happened, I'm sure of it.

"But I'm hearing those two other options for you, and I guess I'm the new girl on the block, here. Sort of the easiest one to rule out..."

"I wouldn't say that at all. And hey, what's so bad about our relationship, if everything just stays the same? With us, I mean. Option one?"

"Oh, Liam, people who really care for each other can't be apart most of the time. I guess we could go on as we've been for a while, see where it leads. But relationships don't stand still. They get closer, or they fall apart. I'm sure you know that." *Sure I do...been telling myself that for a while now.*

"I guess I do, yeah. And I probably couldn't just tread water like that either, long-term." I shrugged again, as if I'd asked a question.

"So, is this a Mexican standoff, Liam? Any way you can tell me which way you're leaning? Can I influence you, one way or another?"

"You already did, Jocelyn. Coming to a warm, bright place out of a cold rain, being fed by a terrific woman I like—right now I'm pretty sure it doesn't get any better than this."

"*Pretty* sure?"

"Well, there's another factor, I'll have to admit." I paused here, trying to marshal my thoughts. This was important, and could be the deciding bit. "Since the accident, I've told you I've gotten a real handle on what I believe. I know you don't buy the religion thing, but it's become really important to me. And it carries a big weight: doing what's right, facing up to my responsibilities, and a lot more. I dumped Sharon, no way around that, without really trying hard enough to make it work. Didn't want to try. I guess I took the easy way out, really, although it didn't seem that way at the time.

"And, taken along with my faith and knowing I'm forgiven, which is now *the* most important thing in my life, I've gotta look at doing what *is* right. If I could only tell what that is."

"Well, I wish I could have a faith like you do, Liam. But I see too many rotten things happening around me—and I've had my share of those—around this messed-up world. I can't see a benign, loving God letting His people destroy each other like we are...greed, anger, violence, poisoning the earth. I'm sorry, but that's just beyond me. My philosophy just has to be treat others as decently as I can, and let it go at that." She crossed her arms, putting a period to her statement.

I let that soak in a while; I'd heard that argument before. Part of Bill Zachman's answer was, again, this life had to be a test of some sort, say of our faith, and what kind of a test would it be if everything went smoothly, with no rough spots—okay, rotten spots? And I guess that meant a person with no faith was just out in the cold. Or hot, as the fundamentalists insisted.

But I wasn't there to argue religion. Wasn't qualified for that one, and would have to travel a long way on my faith journey before I could take that on.

I found I was zeroing in on a handmade vase on a side table. It was a figured piece, by a potter I'd met over beyond Reeds Spring, a face carved in it that looked a lot like him. Name was Al something. More a sculptor than a potter, really. The beard was so real it looked like he'd put actual bristles on the piece. I could almost feel the ridges under my fingers, as he had, creating it. I've never worked in clay, but my fingers really wanted to touch that piece.

Then my eyes were drawn as if by a magnet. I noticed the vase had gotten moved so it was now at the very edge of the table, its curved base flowing into that straight line:

Another tangent.

Keep on with the curve, this curve, familiar now? Or fly off on that line, delineated by space, at table's edge? And just what was the familiar? My deep hollow, my hermit life? Wouldn't stay the same, my life wouldn't stand still. Lives don't.

Relationships don't.

Jocelyn and I were telling each other the status quo wasn't one of the options anymore.

So either way we'd have to break it off, or I'd have to pursue it—her—with the realization that she'd probably never share my newfound faith. Never come to church with me, keep that part of us closed off. Walk that lonesome valley for herself, as the old hymn went.

But what about that, with Sharon? We'd never been religious. Sure, she'd said she was in that church now. Would that last? Was that real? Sounded like it at the time, but here, now, warm on a wintry night, with a woman I didn't fight with, Sharon was very, very distant.

I really needed time to sort this through, the old thing of letting it work itself out. But I sensed that it had to be resolved now, tonight. Been on the table too long already, between us like a wedge.

Or an 800-pound gorilla.

And then I realized something, really for the first time: that this whole thing, from beginning to end, had been put together for me, all of it, by The Man. To get me away from thinking first and always of myself. So it was now time to do what was right for others, old man, *you selfish old fool.* Now why had it taken so long for that to become obvious? Thick-headed, I guess.

Jocelyn had invited me to stay with her this night, and much as I liked that idea, I couldn't do that under false pretenses.

Fish or cut bait, McLeod. And no, this one can't be just for you...

Lightning images: Boswell and me, deep in our tumbled hollow, water sheeting over the falls, the smell of new, green earth enveloping us. Then the high view of the blue, rolling ridges beyond the Caney Creek bluffs. Wind in the cedars, sun on our faces.

Then me: old, bent, confined to my cabin, alone. Jim and Kelly old, too. Everything changed: slow, labored, awash in memories. Then this house, with Jocelyn fussing over me as over an invalid, spending her years tending the shell of me. Then Virginia, and so much of the old routine, good and bad, puttering, slowing inevitably, drawing closer to the same end, no matter the route.

Being alone scared me. Really did, for the first time. So maybe that would cut out the Caney Creek option entirely. So I guessed maybe it came down in the end, to my having to make the choice between these two good women.

Again.

There was the memory, newly sharp after so many years, of Sharon. Needing me, willing to overlook all the baggage I was carrying. Now waiting for me in the house we'd built together. My wife, mother of my children.

Then there was this fine woman standing before me I got along so well with. In the subdued light, her face was soft, framed in that light brown hair. Waiting, too. And all I had to do was reach out to her, draw her to me. I knew the rest would fall into place, here in this warm place out of the rain. I could very nearly feel her body pressed to mine, yielding, becoming a part of me.

Stay with her?

Was that even a question?

Whatever I chose, I knew now I couldn't hack being alone any longer. Man—especially an old man—just wasn't meant to be alone. And I hoped I wasn't just being selfish, this time...

Alone.

Then something Bill Zachman had said, many times, knocked at my head: *"You are not alone. God is with you."*

God. And a Bible quote flashed. Came from right at the end of the Gospel of Matthew. I could see the words, the letters clear, coming up off the page for me, taking on life. Jesus said, *"I am with you always, even until the end of the age."*

Yes.

I rose, drew Jocelyn Summers to me in a long embrace, feeling the firmness, the strength in her, flowing into me. The scent of her hair, the warmth of her filled me with visions of the life we could have together. The joy, to be snatched from the hungry years.

"Goodbye, Jocelyn." Tears stood in her eyes. "May God be with you, dear lady."

I stepped out into the cold.

Into the rain.

~ * ~

The long miles unwound behind us, the gray interstate, the houses and farms clumped in their bare trees, huddled against the chill. Boswell, on the seat beside me, watched this unreal world flash by, winter monochrome, strange. I relived the brief leave-taking, from Jocelyn, then moving the smithy tools to Jim's place, packing, locking up.

Fishing cabin, now.

Yeah, that'll do.

The quick stop at Bill Zachman's place down at the end of the long road at Cedar Creek to say goodbye, the warmth of his big hand on my shoulder, the direct eyes. His blessing, which keeps meaning a lot more, given out of the store of his own pain.

The miles have dragged by, these two days, gray in time spun away behind, my mind ahead. To all the things that wait for me, all the necessary adjustments that will—must be—made if this is to work. Doubts, of course, whether I've chosen the right path. Never be sure of that. Life's not that clear cut, choices not that black and white. If life were easy, it wouldn't be worth living, as C.S. Lewis wrote.

Now at last the mountains rolling down to rounded hills, soft-focus in bare-branch-screened textures, the flash of welcome water falling over ledges. Rushing in meadow creeks. Water, again, enough water to feed the thirsting earth, protect it from the parching sun of summer. How I've missed the blessing of enough water.

The feel of home…drawing, insisting. Christmas lights last night in windows, along the eaves of glowing houses. Once a knot of carolers in a tiny yard, in the smallest of towns where I'd turned off the interstate. I could almost feel the cold feet, see the clouds of warm breath, the reddened cheeks, hands held and holding, singing the joyful season.

Now the Ranger seems to know the way, and it's as if I'm sitting back, watching: automatic turns, stops, familiar hills and curves. Each road I turn into is a little narrower, a little less traveled, than the one I just left. I find myself driving faster as we near home.

Stevenson: "And the hunter home from the hill."

And then at last the long driveway through the woods, tamer version of the Caney Creek track. The familiar trees, glistening in the drizzle that's followed me east. And the glowing windows of the lighted house on its rise among the trees. The house these hands put together.

The welcome quiet from the vibration of the long, long road, the stiffness, getting down onto my feet, feeling the welcome earth communicating itself up through my boots. Boswell jostling past me, eager to check out this new place we've found.

The woman at the open door, light streaming warm around her. The welcoming voices of my wife and daughter.

Home.

Epilogue

I can't pretend everything's been paradise since then. Both Sharon and I have had to work to make our marriage hang together, harder than we ever had before. But we find we can cut each other slack when it's necessary, and gradually that's become a habit, a good one. We've found out we actually like each other a lot.

And we both know we've been guided through that whole rough place in our lives by Someone who really cares. And *I* know I've grown (mostly) past that selfish, crochety old man I used to be. Took a lot to change me, but I shudder to think of the course I was on before. Blaming Sharon for it all was the worst kind of self-centeredness, and I had to lose that, the hard way.

Kyle and Sarah spend a week at the cabin on Caney Creek now and then, fishing, visiting with Jim and Kelly and the folks we'd gotten to know there. They've actually picked some fruit off my dwarf trees up on the hillside. Sharon's even said she'd like to go back for a visit soon, if she can stay at Jim's where there's plumbing. We'll plan it.

I've managed a good garden here, where it isn't threatening to fall off the mountainside. All it's taken, really, is the time and dedication.

Nice activity for a retired guy. We eat very well from my efforts. Have to give a lot of tomatoes and squash away in summer. Almost to the point where I leave sacks of veggies on doorsteps, ring the doorbell and run.

I don't do construction anymore, but I do tinker a lot in the smithy and the workshop. Sharon always has a long list of Honey-do projects for me, and I find I enjoy doing things for her. She's serious about cooking these days, but now and then actually wants some of my stew and biscuits.

But I'm not one bit better with that computer.

Sharon and I are regulars at a little non-denominational church nearby. She's in the choir, a bunch of talented musicians, great human beings whose ministry is music. My contribution to that is to listen and appreciate. And Sharon and I read the Bible to each other some nights.

Boswell has taken on the job of protecting us from the 'possums, skunks, stray cats and other semi-rural Virginia hazards. We go for a lot of walks in the nearby woods. He's managed to terrorize most of the local squirrels and rabbits, at least till his back's turned.

June is engaged to a youthful literature professor she met while in grad school. She'll keep on in the theater, probably teaching somewhere with her Bradley. We look forward to more grandchildren.

I do think about Jocelyn Summers in unguarded moments, and yes, there's some guilt there. You always wonder about the road not taken, what these days would have been like with another person, in another place. *Well, I guess I did take that road actually, for a while at least.*

I remember those pieces of art, crafts she had on that table, and hope that yes, they did represent past relationships, and that another one, the right one, was there now. I wish her well, and I pray for her. But I know I've been shepherded on the right path.

I hope she will be.

Even though we're on a fairly disciplined budget now, we do manage to get away for a spur-of-the-moment weekend or so. Bed-

and-breakfast up in the mountains, or beach house. Romantic really, even for people our ages. And you know, some of the imagined over-the-hill aspects of age are mostly myth, off-the-mark stereotypes.

Speaking of which, tonight Sharon is standing in the bedroom doorway in something that clings to her, looking a lot younger and more desirable than I'd ever imagined she could. She's inviting me, soft light behind her, faint music drifting from somewhere.

I've gotten a little deaf lately, but yeah, I heard that.

Meet Charles McRaven

Charles McRaven is a former Journalism professor, restoration contractor, log cabin and timberframe builder who currently consults on historic structures. He is a stonemason, blacksmith, minister and author of five crafts books and four published novels. He and his wife live in central Virginia.

Other Works From The Pen Of

Charles McRaven

A Piece of Ground – Revolutionary War veteran sharpshooter Stephen Davis searches for the reality of the old saying that all it takes is "Two people and a piece of ground."

Troublesome Creek - Pioneer pursues lost love into Kentucky Territory wilderness, defends missionaries and remote villagers against ruthless marauders.

Letter to Our Readers

Enjoy this book?

You can make a difference.

As an independent publisher, Wings ePress, Inc. does not have the financial clout of the large New York publishers. We can't afford large magazine spreads or subway posters to tell people about our quality books.

But we do have something much more effective and powerful than ads. We have a large base of loyal readers.

Honest reviews help bring the attention of new readers to our books.

If you enjoyed this book, we would appreciate it if you would spend a few minutes posting a review on the site where you purchased this book or on the Wings ePress, Inc. webpages at: https://wingsepress.com/

Thank You

Visit Our Website

For The Full Inventory
Of Quality Books:

Wings ePress.Inc
https://wingsepress.com/

Quality trade paperbacks and downloads
in multiple formats,
in genres ranging from light romantic comedy
to general fiction and horror.
Wings has something for every reader's taste.
Visit the website, then bookmark it.
We add new titles each month!

Wings ePress Inc.
3000 N. Rock Road
Newton, KS   67114

www.ingramcontent.com/pod-product-compliance
Lightning Source LLC
Chambersburg PA
CBHW070625100726
47907CB00007B/1861